Beyond I Do

Will seeing beyond the present
unite them or tear them apart?

Jennifer Slattery

NEW HOPE
PUBLISHERS
Gospel-Centered. Missions-Driven.

BIRMINGHAM, ALABAMA

New Hope® Publishers
PO Box 12065
Birmingham, AL 35202-2065
NewHopeDigital.com
New Hope Publishers is a division of WMU®.

Library of Congress Cataloging-in-Publication Data

Slattery, Jennifer, 1974- author.
 Beyond I do / by Jennifer Slattery.
    pages cm
 ISBN 978-1-59669-417-0 (sc)
 1. Christian fiction. I. Title.
 PS3619.L3755B49 2014
 813'.6--dc23
                         2014014595

Unless otherwise indicated, all Scripture quotations are taken from the *Holy Bible,*
New Living Translation, copyright © 1996. Used by permission of Tyndale House
Publishers, Inc., Wheaton, Illinois. All rights reserved.
    Scripture quotations marked NIV are taken from the HOLY BIBLE, NEW
INTERNATIONAL VERSION®. NIV®. Copyright©1973, 1978, 1984, 2011 by Biblica,
Inc.® Used by permission. All rights reserved worldwide.
    Scripture quotations marked KJV are taken from The Holy Bible, King James
Version.

Editorial: Joyce M. Dinkins, Kristin Easterling, Melissa Hall, Natalie Hanemann,
Bethany Kuhn, Kathi Macias, and Kathryne Solomon

Cover Design: Michel Lê
Interior Design: Glynese Northam

ISBN-10: 1-59669-417-3
ISBN-13: 978-1-59669-417-0

N144123 • 0914 • 3M1

Dedication

To my sweet friend, *Iris Peters,* who showed me what it means to live for Jesus, right up to the end.

Acknowledgments

To my sweet hubby, you saw the writer in me before I did and have always been such an encourager! You continue to bring out the best in me, and I appreciate your commitment to Christ, your family, and sharing God's love with others. Thank you for showing me, day in and day out, what it means to love patiently, humbly, and sacrificially. Though my name is on the cover of this book, we both know I'd know nothing of forever romance if not for you!

To my mother-in-law, *Bea Slattery*, I cherish you not just because you raised the man of my dreams, but also because of all the support and feedback you've offered over the years.

To my *dad*, I'm still skipping and still rhyming. Thanks for instilling in me a love for words and encouraging me to chase after my dreams.

To my *mom,* thanks for teaching me to view others through a "deeper" lens. I hope this tendency comes out in everything I write.

Dr. Andrea Mullins, what a blessing you have been in my writing journey! When I first met you, I was struck by how much you radiate Christ. To all the staff at New Hope Publishers, thank you for making my first book such a wonderful experience.

Joyce, you are such a brilliant, encouraging, and inspiring editor! I'm so blessed to be able to glean from your strong faith and wisdom. You are a wonderful woman of God, and I learn something every time I hear you speak.

Finally, I've had some amazing *critique partners,* and can't thank you enough for all the help each of you has offered from draft one to ten; but *Kathleen Freeman,* you knew you'd get a special thank-you, right? Thanks for encouraging me to follow God's leading in my journey to publication. Cherish you, girl!

Chapter 1

*A*insley's stomach churned as she eased into the Whispering Hills Apartments parking lot. Broken beer bottles and other trash littered the ground. A few tenants had draped sheets across their windows. Other windows were boarded up. One was busted in, shards of glass held in place by silver duct tape.

Please tell me this isn't where Marie Nelson lives. She compared the address Deborah had given her to the rusted numbers on the complex in front of her. This was the place. And from the looks of it, the very place Ainsley shouldn't be, at least, not alone.

Her phone chimed, making her jump. She glanced at the screen. Her fiancé's number flashed. Cutting her engine, she answered. "Hey, Richard. What's up?" She shoved her purse and computer case under the passenger seat.

"Where are you?"

"Doing a favor for Deborah. Why? You need something?" She grabbed her pepper spray from the glove compartment.

"Who?"

As if she hadn't talked about the woman countless times over the years. "Deborah Eldridge, the one who told me about Christ." And kept her from going completely insane or spiraling into rebellion when Ainsley's home life fell apart.

"Sometimes I wonder if you ever really listen."

A pack of muscular and hardfaced men gathered around a navy pickup watched her, causing her already queasy stomach to cramp. There were four of them, two dressed in black with thick chains draped across their neck. The largest was covered, neck and arms, with angry tattoos. She looked away, suddenly acutely aware of her shiny sedan and department store garb.

Oh, Lord Jesus, please keep me safe.

"That Deborah. Right." A keyboard clicked on the other end of the line. Richard was probably working on final edits on his book. "Now I remember. So you're in Smithville?"

"Not exactly. More like . . ." She scanned her surroundings again, her gaze lingering on a used diaper decaying on the ground ten feet away. "More like . . . the Admiral Boulevard area."

Richard made a choking noise, as if spewing coffee. "You're where? Please tell me you are not in the crime center of Kansas City."

He let out an exasperated puff of air. "You are, aren't you?" He muttered something under his breath. "Why must you continue to jeopardize your safety like this?"

"And why must you treat me like a child?"

He sighed. "I'm sorry. I'm just worried. But surely you know how dangerous that area is.

"I'll be fine. It's broad daylight. Besides, criminals and gang members aren't the only people who live in this part of town. There are women and children, senior citizens."

"Yes, I know. I've seen pictures of some of them flash across the evening news — after they've been shot."

She closed her eyes and pinched the bridge of her nose. This wasn't a conversation she wanted to have. Not now, sitting like a bright, shiny target in an this rundown apartment complex's parking lot. "Good-bye, Richard. I'll call you when I get home."

"Tell me exactly where you're at."

So he could come *rescue* her? "Listen, I've gotta go." She ended the call then slipped her cell into her blazer pocket.

Her phone chimed again but she ignored it. Richard was much too sheltered by his high society friends. As her pastor often said, "If you don't know any single parents or folks living in poverty, you need to get out in the real world, because Jesus doesn't need any seat warmers."

It was time she acted on that same advice. She stepped from her car, and a gust of wind carrying the scent of trash swept over her. Moving to her trunk, she glanced around. A man in a low-rider pulled up beside a girl in four-inch heels, a miniskirt, and bikini top.

Please tell me she's not doing what I think she is.

Time to drop off her care items then get home. Grabbing her shopping bag filled with everything from cough drops to orange juice, she locked her car and scurried to unit number 478. A door covered in dirt stood in front of her. Apparently, the only entrance into the complex.

There she stood, looking like a small-town librarian, about to enter into a danger zone. An area known for shootings, rapes, and robberies. So why was she still here and not back in her car headed toward I-70?

Because Deborah said this was important. The woman would've come herself, had she been able. And after all she'd done for Ainsley over the years, this was the least Ainsley could do.

Holding her overstuffed bag and pepper spray in one hand, Ainsley reached for the knob and turned. The door squeaked open, a thick stench of mildew and cigarette smoke permeating the air. A single bulb flickered in the darkened hallway, and it took her eyes a moment to adjust. Surveying her surroundings, bag clutched to her chest like a shield, she searched for an elevator. All she found was a dark stairwell that smelled of vomit.

A verse taped to her bathroom mirror came to mind: *If you try to hang on to your life, you will lose it. But if you give up your life for my sake, you will find it* (Matthew 16:25).

Lose her life, her rights, for Christ. That was fine when it meant holding babies in the nursery or bringing meals. She glanced at her shopping bag. Or medicine to shut-ins. She always said she wanted to live God's adventure, but whenever the chance arose, her fears and insecurities held her back. Not this time. God was giving her the opportunity to put action to her words, and she was determined to see this through.

Finger poised over the trigger of her pepper spray, she climbed up the stairs. *Lord Jesus, keep me safe. Lord Jesus, keep me safe. Lord Jesus—*

A door above slammed shut, and she startled, nearly dropping her bag. Holding her breath, she pressed against the cool cement wall as heavy footfalls descended toward her. A large woman carrying a poodle rounded the corner with a grunt. Ainsley's jittery legs went slack as intense relief washed over her. *Thank You, Jesus.* She offered the woman a shaky smile then faced the remaining stairs with renewed focus. Taking them two at a time, she arrived on the third floor out of breath, heart racing.

Marie Nelson's apartment was three doors down on the left. From inside, a television blared. Ainsley knocked then waited, casting frequent glances down the hall.

No answer. She tried again, louder this time. Muffled yelling erupted from the adjacent apartment, followed by a loud crash. Ainsley knocked again, this time using the flat end of her fist, then her foot. Again, nothing. She started to leave when the television turned off. Once again, she knocked, the yelling in the next residence now louder, clearer.

"Can't even cook fried chicken. What'd I tell you about burnin' my dinner, you stupid cow?" A deep male voice. "You disgust me." There was a high-pitched cry followed by a thud.

Domestic violence? An urge to do something welled within her, battling against her fear. Should she call the cops? Absolutely, but first, she needed to get out of here.

She inched toward the stairwell, ready to bolt. The door to the adjacent apartment burst open, and a lanky man with veins bulging along his arms and chest appeared. Tattooed lettering replaced his eyebrows and dime-sized studs pierced his ears. He smelled of stale liquor, cigarette smoke, and dried sweat. Behind him a woman cowered on the floor, her back against the wall. Sobbing, she covered her face with her hands. A boy, maybe nine or ten years old, crouched beside her. He looked at Ainsley, tear-filled eyes pleading.

She gasped, her heart aching.

The drunken man slammed his apartment door. "What you staring at?" He glowered, his blue eyes boring into Ainsley with such venom, the hairs on her neck stood on end. Holding her breath, she inched backward, stumbling over a crease in the carpet. She dropped her bag, the contents spilling out.

The man looked at her, his upper lip curling, hands fisted. He stepped forward, and she closed her eyes, shielding her head with her hands. His footsteps thudded on the ragged carpet then continued past, soon echoing in the stairwell.

She remained on the ground, trembling.

Marie's door creaked open. "Hello?" An old woman dressed in a lavender housecoat and matching slippers appeared. "You there, did you knock on my door?" She smiled as if completely oblivious to the battle that had occurred in her neighbor's apartment. And the mess of medicine spilled across the hallway floor.

Ainsley's heart hammered so hard, her chest began to burn. "Hi." She scooped her items back into the bag and stood on trembling legs. "I . . ." She looked from the stairwell to the door, now closed, that hid the broken woman and child. What should she do? What could she do?

"You must be Ainsley Meadows." Maria opened her door wider, resting her shoulder against it. "Deborah told me you'd be coming." Her silver hair was pulled into rollers, numerous strands escaping. Her wrinkled face had a yellow tint. Jaundice? Or was that a side effect of chemo?

Ainsley nodded and extended her hand. "Good to meet you."

The woman coughed, a dry, rattling sound then wiped her mouth with the back of her hand.

Ainsley's mouth felt dry. She touched her phone, her fingers resting on the smooth plastic case. Did the woman in the next apartment need help? Was it any of her business? The image of the boy, so young, so frightened, cemented in her brain. She knew what it was like to feel as if the world was crumbling. To wonder if the adults in your world cared. She might not have experienced physical abuse, but she understood intense loneliness, the kind that ate at one's gut and made one wonder if life was worth living. If not for Deborah —

"Don't just stand there looking like a banked trout." The woman winked, making a sweeping motion with her arm. "Come in. Come in." She pulled a wad of tissue from her housecoat pocket and blew her nose.

Ainsley stepped inside, lingering in the entryway. The apartment, a studio, was small but tidy. The furniture reminded her of an old *I Love Lucy* television show, down to the twenty-inch black-and-white television set.

"I brought you cold medicine." She held her bag out then set it on a table pushed against the wall.

"Isn't that kind? I'll tell you what — all that chemo has wreaked havoc with my immune system. Not that I'm complaining none. Just happy to be here, till the good Lord takes me home." She shuffled over and peeked into the bag. "Oh, my! Jelly beans! My absolutely favorite candy. How did you know?"

Ainsley smiled. "Deborah Eldridge told me."

"Such a sweet woman; always does remember the little things." Stifling a cough, she pulled out a bag of lozenges and wrestled the bag open. "Would you like some tea?"

"I . . ." Scraping her teeth over her bottom lip, she cocked her head, listening for sounds coming from the other apartment. Silence. "What's the story with your neighbors?"

Mrs. Nelson wrinkled her brow. "Neighbors? Oh, you mean sweet Wanda and her good-for-nothing boyfriend." Frowning, she shook her head. "Don't know how many times I told her to leave that lowlife. If not for herself, for the safety of her son." She moved to a paisley loveseat and practically fell into it. "But like my momma used to say — God rest her soul — can't help someone who won't help themselves. Still, I pray for her. The good Lord knows how much I pray for her and that boy." She winced as if in pain then grabbed a heating pad from the cushion beside her. Leaning her head back, she closed her eyes.

The woman was tired. Needed to rest. "Listen, I don't want to keep you." Ainsley smiled and pivoted toward the door.

Marie struggled to sit up, her face contorted.

Ainsley raised her hand. "You relax. I can see myself out." With a wave good-bye, she slipped out and continued down the stairs. Once at her car, she glanced toward the apartment building, focusing on the third floor. The young boy she'd seen inside that dingy apartment stood in front of his opened window. He held Ainsley's gaze. An urge to go to him, to scoop him up and hold him close, to protect him and his mother, swept through her. To show him how infinitely loved he was. Like Deborah Eldridge had done for her, back when she was his age.

But what could she do?

Oh, Lord Jesus, please show me what I can do.

Chapter 2

*R*ichard Hollis stopped pacing and checked his watch for the fifth time in as many minutes. It was 6:15, and Ainsley still hadn't returned his calls. All eight of them. How could he show her the danger of her actions? Philanthropy projects were fine, if done through the proper channels. Did the woman have any idea the violence perpetuated in those kinds of areas?

No. She didn't. And he had no intention of allowing her to learn the hard way.

Grabbing his computer bag, he exited his office, locking the door behind him. Not that he knew where to go, except maybe to randomly drive through northeast Kansas City hoping to find her.

His phone rang as he stepped into the hall. He checked the screen. A gust of air expelled from his chest. Finally. "Why haven't you returned my calls? I've —"

"Richard, I need help." Her voice was barely above a whisper and carried an obvious tremor.

His grip tightened around the phone. "Where are you?"

"At Whispering Hills Apartments." Loud music — heavy metal? — sounded in the background. "My rear tire has been slashed."

He cursed under his breath. "I'll be right there." *Ainsley Meadows, what have you gotten yourself — both of us — into?*

A mess, and a potentially dangerous one at that.

There was no way he was going to Whispering Hills on his own. "Get in your car and lock your doors. I'm calling the cops." Building locked and alarm set, he marched toward his Lexus parked in a now empty lot.

"No. You can't do that."

"Don't be ridiculous." At his car, he slipped behind the steering wheel and cranked the engine.

"I'm fine. I just need a new tire."

"Can you hear yourself? Or did you think the nice man who slashed the pretty lady's tires just up and left?"

"Please, Richard, there's a boy here. I feel like . . . if we call the police, I'll ruin my witness. Lose his trust."

Richard scoffed. "No. Getting killed is what will ruin your witness. Besides, you'll never see that boy again." Because there was no way Richard would let her return to that complex. "Now, sit tight. I'll call the authorities, and we'll be there shortly."

He peeled out of the parking lot and headed east on Ward Parkway. First, he called the police, next, a tow truck. An accident backed up traffic on US 71, causing Richard to arrive later, and considerably more upset, than anticipated. Luckily the police and tow truck beat him there and appeared to have everything under control.

Ainsley was talking to a heavy-set officer with blond hair. The man's partner, a squat and balding man, stood a few feet away, chest puffed out, hand on the brunt of his gun. He appeared to be staring down residents who gathered on walkways and cement stairs and poked their heads out opened windows.

Calming himself to a rational level, Richard approached Ainsley. "Are you OK?" Her left rear tire was slashed and deflated, but other than that, her vehicle appeared fine. As did she.

Face downcast, she shrugged, looking to an upstairs apartment window. "Just a bit unsettled."

"And rightly so." There was no need to tell her she brought this on herself, at least, not now. They could talk in great detail about the stupidity of her actions on the drive home. Turning to the officer, he extended his hand. "I'm Richard Hollis." The two shook. "Ainsley's fiancé and the one who reported this incident."

"Officer Hughes." The man dropped a small notebook into his front pocket. "Like I was telling Miss Meadows here, there's really not much we can do in situations like this." He studied a group of teens gathered near a sagging chain-link fence. "No witnesses, least none that'll talk." Tucking a stubby pencil behind his ear, he pulled a business card from his back pocket and handed it over. "Have a good night. And stay safe."

Richard tensed, gangbanger types filling his peripheral vision. When the police left, there was no telling what the thugs would do. And he certainly wasn't going to hang around to find out.

"Come on." He grabbed Ainsley by the crook of her arm and pulled her to his car. "Wait here. I'll grab your things." He started to walk away then turned back around. "Get in and lock the doors."

She glared and crossed her arms but didn't argue. The tow truck driver waited near the rear of his vehicle wearing torn jeans and a T-shirt with the arms ripped off.

Richard approached. "Thank you for coming."

The man jerked a nod and spit tobacco into a plastic foam cup. "Where am I taking this little jewel?"

Richard gave him Ainsley's address and his credit card numbers. After grabbing her purse and briefcase, partially hidden from view, he returned to his vehicle.

She frowned. "Quit treating me like a child."

"Then quit acting like one. Really, Ainsley, what were you thinking? These guys don't play around."

She sat in the passenger seat, staring straight ahead. Five minutes later, when she still hadn't responded, he patted her leg. "Listen, I'm sorry I snapped at you, but you really scared me. They could've hurt you, Ainsley. Very badly, tight-lipped witnesses or not."

"That little boy . . . he looked so sad." Her voice cracked.

"That's not your problem."

She turned fiery eyes toward him. "Then whose is it? His mother's, who as we speak is recovering from being a human punching bag? Or maybe his neighbors', most of whom appeared to be engaged in all manner of illegal activity."

"Listen, I know you mean well. But this isn't your issue. Besides, with your job and our upcoming wedding, you really don't have the time."

She sighed and rubbed her face with her hands. "You're right. I know you're right. It's just . . . I know how that kids feels, is all. I think I could help him, maybe."

"Yeah, and how's that?"

She stared down at her hands. "I don't know. I wish I did."

"That, my dear, is why you are so endearing. Frustrating at times, but endearing just the same." Merging onto I-29, he headed south. "Which reminds me, did my mother call you?"

She frowned and rubbed her temples. "This week, you mean? No."

Richard chuckled. "You act as if she's stalking you or something."

She stared at him for a moment, then gave a slight shake of her head and returned her focus to the street.

"You know, she's just excited about the wedding and wants to make it the best possible."

"I guess. I just wish she'd voice her opinions less strongly. Or become less irritated when I don't accept them."

"You two are getting to know one another, that's all." He continued past industrial buildings interspersed with thick clusters of oaks, poplars, and ash trees filled with maroon, golden, and orange leaves.

"Maybe." She grabbed her purse and pulled out a tube of lotion. The scent of jasmine filled the car when she squirted a blob in her hand. "Does she need something?"

"She wants you to join her and a few of her friends for brunch this Saturday. To discuss potential pianists for the wedding."

"Bummer." She made a mock disappointed face, though her smiling eyes betrayed her. "Gina and I have a shopping date. Maybe next weekend."

Richard's jaw tensed, his grip tightening on the steering wheel. Gina, Ainsley's best friend and a woman who had made it her mission to sabotage Ainsley's and his engagement. He'd warned Ainsley of this numerous times, expressing his concern regarding the friendship. But once they got married, things would change. She'd be much too busy with social functions to engage in such . . . counterproductive relationships.

"How'd the meeting with Dr. Wells go?" He exited onto North Oak, a four lane roadway, and was immediately sandwiched by early evening traffic.

"Not as well as I'd hoped."

"I see." North Oak Market Place occupied a chunk of land to the northwest. Lowe's dominated the northeast corner, and the Northland Fountain created the focal point for Anita Gorman Park to his right. In winter, the central geyser created an ice sculpture captured by countless photographers.

"My boss scheduled an appointment for me with Dr. Senske, tomorrow at 11:00 and sent me home with — "

"Dr. Senske?" Richard raised his eyebrows. "He's one of the most respected and influential psychiatrists in the field."

"So I've heard." She rubbed her face with her hands. "Mr. Holloway made himself quite clear. I produce or he cuts me loose." She shook her head. "It's no wonder most pharmaceutical reps at Voltex don't last past the initial probationary period."

"Once we're married, you won't have to worry about Voltex or the corporate world." Or taking "care packages" to people in low-income apartments. Mother would find much more respectable charities for Ainsley to support. He angled the rearview mirror away from the glare of the setting sun and eased into her cul-de-sac.

"I've already told you, I don't plan on being a house — "

"Who's that?" Richard slowed to a stop. In front of him, two large moving vans filled the street. A royal blue pickup with California plates blocked Ainsley's driveway. At the adjacent house, men in blue coveralls streamed in and out, furniture heaved between them. A large dumpster stood in the cracked driveway, and thick clusters of ivy climbed the rotting porch. "Looks like you have new neighbors."

Ainsley stared out the front window. "Oh. That was fast."

He eased to the curb and let his engine idle. A surfer-type guy wearing jeans and a faded T-shirt stood in the middle of the overgrown yard. The man's dark hair was spiked like one of those GQ models. He wore faded jeans, frayed at the cuffs. He appeared to be directing the movers.

"Excuse me." Richard cut the engine and stepped out.

"Where are you going?"

"To meet your new neighbor." He closed the car door and strode up the sidewalk. A short time later, Ainsley's heels clicked behind him.

Stepping over a pile of crushed boxes, he crossed the weed-covered lawn. A golden Lab splotched with gray lay on the porch. He glanced up and gave a low growl, before letting his head fall.

From behind, Ainsley giggled. "Guess you're neither bark nor bite, huh, killer?"

"Hello." The man approached with an extended hand. "You must be some of my new neighbors."

Richard's eyes narrowed. "Hollis. Richard Hollis." He shook the man's hand with a firm grip.

The guy gave a crooked smile. "Chris Langley." He glanced at Ainsley. "And you are?"

"Ainsley Meadows. I live there." She pointed to her house. "Richard lives downtown, near the plaza."

Richard surveyed the once beautiful two-story home nestled by old growth trees and vibrant mums. Overgrown weeds crowded among them. Ivy clung to the stonework on the front of the house, the chimney, and two pillars supporting the covered porch. "Langley? You're related to property owner?"

"Yep. I'm her son." He shoved his hands in his pockets, his feet shoulder distance apart.

Ah, a freeloader, and clearly someone Richard needed to keep his eye on.

Chapter 3

*M*oving van unloaded, Chris surveyed the clutter-filled living room. Designer furniture sat squeezed between his mother's faded floral sofas and recliners, and boxes were stacked everywhere. He had too much junk. Way too much.

"That's everything." A man in blue coveralls, sweat dripping down his face, handed Chris a clipboard and pen. He scanned the many boxes stacked from floor to ceiling. "You want the guys to help you unpack? We charge by the box."

"No, I got it. Thanks." Chris signed the papers and wrote a check for the final amount, wincing at the total, then handed both over. He really should've gotten a few more estimates before hiring this crew.

"All right then." The man motioned toward the door with a jerk of his head and led his crew out.

Chris followed a few steps behind, stopping at the edge of his porch. He gazed across his overgrown yard to the stone-covered house next door. Light poured from the kitchen window, revealing the faint outline of Ainsley's profile. But then she stepped away, and the light went off.

Unopened mail and business papers covered the table, *Java Bean* printed across the top. His pulse quickened as the reality of his decision—a decision now set in legal stone—settled like a pile of rocks into his brain.

"So what do you think, Rusty?" His dog cocked his head, ears perked.

"Have I gone loopy, trading in my suits and ties for an apron?"

He glanced at the clock. His mom should be finished with her evening meal by now. He grabbed his phone and dialed, trying her private extension first. When no one answered, he called the front desk.

"Shady Lane Assisted Living. This is Heather. May I help you?"

"Good evening. This is Chris Langley. May I speak with my mother, please?"

Heather sighed loudly. "The residents are just finishing up with dinner."

Which meant finding his mother and bringing her to the phone would sap five, maybe ten minutes, from their robotic, check-it-off-the-list schedule.

"I'll wait. Thanks, Heather."

She sighed again, more dramatically this time. "Hold on."

The receiver clanked against something hard before soft instrumental music came on. A few moments later, his mom picked up.

"Hello?" Her voice had the high-pitched tone of agitation, which was normal for this time of night.

"Hey, Mom, it's Chris. Your son."

"I know who you are. What do you want?"

Good. Today was a good day, then. "How are you doing?"

"How do you expect me to be doing? I'm stuck in this horrible place surrounded by people I don't know. I have no idea where your father is. He needs to come soon. I'm tired. I want to go home. Please, call your father and tell him to take me home."

Chris closed his eyes and massaged his forehead. Reminding her of his father's death would only make things worse. "Everything will be all right. I'll be by tomorrow. Sometime after 6:00, after I close down the coffee shop."

"What coffee shop?"

"I sold my practice, Mom." And so went their nightly conversation, but at least this time she remembered his name. For now.

"You did what? Why would you do a stupid thing like that?"

To be closer to you. To make more time for you, like I should've done with Dad. "It was for the best, Mom."

"Your father is going to be very upset, especially after all the money we spent on law school. If you think I'm going to be the one to break it to him . . . if you think . . ."

"You don't need to, Mom. It's fine. Everything's fine."

Rusty lumbered across the linoleum and sat on his hindquarters. He let out a low, sorrowful moan, eliciting a chuckle from Chris. Cradling the phone between his ear and shoulder, he pulled out a bag of dog food and poured a small mound on the floor.

"Sorry, bud, I'll dig your bowl out tomorrow."

"What bowl? I don't need any more bowls."

"No, not for you, Mom. I was talking to my dog. He's hungry, but his dog bowl is buried in my pickup."

"Oh, you have a dog? Do you remember the dog you had when you were in college? Rustin, or Reddie . . . what was his name?"

"Rusty." Chris squatted down and scratched the back of Rusty's ears. "I found him huddled behind some dumpsters my junior year. Dad threw a fit when I brought him home." He laughed. "He threw an even bigger fit when I came back to get him after grad school."

"That's right, Rusty! I remember him. Such a lovely dog. Whatever happened to him, anyway?"

Chris paused. "Are you cheeking your pills, Mom?"

"Am I what?"

"Your medication. Are you playing games with your Alzheimer's pills?"

Something about the nursing staff at her facility didn't sit well with him. Not that he expected them to do a mouth check every time they dished out meds, but his mom deserved better than to be treated like a task between break times.

He needed to get her moved, and soon. But what if the other home, Lily of the Valley, wasn't any different? They promised a six-to-one patient-to-care ratio, but promising didn't make it so. He'd heard, "Oh, we're understaffed today," more times than he could count. In the end, it came down to trust. Whom did he trust most to care for his frightened, disoriented mother?

"Mom, I asked, are you taking your pills?"

"For what? I don't need those things. I'm not sick."

This was the reason he'd moved to Kansas City in the first place—to be near his mom. To make sure she took her medications.

"Carl, I'm tired."

Chris, Mom. The name's Chris.

"I need to find my husband. Do you know my husband? His name is . . . His name is . . ." Her voice trembled.

Chris breathed deep, exhaled slowly. "You get some rest. I'll call you tomorrow."

"You will? Do I know you?"

"Good night." *Love you, Mom.*

He hung up and dropped his phone on the counter. He turned to Rusty. "What do you say, old boy. Wanna watch the stars with me?"

The dog lumbered to his feet then followed Chris outside to the porch swing. Chris slumped against the metal frame. The rusted chains creaked against his weight. A cold breeze whistled through the overgrown maple a few feet away, sending gold and orange leaves fluttering to the ground.

He turned his gaze toward the star-filled sky, a silver moon peeking out from behind a cluster of inky clouds. *Heavenly Father, hold my mom tightly tonight. Help the staff at Shady Lane be patient with her.*

He relished the peace of the cool fall evening and the soothing sound of chirping crickets and cicadas. This had been a good move. Great neighborhood, friendly neighbors. Much different than the high-rise and high-stress environment he'd left. But if his business endeavors failed, he could lose much more than his parents' house.

According to his sister, he was setting himself up for that very thing. He'd just have to prove her wrong.

Chapter 4

*R*ichard stepped out of the elevator into a dark hall. He waved to trigger the motion-activated lights before continuing to his office. Fluorescent lighting reflected off the dark windows lining the hallway. He paused in front of his office, savoring the gold lettering tacked to the door. *Dr. Richard Hollis, Psychiatrist.* After eleven years of schooling, countless hours of clinical research, and enough brownnosing to induce a permanent stain, his labor was beginning to pay off. It'd been a long, treacherous climb, but well worth it.

An image of his father seated behind a thick, mahogany desk, face set in a scowl, flashed through his mind. Words, spoken more times than Richard cared to remember, echoed in his psyche. "You can do better than this, Richard. The weak man settles for mediocrity. While you waste your time listening to music and rotting your brain cells with television, tomorrow's CEOs are at the library, putting forth the effort required for greatness."

Nothing Richard did was good enough. But once his book launched, he could finally look his father in the eye. Presented with an autographed copy from the son he deemed unworthy of more than a passing glance, his father would be forced to acknowledge Richard's abilities. Perhaps they'd even share a celebratory drink.

He unlocked the door and entered the modern yet classically styled office. The dense, chateau carpet cushioned his steps. Breathing deep, he inhaled the rich aroma of soft Italian leather mixed with the faintest hint of ginger wafting from electronic air fresheners.

A quick sweep of the lobby assured him the cleaning staff

had come and gone. It was 6:05 a.m. Mrs. Ellis, his secretary, wouldn't be in for some time, which allotted him blessed silence to work on final book edits.

He crossed the room, gathered the small stack of phone messages from Mrs. Ellis's desk then continued to his office.

He frowned at the first message. Dr. Appello had canceled their engagement and declined Richard's request for endorsement, claiming he didn't have time to read the book. That was inconsequential. Richard wasn't asking for an academic abstract. A quick scan would suffice, followed by a glowing recommendation, of course.

Settling into his office chair, he grabbed his phone.

His publicist never slept past 4:00, and as expected, answered on the first ring. "Hello?"

However, analyzing the results, or lack thereof, Richard often wondered what the man did with his time. "Good morning. Is it too early to discuss publishing concerns?"

"I'm always happy to talk with you, Richard. What can I do for you?"

"Dr. Appello called."

"Excellent! I knew he'd respond quickly, and with his endorsement—"

"He declined." Richard turned on his computer and pulled up his email account. Twenty-five new messages, mostly spam.

"What? Did he say why?"

"He claimed lack of time. Perhaps I should have called him myself." As his father always said, successful results required self-implementation.

"I spoke with Dr. Pioni yesterday and plan to call him back this afternoon, at which time I will invite him to your engagement dinner. I believe you will have more luck discussing the matter with your colleagues then. Face-to-face."

"I hope you're right. Have a good day." Richard hung up and dropped his phone onto his desktop. Things weren't progressing anywhere near how he had planned. Not that bemoaning the matter would do any good. No. He needed to continue to push forward, to focus on the positive. Like his upcoming wedding.

He grabbed a silver-framed photo of Ainsley. Seated on a park bench, her green eyes glimmered in the midafternoon sun. Her olive complexion glowed next to her lilac sweater, giving her the appearance of youthful naïveté. She'd been so timid when they first met, like a frightened cat abandoned one too many times. And yet, beneath her unsophisticated, and perhaps even childish, demeanor hid a sparkling gem waiting to be adored and refined. Yes, he was confident he could mold her into a woman of standing. A wife to be admired, one to make his parents proud.

Ainsley tucked a few granola bars into her briefcase, grabbed a cup of coffee, and rushed down the hall. She pulled her jacket and gloves from the coat closet. The file she meant to read the night before lay on the entryway console, untouched. Sighing, she flipped it open. Twenty-five pages of medical research — not something she could digest during the handful of stoplights between her house and Dr. Senske's office.

OK, so she'd wing it.

As if taunting her, Richard's deep voice filled her mind. *This job is much too stressful for you, my dear. Once we are married, you can spend your time engaged in much more pleasant and rewarding endeavors.*

Right. Such as attending operas and art gallery functions with Richard's mother. No, thank you. Voltex or not, God had much more exciting, eternal things for her to pursue. If only she could figure out what. An image of the sad child staring out of a third-story Whispering Hills apartment came to mind, weighing heavy on her heart. How were he and his mother? She'd probably never know — would never see them again. *Oh, Lord, watch over that sweet boy. Place Your hand upon him.*

Snapping her file shut, she tucked it under her arm then wiggled into her designer knockoff, toe-jamming shoes. Her feet, still tender from the day before, protested. What she wouldn't do for a jeans and tennis shoes kind of day.

After a quick glance in the mirror, she dashed out, locking the door behind her. Spinning around, she tripped over a red Frisbee.

"Sorry about that." Dressed in exercise pants and a faded crewneck, Chris sauntered over with a boyish grin. The navy fabric accentuated the icelike specks in his blue eyes.

She grabbed the Frisbee and winced as her fingers closed around something cold and gooey. Forcing a smile despite a rapidly mounting gag reflex, she handed it over, casually inspecting her hand. "No big deal." Best-case scenario? A glob of mud. She glanced at the old dog lying on Chris's lawn. She wouldn't even consider the worst-case scenario right now, and she certainly wasn't going to smell her fingers.

"I'm trying to get old Rusty off his hindquarters, see if we can't get some blood pumping through those twelve-year-old legs of his." Holding the Frisbee in one hand, he spread his feet shoulder distance apart and crossed his arms. "You know what they say, use it or lose it."

A similar phrase, spoken nearly a decade ago by Ainsley's voice instructor, replayed in her mind. Squelching the thought, she maneuvered around Chris. "As I said, no big deal. You have a good day, Mr. Langley."

Her heels clicked rhythmically on the concrete as she scurried to her car. Fumbling for her keys, she glanced up to find Chris watching her with an odd, almost quizzical expression.

Looking away, she slid behind the steering wheel. She set her files on the passenger seat for easy access at the stoplights and searched the car for her gigantic bottle of hand sanitizer. It lay on the floor, partially tucked under the passenger seat. She grabbed it, squirted a healthy glob in the center of her palm then sat with dripping fingers and no napkin. *Lovely.*

After wiping her hand on the floorboard, she turned the key in the ignition and looped her car around. As she neared the end of her cul-de-sac, her phone rang. Richard.

"Good morning, princess." As usual, a keyboard clicked in the background.

"Sounds like you're already hard at work." On Vivian Road, two kids hiked up the paved bike path, bogged down with backpacks nearly as large as they were. The first fallen leaves of autumn swirled around their feet.

"Since 6:00. I'm working on some final edits, trying to find a better way to tie this book into Telioni's latest research. Or any of the latest research, before my final deadline next Friday."

"So you'll be out of pocket for a while, huh?"

"Maybe a little, but I've reduced my client load. I doubt I'll be taking appointments for some time. And if this book does well, perhaps never again."

"Oh." Rear lights flashed in front of her. She tapped her breaks and tightened her grip on the steering wheel. "I thought you became a psychiatrist to help people."

"Yes, well, we both know how that's turned out." He snorted.

Ainsley bit her bottom lip to keep from responding. His frustration was understandable, considering all the clients he'd worked with, most of whom remained just as messed up now, after years of therapy, as when he met them. If only he'd point them toward Jesus. . . . But reminding him of that would only instigate a fight.

"I wasn't calling to talk about the depravity of mankind, however. I wondered if perhaps you'd be able to join me for lunch. At Marlique's at 1:00?"

"How about somewhere a bit more casual?"

"Like where, the Burger Warehouse?" He spoke through his nose.

Ainsley bit back a giggle as an image of his face, puckered in a disgusted frown, came to mind. "Marlique's is fine. If you think we'll be able to get in. Did you want me to call?"

"Already done." The steady tap of typing resumed. "I'll see you at 1:00."

Click.

Apparently the question had been rhetorical. When had he become so controlling? She'd be glad when everything settled down and the old Richard returned.

Although in all truth, she hadn't seen that Richard in quite some time.

Chapter 5

ome on, old boy. Playtime's over." Chris held the door open for his dog. Rusty lumbered through, his hind legs dragging slightly.

Chuckling, Chris glanced at Ainsley's house one last time before slipping inside. "I don't think we've scored any points with our new neighbor."

Rusty's tail flicked, large brown eyes centered on his master.

"I agree. No sense stressing over it." He scratched Rusty behind the ears then grabbed an opened box filled with miscellaneous junk and carried it into the kitchen.

Rusty followed and sat, ears pointed, a few feet away.

"What, you hungry?"

He yipped, saliva dripping from the corner of his mouth.

Laughing, Chris poured a mound of dog food on the floor. He'd find Rusty's bowl tomorrow. "I know, I know, you're dying here. About to waste away."

Another laugh tickled his throat. What did people say about lonely eccentrics who conversed with their animals? But hey, everyone needed a dash of insanity in their day. Kept it fresh, kept it fun. And slightly pathetic.

He grabbed a cup of coffee and settled himself at the kitchen table. Junk mail, legal documents, and business files covered the surface. He sifted through a large stack of papers until he found the brochure for Lily of the Valley Assisted Living. *"The home away from home, where residents are treated as family."* Sounded great, minus the price. But then again, folks got what they paid for.

He set the brochure aside, thinking of his dwindling

savings. A long list of recent withdrawals filled his mind. And the expenses were just getting started. Maybe buying that quaint little coffee shop on the corner hadn't been such a good idea after all.

No. There was no point second-guessing himself. He'd made his choice. Now he needed to make it work.

Thirty minutes later he stood in the doorway of Java Bean, a box of books in hand. The rich smell of freshly brewed coffee, cinnamon, and chocolate surrounded him. The heavenly aroma contrasted sharply with the rather loud decor. The walls were splattered with a mess of colors, as if someone had tossed a bunch of a paint in a blender then released the lid. Two girls with pale skin, dressed entirely in black giggled behind the counter, steam moistening their faces. A man with a black Mohawk and a large hooped nose ring manned the cash register.

Something told him his employees weren't going to be thrilled with what he planned to do with the place. About as much as a dog loved a muzzle.

"Can I help you?" A third girl, caressing her long, copper hair, flashed a smile. She wore a much too revealing, tight navy blouse fastened above even tighter, low-riding khakis.

"Can I help you?" the girl asked again, with more edge in her voice.

"Hi, I'm Chris Langley, the new owner." He shifted his box to one hand and extended the other to his new employee.

Her perky smile turned into an O, which puckered into a frown when her gaze landed on his box of books and the leather bound Bible lying on top.

"And you are?"

"Candy, like a lemon drop." Her lips popped the last word.

"Good to meet you." He forced an awkward smile and wiggled past her.

People flowed in and out, cream-topped cups in hand. A woman in black leggings and a thick, swoop-necked sweater. Two men in jeans and combat boots. An older woman dressed in orange and yellow sweater.

Smiling at customers as he passed, Chris wove around circular tables covered with laptops, newspapers, and textbooks. Upon reaching the counter, the man with the Mohawk glanced up and gave him a peace sign before turning back to his customers.

Chris tucked his box beneath a shelf lined with various flavors of syrup then faced his crew.

Mohawk Man studied Chris, his face hovering between a smirk and a scowl. "So, you're the boss man, huh?" His smirk broadened as his gaze swept across Chris's green polo and crisp slacks.

"Yep, in the flesh." He surveyed the milk and coffee-splattered area and forced a smile. "And you are?"

The man ran his tongue over his lip ring. "Lawrence. But they call me the L-man."

"Only because loser-man has too many syllables." A girl with black lipstick flicked the guy with a towel.

Chris stifled a sigh and turned to the long line of customers, expecting to see frustration etched across their faces. Instead, they laughed, tossing out a few colorful expletives.

Are You sure this is Your plan, Lord? Because I'm starting to think our wires got jumbled somewhere along the way.

"Now that you all have robbed a good five minutes from my very important, highly productive day — " A woman with long, brown hair and a dress made from thick, colorful wool, like those you see in high-dollar boutiques, interrupted their banter. "I'll take a triple shot, part skim, part whole, extra dash of whipped cream. Oh, and add a bit of vanilla, will you?"

Lawrence scribbled instructions onto a cup. "Quite the slave driver there, Marlina. Got any sugar to go with that vinegar?"

"Only what you give me, lollipop."

The two continued their verbal banter while Chris finished hauling boxes in from his pickup. He stacked his collection of Christian fiction, study materials, sudokus, and a handful of Bibles along a far wall to be distributed on shelves later. Board games would line half the tables and large toy chests would occupy every corner. His final box contained a large collection of

Christian rock, old-time hymns, and a touch of Southern gospel.

Lawrence meandered over and surveyed a box of reading material stacked beside a container of board games. "You've got quite a load there, boss man. You're not planning on making this joint a Sunday School, are ya? Cuz I'd advise you rethink your plans on that one, unless you're looking to flip it to a Jesus joint, turning this oasis into no-man's-land." He picked up a book of inspirational poems, turned it over, then dropped it back into the box. "As in no-man would step foot, let alone fork over their dough, here."

Chris flashed his best smile. "More like a spiritual haven. And I'm not worried about the sales. That's God's department. He'll bring 'em, we'll fill 'em."

Lawrence frowned. "Is that legal?"

"Making this a calm and uplifting environment? Absolutely."

Lawrence studied him for a long moment. "You're not gonna start cleaning house, are you?"

Chris examined the café, taking in the, dark, abstract paintings and angular ceramics lining the windows and shelves. It was enough to make his eyes cross. "Housecleaning, yes. Employee cleaning, no . . . except perhaps in regard to wardrobe."

Lawrence moaned and slumped behind the counter, turning his attention to the growing line of customers.

Box in hand, Chris strolled down a back hall in search of his office. Industrial-sized boxes of flavoring, rolls of paper towels, and reams of cash register tape packed the area. A grungy mop stood beside a bucket full of black, foul-smelling water. Crushed milk containers filled an adjacent trashcan and spilled onto the floor.

A wave of nausea gripped him as the stench of soured milk mixed with overripe trash assaulted his nostrils. *And the next health inspection is?* He really should have paid more attention during his final walk-through, not that it mattered. He was here now. Besides, he had a lot of money riding on this place.

With no backup plan.

A windowless cubicle twice the size of a bathroom stall sat

at the end of the hallway. Manila files and invoices cluttered the dust-covered desk. The place smelled like vomit. Ten minutes of rummaging through old boxes, partially filled coffee cups, and sample bags of coffee beans revealed the culprit. A glass of milk curdled to moldy cheese. Appetizing.

A far cry from the plush, high-end office he left in Los Angeles. But some things were more important than the almighty dollar and a steady dash of prestige. If only he'd learned that before wasting his father's money on law school.

Grabbing the trashcan tucked under the desk, he made quick work of a week's worth of half-eaten food and drink items then leafed through the invoices. Luckily, most had been paid. The others were negotiated in the sale price. After almost an hour of sorting, filing, and tossing, he stretched and stood.

He glanced at the plastic superhero clock dangling sideways on the far wall.

My, how time flies when I'm having fun. The rest could wait until closing. For now, the best place he could be was on the café floor, getting to know his employees and customers.

"Wow, looks like you've been busy."

Chris glanced up. Candy leaned against the doorframe with her hip shoved out, back slightly arched.

He rifled through a stack of papers on his desk, memories of an old sexual harassment case flashing through his mind. A tad paranoid, perhaps, but better safe than sorry.

"Did you need something?"

The girl pouted and twirled a lock of hair around her index finger. "Yeah, there's someone here to see you. She says she's your sister."

Chris exhaled and raked his fingers through his hair. Apparently Matilda hadn't wasted any time tracking him down.

"Thanks, Candy. Tell her I'll be there in a moment."

Candy flashed a plastic smile, spun around, then bounced toward the lobby, long silky hair swinging across her shoulders.

Chris paused at the office door.

Lord, I know You said to turn the other cheek, but somehow I don't think this is the right time for that. Not when Mom's concerned. But even though I'm ready to fight tooth and nail on this one, I'd rather not go into battle today.

Inhaling, he trudged down the hall, stopping at the edge of the counter to scan the bustling dining area. Matilda sat at a corner table near the window, legs crossed, hands folded on top of a large manila folder.

Squaring his shoulders, he crossed the café with long, quick strides.

"Hello."

His sister jumped and turned her head, eyes wide. They instantly narrowed, her mouth pressing into a tight line, as she eyed Chris's coffee-boy attire.

"Good to see —" *No sense lying.* He cleared his throat. "To what do I owe this surprise?"

"Have a seat." She flicked her hand toward the open chair across from her.

"Can I get you something? A caramel latte or an iced mocha?" *A sedative, perhaps?*

Matilda straightened, her gray eyes making a slow sweep from left to right. When she turned back to Chris, her face softened. "Is everything all right? Did something happen at the firm?"

He flipped the vacant chair around and straddled it. "Everything's fine. I told you I planned to make a few changes — after Dad died."

"You need to let that go. So you were . . . unavailable. It was all so sudden. No one blames you for not being there for his surgery."

No one but me. He swallowed, avoiding her gaze. This was not the time or place. Forcing a smile, he drummed his fingers on the table and looked at the manila file clutched in her hand. "So, what do ya got there?" As if he didn't know.

"I'm selling the house. I've already contacted a realtor. I understand that you just moved in, but I'm sure you'll be able to find an apartment easy enough."

"It's not yours to sell."

"I'm also filing for guardianship. I brought the papers with me." She held up the file. "It would be best . . . for everyone involved, if you signed."

"And I told you I want Mom moved to Lily of the Valley."

"I won't allow it."

"Did you look at the brochure I sent?"

"I did, and went a step further, investigating the cost."

Chris leaned back, a derisive laugh bubbling in his throat. "So that's what this is about. You're worried about the bottom line, and now that I'm not pulling in six digits anymore, you're concerned."

Tiny lines formed around her mouth. "Of course I'm worried. About Mom, about the bills, about you. What's gotten into you?"

"Life, Matilda. It might have taken me a while, but I finally figured out life is more than business meetings and courtrooms."

"But you liked practicing law."

"Like an addict likes a hit." He shook his head. "I'm done with the conveyor belt life and basing every decision on the material payoff. It's time I enjoy the blessings God's given me." *While I still have a chance.*

An image of his father's coffin being lowered into the earth flashed through his mind. He blinked it away.

Matilda spread her hands flat on the table. "I know how much you regret not being there for Dad. And I understand how badly you want to be there for Mom, but she's . . ." She swallowed, tears forming in her eyes. "You heard what the doctors said. You've read as many articles on early-onset Alzheimer's as I have. We both know it only goes downhill from here."

"And you're ready to throw her away, is that it?" He spoke much louder than he'd intended, and the room went quiet. Attempting to calm himself, he took in a deep breath and let it out slowly. He needed to stop now before he said something he'd regret.

Matilda dipped her head, eyes downcast, cheeks flushed. "Perhaps we should talk about this another time. When you get off work."

He pushed away from the table, his chair legs screeching on the cement floor. "You can talk till your voice goes hoarse, Matilda. I'm not selling Mom's house, and I'm moving her to Lily of the Valley."

"It doesn't work that way. I've met with legal counsel. A court date will be set soon."

"You wouldn't dare." The last thing any of them needed, Mom especially, was a bitter court battle.

Chapter 6

Music drifted through speakers placed throughout the Zona Rosa outdoor mall. Despite the threat of rain, cars lined the street, and shoppers lugging bags or pushing strollers streamed the walk. Ahead of Ainsley, a large family dressed in tourist attire gathered in front of the 52nd Street Grill, posing for a picture.

"I'm glad we did this." Grinning, Gina looped her arm through Ainsley's. "I've missed you. Between your work, church stuff, and Richard, I feel like we never hang out anymore."

"Sorry."

Gina shrugged.

"That'll change. Things are slowing down." Minus the plethora of reading material her boss continued to assign. Then came wedding preparations.

"Uh-huh. Because you'll have way more time to hang out with me once you're married with a bunch of little Ainsleys underfoot."

"I'll make time."

Gina studied her.

"What?"

"I'm worried about you. About you and Richard."

"Yes, I know, Gina. You've made it quite clear; you don't like him."

"Nor him me, but that's beside the point." She stopped and faced Ainsley front on.

"He's so . . . controlling, and more and more so lately."

Ainsley shook her head. "He's just stressed."

Although Gina continued to hold her gaze for a moment longer, she didn't say more. Which was good, because Ainsley wasn't sure how to respond. True, Richard had been acting like a bear, and he could be very particular on things. Most of the time that wasn't a huge deal. But what about when it was? Would he listen to her, or would he be like his mother, bulldozing his will into a situation?

They continued in silence, past a coffee shop and restaurant and through the grassy area stretched in front of the outdoor stage. Ainsley glanced at a vacant bench seat, feeling a sudden urge to sit. If only she could put the world on hold. She felt completely overwhelmed by all the pressures weighing down on her. She wanted desperately to do something significant, if not for that boy and his mother, then for some other hurting family. She wanted to find a better, less stressful career but didn't have the time or money for more schooling. Then there were all the wedding details: colors, guest lists, where to host the reception, what to serve.

Why did everything have to be so incredibly complicated?

Richard sat at his desk, his gaze shifting between the clock and his opened door. He frowned and crossed his arms, leaning back. Heather McGahana was late. As usual. She was probably checking and rechecking all her household locks and appliances. And yet, she still refused to take her medication.

Why was he wasting his Saturday mornings on this woman?

As long as he was here, he may as well work on book edits, which were extensive. With a sigh, he swiveled to face his computer. But the moment he pulled up the file, the front door clanged open, and Mrs. McGahana's voice shattered the silence.

"I'm so very sorry I'm late. I thought for sure I'd left the burner on, though I also knew I'd checked it numerous times. And then I noticed my tank was only half full, which of course, caused me great concern. With all the, well, never mind. I'm sure you've heard it all before."

"Mr. Hollis is waiting to see you, ma'am." Mrs. Ellis's voice was calm, as usual.

A moment later, Mrs. McGahana rapped on Richard's door and poked her head inside. "I'm sorry I'm late. I thought —"

Richard rose. "Yes, I heard." Crossing the room, he extended his hand, suppressing a grimace with a smile. "Please." He motioned for his client to sit, which she did. After grabbing his leather portfolio containing his pen and notepad, he moved to an armchair across from her. "How have things been? Have you been keeping a journal?"

"To document my feelings, you mean?"

"Yes, but more than that. To begin noticing the circumstances around and potential triggers of your anxiety attacks."

She inhaled, her entire torso lifting and caving on the exhale. "I need to. I really need to. It's just, I'm so overwhelmed with life in general . . ." She shook her head, tears glistening in her eyes. "This disorder steals enough of my time as it is."

"Yes, well, perhaps if you follow the treatment plan, your obsessions will become more . . . manageable, and your time will be freed."

"I don't know. Most days I feel like it's hopeless, you know? It's terrible!" She shifted, tugging first at the back edge of her shirt then at the front. "Some days I feel as if I'm not getting better at all." She went on to list her usual complaints; the same symptoms but different scenarios. "I feel as if I'm a prisoner in my own house. No one understands. Last week, my brother had a birthday party. Of course I was invited, out of spite, I'm sure. Or to give them something to talk about when I didn't show." Her voice hitched. "'Poor, crazy Heather couldn't come again.' And of course, the sane members of my family — as if any of them are — would have to come up with a plan as to how they were going to rescue crazy old me."

"Have you talked with them about your condition? Perhaps if they unders —"

"Oh no! I couldn't do that. I'd never hear the end of it." She went on to tell of a time, two years back, when well-intentioned family members took it upon themselves to "fix" her. Needless to say, it didn't end well.

"Last we talked, I wrote you a new prescription. Have you tried the medication we discussed?"

Her gaze dropped to her hands, and she moved from ferociously rubbing her wrist to picking at her cuticles. More accurately, to picking at the sores where once her cuticles grew. "I researched them online."

But of course, as she had her condition and every other possible ailment in the diagnostic and statistical manual of psychological disorders. "As I told you when we last met, you cannot believe everything you read online. Similarly, just because one person has an adverse reaction doesn't mean you will as well." Why was he wasting his breath? This woman clearly had no intention of listening. Rather, she wanted someone's undivided attention for an hour.

Fifty minutes, actually. With thirty-seven still to go.

Though he feigned interest, nodding at appropriate intervals, asking vague questions at the rare pauses, he let his mind wander to his book.

His editor had concerns regarding a few of his research points and was asking Richard to use alternative sources. As if this wasn't frustrating enough, she also wanted him to delete an entire chapter, calling it repetitious, while adding two others.

"Dr. Hollis, are you listening?"

Richard jerked back to attention, nearly dropping his pen. "Yes. Yes, of course."

"And what would you suggest?"

He flipped through blank pages on his tablet to buy for time, then closed the portfolio and set it on the table. Rubbing his hands together, he stared at her, as if deep in thought. "I have an idea, Heather. One I believe will help you tremendously."

"You do?" She scooted to the edge of her seat.

"I do." He moved to his desk and began rummaging through hanging files in his bottom right drawer. Inside were numerous documents printed off the Internet or received during professional lunches and mental health conferences. Most of them were highly technical; technical enough to keep Heather on Google for some time. If she were occupied by something productive, perhaps she wouldn't feel the need to act out a compulsion.

Regardless, in her current noncompliant state, there was nothing more he could do to help her.

"Here." He handed her a booklet on central dopamine receptors and their involvement in obsessive compulsive disorder. The literature was quite detailed, and as such, should keep her occupied for some time.

Accepting the material, she stared at the title and blinked, looked at Richard, then the title again. "Thank you."

"My pleasure." He looked at his watch. "Unfortunately, our session has concluded."

"It has?"

He nodded, moving toward the door. "I hope you find that information helpful."

"Yes, I'm . . ." She reached for her purse, still casting frequent glances from him to the document. "I'm sure I will."

He opened the door wider. "Good day and good health."

Chapter 7

*A*insley tossed her briefcase onto the passenger's seat and slid behind the wheel. She stared at the glass, four-story medical building in front of her. If only she could take back the past hour of her life.

Dr. Senske's words replayed in her mind, spoken with the warmth of a salamander. "And why should I prescribe Voltex, Miss Meadows, when Neurostockton provides more relief with less risk and half the side effects, at a fraction of the cost?"

And that after she'd explained the results of the double-blind study conducted by Hausenburg University. Had she presented the data wrong or was this medication really that unpredictable? Either way, she'd just lost her chance at receiving a Christmas bonus, the money of which she'd hoped to use for future college expenses.

But for now, she had much greater concerns — like finding a public restroom. If things had gone better at the doctor's office, perhaps she would've used their facilities, but she'd swallowed enough humiliation for one day.

She glanced at the clock — 12:30. That gave her thirty minutes to make it across town during lunch hour traffic. Which didn't leave a lot of time for potty breaks, but if she didn't find one soon, she'd have much bigger problems on her hands.

Easing onto Troost, she scanned the adjacent buildings in search of a bathroom. Hopefully one that didn't totally creep her out — a tall order in this part of town. Five minutes later, she settled on a gas station with peeling paint and a broken sign. She pulled beside a red two-door and stepped out.

A dented Honda with rusted and corroded metal parked beside her, 1980s rock music blaring. A lanky man got out, cigarette in hand. He took a drag then flicked it on the ground, watching Ainsley. Her breath caught, and she froze. It was the man from the apartment. His lips twitched into a cruel smile.

He recognized her.

It felt like forever passed as she stood there, icy feet frozen to the cement, eyes wide.

Lifting his hands like a clawed animal, he lunged forward. "Boo!"

She gave a high-pitched cry and jerked backward, her spine smacking against the car door. Laughing, the man muttered curse words and entered the convenience store.

Ainsley returned to her car and locked the doors. She inspected the man's empty vehicle, hoping to see the boy from the apartment but hoping not to at the same time. She wanted to believe he and his mom were long gone and making a new life for themselves somewhere. As unlikely as that was.

Oh, Lord Jesus, please bring someone into that woman and child's path. Someone safe, someone who can help them.

Continuing to pray, she remained in her car until the abuser was long gone and her churning stomach had settled.

Five minutes later, she perused the sparsely filled isles in search of a token purchase. She settled on a cup of stale coffee then filed behind a long line of customers. The clock on the far wall read 12:40. *Lovely.* Maybe she should call Richard to let him know she'd be late. He'd be thrilled.

The line inched forward one pack of cigarettes at a time until Ainsley stood at the counter.

"That all?" A woman with a blotchy face and dirt-colored hair flashed a millisecond-smile.

"Yes, thank you." Ainsley handed over twenty dollars then waited, fidgeting, as the woman counted out each bill.

She tucked her wallet under her arm and rushed to the door, pausing to study a magazine displayed on a nearby rack. The cover showed a single story log cabin nestled between towering maples. Ivy wove around large, red stones lining the gently sloping landscape.

What is it about this Cabin in the Woods that keeps families coming back year after year? Page 18.

Now that would make a lovely place for a wedding. Absolutely enchanting.

She turned to the cashier. "Are these free?"

The woman squinted then shrugged. "Yeah."

Back in the car, Ainsley set her cup in the console then flipped through the magazine until she reached the featured article.

"Cabin in the Woods, nestled in the heart of Kansas City, is the perfect place for your wedding, reunion, or corporate function."

She smiled as an image of herself dressed in a Victorian lace gown, seated next to a flowering vine, emerged. Yes, that quaint little cabin looked perfect. Oh, she couldn't wait to tell Richard! She set the magazine aside and grabbed her phone in one hand, holding the coffee in the other. Without thinking, she took a large, tongue-scorching sip.

"Ouch!" She jerked her head back and dropped the cup. It ricocheted off the steering wheel to the floor, splattering hot coffee everywhere, including all over her white blouse.

"Oooh! Oooh! Ahhhh!" She pressed her back against the seat, her skin throbbing. Brown stains splattered across her blouse and skirt.

"Great. There's no way I'm going to Marlique's now." She searched her car for tissue, gloves, anything to sop up the sticky mess pooling beneath her. She settled on an old scarf tucked in the glove box and cleaned up as best as she could.

She grabbed her phone, which flew to the other side of the car during her coffee fiasco, and dialed Richard's number.

"Hello?"

Soft piano music drifted across the line. Apparently he was already at the restaurant, likely seated at his favorite table.

"Hey, honey, I'm so sorry, but I've had an accident." She eased onto Troost.

"Accident? What kind of accident?"

"No, nothing like that. I . . ." A giggle bubbled in her throat, gaining momentum with every word. "I'm covered in coffee."

He didn't respond right away. "Coffee?"

Between giggles, she explained her mishap. "So, as you can imagine, I'm not quite up for a five-star restaurant. I'm going home to change."

He sighed. "So lunch is off then?"

"Not necessarily. Why don't we stop by that little coffee place near my house? The crowd might be a bit . . . peculiar . . . but they serve an amazing turkey-avocado sandwich."

Another extended pause. "If you don't want to come to Marlique's, just tell me." His voice took the tone of a father scolding a wayward child.

"Are you serious? Great way to start forever, darling. Accuse your fiancée of lying over something as trivial as turkey."

Richard chuckled. "Of course not. I must be more tired than I'd thought. What time would you like me to meet you?"

"Give me twenty minutes to get home and another fifteen to clean up."

"One thirty it is."

Once home, she traded her starchy dress suit for a softer variety, and headed to the coffee shop. Once again, Richard beat her there, his silver Lexus parked along the curb. She eased between his car and a red convertible, grabbed the coffee-splattered magazine, and got out.

She entered through the back door and headed straight for Richard, sitting near the far wall. "Hi."

"Good to see you." He stood and kissed her cheek.

She smiled and dropped her magazine on the table. "So, what would you like? I'll go place our order."

"I knew our time was short, so I already took the liberty." Sitting, he leaned back, hands folded in front of him. "Two turkey-avocado sandwiches, fat-free mayo, extra sprouts; two salads, no dressing; and two decaf lattes with skim milk."

Ainsley raised an eyebrow. "Wow, thanks. I guess."

He picked up the coffee-splattered magazine with his thumb and index finger. "Evidence of your fiasco?"

She settled into the chair across from him, unable to contain her smile. "Oh, Richard, I found the perfect place for our wedding." She flipped the pages to the article about the Cabin in the Woods. "Ever since I was a little girl, I've had this dream — sort of like Snow White, I suppose, of getting married in a quaint little cabin tucked in the woods."

"You've never mentioned anything of the sort."

"I guess I never put much stock in it, until now. Until this." She pushed the picture of the cabin toward him. "Isn't this place beautiful?"

He studied it. "A delightful place for an afternoon outing."

Not exactly the reaction she expected, but then again, it always took Richard a while to warm up to new ideas. "Or a wedding."

"Now, Ainsley, certainly you can see the difficulties in using such a facility."

"Actually, I don't." She crossed her arms. "Enlighten me."

"I agree with you, this little cabin is quaint. But you deserve more, my love. I already booked the most exquisite location for our wedding and reception."

Ainsley stared at him. "You're kidding, right?"

He shook his head and retrieved his briefcase.

"And when were you planning on discussing this with me? Or are my opinions irrelevant?"

"I thought I'd mentioned it."

"I bet." She rolled her eyes. "From where I sit, it seems you are perfectly content to run the show. Is this how things are going to be for us? You calling the shots and me following like an obedient wife?"

"Don't be ridiculous. I was merely trying to treat you like the princess you are." He produced a glossy brochure. On the front, a towering nineteenth-century cathedral with stained-glass windows stood in the center of a meticulous garden lined with symmetrical shrubs and spiral-trimmed bushes. "Only the best for my beautiful bride."

She studied him for a moment before allowing her tense shoulders to go slack. "This place looks enchanting, really. But I hoped for something a bit smaller, more low-key."

He laughed and bopped her on the nose. "You are simply adorable, my dear, but we both know you deserve much better. Still," he shrugged, "Perhaps we can go to that cabin for a second honeymoon. Or our first anniversary."

Adorable? Like a puppy? "How about we check the cabin out this weekend, then if you still don't like it, we can discuss other options."

"I appreciate your intentions, but I worry a cabin this small will never accommodate our guest list."

"What guest list? I thought we decided to keep things small and intimate."

Richard focused on his BlackBerry. "And I thought we were still discussing the guest list. There are obligations to consider, you know. Certain personalities I need to include, especially considering my upcoming book launch."

"What are you talking about?"

Richard lifted his gaze, his lips pressing into a firm line. She turned to see her neighbor, Chris Langley, standing behind them, laden food tray in his hand, apron tied around his waist.

"Ainsley, Richard, good to see you both again." The corners of his eyes crinkled into a genuine smile.

Warmth crept up Ainsley's neck and face. How long had he been standing there? "Chris, I didn't know you worked here."

"As of today." He arranged the food and coffee on the table then widened his stance, tray dangling at his side, free hand tucked under a muscular bicep.

She cleared her throat, pretending the guy hadn't just caught her and her fiancé on the verge of a squabble. "So, are you settled? At the house, I mean."

"Not by any means. But you know, little by little, right?"

"Well, if you need any help . . ."

"I'm good, but thanks."

An awkward silence ensued.

Richard cleared his throat. "Thank you for your assistance, Mr. . . . ?"

"Langley."

"Langley. We have everything we need."

Chris's eyebrows shot up, his mouth going slack. But then a hint of a smile emerged. "Right. Enjoy your lunch."

Ainsley waited for him to move out of hearing then glared at Richard. "That was rude."

"What?"

"We have what we need? As if he were intruding."

"Well, he was." Richard crossed his arms. "There's something unsettling about that man."

"Like what?" She picked up her latte, inhaling the rich aroma.

He shrugged. "I can't say for certain, but he appears too . . . happy."

"As if that's a bad thing."

He glanced at his watch. "I need to go." Rising, he gave her hand a squeeze then grabbed his food and coffee. "In regard to our wedding location—let's discuss that in more detail over dinner."

With that, he left, leaving Ainsley to reconcile her dreams of the perfect ceremony with what, quite likely, would be a series of mutual compromises. And maybe even a few tears.

Why did weddings have to become so complicated?

Studying her engagement ring, she rubbed the diamond with her thumb. *Lord, am I doing the right thing here?*

Chris tucked his dishrag into his apron and leaned against the counter. Across the café, Ainsley sat with shoulders hunched forward, eyelids blinking so rapidly they looked ready to take flight. She was obviously worried about something. Poor girl. Not that it was any of his business.

He grabbed a dish tub and headed toward a dirty table.

A large crash sounded behind him. He dropped his tub on

a nearby table and turned to see an old woman reaching for a shattered mug. Coffee and salad pieces littered the floor, covered in sticky cream.

"No, please, allow me." He hurried to her side, grabbed her elbow, and led her to a nearby table. She trembled, likely with the onset of Parkinson's. An image of his mother, face contorted with the fear of dementia, came to mind. He shook it away. "I'll clean this up then we'll get you another salad and coffee."

He made eye contact with Lawrence then gave a jerk of his head. The man nodded and disappeared around the corner, returning with a mop and bucket. Offering a smile, Chris began picking up the broken glass. He glanced up to find Ainsley watching him. Once again, he felt a tug to reach out to her, make sure she was OK. But another crash, louder this time and followed by a slew of curse words hurled by one of his employees, stole the opportunity. Suppressing a moan, he wondered for the hundredth time since selling his law practice if he'd done the right thing.

Richard paused in the parking lot of his office complex to read through the Holy Trinity Cathedral brochure again. He really should have spoken to Ainsley before booking it, but he thought she'd welcome the surprise. Wasn't that what women longed for? To be swept off their feet with the unexpected? True, she'd mentioned her desire for a small wedding, but that was her past talking. He'd seen it in countless patients raised in similar circumstances. A life of disappointments made it difficult to dream.

That was why the cathedral was so important. It'd make her feel like a radiant princess, and would go a long way toward replacing that negative self-talk that likely dominated her thinking. She'd thank him for it later.

His cell phone rang, and his publicist's number lit the screen. "Eric, you must have good news for me."

"I . . . well, yes and no."

He stepped onto the pavement, hit the door lock button twice, then strolled across the lot. "I'm listening."

"I haven't had much luck with those television stations we mentioned, but I did manage to secure an interview with a local radio station."

"Which one?"

"KCGW."

"Never heard of them."

"They're an AM talk show."

"What kind of talk — academic or Jerry Springer?"

"Well . . . I wouldn't call them academic. More entertaining, in a rural sort of way."

"How rural?"

"I believe the station is located in Holt. Maybe Kearney."

Richard snorted. "You can't be serious." The glass doors opened in front of him.

"I know they're not your first choice —"

"That's an understatement."

"And yet, it's a start."

This wouldn't do. This wouldn't do at all. Certainly Eric could do better than a small-town, no-name radio talk show. "I'll call you back." He ended the call and tucked his phone into his front pocket.

Inside his office lobby, his secretary sat hunched over her desk, pen in hand, phone tucked between her ear and shoulder. She glanced up and raised a hand as if beckoning him to wait. He paused, shifted; checked his watch.

She hung up. "Heather McGahana called three times already. I told her you're not taking any additional appointments this month, but she says it's urgent."

Richard frowned. There was nothing more he could do for that woman, except perhaps prescribe her new meds. Not that she'd take them.

Candace tore a sheet of paper off a yellow notepad and handed it over.

"Thank you. I'll call her." And suggest she find a new therapist.

Chapter 8

*A*insley sat with her knees pressed together, spine straight. A thick manila file lay on her lap. Plaques and motivational sayings lined her boss's walls, and thick books filled the mahogany shelves. A large, obviously plastic tree stood cockeyed in a ceramic pot, and a novelty plasma ball like those seen in high school science classes, stood on an accent table next to a portable putting green.

Mr. Holloway leaned forward and propped his elbows on his desk. His bushy eyebrows cast dark shadows over his amber eyes. "Tessa told me you haven't made a sale this week. And that you declined the Psychiatrics Mental Health Awareness dinner." He pushed his glasses back with his index finger. "Low sales and declining potentially profitable functions do not go hand in hand. Is there a problem I should be aware of?"

Ainsley glanced at her file lying like a chunk of rock in her lap. Inhaling, she looked up, focusing on Mr. Holloway's receding hairline. "As to the function, sir . . . No, that wasn't the place to start. He wouldn't care about all the hours she'd put in nor all the details she needed to take care of before her upcoming wedding. She cleared her throat. "In regard to my low sales, Voltex appears to have . . ." *Careful, girl. You need this job.* "The psychiatrists I met with prefer a different medication, sir. One they felt carried less risk with more manageable side effects. At a lower cost."

Mr. Holloway's eyebrows pinched together, forming a deep crevice between them. "Did you show them the literature?"

"I did. They felt . . ." She swallowed and spread her hands, palms down, on her thighs. "They felt the study conducted by Hausenburg University was biased."

"Ridiculous." He tapped his pencil on his desk with enough force and speed to snap it in two. "Apparently you are not presenting the study nor its findings effectively." He pushed away from his desk, the wheels of his chair squeaking, and opened a tan filing cabinet to his right. After thumbing through various files, he pulled out a stack of stapled paper. "I thought we went over this in our last sales meeting, but . . ." His voice turned cold. "In case you have forgotten, here are some techniques you should find helpful, the first of which begins with a thorough understanding of the product; something you clearly lack. Take the rest of the day to read this material, and report back to me tomorrow."

She accepted the papers, adding them to the already thick file on her lap. Reason number 578 she had yet to register for pharmaceutical school classes. How could she ever move forward toward a stable career when her boss kept her loaded down? "Thank you, sir. I'll look over these right away." She jumped to her feet.

"Good, because in today's economy, our company must focus on the strongest links in the chain. You know what they say, Miss Meadows."

"Yes, sir. A company's only as strong—"

"We need to weed out the liabilities to make room for the strong." He snipped the air with two fingers. "You are dismissed."

With a final nod, Ainsley dashed out and closed the door behind her. She didn't slow until she'd reached her car.

Oh, Lord Jesus, why must everything be so hard? Maybe I'm not cut out for this job.

Getting in, she checked her phone messages then scrolled through her alerts. Five missed calls from her mom. *Lovely.* Ainsley hadn't heard from her in nearly two years, and now the woman was blowing up her voice mail. So, what tragedy had hit now? Boyfriend number 365 turn toad quicker than expected? When would her mom learn—you can't find marriage material at the local pub? Nor the Quick-N-Go.

She played the first message.

"Hey, sugar drop, I know it's been a while since I called." Her mother's voice exploded across the line. "But you know how it is. Things have been craaaazzzy! I can't believe my baby girl's getting married." She gave a high-pitched squeal. Wincing, Ainsley pulled the phone away and switched ears. "I signed up for a cake decorating class. I saw the most beautiful cake on the *Lisa and Jenny* show this morning. I bet I can make it as easy as . . . well, as easy as a piece of cake." She ended with a high-pitched giggle.

Ainsley skipped to the second message.

"On second thought, what if we had chocolate frosting covered with a variety of rock candy, like they sell in those underground cave stores."

She skipped to the third message, left twenty minutes after the previous.

"On second thought, I might need to take a rain check on that. Like I said, things have been craaaaazzzzy." Must she draw out every syllable like that? "But we'll get together soon, I promise. Oh, by the way, some folks might call looking for me. Do me a favor, muffin, and tell them you haven't heard from me."

What in the world was her mother involved in now? Honestly, Ainsley didn't want to know. With a hefty sigh, she tossed her phone on the passenger seat, ignoring the last two messages. They'd only make her angrier, potentially lose all self-control angry. In the meantime, she planned to turn her phone off and spend the evening sipping peppermint tea while soaking in a hot bubble bath.

She glanced at her work files and sighed.

Reading first; then bath.

She pulled into her cul-de-sac with a contented smile. Home. Oh, how she'd love to hide away in her bedroom with a good book and cup of that tea. Indefinitely. After gathering her mail, she pulled into her garage and collected her things, intentionally leaving her work material behind. She'd catch up on it later, but for one night, just one, she planned to take time to herself.

She flipped through the mail, then stopped.

She'd received a letter from UMKC. This reminded her of upcoming scholarship application deadlines. Applications she'd barely had time to look at. Not that she held much hope in being awarded anything; and even if she was, the monies would only cover a portion of her fees, leaving her to scrimp for the rest.

That meant she'd have to continue working while attempting to complete an insanely difficult coarse load. A fact that made the scholarship application requirements all the more daunting.

Why did it feel like she was boxed in behind a bunch of closed doors? And those that were opened even a smidgeon contained insurmountable hurdles to climb over.

Chris watched Ainsley pull into her garage. He offered a wave but either she ignored him or was too caught up in whatever was causing her deep scowl to notice.

Not that it was any of his business, except for the fact that he wanted to be a good neighbor.

He turned back to his house. Rusty lay on the bottom step, paws extended. His tail flickered as Chris approached.

"Looks like it's just you and me, boy. As always." Chris plodded to the front door then held it open for the arthritic dog.

Massaging the back of his neck, he surveyed the living room. "So, what should I conquer first, unpacking this mound of junk that I really don't need, or turning that college hangout café of mine into a believers' retreat?" He flipped open a box of high school football trophies tucked beneath his old letterman jacket. "This can go in the basement." Hoisting the box into his arms, he wove his way through the cluttered living room. His couch sat parallel to his mother's, The smooth, tan leather a sharp contrast to the faded floral print dotted with decades worth of coffee stains. His heart warmed as an image of his mother standing face-to-face with his father, hands on her hips, flashed through his mind.

"But that thing's a piece of junk, Irene. Why you insist on keeping it is beyond me. It's not like we don't have the money for new furniture."

"Do you know how many Bible stories the children and I read on that couch? How many tears those pillows have caught as your children snuggled into my arms, sharing their tragedies of the day." A playful smile tugged at her lips as she cupped Dad's face in her hands. "Surely age is not a disqualifier, my dear. Because I say things go softer with age, once all the rough edges have been smoothed away."

"Don't think I'm oblivious to your not-so-hidden message, Mrs. Langley." Chris's father grabbed her by the waist and pulled her near, tickling her ribs until her cheeks turned rosy.

He turned to Rusty who sat a few feet away, watching him with droopy eyes. "The couch stays, old boy. At least, for the time being."

Rusty lifted an ear and cocked his head.

"Oh, you don't fool me. I've been talking to you for way too long to believe you don't understand what I say." He walked toward a narrow flight of stairs and paused at the bottom step. "Besides, if I needed anything other than a yes-man, I would've found a cat a long time ago."

Ten boxes later, he relaxed on the front porch nursing a cup of decaf.

The purr of an engine and a flash of lights caught his attention. He turned toward the street as his sister, Matilda, pulled to the curb. The car barely stopped before she stepped out.

"Hey, sis. Nice . . ." He really needed to think before speaking. Or pray for a heart transformation so he could actually say what every brother ought to say to his sister. Even if she resembled a scouring pad.

Matilda, frumpish, with her wooden heels clicking on the walk, clutched a manila envelope in one hand and a black purse in the other.

Stopping a foot from the porch, she crossed her arms. Wine-colored lipstick seeped into the tiny lines around her lips, deepened by her scowl—which had become a permanent fixture following their father's death.

He moved aside and swept his arm toward the front door.

Her frown deepened as she marched up the steps and into the house. She paused in the box-filled living room, eyebrows pinched together.

A perfect end to a tiring day. "Pull up a box." Chris stifled a laugh, the corners of his mouth twitching.

She wasn't amused.

"How about we go in the kitchen. I'll make coffee." He maneuvered around a grandfather clock, two matching end tables, and a box of coffee mugs. Footsteps shuffled behind him.

"This is not a social call."

But of course not, Matilda. I would hate to sully your day with the inconvenience of family and emotions. Oops, already have.

Face puckered, she clutched and released her hands as she surveyed the cluttered table. A brochure for Lily of the Valley lay on top.

Pulling out a chair, he motioned for her to sit down. She perched on the edge of her seat and rested her elbows on top of a lopsided pile of junk mail. Dropping her hands to her lap, she huffed.

"I spoke with my attorney. You and I know it will be much more economical and time-effective if we settle this among ourselves."

Lord, if You want to give me a golden nugget to say here, I'd sure appreciate it.

He handed her the brochure for Lily of the Valley. "I agree. Have you had more time to look at the brochure?"

"I have, in detail and with much thought. I suggest you do the same."

"I understand you're concerned with the price. I'm prepared to cover that." He glanced at a recent and unimpressive bank statement lying on the table.

Matilda followed his gaze and frowned. "And when reality catches up with this midlife-crisis dream chasing? Who will cover the expenses then? I'm sure you noticed the two-year contract required."

"I did, and I am not concerned. God will take care of that."

She sighed. "I have no problem with your . . . radical faith as you like to call it. So long as it doesn't cause harm to anyone else. But when it encroaches on the well-being of others —"

"Let's cut to the chase. I'm being served, is that it?"

Check it, buddy. Don't say something you'll regret.

She lifted her chin and stared down the long shaft of her nose. "If you insist on being so difficult . . ."

He stood. "Then it's good I have a law degree. Thank you for stopping by."

She remained glued to her chair. He walked over to her, placed his hand under her arm, and gently yet firmly pulled her to her feet.

"Well, I never!"

"You have now." He nudged her to the door, her breath heaving in and out like an overdramatic teenager.

"Enjoy the rest of your day." He grabbed a business card from his back pocket and handed it to her. "Your lawyer can call me at this number."

With a gentle push, he eased her across the threshold, offered his best attempt at a smile, and softly closed the door. Laughter bubbled as an image of his sister standing on the other side, face scrunched tighter than a prune, emerged.

Chapter 9

Richard eased into his parents' circular drive and cut the engine. He drew his cell phone from his front pocket. No missed calls, not from Ainsley or his publicist.

Frowning, he returned it to his pocket and stepped out. A gust of wind swept over him as he made his way to the mahogany double door. A familiar uneasiness settled in his stomach as he raised his hand to the bell. The first six notes of Beethoven's Fifth chimed and a moment later, the door eased open.

"Richard, how nice to see you." His mother's silver hair glistened beneath the light of a crystal chandelier. She scanned his wardrobe before meeting his gaze.

"You look lovely as ever." He stepped forward and kissed her cheek. "I told Father I would be stopping by. Is he home?"

She moved aside to let him in. "He's in the basement. I'll let him know you're here." She pressed the intercom button to her right, initiating another melodious chime.

His father's deep voice drifted through the speakers moments later. "Yes, Cheryl?"

Richard straightened and smoothed the front of his shirt. The knots in his stomach tightened like they had when, as a child, he'd awaited his father's chastising hand.

"Richard is here."

"Send him down."

She offered Richard a tight smile. "I do hope you plan to stay for dinner."

He made a deliberate move to check his watch. "I don't have much time."

"Then I suppose we shall eat quickly."

Lowering his gaze, he walked through the foyer, past the formal sitting area to the descending stairs. His feet sank into the plush carpet, and the dim glow of recessed lighting overhead elongated his shadow. He paused at the bottom step. Squaring his shoulders, he lifted his chin and crossed the room.

His father sat in a leather recliner, one leg draped over his knee, thick book in hand. He waited until Richard stood directly in front of him before looking up.

"Have a seat." His father closed his book and set it on the glass-topped table in front of him. "I would say it is a pleasure to see you, but I presume you are not here for pleasure's sake."

Richard sat in an adjacent love seat. "I read your article in *Neuropsychology Today*. I found it quite interesting."

"So you came to discuss the benefits of structural magnetic resonance imaging of the adolescent brain?"

Richard shifted and resisted the urge to wipe his sweaty palms on his pant legs. "A fascinating topic, to be sure. But no, that's not why I came." Although his father preferred the direct approach, Richard longed for a slight buffer period, if only until his muscles uncoiled. And yet, his father hadn't risen to the top of his field by making small talk. "I came to seek your endorsement for my book."

"Really, now, surely you are not asking me to pave your way for you. A man who cannot stand on his own is not ready to stand at all.

"I'm not asking you to pull strings on my behalf. I'm merely seeking—"

"To reap the benefits of my hard work. You're wishing to build your reputation upon mine instead of making a name for yourself. Although as your father nothing would please me more than to see you succeed, it would not benefit you in the slightest if I secured your success for you." He stood. "You're staying for dinner, I presume?"

Richard fought against a frown. Although the idea further knotted his stomach, his father left little room for withdrawal. Besides, one last attempt remained untried. If his mother made the suggestion, through conversation, maybe his father would change his mind. Unlikely, perhaps, but not impossible.

He forced a smile. "Of course." He followed his father across the room and up the stairs. The rich aroma of Salisbury steak and roasted garlic drifted from the kitchen, making his mouth water.

In the dining room, red wine filled three crystal glasses on the dining room table, and a large salad bowl centered the gold-and-maroon striped tablecloth.

His father sat at the head of the table. Locking his gaze on Richard's, he lifted his glass, swirled it, then brought it to his nose. Richard sat beside him and arranged his already straight silverware.

The grandfather clock in the adjacent room chimed.

Moments later, Richard's mother broke the awkward silence when she emerged from the kitchen carrying a platter of steaming meat covered in caramelized onions.

"How unfortunate Ainsley couldn't join us." She set the platter next to the salad. "You did invite her, didn't you?"

Richard forked a slice of meat. "I didn't think of it until just now." A moment after he decided to stay himself. "Perhaps next week sometime."

"Yes, a lovely idea. How is she doing? Did you give her the number of the florist I recommended? They did such a wonderful job with the Doriani wedding. You remember, don't you? Those lilies filled the entire sanctuary with such a sweet fragrance. And not one of them revealed wilting or browning of any kind."

Richard pressed his tongue to the roof of his mouth to keep from laughing as an image of his mother inspecting bouquets as she passed each pew resurfaced. The entire event remained fresh in his memory. Nearly half the women in the cathedral had followed a similar pattern, until each flower and silken ribbon underwent thorough inspections. And as his guest list closely mirrored that of the Doriani's, the flowers at his wedding would likely receive similar scrutiny. Not that it mattered, except to his mother. Which meant it mattered to him as well, unless he wanted to endure her endless lamentations.

"I'll give it to her the next time I see her." He sliced his steak into small squares and stabbed a chunk with his fork.

His mother sipped her wine. "Please do, and mention my plans to schedule a time to meet with Mercedes from Le Veritable Amour Bridal."

"I will ask her, but she may have chosen her dress already."

"On her own? Is that what she said?"

"Quite honestly, we haven't discussed her gown."

"Of course she didn't. She would have told you. Surely she knows how important it is that I be there. It's not every day my only son gets married. Besides, she will need a woman's perspective, and we know how ill-equipped her mother is." She grabbed her wine glass and swirled its contents before taking a slow sip. "How Ainsley managed to mature so nicely is beyond me."

Richard's father dabbed the corner of his mouth with a linen napkin. "It demonstrates the resolve of children, and the benefits of education."

"Yes, well." His mom set her glass down. "Let us not forget, she still has areas in need of growth. Don't you agree, Richard?"

He gave the proper nod and tuned out the rest of the conversation, his thoughts stuck on one question. How much had Ainsley changed? True, she no longer resembled the rather immature, timid, and at times uncouth woman he'd met five years ago. But how deep did those changes penetrate? How much of her mother's flirtatious behavior did she share, and what might awaken that part of her she fought so hard against? Once again, an image of Mr. Langley resurfaced, souring Richard's stomach and causing his pulse to quicken.

Was the security Richard offered enough to keep her?

He finished his wine then pushed back from the table. "I hate to eat and run, but I still have work to finish."

His mother started to stand, but Richard raised a hand. "I'll see myself out."

When he reached his car, he dialed Ainsley's number. It rang four times before her voice mail picked up

"This is Ainsley Meadows. I am unavailable—" A loud, extended beep sounded, followed by a breathless, "Hello?"

"Are you OK?"

"After a mad dash in search of the phone, yes." She laughed. "What's up?"

"I . . . was just checking in."

"Oh." Her voice sounded flat, almost as if he'd annoyed her.

"How did you spend your evening?"

"Reading through Voltex material." She paused. "Is everything all right, because you sound tense?"

"Do I? I'm sorry. Preoccupied, I suppose. You get some sleep. I'll call you tomorrow."

Ainsley poured herself a cup of coffee, added a healthy dose of vanilla creamer, and meandered to the living room. Kicking her slippers under the coffee table, she grabbed her Bible. Feet tucked beneath her, she curled into the corner of the couch. She glanced at the manila file lying on the coffee table, partially read—as much as she could stomach, anyway, without turning her throbbing headache into a full-blown migraine. But there was always tomorrow, after church.

It was already 7:30 p.m. Where had the day gone?

Resting her Bible in her lap, she ran her hands across the smooth leather. No matter how hectic her day, no matter how imminent her failure, God's Word remained a beacon of truth to which she could always turn, a shelter of love beneath which she could always hide. As a child, the promise and assurance of God's presence carried her through many tear-filled nights. In those moments when everyone else failed her, God alone remained.

Did the young boy at Whispering Hills know this? That God loved him, was watching over him, and longed to be known by him? If only Richard shared her passion for helping hurting children. Imagine the lives they could impact. Imagine the souls God could save through them. Tears pricked her eyes as she held her Bible close, too many thoughts warring in her brain. *Help me focus on You, Lord. Draw me into the divine romance tonight.*

Eyes closed, she waited until the tension eased from her neck and shoulders. Then, she flipped through the thin pages before landing on Jeremiah chapter 9. *Lovely, the weeping prophet.* Not exactly the dash of peace she needed. You have sinned. You're going to die. Repent. Repent.

No disrespect intended. She started to flip the page again, moving to the New Testament, when her eyes landed on a phrase that gave her pause. *How can light live with darkness?* It was from 2 Corinthians 6. She'd underlined the entire passage, from verse 14 to 17 years ago during a purity class at church.

Don't team up with those who are unbelievers. How can righteousness be a partner with wickedness? How can light live with darkness? What harmony can there be between Christ and the devil? How can a believer be a partner with an unbeliever? And what union can there be between God's temple and idols? For we are the temple of the living God. As God said:
"I will live in them
    and walk among them.
I will be their God,
    and they will be my people.
Therefore, come out from among unbelievers,
    and separate yourselves from them, says the Lord.
Don't touch their filthy things,
    and I will welcome you."

She'd written a date in the margin, along with the note: *Christians must not marry non-Christians.*

Her heart pricked as an image emerged. It was of Richard standing amidst his social crowd, chin lifted, a politically correct smile in place. But that didn't make sense, not considering the complete lack of peace the image brought. It was as if God was warning her of something, but why? Richard was a Christian . . . wasn't he?

Chapter 10

*T*ote bag draped over her shoulder, Bible, journal, and favorite pens tucked inside, Ainsley exited her car. Standing in front of the thick cluster of trees encasing Smoke and Davey's bike trails, she inhaled the sweet, earthy air. Puffs of clouds clung to the tops of the trees, beams of golden sun piercing through them.

Inching down a sloped dirt pathway, she left the parking lot behind and entered one of her favorite places in Missouri. A place where, as a teen, she'd spent many long summer afternoons when she'd needed a place to escape. To pray. Like she did now.

She followed the path to the left. Winding up a hill, she crunched leaves and twigs under her feet. She reached her favorite childhood hiding spot, a fallen tree resting on a stump, and nestled among bushes and branches. It had experienced more decay, and was covered in red, flower-like mushrooms and thick moss. But that only made it more beautiful, more enchanting.

She cleared some wood dust and sat, pulling a leg to her chest. She grabbed her Bible and laid it open before her. *Oh Lord, why does it feel like everything is falling apart? My engagement, my job. I know You have a plan in all this. A plan for me.*

At least, I hope You do.

She pulled out her journal and flipped to a clean page. As a kid, whenever she had to make a tough decision, she'd list the pros and cons. That didn't seem appropriate now. Instead, she closed the pages and returned the book to her tote. Moving to rest her back on an adjacent tree, feet propped on the log, she closed her eyes.

Lord, why do I feel so unsettled? It shouldn't be this way.

Not if she was truly in love. Nervous, maybe, but not so ... uncertain. Full of doubts.

What did love feel like anyway? According to her mom, it came in with a whoosh and left you heady and all fluttery inside. For a time, until another whoosh came along.

If that was love, Ainsley wanted nothing to do with it. Even so, she wanted more than ... than ... whatever this was she had going on with Richard. Things felt so strained lately, like she was trying to go one way and he was holding her back. Trying to force her into a mold she'd never quite fit.

A year ago, she thought she could; desperately wanted to. She'd even looked forward to being a psychiatrist's wife with country club membership, high-society gatherings, and charity functions. To a life of stability, predictability. But now ...?

Voices drifted toward her, followed by the slow shuffle of approaching feet. She glanced up to see an older couple walking hand in hand. The man, bald except for fluffs of hair around the base of his skull and ears, held a walking stick. The woman was hunched over with what appeared to be osteoporosis. They were both wrinkled and gray, and obviously very happy. Happy and in love.

It was a love she saw often on Sunday mornings, when couples came together to worship their risen Savior. It was a love she'd never seen growing up, not in her home anyway.

No, what her parents had was something entirely different. She didn't know what it was, exactly, but she knew with certainty what it wasn't.

Then again, neither of them were Christian. She thought of the passage she'd read the day before and a sense of apprehension swept over her.

Lord, what are You trying to tell me? Please make it clear; help me to understand Your perfect wisdom.

She grabbed her Bible from her tote bag and opened it to 2 Corinthians 6, marked by an index card tucked between the pages.

She read the passage again, then again, the words *unbeliever* and *darkness* standing out to her. Once again, she got the sense that God was trying to tell her something.

Why did Richard come to mind whenever she read that passage? He went to church, most Sundays. Come to think of it, he'd never been terribly regular about it. In fact, he hadn't been in some time, and he wasn't involved in a men's group of any kind. Then again, neither were half the men in the church. That certainly didn't mean they weren't saved.

But she wasn't concerned with all the other men. She was, however, incredibly concerned with her fiancé's faith. Where did he stand spiritually?

Maybe she was making way too much out of this verse, but the prick in her heart told her otherwise.

Ugh! She couldn't think about this anymore, not today. It was driving her crazy.

She needed some Gina time, and lots and lots of chocolate. Grabbing her phone, she dialed her friend's number. Unfortunately, she got her voice mail.

"Hey, girl. So, I'm sort of having a bridentity crisis here. Could use a laugh. Call me."

Later that evening, Ainsley sank into her couch, feet tucked under her, a warm cup of tea in hand. The doorbell chimed. She answered it to find Gina standing on the other side, filled paper bag in her arms. "Wow! So, who's the hottie?"

Ainsley rose on the balls of her feet and glanced across the yard. Dressed in exercise gear and running shoes, Chris stretched beneath a pale streetlight. He looked up and grinned. She offered a brisk wave then dashed back inside.

"Ah, so you've noticed then." Gina's eyes danced with laughter. She walked to the kitchen.

Ainsley followed. "I've done nothing of the sort. In case you've forgotten, I'm engaged." She held up her hand, the sun catching her diamond, reflecting in rainbow colors.

Gina set her bag on the counter and began to unload it. Two movie rentals, a box of brownie mix, eggs, butter. "Oh, yes, how could I forget the reason I'm here?" She shot Ainsley a wink. "So, what's with this identity — excuse me — bridentity crisis?" She paused with her hand still in the bag then pulled it out and shoved the package aside. Turning to lean against the side wall, she crossed her arms. "Spill it, girl."

Ainsley sighed and pushed her hair from her face. She relayed the passage she'd read over a half dozen times. "I can't shake the feeling that God's trying to tell me something."

"I'd agree."

Ainsley waited for Gina to elaborate, not that she needed to. Her friend had made her feelings regarding the engagement clear on numerous occasions. Up to now, Ainsley had chalked that up to overprotection or maybe a resistance to change, but now she wasn't so sure. "Oh, Gina, this is all so confusing. I'll admit, he's been acting like a royal jerk, but he's got a lot going on, you know?"

Gina pulled herself up on the counter, sitting so her legs dangled over the edge.

Ainsley moved to a kitchen chair and flopped into it. "No one, no relationship, is perfect."

"Uh-huh."

"So when does one overlook faults and persevere, show patience, and when is it time to walk away?"

"You want my honest answer? Because I say you should've walked away years ago."

"My biggest question is, why am I feeling all this now? I mean, we've been together for five years! Surely that means something."

"Yeah, it means you're more loyal than my mom's St. Bernard. But you know what they say about displaced loyalty, right?"

"No, what?"

"Yeah, neither do I. But what I do know is that once he slips that ring on your finger, it'll be too late."

Ainsley traced her finger along the edge of the counter. This conversation — thinking about her engagement in general — made her anxious, and that concerned her greatly.

Ready for a subject change, she grabbed the DVD and flipped it over. "What's all this?"

"Girl's night out at the Meadows', large amounts of chocolate included." She pulled a bowl from the cupboard and set it on the counter. "You know, maybe you two should go to premarital counseling."

"He won't go. Says we don't need it, him being a psychiatrist and all."

"And I, and Pastor Leoffold, say you do." Gina faced Ainsley head on. "You need to be absolutely sure you're making the right decision, because you only walk down the aisle once."

"Unless you're my mom."

Gina laughed. "Ouch! True, but ouch just the same."

"Although, in her defense, at least she ditches before the vows, most of the time, anyway. A habit I appear to be mimicking."

"Double ouch." Gina dipped her finger into the brownie mix and stuck it in her mouth.

Ainsley copied her. "But enough about my love life. Let's get to eating."

"Absolutely! Because you know what they say, all work, no play makes for a very boring Ainsley." She bopped Ainsley's hip with her own then glanced out the window, head angled slightly. "Of course, we could always pack a picnic and head to that biking trail down the street."

"Oh, no. Crafting and baking is fine." She poured two cups of coffee and brought them to the kitchen table.

Gina moved to the window and raised on her toes. "Oh, look! Here comes your 'adorably cute in a ruggedly masculine way' neighbor now." She grinned. "You won't mind if I get to know Mr. Hottie with the California plates, will you?"

"You've been checking him out, have you? Already stalked out where he's from?" She lowered her eyebrows in mock rebuke then flicked her hand. "Have at him, my dear."

"Great! Let's see if I can't dish out a bit of that southern charm Gramma Zoe used to feed us."

"You, a Southerner?"

"It's not in the location, my friend, but in the presentation." Gina batted her lashes. "Come on, I'll show you how it's done." She grabbed Ainsley's elbow, dragged her outside, and to the end of the sidewalk. Chris approached, half-jogging, half-walking, his dog slumping behind him.

He stopped at the curb and offered a lopsided grin. "Hey, there."

"Hi, I'm Gina. And single."

Chris's eyes widened and Ainsley's cheeks flushed hot. She pinched Gina's arm.

"Ouch!"

Ainsley cleared her throat. "Please excuse my friend. She doesn't get out much." She glanced at the dog sprawled on the ground, panting. "I take it your friend here wasn't up for the run?"

"He made it about three blocks, poor guy. I should probably let him stay home, but—"

"Yeah, I know, use it or lose it." Ainsley smiled.

Gina elbowed Ainsley's side who countered with a warning glare.

"We better get going."

"Right," Gina said. "To cook those brownies. We'd love to bring you a sample, if you like chocolate."

"I love it." He gave a thumbs-up sign.

"Perfect." Her eyes sparkled. "Come over in about a half hour."

Ainsley glared at Gina, but she waited until they were well out of earshot to unload. "What were you thinking? Chris can't come over! What would that look like?"

"What do you mean?"

"I'm an engaged woman. I can't have strange men in my house. What would Richard think?" She threw open her front door and stomped inside.

"So invite him." Gina followed half a step behind. "Oh, I forgot, Mr. Suit and Tie is at a formal function. Maybe next time." She snapped her fingers. "That's a great idea! Let's do a double date. Like next Friday. How does that sound?"

Ainsley spun around. "You're kidding, right?"

The twinkle in Gina's eyes betrayed her innocent smile. "Yeah, it'd be great. You and your beau, and me with my new-found hottie. Like the Three Musketeers, only with four." She grabbed the box of brownie mix and studied the baking time on the back. "Now let's see about getting this batch of hip-increasers done just right."

"Gina Rose, what am I going to do with you?"

Gina looped her arm through Ainsley's and gave a squeeze. "Just love me, my dear. Just love me."

Chris chuckled as he watched the girls leave. Gina nearly skipped behind Ainsley who walked briskly with shoulders squared, arms swinging at her sides. Those two were interesting, to say the least. He turned to Rusty. "Something tells me I'm in for quite an evening, old boy." His stomach rumbled. "And a tasty one at that."

Taking the steps two at a time, he opened the front door and waited for Rusty to lumber through. A slight bounce marked his step as he made his way to his bedroom and a rather large basket of unwashed clothing. He lifted his arm and sniffed, nose crinkling.

Rusty slid to the floor, his head resting on his front paws, sappy eyes following Chris's every move.

"So, you think I've got time for a shower and a load of wash?" He glanced at the clock. "Shower, yes. Laundry?" He moved to a stack of boxes and pulled out a wrinkled shirt. "Which would be better, a stinky old, coffee-splattered work shirt, or one creased in the shape of an octagon?" He dug deeper in the box until he found a pair of jeans then set both on the dresser. "Octagon and stiff jeans it is, old boy. But the real question is, why do I care?"

On second thought, maybe it'd be best not to go at all.

No, he said he'd be there. A man needed to honor his word, right?

About thirty minutes later, he stood on Ainsley's front steps ringing her doorbell. Gina answered right away. Ainsley followed a few steps behind, cheeks pink, likely from standing over a hot oven. The hint of a smile graced her delicate features, adding sparkle to her green eyes.

He shifted and glanced from one girl to the next. Perhaps he misunderstood? Oh, brother, now he looked like an idiot. An idiot in an octagon shirt.

"Come in!" Gina flung open the door and moved aside.

Chris smiled and stepped forward, inhaling the sweet scent of freshly baked chocolate mixed with cinnamon. A red candle burned on the coffee table next to three tiered books.

Ainsley paused, palms pressed together. Her mouth quivered as if she wanted to speak, but then she dashed back into the kitchen.

"Have a seat. Make yourself at home." Gina cupped her hand around his elbow and guided him to a cream-colored sofa. "Do you like to read?" She picked up a book and studied the cover — *Real Women, Real Issues, Unreal Faith* — then set it down. "What do you want to watch?" She turned on the television. A maxi-pad commercial came on. After flipping through four channels, she handed him the remote. "Here. I'm going to see if Ainsley needs help." She darted out of the room.

Chris leaned against the leather cushions and propped an ankle on his knee. Nice place, comfortable yet classic with earth toned furniture, candleholders on the mantel, and a vase of dried foliage. Pictures, some of people and others of country landscapes, decorated the walls and two end tables. He surveyed the earth-toned furniture and scanned the pictures lining the end tables and mantel.

Muffled voices drifted down the hall, followed by giggling. He leaned sideways, trying to make out the words.

"You can't just leave him out there."

"Why not?"

"What do you mean, why not? You invited him. Go entertain him."

"I will, as soon as I pop the popcorn."

The steady hum of a microwave followed by rapidly popping kernels muffled the rest of their conversation. Chuckling, Chris turned his attention to the television. If nothing else, he could catch a few minutes of ESPN. No small blessing, considering his cable wouldn't be hooked up for another week.

Ainsley walked into the living room holding two DVDs in her hand. "So, *The Heart of Sisterhood* or *True Love Waits*?"

Gina followed with a plate of steaming brownies and a mammoth bowl of popcorn. "Sorry about the movie choices, but . . ."

"We weren't expecting company." She shot Gina a glare then turned back to Chris, her face softening. "Not that I mind, of course."

"Of course." Chris planted both feet on the ground and cracked his finger knuckles. Could this get any more awkward? Maybe it was time to find a polite way to excuse himself.

"So?" Ainsley stepped closer, carrying the soft scent of lavender. Her eyes were a deep green, the irises encircled by a faint brown.

Chris looked from her to Gina. "Whatever you ladies prefer. I'm just here to taste the brownies, remember?"

Ainsley blushed and lowered her lashes. Gina set the brownies and popcorn onto the coffee table and plopped onto the couch next to Chris. He shifted left, realizing much too late that he had positioned himself in the center of the couch, leaving Ainsley only one place to sit. If she wanted to be able to see the television anyway.

"Take a seat already." Gina grabbed a handful of popcorn. "Or are you going to stand there all day."

Chris suppressed his mirth as Ainsley shot her friend yet another piercing glare. Poor girl. If he had any manners at all, he'd leave and put her out of her misery. Instead, he scooted to the edge of the couch and offered what he hoped to be a friendly, nonthreatening smile.

Ainsley set the movies down and perched on the edge of the cushion. "How about we play a game instead?"

Gina sprang to her feet, her thick, auburn hair swooshing across her shoulders. "Good idea! I'll get On a Dare."

Ainsley's eyes widened. "On second thought, talking is good. Chris, are you enjoying Kansas City?"

"Minus the thunderstorms and rapidly plummeting temperatures, yes, I am. Thanks for asking."

Gina sat on the couch and pulled a leg to her chest. She rested her chin on her knee and angled her head in Chris's direction. "That's right. You're from California, aren't you?"

Chris raised his eyebrows. Apparently they'd done some digging, Sherlock Holmes style. Flattering, even if a bit creepy.

Ainsley folded her hands in her lap and straightened her spine, the pink hue in her cheeks deepening. "Your license plates."

"Right." He grabbed a brownie, tore off the corner, and popped it in his mouth. "So, what about you ladies? Are you both from here?"

Gina shook her head. "I'm from Michigan, although I've been here long enough to wear the native badge with honor." She giggled. "But Ainsley is."

"Third generation Chiefs fan." Hugging a throw pillow, Ainsley leaned back.

Chris smiled. Nice to see her relax a bit. Now he needed to make sure he didn't say anything to throw her back into that shell of hers.

"What brought you to Kansas City?" Golden hair framed her face like a halo.

Looking away, he cleared his throat. "My mom. She has early-onset Alzheimer's. I wanted to be closer to her, to make sure she gets the care she needs. And to try to fix some of the damage those college kids did to the house."

Ainsley's brow furrowed. "Are you planning on selling it?"

"Honestly, I don't know." An image of a scowling Matilda came to mind. He blinked it away, and the surge of bitterness it aroused. "But enough about me. So, Ainsley, what do you do?"

"I'm a pharmaceutical rep for Voltex."

"That's interesting. You don't strike me as a saleswoman."

"She's not a very good one, that's for sure." Gina tossed a popcorn kernel at her friend.

"Ainsley's about as outgoing as a turtle on a stormy day."

She shot her friend a glare. "Aren't you the clever one?" She shrugged. "But she's right, the job has required a bit more sugar-shoveling than I anticipated, which is why I'm hoping to go back to school, as soon as finances and my schedule allows."

"And I keep telling her to follow her first love," Gina said.

Chris looked at her. "Which is?"

Ainsley's frown returned, even deeper than before.

Gina appeared not to notice. "Singing. Ainsley has the voice of an angel."

"Really?" His gaze drifted to her small, rose-colored lips.

She lowered her lashes and shrugged. "I've been known to sing on occasion."

"That's about the only time you'll see this turtle poke her head out." Gina shot her a wink. "You'd have to see it yourself to believe it. Put a microphone in her hand, play a few piano keys, and suddenly the girl's . . . Gina's nose wrinkled. "The girl's . . . She let out an overdramatic sigh. "OK, so I'm out of cute slogans here, but the girl's on fire, let's just leave it at that. She'll be leading worship in a couple weeks down at the North Kansas City Ray of Hope, a women and children's shelter. You're invited, if you'd like to come. I imagine they could always use a few more hands."

"Gina!" Ainsley hurled her pillow at her friend but it hit the bowl of popcorn instead, sending kernels flying.

Gina giggled. "No, seriously. It'd be fun. Richard's coming, right?"

"Um . . . maybe." She shot Gina a nonverbal message.

Gina's eyes rounded. "Oh, right." She mouthed the word, "Sorry," and then both girls grew awkwardly quiet, suddenly focused on the spilled popcorn.

Not surprising, Gina broke the silence first. "Anyway, we'd love to have you."

Chris stood. "Look, it's been nice, but I should probably —"

Gina jumped to her feet. "Leaving already?"

Chris looked from one girl to the next, feeling like Pee-wee Herman stuck in the football team's locker room. "Yeah, I've got . . . stuff to do."

Gina's glossy lips twitched toward a frown before stretching into her normal bubbly smile. "Right. So, I'll call you later with the details. You can meet us here the evening of."

"I . . . He started to politely decline but Gina nudged him toward the entryway, stealing all cohesive thought from his brain.

"Thanks for stopping by." Opening the door, she flashed a toothy smile then gave him a gentle push over the threshold. "See you on the twenty-second."

A gust of wind swept across his face as the door closed in front of him.

He didn't know whether to laugh or moan. Gina was beautiful, in a spastic, explode all over you, sort of way . . .

Oh Lord, what have I gotten myself into?

Chapter 11

*R*ichard stared at his blank computer screen, the letter he intended to type no longer important. Swiveling his chair, he inspected his tidy desk, pausing to study a photo of Ainsley. A delicate, almost childlike smile spread across her sun-kissed face. He grabbed the frame and focused on her deep-green eyes. How long had it been since he'd seen her face light up? How long since he'd heard her easy laughter? Sighing, he rubbed his forehead and swallowed against a knotted stomach. Less than six months until their wedding and she was growing distant. He could see it in her eyes, feel it in her touch.

With a shove of his foot, he rotated his chair to face the long, tinted window behind him. A thick layer of smog clung to the tops of the adjacent factories, further darkening the already cloud-filled sky. A distant train bellowed in the distance, followed by the high-pitched screech of wheels scraping against metal railings.

What if Ainsley broke their engagement? No, she wouldn't do that. Not now, after years of courting followed by months of planning. All women worried, Ainsley most of all. And considering her background, and all the games her mother played, he certainly couldn't blame her occasional emotional distance. Which was precisely why she needed him. No one else understood her like he did.

She knew this. He just needed to remind her in a way that she could understand, that would override her normal distrust.

He had thought, after five years, they'd moved past that.

With a sigh, he rose and paced the room then turned to his bookshelf. Leather-bound volumes stood erect between marble book ends. *Neurology and Neuropsychology in the Twenty-first Century, Applied Behavior Analysis, Understanding Psychosis of Varying Degrees, Effective Behavior Modification for the Adult Patient.*

He selected a small, green text outlining various techniques used to counter the negative effects of dysfunctional familial interaction on the human brain. He flipped through the pages but found nothing helpful.

Snapping the book shut, he resumed pacing. After five minutes of evaluating various behavior-modification techniques, all inappropriate in this case, he settled on a timeless course of action: flattery accompanied by a lavish dose of roses and flickering candlelight.

He strolled back to his seat, chuckling at the simplicity of life, and his rather absent-minded mistake. With his impeding deadline and all the wedding details, he had allowed their romance to slide.

Settling into his leather chair, he turned to his computer and typed *Kansas City Florist* into the search engine. He skimmed the various photos. Roses seemed too predictable. Tulips too formal. He clicked on an image of a bouquet made from varying shades of purple carnations and smiled. Perfect. Now for a flowery message to go along with it. He pulled up another window and navigated to a familiar site: Prose and Quotes for the Lovesick Soul.

Less than five minutes later, a delicate arrangement with words able to bring tears to even the hardest of hearts awaited delivery. He smiled, imagining Ainsley's wide-eyed response when she received the flowers.

"I know you're right, Deborah." With her earpiece in place, Ainsley pulled into her tree-lined neighborhood. A steady wind moaned through the trees lining Ainsley's cul-de-sac, sending red, orange, and gold leaves flittering to the ground. "Thanks for listening. And for being such a great support."

"My pleasure, dear. I'll be praying for you, and for Richard.

I know this is hard, but God will show you what to do, although from the sounds of it, He may have already. If your suspicions are correct."

"Yeah, I just hope things don't get ugly."

"Me, too, dear. Me too. On another note, how are things with you and your mom?"

Ainsley released a gush of air. "Same. Maybe worse. I'm probably not doing anything to help the situation." Last Sunday, Pastor Leoffold had urged his congregation to love the unlovable, to reach out even to those who spurned your affections. Which was great when talking about co-workers or annoying neighbors. But her mom?

"You know, you can invite her to the fall fest. Might be a safe . . . icebreaker. Pray on it."

If she did that, she'd be stuck, because she already knew what God wanted. It was the doing that was hard.

An occasional gust rocked the frame of her car. A thick blanket of clouds dimmed the sun to a dull orange, casting a soft glow over the neighborhood. Old growth trees, their twisted and gnarled branches stretching across the street, cast elongated shadows across the road.

Easing her car around, she pulled along the curb and lowered her window. Wind swept through her hair, sending a shiver down her spine. She reached into her mailbox and grabbed the thick stack of envelopes and newsprint shoved inside.

To her left, Chris hunched beneath a sagging oak tree, gathering severed branches and throwing them in a pile.

He waved. "If this is Missouri's fall, I dread winter."

"You'll get used to it in a year or two." With a friendly nod, she eased into her driveway then stopped, letting her car idle. *As much as I don't want to do this . . .* She glanced toward the cloudy sky. "You know I'm doing this purely out of obedience, right?"

She sighed and called her mom. Luckily she got her voice mail. "Hey, it's me. Our church is having this . . . thing, and I wondered if you'd want to come. Canning, making applesauce, crafts, that sort of thing." She gave the date, time, and location, then ended her call. There. Now she could spend the rest of her night in peace without feeling guilty for being perhaps the most hateful daughter ever.

She clicked her garage door opener. Nothing happened.

Lovely. Mental note: buy replacement batteries, preferably before blizzard season hits.

Setting her car in Park, she gathered her things and jumped out. Her spine angled sideways, painfully pulled groundward by her overstuffed tote. Lengthening her stride, she fumbled for her keys and hustled to the front door to beat the approaching storm clouds. Tiny flecks of moisture swirled through the air, misting her face and causing her teeth to chatter. Halfway up the walk, her left heel hit a wet patch and flew out from under her.

"Ahhh!" Her leg fought to go in two directions, wrenching her angle. A sharp pain exploded through her knee as her skin scraped against the pavement. Sitting on the damp ground, she rubbed her throbbing ankle then lunged toward the scattered pile of papers that spilled from her tote. Sheets flew across the yard, carried by the wind. Gritting her teeth, she pulled herself to her feet then hobbled toward the mass of papers.

"You OK?"

She glanced up, cheeks burning despite the cold. Chris stood in front of her, crinkled papers in hand. Before she could answer, he dove toward another fluttering sheet that settled into an oil-topped mud puddle.

He held it up with a lopsided grin. "Hopefully this wasn't too important."

She hobbled over, snatching up stray papers along the way. "Oh, just a memo from my boss."

He tucked the pile of papers under one arm and supported her elbow with the other. "That was a nasty fall. Think you sprained something?"

She shook her head and fought against his support until another twinge of pain nearly buckled her knee. "I hope not."

His hand gripped warm and strong around her arm, bearing a good deal of her weight as they walked.

Once they reached her doorstep, he waited as she searched for her keys then handed over her mud-splattered papers. "Gotta love Missouri weather, huh?"

"You do?" She smiled. "Thanks for the help. Sorry to be such a bother." Her papers rustled and her hair whipped around her face.

He shrugged. "No bother." He glanced at her three-inch heels. "Although you might consider wearing sneakers until spring."

She flushed. "Yeah, maybe so."

"Let me help you in."

"No, thank you. I'm fine, really."

He stared at her for a moment then shrugged. "OK. Hope you feel better." With a dip of his head, he traipsed back to his yard, where he quickly resumed his tree-limb pickup duty.

Ainsley slipped inside as another gust of wind swept over her. She limped into the living room and deposited the mail and her papers onto the coffee table. Dropping her tote to the floor, she collapsed into the sofa.

Her cell phone buzzed but she ignored it and sifted through letters and bills instead. A pale-green envelope labeled *Collection Notice* caught her eye. Her stomach soured as she read the return address: Chief Financial Visa.

"Some folks might call looking for me."

"Mom!" She tore open the envelope and scanned the page. The dollar amount printed at the bottom glared back at her. Adrenaline surged through her as she reached for her phone. Landing on her mother's number, she hit Dial, breathing deeply in an effort to calm herself. The ringtone grated against her ear. After five rings, she started to hang up when her mother answered.

"Hello, pumpkin. I'm so glad you called. I got your message, and that sounds like such a lovely party. Unfortunately, I'm not sure if I'll be able to make it. But I'll let you know."

"Mom, what's going on with your Visa?"

"What Visa?" Either her mother was playing games or more than one creditor was tracking her down. Most likely, the latter.

"The one I cosigned on."

"Oh, that. I've got a new card now." She launched into a long story of cash rewards and low-interest rates.

Heat climbed up Ainsley's neck and down her arms like bolts of electricity ready to spark. "What do you care about interest rates? You never pay your bills anyway."

Her mom went silent, amplifying Ainsley's breathing. When she finally spoke, she used her, "look who's crabby now" tone. "Have you had a tough day, honey? Did someone say something unkind? I know how sensitive you can be, especially when it's that time of the month."

"No, Mom, I'm not PMSing. Seriously, everything isn't about hormones."

"Oh, honey, I'm sorry. You and Richard had a fight."

"No." It'd be easier talking to a slab of plywood. "I received a collection notice for your Visa bill. You have an outstanding balance, and you need to pay it."

"I will, dear, as soon as I catch up on a few things."

"Like what? Stocking your lipstick drawer? If you default, I'm responsible for every penny. The extent of your irresponsibility never ceases to amaze me. Sometimes I wonder who's the parent here."

"Ainsley Meadows, what is with you today? You're being downright hateful. You know how hard it's been since your father and I —"

"It's been fifteen years, Mom." Followed by nearly as many men, each one slimier than the previous.

"Fifteen years of starting over, scraping by, and scrambling for every dime. I know it's hard for you to understand, being engaged to a man like Richard and all. I'm so glad you found him. He's as opposite to your father as you can get. Responsible, mature, driven."

Ainsley's breath caught as her mother's words settled deep. It was true. Richard was nothing like her father. Wasn't that what she'd always said? Normally, the thought brought consolation, peace. But now?

Was that why she accepted his engagement? Because he was predictable? Safe?

She shook her head as if doing so would clear her inner tumult and gripped the phone tighter. "Let's stay on topic, Mother. According to the notice, you have thirty days to make a payment before it goes to collection."

"They're just trying to scare you, dear. Besides, it goes off your record in seven years."

"I'm not playing these games, Mom. Pay the bill." She hit Call End, snapped the phone shut, then slumped further into the sofa.

Did her mom care nothing for her at all, other than what she could get from her? Tears stung her eyes as painful memories surfaced. How many times as a child had she waited up for her mom, aching for a sympathetic ear and a warm hug—for any sign of affection at all—only to fall asleep alone. In a silent house. Her mother would never change. The sooner Ainsley realized that, the better.

Her Bible lay on the edge of the table, the long, silken ribbon tucked between the smooth pages. She grabbed it and flipped it open to Jeremiah 31.

"I have loved you with an everlasting love; I have drawn you with unfailing kindness."

She closed her eyes as a sense of peace washed over her.

Yes, God, You have loved me. Throughout my life, You alone have proved faithful and true.

Her doorbell rang and she glanced toward the partially cracked blinds of her living room window. A bright-green van parked in front of her driveway. Pushing to her feet, she hobbled to the door and peered through the peephole. A woman with long, blonde hair that blew about her head like sugar in a cotton-candy machine stood on her front step. She clutched a bouquet of carnations. Her torso hunched forward, her arms raised in a protective shield around the flowers.

Ainsley opened the door. "Hello."

The woman smiled through her swirling hair, pushing it from her face with her forearms. "Are you Ainsley Meadows?"

"Yes."

"These are for you." She thrust the flowers forward.

"Thank you."

Closing the door against the wind, Ainsley pulled a small, cream envelope from a plastic holder and turned it over to read the words printed on the back.

As fragrant as a thousand flowers upon the hill, as delicate as the petals that stir in a springtime breeze, your angelic smile awakens me and stirs me still. Forever yours, Richard.

Forever . . . the word echoed in her mind, adding weight to her chest. How could such a tender token of love cause such angst?

Forever was a long time.

She and he were so completely opposite. In everything, and their differences appeared to be widening rather than merging. He liked formal dinners and attending parties with academics, where she preferred to stay home reading or watching television. But even more than that, she loved going to church, reading her Bible, spending time with wonderful older women in the faith. That was where she drew her strength, found her peace. Richard almost seemed to feel the opposite, bristling when the conversation turned spiritual, turning down opportunities to serve or spend time with other believers.

What would happen once—if—they had children? How could she expect her children to seek after a God in whom their father appeared to show no interest?

She turned her face heavenward.

I'm listening, Lord. It took a while, but I'm listening now. Please give me the strength to do what I must. This wasn't something she could put off anymore.

She grabbed her phone and dialed Richard's number.

He answered on the second ring. "Let me guess, my little surprise arrived."

"Well, yes, and thank you. But that's not . . . Richard, we need to talk."

Chapter 12

*A*insley sat on a barstool in front of the window of Jalapeno's and Burritos, a family-owned restaurant halfway between her place and Richard's. Her stomach knotted as she mentally rehearsed the conversation she was about to have.

She spent the next ten minutes sipping her drink — to keep stomach acid from bubbling up her throat — and watching cars pull in and out of the parking lot. Another five minutes and Richard's Lexus rounded the corner. He parked in the farthest stall, one where his car was least likely to get dinged.

Not long after, he entered the restaurant dressed in a button-down shirt and pressed slacks, leather briefcase in hand. After a quick scan of the dining room, his gaze landed on Ainsley, and he offered a stiff smile.

He walked toward her with stiff, almost rhythmic steps. "You look lovely today." He leaned forward to kiss her. She turned her head, offering her cheek.

"Thanks for meeting me." She motioned to the barstool beside her then glanced toward the counter. In cafeteria-style fashion, patrons were lined from the door to cash register, trays in hand. "You hungry?"

Richard shook his head. His Adam's apple shifted with what appeared to be a nervous swallow. "What's this about, Ainsley?" His eyes searched hers, and her heart tugged at what appeared to be genuine concern. Or perhaps insecurity, neither of which she'd seen from him in some time. "Is everything all right? Did I do something to upset you?"

She ran her nail along the edge of her napkin. "I've been . . . I have some questions." She looked at him, held his gaze. "Questions we should've discussed long ago."

"OK." Straightening, he folded his hands in front of him.

"Where do you stand, faithwise?"

"Excuse me?"

"How do you feel about Jesus?"

He wrinkled his brow, giving his head a slight shake. "Forgive me, but your question surprises me. Have I done something to make you question my integrity?"

"Not exactly, more like your . . . (heart)." But saying that seemed too harsh.

His smile widened as he placed his hand over hers. "You're nervous and overwhelmed. That's understandable, and as such, you're looking for some sort of . . . confirmation. Is that it?"

She pulled her hand out from beneath his and turned to face him. "I'm concerned that we aren't as compatible, spiritually, as I previously assumed."

"But of course we are. I have no problem with your women's gatherings, holiday rituals, or biweekly church attendance."

"Maybe not, but I have a problem with yours. Lack of, I mean."

He stared at her for a moment. "I'm afraid I don't understand."

The more they talked, the more she realized just how true those words were. That was what made this discussion all the more difficult. He truly had no idea why she was even having this conversation, why his faith status was so incredibly important.

"My dear, if you're looking for a billboard to fall from the sky saying, 'He's the one. Marry him . . . '" He chuckled in a way that made her nerves ignite. "Well, it's not going to happen. I really believe God has much more important things to worry about than whom you or I marry."

"That is where you're wrong, Richard. God is incredibly concerned about every detail of our lives, including whom we marry, of that I am certain."

"Really?" His eyes narrowed, his former mirth replaced by an underscore of sarcasm. "And you believe He's revealed this to you. Is that it?"

She bristled. Had he always been this condescending? "If

you really must know, I've received numerous *signs* that indicate marrying you truly isn't God's design."

His face hardened. "Then tell me, who does God intend you to marry?"

"A Christian. Which leads me to my original question: Where are you spiritually?"

"You're being absurd. I go to church. Maybe not as often as you like, but I go."

"And why is that?" She crossed her arms. "Because you've fallen madly in love with Jesus or because you feel it's the responsible thing to do?"

"Not everything is about emotional responses, Ainsley."

She stared at him, trying to make sense of his statement in light of his personality. True, some were more emotional than others; and Richard was certainly more of the logical, calculating type. But even so, Jesus Christ had died for him; to have an intimate relationship with him. Surely that warranted heartfelt love in return. Perhaps she had phrased her question wrong. "Let me put it this way. Who is Jesus to you?"

"What do you want from me? You want me to go to church more? Fine. You want me to donate to charities, to serve in the nursery? Tell me."

"You don't get it, do you? Christianity isn't about *doing* anything. It's about accepting what Jesus Christ has already done."

He offered nothing more than a blank stare, confirming her suspicions. But even so, she couldn't walk away. Not yet. Not without at least pointing him to the gift of eternal life.

"Don't you see? That's the beauty of grace. We can't earn it. None of us could ever do enough good deeds to earn God's favor or pay for our sins — "

His phone rang. He pulled it from his shirt pocket and checked the screen. "Excuse me, but I have to get this."

Ainsley nodded with a sigh. He hadn't been listening anyway. Not really. And though she'd received her confirmation, the moment felt anything but victorious. Clearly, Richard wasn't the man she'd thought he was. Or maybe more accurately, had hoped he was. Because looking back, she'd seen hints of this all along. She'd just been too stubborn — too focused on following her detailed life plans — to acknowledge them.

"I did this morning." He moved a step back, shooting Ainsley an apologetic smile. "No. I'm away from my computer, but I can send it this evening." He checked his watch. "Fine. I'll have it to you within the hour."

Facing Ainsley once again, he returned his phone to his pocket. "I am so sorry. I can tell this concerns you a great deal, and I'd really like to discuss this further. But I must take care of something. I'll call you?"

As if having this conversation a second time would do any good.

She couldn't marry him. That was so very clear now.

Chapter 13

*T*hank you for coming in, Miss Meadows. I trust you know the way out?"

"Yes, doctor." Ainsley stuffed her brochures into her tote and stood. Squaring her shoulders despite the sinking feeling in her gut, she crossed the room with long, deliberate strides. A dull ache permeated her right ankle, still tender from the day before, but she gritted her teeth against it.

Women in pale-blue scrubs crowded the nurse's station, clipboards in hand. They glanced up as Ainsley passed then returned to their conversation. A man with black hair streaked with gray followed a nurse practitioner down the hall, biting on his nails. He mumbled as he walked, his eyes shifting right to left like a movie clip on instant replay.

Ainsley continued through the lobby and toward the thick metal elevator leading to the parking garage. As soon as the doors closed, she checked her phone for missed calls. Three had come in—two from her mom and one from Richard. Had he thought about what she said? Prayed over it? And if he had?

She wasn't sure how to feel about that. It was as if her heart had suddenly shifted. She cared for him, longed to see him come to know Jesus. But other than that . . . She shook her head as her phone rang with yet another call from Richard. Though tempted to hit Ignore, she knew she needed to conclude their previous conversation.

"Hi."

"Good morning." He paused, his breath echoing through the line. "Listen, I know how important religion is to you. I want to assure you that I am behind you 100 percent.

Whatever you want to do. This doesn't have to be a deal breaker."

She closed her eyes and leaned back against the headrest. Why did this have to be so hard? *Lord, please show me what to do.*

Except He already had. Things couldn't be any more clear. Even so, she couldn't break up with Richard by phone.

"Can meet for lunch."

"That sounds great." His voice lifted with a hope that broke her heart. "At Pierre's? I can be there in thirty minutes, with a surprise." He hung up.

Frowning, Ainsley dropped her phone in the console. This wasn't going to be easy.

Heading south on 69, she wove through lunch-hour traffic until she reached Broadway. Thick storm clouds hovered near the downtown skyline, casting the city in a blanket of gray. Pedestrians dressed in thick jackets streamed up and down the sidewalk. Others flowed in and out of stores, cheeks red, bags in hand.

As expected, Richard beat her to the restaurant, his Lexus parked along the curb. She paused to say a quick prayer for courage and kindness to say what she needed to. Limping her way inside, she gritted her teeth against the pain pulsating through her ankle.

The maître d', a tall, well-groomed man wearing a suit and tie, greeted her with a smile. "Good morning, Miss Meadows. Mr. Hollis is waiting. Follow me."

Nodding, she hobbled past a stone-covered fireplace surrounded by suede furniture to a formal dining area. Men and women dressed in business attire gathered around white-clothed tables, the warm glow of flickering candles illuminating their features.

Richard sat at a far table near the window, and apparently, he had company.

Lovely.

Richard stood to meet her, his smile and stance stiff. "Hello, beautiful." His forehead wrinkled. "Are you hurt? You're limping."

Heat pricked Ainsley's cheeks. He'd only noticed just now?

But then again, the last time they met she'd remained seated. "It's nothing." She turned to the men seated in front of her and waited for Richard to make introductions.

"You remember Dr. Lizenhower?"

Two balding men in matching pinstriped suits stood. Ainsley forced a smile and extended a hand. "Of course. From the Midwestern Neurological Research Center, right?" So much for having that heart-to-heart. Now what? Pretend like everything was OK then schedule a second meeting?

"Correct." The man puffed out his chest and ran a hand over his charcoal tie.

"And this is Dr. Shevell from North Kansas City Neurology."

The three looked like chiseled replicas, from their tight smiles to their crisp dress shirts. Their raised chins and nasally tones promised a rather uncomfortable lunch.

Eyes narrowed on Richard, she fought to keep the frustration from her voice. "I didn't realize you had a meeting."

"I arrived early and while in the lobby, struck up a lively conversation with these brilliant gentlemen. I invited them to join us, and they graciously accepted."

Dr. Lizenhower nodded. "Yes, yes, indeed. And Dr. Hollis was just about to tell us more about his book."

Ainsley suppressed an eyeroll and reached for her chair.

Richard beat her to it. "Allow me, my dear." He slid it out with one hand and took her coat with the other. "You should tell these gentlemen about the revolutionary new psychotropic drug Voltex Pharmaceutical's developed, bearing the same name. It really is quite unlike anything that's currently available."

"Really?" Dr. Lizenhower raised an eyebrow. "Do tell, Miss Meadows."

No sense wasting an hour. Attempting to make the most of an irritating situation, she launched into her oft-repeated pitch.

"Sounds intriguing." Dr. Lizenhower pulled a business card from his front pocket and wrote something on the back. He handed it to Ainsley. "I would be interested in hearing more. Why don't you call my secretary to set up a meeting?"

"Thank you, sir. I'll do that." She glanced at Richard, careful to keep her face void of emotion.

He cleared his throat. "As I was saying earlier, gentlemen, my book explores the stigma associated with mental illness in terms of how it relates to children. In many ways, I address the nature versus nurture debate, approached from a unique angle. To what extent is irrational behavior learned, and what can we as a society do to address the problem? Because it is clear, this problem is affecting society as a whole."

"An interesting topic well worth discussing, Dr. Hollis." Dr. Lizenhower crossed his arms. "And an area in need of further research. What do you propose?"

As the men continued to discuss the development of the human brain and its role in psychopathology, Ainsley stared into her water glass. She needed to find a polite escape route before her brain went insane due to utter boredom.

Although her thoughts drifted, she caught Dr. Lizenhower's brisk rebuttal. "I'll skim the pages as I have time." He spread his linen napkin across his lap. "However, and please forgive my forwardness, it sounds like your book offers theories, and unsubstantiated ones at that, rather than solutions."

Richard leaned forward, eyebrows pinched together.

Dr. Lizenhower glanced at his colleague and shrugged. "But as I said, I'll take a look at it. Well, more likely, I'll ask one of my graduate students to review it."

When the conversation shifted to a stilted discussion of etiology and pathogenesis, Ainsley checked out. Stirring her ice with her straw, she surveyed the busy restaurant. Two women, the younger dressed in maroon from her pointed shoes to her knit sweater, the other in all black, appeared to be engaged in a rather heated conversation. Behind them, sat an elderly couple. As they ate, they watched their plates, never once looking at the other. Neither spoke. Neither smiled.

Till death do they part.

"Shall we?" Richard's question jolted her back to the present. She glanced up. "Um . . . sure."

The men stood.

After everyone said good-bye, Richard guided her through the restaurant and to her car.

She spun around and glared. "So, was that your surprise? Richard Hollis saves Ainsley's career once again?"

He smiled. "You are so cute when you're frustrated, but of course not. I understand how you value your independence, and I would never do anything to cause that pretty little face to pucker." He traced his gloved finger across her upper lip. "I merely lined up an appointment. The real work of turning the meeting to profit is up to you."

"If only it were that easy." She sighed and tucked a lock of hair behind her ear. "Listen, Richard, we need to talk." Squaring her shoulders, she ushered the courage to look him in the eye. "This isn't working."

He froze, his face slack, his mouth slightly ajar. But then he smiled and placed his hands on her shoulders. "My dear, you worry way too much. As I told you before, everything is going to be fine. I promise." He leaned forward to kiss her, but she stepped back and out of his reach.

"Richard, please."

"Close your eyes."

"Not now. I need you to hear me."

"Let's not fight. Here, this is for you." He held a heart-shaped diamond pendant dangling from a gold chain in the air. "A delicate locket for a delicate lady. Do you like it?"

"Don't make this any harder than it has to be." She swallowed, wishing she could think of an easier way to say this. "I can't marry you. I'm sorry, but it's over." She pulled her engagement ring from her pocket and handed it over. He stared at it, making no effort to accept it, so she set it on the ground by his feet. Standing, she turned to leave but he grabbed her wrist.

His eyes turned hard. "No. It's not over, my love. We'll get through this. I promise you that."

Chapter 14

*A*insley sat along the far wall in Pancho's Village, an old-style Spanish restaurant located in the heart of Parkville, a close-knit community five miles north of downtown Kansas City. The aroma of cilantro and steak fajitas surrounded her with warmth. Breathing deep, she leaned back in her chair and watched pedestrians pass her window, heading to or from one coffee house, shop, or boutique to another.

How many afternoons had she and Deborah spent here over the years, eating enough tortillas to produce a bellyache? When done, they'd meandered through the stores and galleries, pausing to nibble on chocolates and to smell the handmade soaps and candles.

Ainsley's favorite was the Parkville Antique mall, a 500-square-foot building filled with vintage furniture, hand-sewn lace dresses and satchels, and wicker baskets. She loved sifting through old black-and-white photographs, imagining the stories behind the pictures. Lives long forgotten except by those whom they had touched.

She wrapped her hands around her coffee mug and breathed in the rich aroma. Things might have been rough growing up, but God had been faithful. He'd provided so many people to help her along the way. So many moments of joy and peace.

Footsteps approached, and she glanced up to see Deborah dressed in her familiar red jacket and yellow clogs. She wore her hair short, the ends flipped out. Her circular reading glasses balanced precariously on the tip of her slender nose.

"Hi." Ainsley rose to meet her.

"My sweet girl." The woman embraced her, the scent of cherry-blossom lotion filling Ainsley's nostrils. Grabbing her hands in her own, Deborah stepped back. "You look as beautiful as ever, although," she cocked her head, forehead creased, "you're not sleeping well, are you?"

Ainsley shrugged and gave a sheepish smile. "Well, you know. Failing miserably at my job, dealing with my slightly insane mother, and breaking off a five-year relationship months before my wedding has a way of keeping one up at night."

"A lot to process, I'm sure." She shucked her jacket and purse, draped both over her chair, and sat. "Mmm . . . She reached for a chip and dipped it in the guacamole Ainsley had ordered, "I'm starved. Oh, I almost forgot. I brought something for you."

She rummaged through her purse and pulled out a pink, pocket-sized book. She handed it over. The title read: *Daily Nourishment for a Woman's Heart.* "I discovered this little gem a few days ago. Bought one for both of us."

They made small talk until their order had been taken and the chip basket emptied. That was Deborah's way. She never dove into the meat of their discussion until they'd had a chance to build a buffer. That used to drive Ainsley insane, back when she was an impatient and highly emotional teenager. But now she cherished every moment.

"So," Deborah folded her hands on the table and leaned forward, her blue eyes centered on Ainsley's. "Enough about my dying blue spruce, overgrown vegetable garden, and plantar fasciitis." She smiled and patted Ainsley's hand. "Tell me about you and Richard. How did he take the news?"

Ainsley traced her finger along the rim of her ice water. "Not as well as I'd hoped; but if I'm honest, no worse than expected." She picked at a loose thread in the tablecloth. "We both know how bullheaded he can be." She paused. "And how indecisive I can be."

"And yet, I suspect you have a very good reason for ending the engagement."

Ainsley nodded and told her friend everything — from the passage she'd read to Richard's evasive behavior every time she asked about his faith walk. "Obviously, we're headed in different directions. Our marriage would've been a mess."

"Believe me, I know. I've seen way too many endure the pain of living with an unbelieving spouse. A growing number of ladies today don't appear to consider that most important piece until after they've made a lifelong commitment." She shook her head. "They must not realize what a big deal marriage is. In Scripture, we're told through marriage, two people become one. It's a beautiful thing and a powerful representation of Christ's love for us, His followers. But when couples aren't united spiritually . . . Marriage is hard enough." She patted Ainsley's hand. "I'm just glad you listened to God before Richard slipped a ring on your finger."

Ainsley's cheeks heated, and her gaze fell to the table. In truth, she'd spent very little time praying about this engagement, or her and Richard's relationship at all, until things started getting tense. But not anymore. From now on, Christ would be the center of all her decisions.

Deborah opened her mouth as if to say something, but was interrupted by the waiter. The girl, maybe seventeen years old, had wispy, blonde hair pulled into two side braids. After delivering a steaming, cheese-covered enchilada to Ainsley and a taco salad with extra sour cream to Deborah, she left.

She held out her hands. "Shall we pray?"

Ainsley nodded, and, with their hands clasped, bowed her head.

"Holy Father, what a blessing it is to watch Ainsley grow spiritually and to see her seek after You and Your wisdom. We know You have a plan for her — a wonderful, glorious, fulfilling plan. Not only for her, but for her future husband as well. Thank You for making Your will clear to her in regard to her relationship with Richard. Please continue to guide her, and above all else, stir within her a passionate love for You, Your truth, and Your redemptive mission."

Deborah dropped her hands and reached for her napkin, which she opened and placed on her lap. "Now, what is it you're concerned about?"

"Besides the fact that Richard could very likely turn hateful on me?" His cold expression and icy tone the day she broke their engagement came to mind, causing her stomach to tighten.

Deborah raised an eyebrow. "Oh? You aren't frightened he'll harm you, are you?"

"Not physically, but financially, maybe. He has a lot of connections. If he wants to, he can make life miserable for me."

Deborah pulled on the loose skin under her chin. "I suppose that is a concern. And yet, there's not much you can do about that, except perhaps pray." She shrugged. "Then trust God to work it all out." She speared a tomato with her fork. "Where do you see yourself in ten years?"

"To be honest, I have no idea. I'd like to think I'd be working as a pharmacist with a national chain, or maybe..." She exhaled, rubbing her temples. "Right now I'm just trying to pay the bills."

"God wants so much more for you, my dear. So very much." Deborah moved her glass aside. "If you could do anything, knowing God would stand behind you 100 percent, what would that be?"

She thought of the boy and his mother, and his mother, of the countless women and children like them, and a searing pain shot through her heart. With a quivering voice, she said, "I'd share God's love with hurting children. Hurting families."

"Hurting kids, like you once were."

Tears pricked her eyes. The emotion surging within her surprised and scared her. "I hadn't realized how much I long to do that until this moment."

She spun a thick string of cheese around her fork then set it down. "You know that kid from the apartment? The one who lives next to Marie Nelson?"

Deborah nodded, her smile fading. "Yes. Little William. I pray for him often."

"Do you think I should reach out to him?" There had to be

a reason she couldn't shake the image of the child staring at her from that third-story apartment window. "To him and his mom?"

Deborah looked at Ainsley for a long moment. When she spoke, her voice was soft. "They're gone, sweetie. The landlord evicted them over a week ago. Threw out all their belongings."

"What?" She croaked the word out, her throat suddenly dry. "Where'd they go?"

"I don't know. I wish I did."

With the radio turned to her favorite Christian station, Ainsley headed home. Halfway there, her phone rang. Gina's number flashed across the dash.

Ainsley answered the call through her car's Bluetooth system. "Hey. What's up?"

"You OK? Because you kinda sound like your best friend died, and I'm still kicking."

"Got a lot on my mind is all." She reached the Missouri River and one of her favorite architectural designs in Kansas City, the Christopher S. Bond Bridge. Massive cables extended from a delta-shaped pylon that rose 315 feet above the river to the end of the bridge on either side. At night, the structure lit up, casting silver light on the velvet water below.

"How'd lunch go?"

Ainsley told Gina all about it, including William and his mother's eviction.

"Wow. What are you going to do?"

"What can I do? I certainly can't track them down. The child could be anywhere." Stuck in foster care, with his mom in some other section eight apartment, maybe even on the streets. Or running with gangs. Kids like him were a perfect targets for drug dealers. "All I can do is pray. And, hopefully, figure out what all this means. I know God has a plan in this, an action plan. A way for me to *do* something."

"I get it, and I'm sorry, Ains. On another note, what's the latest with the Richard drama? Has he told his mom yet? She's shucked out thousands of dollars already, hasn't she?"

Ainsley groaned. "I hadn't even considered that. Oh, I hope she hasn't. I feel like such a jerk."

"Sounds like you could use some retail therapy. I hear Dillard's is having a sale."

"No. More like a night in. With a giant tub of chocolate chunk ice cream. What do ya say? You free Friday?"

"Um . . . sure. Let me just . . . yeah, no problem."

"You have plans, don't you?" Ainsley stopped at the entrance to her neighborhood to let two elementary aged kids cross on their bikes in front of her.

"Um . . . sort of. I set up a bowling thing with Chris. But I'll totally cancel. You're much more important."

"No. Go. No reason both of us should be miserable this weekend."

Chapter 15

Chilled wind slammed Chris in the face when he stepped out of his warm house and down his porch steps. The sun poked over the horizon, casting the neighborhood in a golden glow. From the looks of it, a nasty storm was brewing. He paused in front of Ainsley's yard. Light radiated from the kitchen and a back window. Other than that, there was no sign of her long, blonde curls and soft, heart-shaped face.

Most likely, she'd already left for work.

He continued on, past two-story brick houses with shake roofs and detached garages. Smoke pumped from a few stone chimneys, dark plumes dissipating into the pale-blue sky.

On the corner, a man wearing a gray beanie pulled over his ears, tufts of black hair peeking out, hacked at an overgrown flameleaf sumac. He littered his lawn with the bright-red foliage. A few feet away grew large clumps of purple fountain grass, their feathery tips waving in the wind. An old woman sat in a rocker on the porch, a crocheted blanket draped over her shoulders. Watching the man, she sipped from a mug.

Chris thought of his mom. Hopefully the staff at Shady Lane would keep their eye on her tonight. He didn't need her wandering the streets of Kansas City, disoriented, during a storm. Didn't need her wandering the streets period, but tonight even more so.

A sudden urge to drive to the nursing home, scoop her up, and bring her home, swept over him. Reality followed on its tails. What did he know about Alzheimer's, other than the articles he'd read? His mother required more care than he could provide — more than Shady Lane provided as well.

His old pastor would've told him to trust in God, to surrender his mom into God's care. But that kind of trust was easier preached than followed. "Achoo!" A sneeze sounded to his left.

He turned to find an old man huddled in a thin, torn blanket. The man held his gaze then buried his face in his knees.

Entering the café, Chris paused, cold wind pressing against his back while forced heat flooded his face. He glanced at the clock on the far wall then back at the shivering man. Most likely, customers wouldn't start streaming in for some time yet. Even so, he had plenty to do before opening.

His tasks could wait. Chris faced the man and opened the door wider. "Good morning. You want a cup of coffee?"

The guy looked up and scrunched his face. A moment later, he clutched his blanket around his neck and jumped to his feet. "Ye-e-e-s sir!" His teeth chattered.

He entered, carrying with him the stench of urine and body odor. Still shivering, he stood in the center of the café, eyes darting back and forth like caged crickets.

"Excuse me for a moment." Chris disappeared behind the counter, reappearing with a handful of rags. He placed them on a nearby table. "If you wanted to clean up, run some warm water over your hands and face, bathroom's that way." He pointed toward a short hallway edging the north side of the café.

The man looked from the rags, to Chris, then back at the rags. With one swift movement, he grabbed the mound of cloth and dashed into the hall.

Chris smiled, humming softly as he rounded the counter. He pulled a gallon of vitamin D milk from the fridge, poured it into his mixer, and added two scoops of protein. After making a vanilla latte, he topped it with whipped cream. He grabbed two scones from the bakery case and set them where the rags once lay. Next, he found a small pocket Bible and a gospel tract and set them beside the scones.

After making himself a cappuccino, he popped a gospel CD into the surround sound stereo system and started unloading boxes.

Feet shuffled across the stained concrete, paused, then shuffled again. Chris glanced up and smiled. The man sat at the table, scone in hand, watching Chris. The guy left as soon as he finished eating, and Chris paused, books in hand, to offer up a silent prayer.

Lord, thank You for giving me an opportunity to demonstrate Your love today. Please watch over my new friend.

He distributed books among the shelves lining the far wall, placed a few along the window sill, and the rest on tables. Hopefully his patrons wouldn't hot finger them, but that was the risk he was willing to take. It'd be rather ironic, really, for some-one to steal a Bible. Almost comical.

Next, he called the local paper to find out why his print ad and coupon hadn't run.

"Your name again?"

Chris gave it along with that of his coffee shop. A keyboard clicked in the background then stopped.

"Yes, I see it now. It looks like you missed the deadline, but we've got it lined up for this Sunday."

"Great, thanks." Better late than never, but a print ad alone wouldn't cut it. Nor were his social media efforts. It didn't help that all his "friends" lived on the West Coast. They could share coffee shop updates nonstop; it wouldn't bring people in. Next step, canvassing the area, especially local businesses, with flyers and two-for-one deals.

By the time his employees arrived an hour and a half later, most of the reading items had been distributed and he was half-way through his third CD.

Lawrence walked in and scowled. "Oh, man! Not the Jesus music, dude."

Chris centered a checkerboard on a back table. "Give it a minute, L-man, see if it doesn't grow on you."

"Like cancer, you mean? Or the bubonic?"

Candy waltzed in a moment later smacking a wad of gum. "Whoa, what happened in here?" She moved to the closest table, picked up a pink-and-blue devotional, then set it down. "Did I miss the April Fool's memo or something?"

"No joke." The twinsy girls, self-named for their tendency to dress completely alike, down to nail color and hair style, stood shoulder to shoulder, arms crossed.

Chris chuckled. "Good morning, everyone. Feel free to make yourself a cup of coffee. We'll open in about twenty minutes."

"Yeah?" Lawrence rounded the counter. "And we'll close almost as quickly, if you don't turn that Sunday morning garbage off." He grabbed a coffee mug from the rack. "Oh, wait, I get it. You're turning the place into a comedy club. Right."

"Better watch it, L-man." Candy lowered a brow. "You're liable to get yourself fired with that kind of lip." She angled her head and twirled a lock of hair with her finger. "As for me, I don't care what kind of music you've got going, or . . ." She glanced at a box of a board game on an adjacent table. "What silly games you want people to play, so long as I get mine. It's all in the green, baby." She rubbed her fingers together and laughed.

"Great. We have an understanding then." He straightened a few sugar packets and moved to the condiment bar to check napkins and cinnamon shakers. "Almost forgot. Have you all liked our new Facebook page?"

They responded with blank stares. "If you could do that, I'd really appreciate it."

"Dude, no one's going to pay attention to that." Lawrence ran his hand along the top edge of his Mohawk. "You want to bring people in, you need to do some sort of promo. A photo thing. Like . . ." He drummed his fingers on a nearby table, jerking his head one way then the other as if his brain cells moved in time to high-tempo music. "Like maybe a 'Show us why you love coffee' campaign."

"Oh, I get it! That'd be perfect! People could send in photos of themselves in their nighties or up late studying — "

"Except we close at 10:00 p.m." Lawrence cracked his knuckles one by one. "But I like the jammies thing." He raised an eyebrow, giving Candy a suggestive smile. "So, Miss Lolly-dolly, what kind of pic you gonna send in? Cuz I'm thinking you've got some slinky-dinks that would bring folks in for sure."

Chris cleared his throat. "Pictures probably aren't the best idea. But if you have any other ideas — G-rated — shoot them my way. In the meantime, I'll continue pursuing the regular, old-school marketing channels."

He started to return to the counter when the door chimed open.

Stepping inside the Java Bean, Ainsley paused to take in the dramatically different atmosphere. The psychedelic artwork had been removed, replaced with softly hued paintings of children running through meadows and horses grazing in green valleys. Christian rock poured over her, adding an extra lift to her heart. The furniture had been rearranged, and a few softer pieces had been added.

The tables were lined with a rather odd assortment of board games and reading material — odd, yet inviting, in a childish sort of way. Standing in the center of it all wearing a sheepish grin and holding a coffee-stained rag stood Chris Langley.

Nervous energy nibbled at her gut.

"Ainsley, good to see you." He looped his thumbs through his leather belt. "Let me guess, vanilla latte, skim milk, no whip."

A smile tugged at her mouth despite her best efforts against it. He remembered what she'd ordered the last time she was here?

With Richard.

Forcing the thought aside, she inhaled the rich scent of vanilla and fresh brewed coffee. "That does sound tempting." She pulled off her gloves and tucked them into her purse. "Is that what you recommend?"

"Actually, I recommend pumpkin spice." He led her to the counter, void of customers.

A man with the Mohawk shuffled forward. "Hey, y'all, we got a customer. Alert the press."

Ainsley surveyed the sparsely populated dining room. "Are things that bad?" Eyes wide, she sucked in a breath of air. "I'm sorry. That's none of my business."

Chris flicked a dishtowel against his free hand. "No worries." He glanced toward the entrance. "Guess the customers weren't a fan of Praise-turnative."

"I see." She cocked her head, listening to Chris Tomlin's rich voice pouring through the speakers. It was one of her favorite songs. "Well, I find the changes you've made absolutely delightful."

Chris grinned, looking like a little boy who'd made his first basket. "Do you? Well then, I hope you'll stick around and enjoy the ambiance."

Her stomach did an odd flip. "I . . . no . . . I'm sort of in a hurry." She turned back to the man behind the counter. "I'll take a . . ." Her cheeks warmed as she fumbled in her purse for change. "Skim mocha, please."

Five minutes later, with steaming drink in hand, she sat in her car, staring back at her rather confusing neighbor. Richard was right; there was something different about him. But not in the way he'd insinuated.

Chapter 16

*R*ichard paced his office, phone in hand. He'd called Ainsley's number, got her voice mail, hung up, then called again. She couldn't do this. Not after all the money his parents had spent. After all the invitations that had gone out.

This wasn't good. This wasn't good at all. She was having prewedding anxiety is all.

He scowled. Anxiety that nosy pastor of hers had probably either created or exacerbated with all his "born-again" nonsense. Apparently, it wasn't enough for Richard to agree to go to church, every Sunday even, if it came to that. Nor was it enough that he allowed Ainsley — and, in fact, gave her his blessings — to do the same. No. Clearly that man expected some sort of sprinkling or dunking.

Ridiculous.

Ainsley needed him. Deep down, she knew this. Otherwise she'd end up just like her irresponsible, ideological mother, bouncing from job to job and man to man until Social Security kicked in.

He glanced at the satin box sitting on his desk, her very expensive engagement ring tucked inside.

Oh, sweet Ainsley, why must you sabotage every good thing that comes your way?

He tried her phone again. Nothing. He redialed.

Two more attempts later, she answered.

"Richard, you must stop this. You're becoming obsessive."

"Ainsley, please. I'm concerned for you. We really must —"

"If you don't stop harassing me, I'll change my number."

He froze, his hand tightening around his phone. A muscle in his jaw cramped, sending a jolt of pain up his temple. He was pushing too hard. Time to soften his approach.

"I've been think—"

The line went dead. Well, then, if she wouldn't come to him, he'd have to find a way to get to her.

Ah! Their online planner. He talked her into using Mitzo, a shared calendar, when they first began planning their wedding. She'd probably forgotten all about it, and that he had it linked to her phone calendar and email accounts.

He moved to his computer and clicked to the downloaded app, navigating to her daily agenda. She had a few meetings this morning. But that would be too soon. No, he needed to give her time to cool down.

But by Thursday, she'd be in a much better mood, and she had an appointment near the Plaza that day, at 10:30. Perfect.

He closed out the window and called to his secretary. "Mrs. Ellis, please contact Panache Chocolatier and instruct them to prepare a large gift pail. Have them charge this to the office Visa. Let them know I'll pick it up in a few days. Make sure they understand I will be in a hurry and will not want to wait in line."

"Yes, sir."

Thursday morning, he parked in front of a glass-walled medical building, Ainsley's car in sight. Flipping on his radio, he leaned back against the headrest and waited. Gershwin's piano concerto soothed away his frustrations, ushering forth his analytical side.

Fifteen, maybe twenty minutes later, she exited the building dressed in a lavender sweater, knee-length skirt, and flats. Soft curls framed her delicate face, her cheeks a delightful pink. She was so incredibly beautiful. She still favored her left ankle, although most of her limp was gone.

Grabbing the pail of candy, Richard slipped out of his Lexus, easing the door closed. Lengthening his stride, he met her at her car. "Ainsley."

Startled, she whirled to face him, her eyes wide. "Richard."

She looked from him to the candy then back to him and crossed her arms. "What are you doing here?"

He forced what he hoped to be an endearing smile. "I realize you are upset, and I completely understand, but I'm concerned with the way we've left things. With where things are going." He stepped toward her; she stepped back, maintaining the distance between them. "You know as well as I how important it is to discuss these things."

"I'm done discussing."

"I have something for you." He held out the pail of chocolate. "Something sweet for my sweet."

"Richard, please." She placed one hand on her car door. The other clutched her computer bag.

"Can we go for coffee? There's a wonderful café down the —"

"Stop." She raised her voice and her hand. "What part of 'It is over' don't you understand?"

He tensed, heat shooting through his veins. "There's no reason to become so emotional."

"Then listen to me. Watch my lips." She pointed to her mouth. "I won't marry you, Richard. And no amount of phone calls, cards, and presents will change that."

"I'm sorry, Richard. I truly am."

The ungrateful, inconsiderate —. Nerves in his neck and jaw firing, he narrowed his gaze. "Are you?" He made no attempt to hide the edge in his voice.

"I am."

"Then I suggest you think long and hard about what you're doing here." He trembled as he fought to maintain self-control.

She shook her head. "I wish you the best." She started to slip inside her car.

He lunged for her and grabbed her arm. "Wait!"

She whirled around, her eyes hot. "Let go of me. Now."

Blood pulsated in his ears and the tips of his fingers, pressed firmly against Ainsley's smooth skin. He couldn't let it end like this. He refused.

A car door slammed, and heavy footsteps approached, but

the sound barely registered. He continued to grip Ainsley's arm, his vision narrowing on her thin, quivering lips.

A shadow fell over him. "This guy bothering you, miss?" Outweighing Richard by at least fifty pounds, a bulky man in a camouflaged jacket moved to Ainsley's side, gaze fixed on Richard.

He maintained eye contact without wavering. "This does not concern you."

"Wrong answer." The man wedged closer, close enough for Richard to feel his hot breath on his face.

As the two remained in a nonverbal standoff, another car pulled into the lot. Its owner, a balloon of a man with a shiny bald head and a mustache that curled out at the ends, joined the fray. He stood two feet back to Richard's right, giving no indication he planned to leave.

Richard's grip slackened.

Ainsley jerked her arm away, staring at him with cold eyes. "Thanks for confirming my decision." She turned to the man in camouflage. "Thank you for your help," then eased into the driver's seat. Her door locks clicked and her engine roared to life. Her car lurched backward, she turned, and peeled out of the parking lot, leaving Richard to stare after her.

Chests puffed and arms bowed in a muscle-man stance, the men continued to stare at him. Smoothing his shirt, he looked from one man to the next. "As entertaining as this rather base display of masculinity is, I have much better ways to spend my time."

He turned toward his car, but Mr. Camo stopped him.

"You're not going anywhere. Not till that gal you were harassing is long gone."

Richard snorted. "*Harassing?* For your information, that *gal* is my fiancé."

"Whatever you say, buddy. You're still not going anywhere. Not until I'm sure that woman's put plenty of distance between you two."

Richard fisted his hands, fire raging within. There was nothing he could do but comply.

For now.

Chapter 17

*S*aturday morning, pebbles pelted the sides and undercarriage of Ainsley's car as she continued down the gravel road she hoped led to Beverly Pugh's place. She gave up on using her GPS a long time ago. Apparently, satellites grew fuzzy the farther one ventured into cow country. Unfortunately, the directions Mrs. Pugh gave weren't much better. *"When you hit a fork in the road, turn left. Not sure if there's a street sign there. Nope. I'm sure there's not. It was knocked down by a drunk driver last year some time. Should be a long, barbed wire fence extending a quarter mile of the way or so."*

The only highlight of her wasting over an hour driving past one farm after another? It looked like she might be able to avoid her mom after all. If the woman wasn't equally lost, she'd already given up and returned home. Maybe this obedience thing wasn't so bad after all.

Probably not the most Christlike attitude she could have, but at least she was trying. Sort of. Inwardly cringing, she glanced toward the ball of fire hovering in the pale-blue sky. *I'm sorry, Lord. Help me be more . . . gracious. Forgiving.*

The word stung.

Thank goodness Richard hadn't called. Not since their parking lot fiasco. Maybe he finally accepted the fact their relationship was over. Although as stubborn as he was, she doubted it.

She looked at the hand-drawn map Deborah had given her for the tenth time. How many gravel roads cutting through cornfields could there be? She surveyed her surroundings, with farmland stretched in every direction. Apparently a lot. The houses, however, were few and far between.

Seemed the smartest thing to do at this point was turn around and head home. She reversed her car, heading south on what she assumed to be Old Creek Lane. Less than a mile later, a single-lane dirt road appeared on her right. It was flanked by tall, golden grass, and a rusted metal gate marked the entrance. Three orange balloons and a handwritten sign verified Mrs. Pugh's residence was but a few more potholes away.

The road took her to a two-story log cabin centered in an open field. Half a dozen vehicles filled the driveway and adjacent grassy area, Deborah's twenty-year-old Volvo among them. Ainsley pulled in front of an old red barn and cut the engine.

Stepping out into the crisp fall air, she inhaled the sweet scent of fresh cut hay and baked apples. Firewood was stacked along the left of the house, a primitive vegetable garden next to that. Behind this stretched a fenced pasture where a caramel-toned Pinto and a speckled calf grazed.

Ainsley stepped onto the wraparound porch, the wood creaking beneath her. Laughter poured from the opened windows, Deborah's among them. Smiling, she opened the screened door and rapped on the wood behind it. It opened with a whoosh, releasing a warm gust of cinnamon-spiced air.

"Hello!" Mrs. Pugh engulfed Ainsley in a hug then pulled away, looking behind her. "Is your mother coming?"

She suppressed a frown. "Don't know."

"No matter. Come in, come in."

She ushered Ainsley into a room filled with pumpkins, scarecrow statues, and burning candles. Handmade quilts draped over checked furniture and framed embossing hung on the wall. Women of all ages and sizes filled the room, some doing needlework, others peeling apples at a long table pushed near the side wall.

"Look who finally arrived." Beverly placed her hands on Ainsley's shoulders. Heads turned, hands stopped, and smiles grew.

Deborah rose to greet her. "So glad you could make it. I was starting to get worried."

"Yeah, me too."

"Do you think your mom will have any trouble?"

Ainsley tensed, her gaze shooting to one of the open windows framed by floral curtains. She shrugged.

Deborah rubbed her thumb knuckle under her chin. "Hmm . . . If she doesn't show within the hour, maybe we should go looking for her."

Ainsley turned and approached the women sitting at the table. She knew most of them from her years in Sunday School. There were five in all, each over sixty, and four of them still faithfully serving in the church. The women smiled up at her, their eyes bright in their wrinkled faces.

Magdaline Armstrong, a hunch-backed woman well into her eighties, scooted over and patted the bench seat beside her. "Haven't seen you since you were knee-high." She held an arthritic hand four feet off the ground. "You still hiding candy in your pockets?"

Sitting, Ainsley shook her head. "Absolutely not. I've got a purse now." She raised her tote.

This got everyone laughing, which soon set some to coughing and blowing their noses into lace-trimmed handkerchiefs. Once her hacking subsided, Magdaline slipped an arm around Ainsley's back. "Well, I've missed you. Can't get these old bones to church as often as I'd like. But the ladies here keep me grounded. Ain't that right, Dottie?"

The woman across from her nodded. "We visit Magdaline once a week and bring the Good Book with us." She raised a cracked, leather Bible, and numerous heads nodded. Making eye contact with Ainsley, she pushed a bushel of apples across the table and tossed over a peeler. "Better get working, kiddo. We've got a lot of orders to fill this year."

Ainsley raised an eyebrow. "Orders?" She grabbed a piece of fruit in one hand, a peeler in the other.

"Uh-huh." Deborah lifted a notepad filled with names, addresses, and tally marks. "We're selling our goods — apple sauce, pie, knitted blankets." She made a large sweeping motion with her arm. "To earn money for Rachel's House."

Ainsley paused in midpeel. "What's that?"

"A ministry for pregnant moms." Magdaline drew her peeler across her apple with a shaky, contorted hand.

Ainsley watched her for a long time. She grimaced with each stroke, as if it caused her pain, and yet, she continued. The woman had been through a lot. Battled breast cancer in her thirties, had her gallbladder removed ten years later. Buried her husband a week before their fiftieth anniversary, lost their farm a short time later. Now she lived in a rent-controlled studio apartment. And yet, here she sat, working with her arthritic hands to help someone else. And based on the radiant smile she gave everyone who looked her way, it filled her with immense joy to do so.

Meanwhile, here was Ainsley, with her rent paid, money in the bank, and a steady job — at least for now. And she was more miserable than ever. What did Magdaline have that Ainsley lacked?

Turning her apple in her hand, she thought about a memory verse Deborah often recited. *Whoever wants to save their life will lose it. But whoever loses their life for me will save it.*

A loud knock jolted her attention to the front door.

Ainsley's mother's bellowing voice followed. "Hello?" She banged again. "Hello? Hello-hello-hello, anyone gonna let me in?"

"And that would be my mom. Excuse me." She and Deborah exchanged glances and the two of them rose and crossed the room. Deborah opened the door to find Ainsley's mom on the stoop dressed in leggings, black leather boots, and a glittery sweater dress. She smelled as if she'd been dunked in a perfume factory distiller. A large, zebra print purse hung from one arm, a tote tilled with fake flowers and scraps of tissue from the other.

She stepped inside and smoothed a stray lock of hair from her face. "Talk about the middle of nowhere! What do the people in this town have against street signs? I thought I'd never find this place."

Now wouldn't that have been nice? Forcing a smile, Ainsley allowed her mother to hug her before moving aside. "You remember Deborah Eldridge?"

Her mother eyed the woman then nodded. "Yes, of course. Your old third-grade teacher. How nice to see you." She surveyed the area, her gaze lingering on two baskets, one filled with gourds, the other with giant pine cones, placed on the brick mantel. "Now isn't this quaint?" She took Ainsley's hand and gave it a squeeze. "This will be fun."

Ainsley tried to return her mother's smile, but her cheeks were beginning to ache and her stomach felt as if it'd been tossed in a blender. *Please don't do anything to embarrass me. Or offend these sweet ladies.* Hands clasped in front of her, she led her mother to the long table covered in fruit bowls, apple peelings, and cinnamon sticks. A stack of sticky labels and permanent markers were spread out at each end of the table.

Small talk followed as the ladies introduced themselves, sharing where they lived and how long they'd been participating in the fall event. Then, they talked about the various projects they were doing, inviting Ainsley's mom to join them.

"So many wonderful endeavors to choose from." Dropping her belongings on the floor, her mom fingered a lace doily. "But since I came to spend time with my wonderful daughter," she flashed Ainsley a smile, "I'll do whatever she chooses. What are you working on, darling?"

Ainsley shrugged. "Peeling apples, I guess."

She and her mother sat, and the women handed them each a peeler and pushed a fruit bowl between them. Her mother grabbed an apple and rolled it around in her hand. She looked at the stack of labels. "I love how you all work together. Support one another. I for one am thrilled I could help out. You know, I'm something of an entrepreneur myself."

The women stopped working and stared at her. Ainsley and Deborah exchanged glanced.

Ainsley almost hated to ask. "What are you talking about, Mother?"

She laughed. "Oh, you know, dear. I've participated in numerous business ventures over the years. Surely you remember my catering business."

"Not really." Unless she was referring to the time when she printed off a bunch of hand-typed menus and delivered them to all the neighbors. Or maybe when she sold sandwiches at a garage sale.

"I hit a few hurdles and setbacks. Tried a few things, tweaked some others. But I've always felt if only I had more support . . ." She looked at Ainsley and shrugged. "Anyway, I hope you ladies have more luck than I did. It's sad but true, this economy is a bear for the small business owner."

"This isn't a business, Mother. These ladies are going to sell their wares to help raise money for a ministry our church supports."

"Oh." Her mother's eyes widened. "What a thoughtful gesture."

Magdaline nodded. "We do this twice a year, once in the fall and again in the spring, same ministry each time." She went on to explain what the Rachel House did, who they helped, and why they needed financial support. "It's a community affair. We do the baking and making, others do the purchasing, often donating well over the suggested prices." She smiled. "It's wonderful to know our baked goods can help bring hope to those young women."

"And tangible things like food and clothes." Deborah grabbed a bowl full of peeled apples. "You'd be surprised how many of those ladies don't have coats to get them through the winter."

Ainsley immediately thought of William and his mother, living who knew where. Hopefully they'd found somewhere else to stay. But what if they hadn't? The winters in Kansas City could be so brutal. "What a wonderful thing you all are doing." Her mom wiggled off the bench and moved to a central location where she could see the kitchen, dining table, and living room. "I'd love to order a few pies." She glanced at a stack of quilts draped over a standing towel rack. "And some blankets as well."

Sweeping through the room, she hit shopping mode and had soon gathered a large number of items.

Ainsley quickly drew to her side. "Mom, you really can't afford this right now."

"Oh, don't be ridiculous, sweetie. It's good karma."

Heads turned, but luckily, no one said anything. Neither did Ainsley. The last thing she needed was to launch a philosophy debate.

Her mother rummaged through her purse and pulled out a purple change purse. She opened it, frowned, then snapped it shut. "Hmm . . . Seems I left my cash at home." She plunged her arm back in her purse. "Do you take checks?"

Ainsley grabbed her mother's wrist. "Mom, stop."

Her mother glared and jerked her hand away. "What I do with my money is none of your business, child."

"Actually, it is. And I have a collection notice sitting on my coffee table at home to prove it."

Her mother's hand flew to her neck as her gaze swept the room. She gathered her things, slinging a bag over each shoulder. With a deep breath, she straightened. "Perhaps it'd be best if I leave."

"Perhaps it would." Ainsley's temperature rose, every muscle in her body constricting.

She followed her mother out. Hugging her torso, she leaned against the wooden column and watched her mother's car disappear down the gravel road. A plume of dust kicked up behind her.

The door creaked open, and Deborah came to Ainsley's side. She placed an arm on her shoulder and gave a gentle squeeze. "You OK, kiddo?"

"I hate that I let her get me so worked up. Why does she always bring out the worst in me?"

Deborah studied her. "I suspect it's more like she's stirring up wounds from the past."

Chapter 18

*R*ichard's spine grated against the backing of the hard, plastic chair and the pungent odor of lemon-scented cleaner stung his nose. He checked Mitzo, the online calendar again. Ainsley had deleted all her appointments and withdrawn from the account. A growl welled up inside him. Stupid woman. How long did she intend to continue this maddening game? But he couldn't think about that now. It'd get him worked up and could potentially sabotage his interview. As insignificant as it — and the radio station it would air on — was.

He scanned the boxlike lobby of KCGW AM. Except for a handful of paper certificates and old newspaper clippings framed in plastic, the dingy, white walls remained barren. A small, wooden end table sat beside him, five-year-old magazines strewed atop it.

Across the way a woman with carrot hair and purple-framed glasses chomped on a mouthful of gum, causing her fleshy underchin to quiver. "Mr. Showtoe will be here shortly."

Richard glanced from his watch to the window behind him. Three cars dotted the small, cracked parking lot. Why in the world had he agreed to this deal?

Because Eric couldn't land him anything better. Maybe he needed to find a more qualified publicist.

The door beside him opened and a balding man with tufts of hair sprouting from his ears wobbled in. He held a tarnished briefcase in one hand, a partially eaten sandwich in the other. Wiping his mouth with his sleeve, he left a trail of mustard on his pale-blue and green-striped shirt. "You must be Mr. Hollis." He set his briefcase on the ground and extended his hand.

Richard rose and fought against a nose-scrunching frown as the stench of garlic and onions wafted over him. "That is correct."

A sticky hand closed around his and pumped his arm.

"I'm Frank Showtoe, host of *Let's Talk About It*. Follow me." He jerked his head toward a narrow, dimly lit hallway to their left and picked up his briefcase.

Richard rose, smoothed the front of his designer shirt, and followed. They stopped in front of a wooden door flanked by thick glass windows. Inside the room, a woman with spiked blonde hair and more lipstick than a circus clown hunched over a microphone.

Mr. Showtoe touched a finger to his lips then eased the door open. Richard followed and leaned against a pale, white wall. The woman gave Mr. Showtoe a nod and Richard a wink, then turned back to the mike. She closed her broadcast with a catcall that made Richard jump.

"Woot-woot! And you heard it here first, on *Jewels Among the Junk Pile*, digging through other people's trash for pleasure and profit. Make sure to come back next Tuesday to meet Mr. Trashcan himself, Sigmund Stashaway." She clicked a button then spun around, her lipstick cracking as her mouth slid into a toothy grin. "Frank, my man, who's your buddy?" Her seat screeched as she stood, revealing a gaping tear extending the length of the seat cushion.

Mr. Showtoe tucked his briefcase beneath an elongated table covered in various radio gear. "This is Mr. Hollis — "

"*Dr.* Hollis." Richard puffed out his chest.

"Excuse me. Dr. Hollis, author of *The Schizophrenic Next Door: Societal Solutions to the Age-Old Problem of Dysfunction*."

The woman's face scrunched. "Oh. Interesting, I'm sure." Her voice held a nasally tone. She paused, inspecting Richard's attire before meeting his gaze.

He lifted his chin. "It is rather complicated, based on years of research."

"I'm sure." She stared at him a moment longer then turned and grabbed a gigantic gold and silver sequined purse from beneath her chair. Clonking out of the room, she winked at Richard then disappeared down the hall. The rhythmic clicking of her heels grew steadily fainter.

Mr. Showtoe pulled a folding chair from the wall and flipped the seat down. "Make yourself comfortable. I'll start us off."

Richard sat, spine erect, hands folded tightly in his lap, and waited for the rather annoying theme music to swell and fade.

Mr. Showtoe's blaring voice followed. "Good morning, ladies and gentlemen. Welcome to *Let's Talk About It*, where real life meets the airwaves. Today I'm pleased to introduce you to Mr. Halls, author of the soon to be released *Your Schizophrenic Neighbor*. Mr. Halls, thank you for joining us. Before we begin, why don't you tell us a little about your book? Does it stem from personal experience?" He laughed, his jowls shaking. "Give us a glimpse of your neighborhood."

Richard's jaw tightened, his back molars grinding. "It's Dr. Hollis, and the book is entitled *The Schizophrenic Next Door: Societal Solutions to the Age-Old Problem of Dysfunction*."

"Right, sorry. A fascinating topic. You must live in my neighborhood." He laughed again, sending ripples through his gut. "But seriously, tell us, why did you write a book about schizophrenic neighbors?"

Richard shifted and cleared his throat. Eric and he needed to talk, as soon as this sham of an interview concluded. "This book is not about schizophrenic neighbors, per se, although studies estimate 2.2 million Americans suffer from the illness, so it is quite possible many in your audience do indeed have a schizophrenic neighbor, family member, or friend."

The interview progressed, Mr. Showtoe continually turning it into a comedy show while Richard countered with sound data. After thirty minutes of back-and-forth banter, Richard's self-control wore thin. Luckily, Mr. Showtoe turned the broadcast over to callers before Richard said anything he'd regret.

"Our first caller is Buddy Landers from Holt, Missouri. Hey, Buddy, thanks for listening. Do you have a question for our good doctor?"

Static crackled across the line, followed by a heavily accented, clearly slurred voice. "Not a question, more of an observation." Laughter sounded in the background. "I'm just wondering how I can get me some of this schizophrenia."

Richard frowned. "I'm sorry, I don't understand what you mean. Are you asking where you can buy the book?"

The caller snickered. "No, man. That thing would make my head hurt, and I got enough headaches as it is, but that trip — hearing voices, seeing things, jamming in my own world — that I can dig. Wild!" Laughter — from the caller and at least three others — came through the line .

Richard's hands clenched, his nails digging into his palms. "This is not a comical matter. It's a serious mental illness that must be addressed." He launched into his oft-rehearsed speech, but Mr. Showtoe cut him off with another caller, a woman this time.

"Dr. Hollerk, have you researched the benefits of fish oil and iodine on the human brain?"

"It's Dr. Hollis, and no, nor does my book discuss alternative medicine."

The woman went on about various nutritional supplements and how they provided cures for everything from mental illness to stage four brain cancer. Richard tuned her out and watched the second hand of the clock tick by.

This was the longest, most unproductive hour of his life.

By the time the interview ended, a dull ache, birthed in his right temple, spread to every cell in his brain.

The door behind him squeaked open and a man dressed in torn jeans and a paisley shirt waltzed in wearing headphones and carrying a large fill-and-go soda. Mr. Showtoe snapped on the theme music, flicked a few switches, then rose. He and Mr. Paisley exchanged a nod.

"Let's schedule a follow-up, for after your book launches." Mr. Showtoe glanced at a paper calendar tacked to the wall. "When does it hit stores, again?"

Richard moved to the door. "I'll have my publicist call you."

Chris counted the money in the cash register while Lawrence mopped the floor. The twinsy girls huddled in a far corner smacking gum, which he told them hours ago to spit out. Candy leafed through various books lining the far window. And the customers? They hadn't seen any in over thirty minutes. All day, maybe a dozen folks had walked through that door. Had he tried to make too many changes too fast? And what about all those advertisements he'd sent out?

He really should've taken some basic marketing classes before buying this place. Or maybe hired on a manager.

Was it too late? Considering how close his bank account hovered near the red, yeah. But if he didn't figure out something soon, this place would go under.

"Guess we won't be getting a year-end bonus this Christmas, huh, bossman?"

Lawrence propped the mop handle upright and rested against it. "Warned you this would happen. Like I always say, no sense fixin' what's already rockin' and rollin'. Unless you want static, which is what you got here, my man." He swept his arm to indicate the empty seating area.

Chris stuffed the money in the bank bag and slammed the drawer shut. "That's really not your concern, now is it?"

Lawrence raised an eyebrow. "Touchy. But hey, what do I care if you tank the place?" He dipped his mop into dirty water then plopped it onto the floor.

"You need to dump that and get clean water." Chris scowled and stomped toward the girls who grew silent when he approached. "And you two, the glass is past clean. Tessa, make sure the napkin holders and spice shakers are full then sanitize the tables. Selena, I want you to clean the bathroom."

The girl's face puckered. "Nasty. How about I help Tessa with the tables?"

"How about you do what you're told?"

Her eyes widened then narrowed into a scowl. "I don't need this garbage, not for minimum wage and . . ." she lifted a Mason jar on the counter and let it drop with a clang, "zero tips." She turned to her friend. "What do you say, Tessa, think Starbucks is hiring?"

Tessa ran her tongue over her lip ring and shrugged. "Worth a shot."

Their long, jet-black hair swung across their shoulders as they waltzed out. Selena paused at the door to throw Lawrence a kiss and Candy a wave. "It's been real, man, but you know."

"Yeah, a real dud." Tessa giggled and spun around. The door closed behind them.

Chris turned first to Candy then to Lawrence. "You two can take the rest of the night off. I'll finish up here."

"Sounds good to me." Lawrence pushed the mop bucket aside with his foot, splashing water onto the floor.

Chris tucked his money bag under his arm and stalked off to his office. Dropping his meager proceeds onto his desk, he sank into the chair. Concerns for his mother and the upcoming guardianship hearing jumped to the forefront of his mind. Years of law practice told him what to expect if things didn't turn around soon:

"Medicare does not pay for such a facility, Mr. Langley. How do you propose to cover the residency fee?"

Three months ago, he could have offered his savings. Twelve months ago he could've called his dad for advice. His dad always said his impulsive nature would do him in one of these days. Only this time, his actions could hurt his mom. Badly.

Swallowing hard against a lump lodged in his throat, he grabbed his Bible from a nearby shelf and flipped it open to his life verse, scrawled on a 3-by-5 card tucked between the pages.

Isaiah 31:1, *What sorrow awaits those who look to Egypt for help, trusting their horses, chariots and charioteers and depending on the strength of human armies instead of looking to the* LORD.

Closing the Bible, he bowed his head. *Lord, even though everything I see points to the contrary, even though my bank account dwindles as this once thriving café struggles to stay open, I will trust in You and not my abilities or my savings account.* He swallowed, unable to verbalize the words taking hold in his head. After a moment of internal struggle, he began again. *Lord, I surrender to You—this shop, my finances, and . . . and . . .* An image of his mother, seated at a noisy table, eyes filled with fear, came to mind, drowning out his final words.

Opening his eyes, he gathered a stack of papers and his money bag and left. His footsteps echoed in the hall. He paused at the door to scan the empty tables one more time then flicked the switch.

Chapter 19

*A*insley curled into the corner of the couch and popped a handful of popcorn into her mouth. Gina sat beside her with a blanket wrapped around her shoulder and a steaming cup of cocoa in her hands.

She took a drink, marshmallow foam clinging to her top lip. "Sorry about what happened with your mom."

Ainsley shrugged. "I didn't really expect any different." And yet, she'd hoped. "I know we're supposed to be patient, loving, but . . . how long do I have to keep trying?"

Gina looked at her for a long moment. "You probably don't want to hear my answer."

Ainsley sighed and pulled her leg to her chest, resting her chin on her knee. "Yeah, I probably don't." She ran her hand up her shin. "Why does life have to get so messy? My mom, that kid from the apartment, Richard."

"Speaking of, what are you going to do?"

"I don't know. Pray he gets over it. Finds someone else."

"You freaked out? I would be."

"No. He might be a bit on the obsessive side, but he won't do anything stupid. He'd never tarnish his reputation."

"Maybe you should sign him up for some online dating thing."

"Gina!" Ainsley hurled a throw pillow at her, nearly spilling her cocoa.

"Hey, it'd give him someone else to obsess over. You have to admit, that would be hilarious! Can you picture it? All these women showing up on his doorstep." She giggled.

"Especially if you fudged a few things, like age, interests, you know."

"Your immaturity never ceases to amaze me, my friend."

Gina grabbed a *Southwestern Cuisine* magazine off the coffee table and flipped through the pages. "This looks scrumptious!" She showed Ainsley a picture of Cornish game hens sprinkled with rosemary. "Although I doubt my mom would ever go for something like that, not for Thanksgiving anyway. I've been meaning to ask, you wanna join us this year? I know we can get a little crazy, especially when aunts and uncles start playing Pictionary or . . ." she framed her face with her hands, "charades, but considering the drama your parents typically launch at these types of gatherings . . ."

"You don't know how much I wish I could take you up on that offer, but there'd be even more drama if I didn't show. Not just from Mom and Dad."

"Why does your dad come anyway?"

Ainsley frowned at the memory of her parents hurling hateful words at a Fourth of July picnic a few years ago, faces redder than a rotten watermelon. "I think it's great that he comes. It's the plastic floozy hanging on his arm that gives everyone heartburn." Something she was beginning to experience just thinking about it.

"Sorry, Ains. Like you need more drama, huh?" She grabbed a handful of popcorn.

Time for a conversation change. "So, how are things with you and Chris?"

Ainsley frowned, nibbling on the edges of a popcorn kernel.

"What's wrong?"

"I don't know. I guess I just feel a little . . . weird about the whole thing." She grabbed another handful of popcorn. "I mean, he's hot and everything, but I'm not sure the spark's there."

"Great. Then I've still got someone to hang out with on Friday nights."

"Oh, no! Don't start forming a loser club on me now!" She made an L with her hand and pressed it to her forehead. "I haven't given up on the guy. I'm just keeping my eyes open, that's all. Not that I wouldn't pull a freak-out if he happened to call me."

"What do you mean you're keeping your eyes open? For what — another California hottie to come your way?"

"Maybe." Gina stood and strolled to the window, poking her finger between the blinds. "Or maybe a rugged Utah man, or a GQ New Yorker."

Ainsley pushed the popcorn bowl to the center of the table and wiped her hands on her pant legs. "Gina Rose, how you and I ever became friends is beyond me. We're like . . ."

"Salt and pepper." She grinned. "Totally opposite, but perfectly complementary." Meandering back to the living room, Gina grabbed a brochure off the end table. "UMKC. So you're still planning on going to pharmacy school, I take it."

Ainsley nibbled on a kernel of popcorn. "Maybe, if I can afford it."

Gina plopped on the couch beside her and skimmed the brochure. She studied Ainsley for a long moment. "If you want my honest opinion, I can't picture you as a pharmacist. You don't seem the type."

"Really? What type do you envision pharmacists to be? Or, more importantly, what role do you think I'm best suited for?"

"Honestly? The first time I heard you sing, and watched your eyes light up as the melody took hold of you, I knew God created you for that purpose." She twined her fingers and cupped her knee. "You know, I know somebody who knows somebody who knows somebody in the music industry. If you'd like, I could make a few calls."

Ainsley huffed. "You may as well tell me to join the circus. No, that's not a good analogy. Circus performers get paid. More accurately, you're telling me to jump on one of my mom's rapidly changing bandwagons." She smiled. "Now that would be comical, her and I. You know she'd be all over it too. For about ten minutes, before launching into another endeavor like jewelry making or fudge-factory ownership."

"So, because your mom's . . . ," Gina's forehead wrinkled, "because your mom lacks follow-through, you can't pursue your dream?"

Ainsley lowered her gaze and chewed on her bottom lip as dreams long since forgotten nibbled at her heart.

Planting her feet on the ground, she grabbed the brochure and flipped it over, pointing to the black lettering printed on the back.

"'According to the Department of Labor, employment opportunities for licensed pharmacists are expected to increase by 17 percent. As the median age of Americans continue to increase, the demand for pharmacists will increase as well.'" She dropped the brochure onto the table. "The best recession-proof job around!"

"Uh-huh, so you're playing it safe."

"Since when is that a bad thing? I'm making wise choices and choosing level paths for my feet."

"And fighting against that dream God placed in your heart years ago, before fear drowned it out. Is any decision wiser than following God's plan, regardless of how irrational it appears to be?"

Chapter 20

Chris leaned against a bowling ball rack and fumbled with his car keys. Gina sat beside him in faded jeans and a lavender shirt. A few strands of auburn hair escaped from her silver barrettes, framing her face in soft wisps.

"So . . ." He shoved his hands into his pockets and rocked on his heels.

"So . . ."

"You wanna go first?"

"Yeah, OK."

Great conversation starter. Next he could ask her shoe size. Twirling his straw in his soda cup, he watched her glide across the floor. The girl was cute, in a take-your-sister- to-lunch sort of way, but he didn't feel a spark. Not even a flicker. Although the fact that his thoughts kept drifting to Ainsley and her delicate smile didn't help.

Only problem—Ainsley wore a giant rock on her finger, making his attraction to her almost creepy. Further complicating the matter, here he was dating her best friend. *Way to create a soap opera, Mr. Casanova.* Almost made him feel like a cocky frat boy cruising the college campus for unsuspecting prey. Yep, *Jerk* with a capital *J*. A regular live-like-Jesus moment. Truth was, he wasn't even interested in dating. He had enough to worry about keeping his coffee shop afloat and his mother cared for.

What now? Wear a cheesy smile on his face and play gentleman until his emotions matched or politely excuse himself before inflicting real damage?

A group of men dressed in flannel shirts and sweat-stained cowboy hats bellowed in the lanes beside them, curse words flinging like popcorn kernels from an iron kettle. Gina jumped when a man with a ruddy complexion and a belly bigger than an overinflated tire slammed his fist on the counter. Foul language exploded from his bearded face.

Chris turned toward her. "You wanna leave?"

"No, it's fine. You're up."

They bowled a full game, their conversation progressing from, "Do you think it will snow?" to "What's your favorite television show?" After an hour, their date resembled a formal interview—and a failing one at that.

He fought the urge to check his watch and shifted in his seat. "So, where do you work?"

"B&R Accounting, downtown."

He nodded. Another great discussion launcher. But at least it beat awkward silence—minus the crashing pins, hollered swear words, and occasional he-man battle calls echoing all around him. "I suppose you like numbers then."

"I don't know about that. But I do enjoy receiving a steady paycheck. You know what they say, there are two guarantees in life, death and taxes."

"And illness." Genius addition. A Shakespeare duplicate. "Your turn."

He sprang to his feet, walking to the ball return slowly as his mind searched for something a bit more interesting to say. Employment, childhood residence, and major weather trends in the state of Missouri and California sufficiently covered, he sifted through the remaining icebreakers he used to hear at suit-and-tie functions.

Had it really been that long since he'd gone on a date? So many years of dollar chasing he had forgotten how to relate to beautiful women?

Or perhaps she wasn't "the one." The thought unsettled him, as if indicating the one waited in the wings. Which was far from the truth. He had enough to deal with watching out for Mom and keeping Matilda, with her constant threat of court proceedings, at bay.

Then why was he here? Now that was the question of the decade.

Ainsley pulled into her driveway and studied the houses on either side of her. The windows were dark minus the occasional flash of a television set. The motion sensor lights above her garage came on, accentuating the dark shadows encasing her front door. She'd never been a fan of the dark. Everyone said it'd get easier after she'd been on her own for a while. It hadn't.

Once inside, she locked her door and turned on a fair number of lights. Tea beckoned. Moving to the kitchen, she brewed hot water then rummaged through her fridge for edible leftovers. Ten minutes later, hot drink and fruit plate in hand, she ambled to the living room to spend the evening buried in work. Not the most exciting way to spend a Friday night, but it wasn't like she had anything else to do.

With her engagement officially terminated, her frequent joke of turning into an old lady surrounded by cats seemed unnervingly plausible. She thought of Chris and Gina, laughing and having a grand time down at the bowling alley. They'd probably fall in love, get married, move into a two-story house with a white picket fence, have 2.5 kids.

While Ainsley spent the rest of her life with her most faithful companion — Ben and Jerry's chocolate chunk ice cream.

She grabbed the remote and flicked through the channels. Friday night television stunk, probably because producers knew most people had better things to do than watch TV. Besides, what she needed most was a bit of praise music to counter the gloom settling in her heart — all self-inflicted.

She exchanged television noise with praise music. Closing her eyes, she leaned against the couch cushions as "Silent Night" poured from her speakers. At the end of the song, the broadcaster cut in.

"I love that song, not just because it speaks of God Incarnate coming to earth as a helpless babe, but because it reminds me of my grandmother who passed away two years ago. This was her favorite song, and every year in preparation for Thanksgiving and Christmas, she and I baked dozens—and I mean dozens—of cookies, most of which were supposed to go to family and friends, but unfortunately, well . . . you know." The broadcaster giggled. "There are so many things I love about the holidays, but the family memories most warm my heart."

Tears stung Ainsley's eyes as a similar memory shared between her and her mom surfaced. How could recalling the past warm and break her heart at the same time? She pulled her phone from her back pocket and flipped through her contacts until she got to her mother's number. Her finger hovered over the Dial button.

Likely her mom was out with her latest guy friend, spending money they didn't have, whispering soon-to-be broken promises to one another. Because that's what her mom did—made and broke promises, leaving a trail of broken relationships in her wake.

A message spoken by her pastor the week before came to mind. "Love is patient, taking people as they are. Love is kind, filled with tenderness and concern for others, yes, even the unlovable. But most of all, love is initiating, taking the first step to reach out, with no strings attached, expecting nothing in return."

She sighed and grabbed her cell phone again. "Fine. I'll try it. I'll stick my neck out one more time, but if Mom bails on me again, I'm done. Do you hear me, God? Done!"

OK, maybe giving God ultimatums wasn't a wise course of action. After offering a heartfelt prayer of apology, she dialed her mom's number then waited, gnawing a cleft into her bottom lip.

"Ainsley, hello." The tension in her mother's voice was palpable.

"Listen, I'm sorry for the little spat we had the other day."

Her mother didn't respond right away, and when she did, her voice sounded tight. Reserved. "I appreciate that."

Another extended silence followed. Ainsley closed her eyes and rubbed them. Then, taking a deep breath, she plunged forward. "What are you doing?"

"I'm about to head to bed. Why? Is everything all right?"

"Yeah, everything's fine. I just . . ." Why bother? *As far as it depends on you. Love initiates, reaches out, even to the unlovable.* "I was going to invite you to a movie, but maybe next time."

"What a lovely idea. I haven't been to the theater in so long. And I certainly don't need to fall asleep so early. I'm much too young for that. Or at least, that's what I tell my neighbors."

Her giggle made Ainsley smile, reminding her of a time when the two of them used to snuggle in her mother's bed, pillows propped behind them and a large bowl of candy between them.

"Great. I'll pick you up in a few." She hung up and dropped her phone onto the seat cushion beside her. She didn't know whether to laugh or call back to cancel. Her conflicting emotions didn't make sense. For years she mourned over her mother's inaccessibility, and now, she had the opportunity to connect with her one-on-one and her stomach knotted. Why?

Because once she allowed hope to blossom, it would hurt all the more when her mother let her down.

Lord, this one's on You. Either radically change Mom or barricade my heart, because I'm going out of obedience here. And I really can't handle another letdown right now.

Twenty minutes later she pulled into her mother's apartment complex and jumped out. A smile tickled her lips as she hastened up the sidewalk and to the stairs, taking them two at a time. Her mom met her at the door wearing a fluffy pink sweater and a jean skirt. A circle of rouge dotted each cheek.

"Oh, my sweet muffin, this will be so much fun." She grabbed Ainsley's hands and squeezed. "I can't remember the last time you and I had a night out, just the girls."

Not counting parent-teacher conferences or the occasional let's-make-Dad-jealous, outing? But things would never get better between them if Ainsley didn't release her bitterness.

Lord, help me forgive her. Let us start fresh tonight.

They arrived at the movie theater to find a packed parking lot.

Ainsley checked the time on the dash — 8:20. "Do you want me to drop you off at the door? Because I'm thinking I'll have to park across the way at Mickey D's."

Her mom shook her head, her auburn hair dancing across her forehead. "I'll go with you."

Not finding anything closer, Ainsley parked near an overflowing dumpster behind McDonald's. Her mom chattered like a sugar-saturated child. By the time they reached the entrance, her enthusiasm rubbed off on Ainsley, provoking more than a few giggles. A gust of warm, popcorn-scented air swept over them as they stepped inside.

"A week before Thanksgiving and already they've got their Christmas tree up." Her mom pointed to a small display sitting in the far corner, partially hidden by a ten-foot movie billboard. "Take a look at those decorations." She looped her arm through Ainsley's and pulled her toward it. Handmade ornaments draped from the thick branches, surrounded by gold and silver tassels. The sign below read: *Donated and decorated by Veritas Academy.*

Her mother fingered a paper angel. "Do you remember when we used to make ornaments from salt dough?"

"Absolutely, and the time I tried to eat one, thinking it'd taste like a soft pretzel."

"The look on your face." Her mother laughed. "Your lips about disappeared, they puckered so much. You know, I still have a few of those ornaments in a box somewhere."

"You do?"

"Mmm, hmm. One you gave me when you were five, shaped like a heart, painted in a rainbow of colors."

Ainsley giggled. "I remember. It was quite . . . interesting."

"It was beautiful." Her mother grabbed her in a sideways hug. "You know, we really ought to do that again, for old time's sake."

"Do what? Eat salt dough or pretend to be drugged-out hippie artists?" She offered her mom a lopsided grin. It felt good to joke with her like this, to laugh together. When had they last done that? When had they last enjoyed one another's company period?

"Make bakeable ornaments. What do you say?"

"I say I'm twenty-nine and a little too old for arts and crafts."

"Oh, come on. Humor me. It'll be fun."

Ainsley smiled. "You're right. It would be."

Chris and Gina gathered on the curb, a brisk wind stirring their hair and sending a chill up his spine.

She turned up her collar, shifting from one foot to the next. "This was . . . nice. Thanks for inviting me."

"Thanks for coming." Standing at a respectable distance, he shoved his hands in his pockets.

Now what? Offer to call her? Was that what he wanted? No, unfortunately, as beautiful as she was, he felt nothing. Nada.

She sighed, scrunching her neck deeper into her collar. "This isn't working, is it?"

Chris exhaled, his tense muscles relaxing. "I don't think so. I mean, it's been fun and all."

"Yeah, I get it." She laughed. "Guess I'll see you around?"

"For sure. At the shelter, right?"

"Definitely."

He offered her a polite, sideways hug then returned to his car. By the time he reached it, Gina had already slipped inside her house. Such a beautiful girl. A Christian. One who appeared to have a servant's heart. By all accounts, a woman any man would be pleased to call his own. Apparently, any man other than him. But at least they figured that out before things became complicated.

Chapter 21

A t work Monday morning, Ainsley massaged the back of her neck. The day felt like it was dragging on, and she'd made little progress on the ever-growing mound of files in front of her. This job had turned from a frequent headache to an all-out migraine. And for what? A company car and a steady paycheck? Granted, two very necessary things, but still. On days like this she envied her mom's carefree, job-hopping, attitude. Not counting the collateral damage it caused for Ainsley, to which her mother appeared oblivious.

Would that change, now that she and her mom had started getting along?

She scoffed. They went to one movie, and yet, it was a start. Right? But what would happen when another debt collector came calling and bitterness swallowed any positive feelings their little outing had created? Sighing, she fished through her desk until she found her mother's last credit card statement. Fifteen dollars over the maximum. A statement she wouldn't have seen if not for the collection notices streaming into her mailbox.

But at least her mom hadn't asked her to cosign for a while, which likely meant things were going well with her and her latest guy pal Stephen. Miracle of miracles.

And aren't I the perfect example of a Christian daughter? So much for honoring her mother and father. Not that she felt it necessary to bail Mom out. But eventually she needed to be able to think about the woman without going into fight-or-flight mode.

At some point she needed to give her mother the opportunity to change.

Maybe their Christmas ornament making would help.

An old Sunday School verse trailed her thoughts. "For yet while we were still sinners Christ died for us."

Uncomfortable with the feelings of guilt the verse aroused, she flipped through the abstracts on her desk in search of a diversion. Halfway through a document on the benefits of serotonin reuptake inhibitors her office phone buzzed; the button for her boss's extension flashing.

She answered. "Good morning, Mr. Holloway. What can I do for you?"

"Come to my office."

"Certainly." Closing her partially read files, she stood. She paused to smooth wrinkles from her blouse and skirt. Then, squaring her shoulders, she exited and proceeded down the hall. A growing uneasiness settled in her gut as she peered through Mr. Holloway's office window. He sat hunched over his desk, thick eyebrows pulled in a rather ominous scowl.

He glanced up when Ainsley entered and jerked a hand toward the empty seat in front of him. "Sit."

She perched on the end of her chair, hands cupped over her knees. "Is everything all right, sir?"

He shoved a manila folder toward her. "Your results are less than impressive, Miss Meadows."

Ainsley swallowed. "Yes, I know, sir. I've been reviewing the latest literature, including the double-blind study conducted by Dolson University of Health Sciences. I also reviewed the ten steps to effective presentations you sent via email and plan to implement them immediately. Next week, I have three very promising meetings lined up—"

He held up his hand and shook his head. "I'm sure you understand, we can't afford to maintain liabilities."

She blinked. Liabilities? Is that how he saw her? "I understand, sir, and I certainly do not wish to cause harm." How did that work anyway? As if her lack of sales in some mysterious way damaged the company? Failed to help, maybe, but damage? Hardly.

"You're fired."

Seriously? No "I'm sorry to inform you" or "I wish you the best. Call me if you need a recommendation"?

He pulled a pen from the holder on his desk and a slip of paper from a nearby cabinet and shoved them her way. "Read and sign."

Her mouth went dry, all her upcoming bills swirling through her brain. Her vision narrowed on the blocked letters in front of her.

TERMINATION OF EMPLOYMENT AGREEMENT

She skimmed the terms and conditions laid out before her.

. . . the employment relationship is to be terminated. Any severance payment provided for in this Agreement will be made after the Agreement has been signed by all parties.

REASON FOR TERMINATION.

. . . consistent failure to meet job requirements . . .
. . . effective immediately . . .

Silence dominated the office. This couldn't be happening. Not now. Should she fight for her job? Convince Mr. Holloway she'd do better? Or take her severance pay and run? If only she had another job to run to.

Lord, please tell me You've got this one covered.

Her hand trembled as she scrawled her signature on the bottom line, thus sealing her fate. She set the pen down and pressed sweaty palms against her thighs.

This also meant no more late-night study sessions cramming to keep up with the latest research. No more nerve-wracking doctors' meetings. No more hostile phone calls from Mr. Holloway. No more Mr. Holloway period. If not for her money concerns, she might consider this an early Christmas gift.

She stood and looked her boss in the eye.

"It's been . . . interesting." She extended her hand.

Face stoic, Mr. Holloway returned the sentiment. "Well, then. Thank you for coming in. Have a great day."

"I will."

According to the cliché, closed doors meant new ones opened. She hoped that was true.

Chris paced his kitchen, looking from the clock to his phone, then back to the clock. The oft-recited phrase, "What would Jesus do?," echoed in his mind. If only his conscience had an off switch. Besides, inviting his sister to join him at Shady Lane for Thanksgiving went against every ounce of reason he possessed. Her snippy comments, pursed lips, and deep-set scowl would only aggravate their mother.

But they were family, whether he liked it or not. With a clenched jaw, he grabbed the handheld receiver and punched in Matilda's number.

"Hello?"

"Good morning, Matilda. How are you?"

"Fine."

Nothing like a lively conversation to ease the tension. "Are you heading to Shady Lane today?"

"Of course."

"When?"

She took an insanely long time to answer. "Two, why?"

"I'll join you. See you there." He hung up before Matilda could object or lay any "ground rules."

For the next hour, he ambled through the house clearing away dirty dishes, unpacking a few boxes, and whittling away at a mountainous pile of laundry. By 1:30, his agitation had subdued to a manageable level.

Gathering his things, he paused to scratch Rusty behind the ears. "I'll catch you in a few hours, old boy."

Rusty's tail twitched.

Chris grabbed his car keys from the counter, his gaze landing on a stack of bills lying beside his recent bank statement. A long list of withdrawals and debits filled the page, depleting his savings. If, by some miraculous intervention, his sister conceded to his wishes and moved their mother to Lily of the Valley, and he didn't have the funds to pay for it . . . He shook his head. He wouldn't let that happen.

Somehow the old saying "God is never late but rarely early" failed to bring comfort, especially with the impeding court date.

Maybe if he'd spent more time praying before purchasing the coffee shop . . .

Hand on the doorknob, he swallowed against a surge of uneasiness as a disturbing question surfaced. What would he do if forced to choose between the café and a loving, peaceful environment for his mother? Neither choice settled well and both required sacrifice. One meant sacrificing time with his mother and abandoning his mission. The other meant robbing her of a chance of peace.

Of course, if Shady Lane terminated Heather, their harsh, uncaring, nursing assistant, they'd terminate his problem as well.

Taking the back roads through the city, he arrived at the nursing home twenty minutes later. The wind swept cotton-ball clouds across the sky, revealing patches of blue. Near the door, he passed a woman with three young children, gathered beneath the awning.

The youngest, a boy with rosy cheeks and pale-blue eyes frowned and stomped his foot. "But I don't want to go." Chubby fists clenched at his sides.

Hands on the boy's arms, the mother knelt in front of him. "I know this is hard for you, but Gramma needs us. And I need you to be a big boy."

She met Chris's gaze when he passed. He dipped his head and offered a slight smile. Once inside, he paused a few feet from the nurse's station and glanced about the small formal sitting area. Wilber, a baldheaded man with a crooked nose, snored in a nearby wheelchair. Darla, a scowling woman with short, silvery hair, manned a bench on the far wall, arms crossed.

As he continued down the hall toward his mother's room, the tension alleviated during the drive bubbled to the surface.

With each step, he repeated his stay-out-of-the-ring mantra. Matilda could only get under his skin if he let her. Besides, now wasn't the time to discuss legal matters. Certainly she realized that.

He reached his mother's room. Soft music drifted from beneath the door, mixed with his sister's almost maternal voice. Leaning closer, he strained to catch her words. He couldn't make them out. Breathing deep, he eased the door open and stood, frozen.

Before him sat his mother, nestled in her recliner, feet propped, while Matilda massaged lotion into her hands and forearms. She hummed softly. His mother's head sagged to one side, propped by a pillow, her eyes closed.

Matilda glanced up and held Chris's gaze. He blinked, swallowing hard. He crossed the threshold and eased the door closed behind him. Tiptoeing across the charcoal carpet, he sat in a folding chair and watched his sister.

A soft melody poured from Matilda. The same song his mother used to sing to them when they were young. He closed his eyes and drifted back to a time when the four of them snuggled beneath thick blankets on the couch.

Chapter 22

*a*insley pulled behind a teal Volvo and gripped the steering wheel with both hands. Her stomach did a 360, her adrenal glands on full alert in anticipation of the hidden battle she soon might face. Barbs hurled beneath plastic smiles as her parents fought for answers to the winning question: Which parent did she love most? And manning the outer ring came Aunt Shelby and Great-Aunt Fiona with their forced reconciliation and "can't we all just get along" mentality. News flash: No, they couldn't, and her parents had court papers to prove it. At least Thanksgiving only came once a year . . . followed by Christmas, Easter, and the Fourth of July. Ugh! Almost made Ainsley want to join a commune.

A tap on her window made her jump. She turned, her forced smile already cemented in place. Brooks, a lanky sixth-grader, and Chaz, his seventh-grade mirror image in nearly every way, huddled near her door. Their eyes shone bright beneath matching skater haircuts.

They moved aside to let her out then stiffened beneath her embrace. "My two favorite second cousins." She ruffled their hair and stepped back to scan their fluorescent skinny jeans topped with graphic tees. "Aren't you guys freezing? Where are your jackets?"

"Uh-uh. It's like forty-some degrees, you know."

"Yeah, regular beach weather." She rounded her car and pulled bags of chips and sodas from her trunk. The boys scurried to her side. "So, you gonna hop in the lake after dinner?" She handed them each a bag then retrieved the remaining two.

Chaz and Brooks exchanged looks, an ear-to-ear grin widening their faces.

"That'd be sick!" Brooks raised his hand, and Chaz slammed him with a high five. "Wanna? Polar diving, bro."

"Polar diving." Chaz wrinkled his brow and nodded his head slowly in a John Travolta meets Justin Bieber simulation.

A door slammed and they peered down the car-lined street. Ainsley's father escorted a bleached-blonde woman in a crisp, knee-length skirt.

Ainsley spun back around and offered the boys a shaky smile. "Mind if I join you?"

Their mouths slackened. Chaz shifted. "I . . ." He looked at Brooks whose face wrinkled.

Ainsley giggled and gave them a sideways squeeze. "Just kidding." A woman can only handle so much torture in one day, although which scenario — diving into icy water or sitting in an equally iced living room — proved most torturous remained to be seen. "But how about you wait until after I leave to turn hypothermic? I'd hate to have your parents ban me from these fun family get-togethers." On second thought . . . Ainsley smiled.

The boys' faces relaxed into smiles once again and Brooks flung his chin-length bangs out of his eyes. "OK. See ya.'" And off they went, bouncing and bobbing like a pair of hyperalert squirrels scampering through a golf course.

"Hey there."

Ainsley tensed at her father's used car salesman's voice. *Ready or not, it's diplomat time.* Maybe she'd find a use for all that pharmaceutical rep training after all.

"Ainsley, dear, you look beautiful as ever." He wrapped her in a hug, smooshing her face into his heavily cologned chest. "You remember Iona?"

Ainsley stifled a frown as Barbie extended a ring-filled hand, dime-sized costume jewels glittering in the sun. Did Save-Mart have a sale? "No, Dad, I don't believe we've met." Not surprising, considering she and her father rarely spoke. "Good to meet you, Iona."

"So you're the brilliant pharmaceutical rep your father always talks about?"

"Not anymore. I was fired."

"Oh. I'm sorry to hear that."

Her dad's eyebrows shot up for about half a second before smoothing back to his easy smile. "So, where's Richard?"

"Don't know. We broke up." She regripped her grocery bag, her sweaty palms working against her. "Guess we better get in before Aunt Shelby sends a search party."

She turned around. With long strides, she crossed the street and hurried up the walk, leaving a minimum of three feet between her and the glitter and glam duo. Unfortunately, they caught up with her at the front door.

She suppressed a groan when Iona cooed over everything from the rocks lining the walkway to the type of grass in the yard. Yes, they were lovely. Gray, red, and, yeah, black river rocks. Just wait until she saw the tan carpet and linoleum flooring inside.

Lord, I really need some Spirit saturation here, before I pop a vein. Love, joy, peace. Love, joy, peace. Although she'd settle for peace.

The door creaked open and Ainsley's mother met them with a much-too-wide smile and slightly pinkish hair. Apparently, she went the do-it-yourself route again.

"Chuck, how nice to see you." She examined Iona, face bunched in what almost resembled a smile, her right cheek twitching. She turned to Ainsley. "You didn't tell me you brought a friend. Is this one of the young ladies you mentor, dear?"

Ainsley rolled her eyes and pushed past her. "I'll leave you all to get acquainted." She maneuvered down the hall, past the crowded living room, and into a tiny kitchen crammed elbow to elbow with women.

Pamela, her second cousin twice removed, met her at the island dressed in a cream sweater embossed with a squash-filled cornucopia. "What have we here?"

Ainsley set her bag on the counter and the two of them began unloading and lining the contents across the counter.

"Snacky-type stuff. To help with that weight loss goal of yours." Ainsley shot her a wink and held up a bag of deep-fried veggie sticks.

"That'll go great with my high-calorie, saturated, chemical-infused dip."

"Perfect."

Perhaps if Ainsley stayed in the kitchen with Pamela and the veggie sticks, she could avoid the high school drama circulating at the other end of the house.

Unfortunately, her mom and Iona appeared a moment later, faces donned with identical beauty pageant smiles, shattering Ainsley's hopes of temporary reprieve. Her dad and her mom's slug, Stephen, followed a moment later, beer bottles in hand and chests puffed out so far you'd think they inhaled helium.

Love, joy, peace. Love, joy, peace.

Why did she allow her parents to get her so worked up? Did it really matter how they acted, what they thought, or how many mannequins they draped on their arms?

"So, Stephen, where do you work?" Ainsley's dad dipped a celery stalk into a container of ranch then popped it in his mouth.

"I fix trains." He raised his arms slightly in a Popeye stance and lifted his chin, his ear-to-ear comb-over shifting like a flap of fabric.

Ainsley's dad countered with a few hidden barbs, but Ainsley ignored them and dashed out of the room before her parents found a way to drag her into the conversation.

In the living room, Aunt Shelby fluttered around the room, food tray in hand, while the men huddled around the television set. Ainsley found an empty seat next to her cousin Shannon and her pudgy-faced, blue-eyed baby girl. Shannon's toddler, Davey, lay on the carpet a few feet away, his wispy blond hair charged with static electricity. Skye, his father, a long-haired man with soft blue eyes, lay across from him, propped on his elbows.

"Ainsley, how are you?" Shannon shifted her daughter to her other knee, her leg bouncing.

"I'm good. And you look excellent. Don't tell me this precious bundle of joy is letting you sleep already." She reached out a finger and the baby latched onto it, sparking a sudden longing deep within her heart. She blinked, turning her thoughts off pattering of feet that would never fill her home and onto her cousin.

"Thanks to Skye." Shannon glanced at her husband, the skin around her eyes crinkling. "He takes the kids from seven on, and I hit the pillows. About ten, he wakes me up for Ayana's nightly feeding. I put her to bed shortly after, and sleep for another three to four hours."

"Wow, what a saint."

"Absolutely. I keep telling him God's got a whole slew of rewards waiting for him when he gets to heaven."

"I knew dirty-diaper patrol earned me something." Skye winked then poked Davey in the ribs, evoking a squeal.

"Would you like to hold her?" Shannon held the baby out to Ainsley.

She wrapped her arms around the infant's soft back and kissed the top of her head, inhaling the sweet scent of baby oil. The baby reached up and brushed her chin with chubby, featherlight fingers.

"So what about you and Richard? You two started talking family yet?"

"We broke up."

"Oh, sweetie, I'm so sorry. Are you all right?"

Ainsley shrugged and cradled the baby to her chest. "It was for the best. Richard's a great guy, just not for me."

Shannon nodded. "I know exactly what you mean. Before I met Skye, I thought for sure I'd never get married—had the whole all-guys-are-jerks mentality going on. Then we met, and I knew God brought us together, like Skye dropped straight from heaven, a perfect gift designed just for me."

"Thanks to all that love potion I fed you during our first date." Skye chuckled then turned his attention back to his son.

Ainsley laid the infant in the crook of her arm. The song she and Shannon used to sing as they sat on her parents' fence railing on hot summer nights mocked her. *First comes love, second comes marriage, then comes a baby* . . .

For some, the rare fairy-tale few like Shannon and Skye. Apparently Ainsley had failed the Cinderella Meets Prince Charming training session.

Chapter 23

*R*ichard sat in the Crestline Country Club parking lot and scanned the adjacent cars. Mr. and Mrs. Doriani's green Mercedes parked near a row of golf carts, two cars down from the Berlows' gold Cadillac Seville. Across the lot sat the Robinsons' navy Jaguar, tucked beneath the shade of the driving range shack.

Richard studied his reflection in the mirror and smoothed his hair. And so the performance began. Lifting his chin, he stepped out of the car and crossed the asphalt in long, deliberate steps. A party of five exited the clubhouse, talking among themselves. He nodded and moved aside. Through the window, he watched his mother sip a glass of champagne, her torso angled toward the putting green. She wore a red blazer, her silver hair swept up. His father sat beside her wearing his usual scowl.

Richard opened the door, and a blast of heat rushed over him, stinging his eyes. Blinking and peeling off his jacket, he approached the hostess stand.

The hostess smiled. "Good afternoon, Mr. Hollis. Your mother and father are already here. Follow me."

They wove around linen-covered tables, the aromatic scent of sautéed mushrooms and roasted garlic drifting through the air. When they reached his parent's table, his mother stood to meet him.

"Richard, so glad you could make it." She kissed his cheek then glanced around. "Where's Ainsley?"

He pressed the soles of his feet into the maroon carpet to prevent fidgeting. "I'm afraid she couldn't make it." He turned to the others seated around the table, shaking each hand in turn before settling into one of two open seats. Grabbing the menu in front of him, his mind worked for a plausible excuse to explain Ainsley's absence. Luckily, the waitress appeared, alleviating the problem.

"What can I get you to drink, Mr. Hollis?"

"I'll take a bourbon sour." He turned to Mr. Burlow before anyone could ask further questions. "I'm pleased to have a chance to talk with you. I've heard excellent things about your company. Is it true you plan to merge with Toliech Inc.?"

The man nodded and launched into an extensive dissertation on textiles while Richard feigned interest. Unfortunately, the reprieve was short-lived. By the time the waitress brought Richard's drink, the topic returned to him and Ainsley.

"So," Mrs. Burlow turned her golden eyes on him. Flecks of mascara dotted her wrinkled cheek and settled into the creases beneath her eyes. "You mother says you and your fiancé plan to wed at the Holy Trinity Cathedral?"

"I've made reservations."

"A lovely facility. As you know, that's where we held our son's christening."

He nodded and clinked the ice in his glass.

Across from him, his mother sat poised and erect. "Yes, it is lovely, and the flower arrangement Mr. Adele and I discussed will complement the sanctuary well."

Mrs. Doriani's face puckered. She pressed her lips together and glanced around, as if uninterested. Richard almost laughed. Was she worried his wedding would outshine her daughter's? His smile faded as the memory of Ainsley's narrowed gaze resurfaced, followed by her biting words. *It's over, Richard.*

Keeping his expression blank, he returned his attention to the conversation.

"Have you hired a photographer yet?" Mr. Doriani pulled out his wallet and flipped it open. "You may remember, we used Elite Photography. They did an excellent job, and demonstrated extreme patience." He chuckled. "Which, considering Jessica's rather impetuous demands, proved no easy task, I am sure."

Mrs. Doriani frowned, deepening the lines fanning from her mouth. "Impetuous? Because she valued her wedding and expressed a clear desire for how things should be decorated and the ceremony conducted?" She turned to Richard's mother with a stiff smile. "Regardless, I am certain Elite Photography is booked."

She lifted her chin. "Perhaps, but I imagine he'll be able to work us in." She touched her husband's arm. "Remind me to call Mr. Jacobs, will you, dear. I believe I still have his personal phone number somewhere." She lifted her glass. "He and his wife are very dear friends."

The men dominated the rest of the conversation like gladiators hurling iron mallets. At first, Richard joined in, until it became clear his diminishing practice and small book deal with an unknown publisher placed him on less than equal footing. Although none of the men laughed outright, their eyes danced with silent mirth. All except his father. Clearly, Richard embarrassed him.

Richard placed his hands flat on the table, palms down, and focused on his plate. Once his parents learned of Ainsley's decision, he'd never hear the end of it.

Which was why he needed to do whatever it took to change her mind.

The sun set quickly behind the brick industrial buildings on either side of I-35, the dark of winter settling across the city like a heavy cloak. Ainsley's breath came out in a thin fog, her teeth chattering.

What a waste of time. Why did employers schedule interviews when they already had someone in mind for the job? She grabbed her planner and flipped through the pages. Her next interview wasn't for another two weeks, and each day in between her savings dwindled.

So much for pharmacy school.

She cranked up the heat, clenching her jaw as cold air flooded her face. The car didn't heat up until she exited the freeway onto North Oak. By then, it had begun to drizzle, the dark clouds on the horizon suggesting a storm approached.

A young man, no older than twenty, stood, shoulders hunched, on the side of the road. Dressed in jeans, what appeared to be workboots, and a thin hoodie, he shivered. He held a cardboard sign that read, "Veteran. Please help." A raggedy backpack lay at his feet.

She searched her car for a water bottle or cereal bar. Nothing, and her purse was empty — the one downfall of living off ATM cards. She really needed to keep something on hand, maybe sandwiches, or crackers.

Avoiding his gaze, she merged onto Vivian then turned into her cul-de-sac. Chris stood at the end of his driveway, a large bag in his hand. He glanced up as Ainsley approached and offered a nod. She waved and pulled into her driveway. Her tires crunched as she eased into the garage. She parked, stepped out, and surveyed the dark cement behind her.

Tiny salt crystals glistened in the dim lighting. Planting her hands on her hips, she studied the driveways on either side of her, all glittering. Tucked beside Chris's garage stood another bag and a shovel.

A modern-day good Samaritan, perhaps?

After her day of rejections and disappointments, it felt like a ray of sunshine sent from God Himself. And maybe it was His way of reminding her He was watching, helping.

Chapter 24

Friday afternoon, Ainsley grabbed a pen and pocket notebook then flipped through the church directory. She needed to call Ned, the youth leader, to find out how many students had committed to helping her prepare the dinner for the shelter and what items they were bringing. Hopefully they planned to cover most of the meal, because a chef, she was not.

Having found his number, she dialed.

"Ainsley, hello. What's up?"

"Hi. I'm calling to see how many kids signed up to help me tonight."

"With what?"

"Ha, ha. Funny. I hope they planned the main dish, because a tossed salad is about as creative as I get."

"Dude, I totally forgot."

"Good thing I'm reminding you then. Let's hope your students didn't forget as well."

"No, I mean I forgot to ask them."

Ainsley stiffened. "You're not serious."

"I'm so sorry. Things have been crazy getting ready for Christmas and everything."

"So call them, quickly."

"I'll try, but with such short notice, if I were you, I'd move to plan B. I'd help you, but tonight's the tween ice-skating party, and I'm already short a few drivers."

What a nightmare. Cook for sixty, maybe seventy-five people? There was no way.

After ending the call, she tried Gina. Got her voice mail. Of all the times for her friend to be unavailable.

"It's Ainsley. I have an emergency. Any chance you can stop by a few hours early? I need some recipe-planning help and someone to cook ten, maybe twenty pounds of meat." A food donation wouldn't hurt either, except Gina was nearly as broke as she was. "Call me as soon as you get this message."

After flipping through numerous recipes and calculating the potential expense in her head, which well exceeded her unemployed budget, she settled on sloppy joes. Adding chips and store-bought cookies and she'd be good to go. Only problem — what would she cook the meat in?

She sifted through her cupboards and placed every pan and baking dish on the counter. There were enough to fill her tiny 1970s oven five times over.

Chris added the long list of expenses and compared it to his weekly proceeds for the third time. No matter how he worked it, he came up short, and on payday. He grabbed the phone and called his bank.

"Good morning, F&C Financial. Can you hold, please?"

Elevator music played across the line before he could answer. A moment later, the woman returned. "May I help you?"

"I'd like to confirm my actual balance."

"What's your account, sir?"

He pulled his bank ledger from his desk drawer and read the numbers printed along the bottom.

"This account is already at the minimum. Do you want to close the account, sir?"

"No, I want to transfer from my personal savings to my business account."

"How much would you like to transfer, sir?"

He looked at the number circled in red at the bottom of a yellow notepad. "One thousand, two hundred, seventy-five and — . Twelve hundred dollars, please."

Transaction complete, he pushed away from his desk. He paused to listen for the sound of chattering customers out front. The few voices he heard were quite the letdown.

Lord, don't leave me hanging here. I'm not asking You to make me rich, but it'd sure be nice to stay out of the red.

He plodded down the hall toward the soft instrumental music pouring from ceiling speakers. Lawrence sat on a stool a short distance away picking at a nail. Candy sat in a corner sofa flipping through a small pocket devotional.

Hooking his thumbs in his belt loops, Chris surveyed the café. A couple sat in the far corner, huddled together over a computer screen. Across the room, a woman nursed a small coffee while two toddlers sifted through the basket of toys nestled in the corner. An older couple sat near the side door, shopping bags at their feet. All told, they'd made enough to pay for the day's use of electricity, maybe.

Lawrence approached and ran a coffee-stained dish towel over an already clean table. "So what do you say, bossman? Wanna join Candy and me for a game of twiddle your thumbs while we watch the spiders spin webs?"

"Things'll pick up soon enough."

"Listen, man, I appreciate what you're trying to do here, but we're running low on green."

"It won't crash, Lawrence, I have faith."

"Yeah, well, faith doesn't pay the bills. I've got another job, starting Monday. Had to take it while it was there to take, if you know what I mean."

Chris raked his fingers through his hair. "I understand." He held his hand out to Lawrence who looked at it, shrugged, then accepted the shake. "If you change your mind . . ."

"Need me to stick around? Cuz if not . . ."

"No, go ahead."

"It's been interesting." He punched Chris in the shoulder. "I'll be back later for my check."

The rest of the afternoon wore on slowly. Candy meandered around the tables, occasionally pulling books from the shelves.

She flipped through them, read a page or two, then put them back.

It wasn't exactly the urban revival he hoped for, but Candy was better than none.

His stomach soured as he thought of his mother sitting in her tiny five-hundred square foot nursing home apartment. What he wouldn't give to move her to Lily of the Valley; but if he moved her, and the café tanked, he'd only have to move her again. Maybe Matilda was right.

No, he refused to believe that. There had to be a way, even if it took every last cent he had.

By 2:00 the cafe was nearly empty. The next rush wouldn't come until 4:00 — if at all. Lot of good all those ads he placed with the paper did. He might as well take a few hours off. It was well past time he unpacked some of the boxes crowding his house. In truth, a garage sale was in order, come spring, but the thought of selling his parents things made him ill.

He turned to Candy. "Think you all can handle the place for a few?"

She shrugged.

"Great. I'll see you later."

A fierce wind swept over him when he stepped onto the sidewalk, the faint glow of the sun hidden by a thick cloud layer. A couple strolled by smiling and holding hands. As he watched them, an image of Ainsley surfaced unbidden. She had such a sweet, gentle nature. Her fiancé was one lucky man. Hopefully, he realized that and treated her accordingly.

Diverting his thoughts, he gripped the collar of his jacket tighter around his neck and headed home.

A pack of geese flew over head, their loud honks and cackles mingling with the low moan of the December wind. It slowed to a gentle breeze by the time he reached his neighborhood. Walking up his drive, he stopped, laughing at Rusty's moist nose pressed to the living room window. The dog met Chris at the door with ears perked and tail wagging.

Chris dropped to one knee, rubbing both sides of the dog's face. "Missed me, huh?" He stood and glanced around. "Where's your Frisbee?"

Rusty cocked his head but made no effort to retrieve it. Rather, he inched past Chris to the porch then down the steps.

Shaking his head, Chris crossed the room, grabbed the half-chewed piece of plastic, then met his dog outside. "No being lazy on me, old boy. We gotta keep those legs of yours moving." He tossed the Frisbee. "Go get it."

Rusty stared at him then slid to the ground.

He laughed. "Bet you'd move faster if I brought out some bacon."

An engine hummed behind him, and he spun around. Ainsley sat behind the driver's wheel of her tan two-door. Chris stepped aside to allow her to pull into her driveway.

She waved, opened her garage door, and pulled inside. A moment later, she popped the trunk, revealing two large metal pans.

Chris sauntered over. "Do you need help?" Rusty followed then parked himself at the edge of her driveway.

Chewing her bottom lip, she glanced at the pans. "I . . . Yeah, maybe so." Her soft smile emerged. "If you don't mind."

"Not at all." He stepped forward and lifted a gigantic slow cooker.

She unloaded a bag of groceries from the backseat. "Can you put that in the kitchen?"

"Sure thing." Her car looked jam-packed with food. "This for the shelter?"

She nodded.

"If I didn't know better, I'd say you were trying to cook the meal all by yourself."

Still smiling, she rolled her eyes. "Long story."

He angled sideways to make it through the backdoor, careful not to step on the black electric cord trailing him. Ainsley followed.

"Where would you like me to put this?"

She deposited her groceries on the counter and motioned toward a center island. "Right there is fine. Thanks."

"Not a problem. How many people are you planning to feed?"

"I'm not sure. Maybe seventy-five."

"Wow. Need help? I'm not a fantastic cook, but I can whack a tomato or two."

She studied him for a moment then surveyed the three ten-pound tubes of ground beef sitting next to packages of hamburger buns. "Ever cooked sloppy joes from scratch? I couldn't find premade sauce."

"Unfortunately, no. But I can stir or chop up a head of lettuce."

The doorbell rang.

"Excuse me." She crossed the kitchen and disappeared around the corner, returning with an adult and two teenagers, each carrying a plate of cookies. The mother appeared to be in her late forties and had long brown hair parted down the middle. Permanent laugh lines had formed around her eyes and mouth.

"This is Norma Qualls and her daughters, Amanda and Sammie." She indicated each in turn. "Apparently, they heard I'd be cooking all by myself and hurried over to rescue me." She introduced Chris next, adding, "I finagled him into helping me." She flashed him a grin, which he returned.

The foursome made small talk for a while. Apparently, the girls loved to cook, although to date, their culinary efforts had centered around taco salads and macaroni and cheese, which, according to Amanda, had been a colossal fail.

"The cheese just clumped together." Amanda popped a cucumber slice in her mouth.

Their mother laughed. "Now, if you still want us after listening to all our credentials . . .

Ainsley grinned. "Absolutely. In fact, you'll fit right in. Follow me." She led everyone into the kitchen to await orders.

"So, what's this place like, anyway?" Amanda leaned against the counter. "Because we're kind of nervous."

Ainsley smiled, her face lighting up with a tenderness that

was captivating. "Honestly, this will be my first time as well. But from what I hear, it's amazing. Life-changing. Going, I mean. To be part of what God is doing for these poor women, to show them the gentle love of Christ." She swept her gaze from Chris to Norma then extended her hands, palms up. "We should pray."

"Great idea." Chris stepped closer, taking her soft, small hand in his. His gaze fell to her hand. Had she taken off her engagement ring . . . to cook, or . . . ? His pulse quickened, but he quickly pushed the thought aside. Extending his other hand to Norma, who closed in on his left. The four formed a circle, and Chris bowed his head.

Silence followed. Were they wanting him to say the prayer? As if in answer, Ainsley's sweet voice followed:

"Holy Father, thank You so much for bringing Chris, Norma, and her girls to help me. I was so nervous. And yet, once again, you showed me just how faithful You are, always ready to help the moment we take even the smallest step of obedience." She paused, her deep breath audible. "Help us to be a blessing to these women. Help us to do more than bring them food. Help us to connect with them, to show them Your amazing love and grace. In the name of your sweet and victorious Son, Jesus, amen."

A chorus of amens followed, but no one made an effort to move. Rather, they continued to stand in their circle, arms dropped to their sides, faces pensive. It was as if weight had been added to their endeavor. They weren't merely providing a meal. They were reaching out to fellow human beings. Mothers and children who had been stripped of everything. Maybe even their dignity.

Chris swallowed, thinking back to his life in Southern California. The homeless had been so prevalent, they faded into the scenery. How many had he walked by without giving them so much as a second glance? Without even being aware of their presence?

Worse than that, there had been many times, way too many, he'd seen them and their needs but continued on, too busy, too focused on himself, to offer even a bottle of water.

He'd been so incredibly selfish for way too long.

Help me do different, Lord. To be different. Starting now.

He glanced across the room to Ainsley who stood at the counter flipping through what looked like an old cookbook. Slips of paper stuck out of the pages, some of which had come loose from their binding and slipped out, only to be shoved back in.

After a few minutes, she snapped it shut and whirled around to face her crew. "There's everything from lamb stew to meatless lasagna but not one recipe for sloppy joes. Go figure."

"Maybe do a Google search?" Norma pulled out her phone.

"Great idea!" Ainsley beamed. "Hold on while I grab my laptop." She dashed out, returning with her computer which she plunked on the counter. Her fingers flew over the keyboard.

Norma crossed the kitchen to the table where bags of groceries waited. She peeked inside each in turn. "Salad fixings. Perfect." She pulled out a head of lettuce. "While you do that, the girls and I will work on the salad." The doorbell rang, and Ainsley shot her guests a grin. "Lookie there. More helpers, you think?"

Chris shrugged, amused to see an almost childlike side of Ainsley. It stirred his heart in a way that felt quite uncomfortable, especially considering the woman was engaged. Did her fiancé realize how lucky he was?

"I'll get that." Norma handed the lettuce to her daughters with the instructions to wash it and padded to the door. A moment later, a click sounded, followed by creaking hinges and Norma's cheerful voice. "Richard, hello!"

Ainsley whipped around so fast she nearly knocked her computer off the counter. She stared through the kitchen entryway, her face going from shock to a frown. She turned to her guests. "If you'll excuse me."

Chris watched her go, intrigued. That wasn't how one normally behaved when the love of their life appeared. Relationship trouble maybe? Not that it was any of his business. The fact that the idea brought a wave of pleasure only proved how incredibly selfish and sinful he was. That girl was as far off limits as one could come.

Chapter 25

*A*insley hurried to the door, making it there just as Richard stepped across the threshold. "Pardon us, Norma. Richard and I have something to discuss."

"Certainly." The woman excused herself with a smile and a nod and returned to the kitchen.

Ainsley faced Richard, arms crossed. "What are you doing here?"

He offered her a much too smooth smile. "I told you I'd help you serve at the shelter."

"But that was before . . . This is inappropriate, and you know it. You need to leave."

"I am merely wanting to help the less fortunate in our community, my dear. Surely you will not fault me for that. Nor hinder my acts of goodwill."

"Right. Out of the goodness of your heart." She glared. "If you seriously think this will somehow change my mind about us —"

"Surely you do not think I'm that juvenile. Or manipulative."

Her tense muscles relaxed a little as she determined to hear him out. Not to jump to conclusions. Just because God had said no to their marriage didn't mean she couldn't be civil to the man.

"I signed up to help with tonight's preparations, and I intend to honor my commitments." He paused. "But to speak to your initial . . . accusation, yes, I do think it's important to help those in need. My entire career is centered on that."

She massaged her temples. She wasn't so sure he was telling the truth about his intentions, but he had signed up. And this was a church-sanctioned event. Who was she to set the rules regarding who could help and who couldn't? Except they were baking at her house, and Richard being a part of that felt wrong.

Or was that her pride talking?

"We're adults here." He glanced past her toward the kitchen, and his smile wavered. "As such, I would expect we can serve together on this project."

Her cheeks warmed at the chastisement underlying his words. As much as she hated to admit it, he had a point. She was probably blowing this—him being here—way out of proportion. Besides, he couldn't weasel himself back in if she didn't let him.

"Fine." She threw her hands up. "But don't act stupid."

She turned and stomped into the kitchen. Richard's heavy footfalls followed.

Then, ignoring him completely, she turned to her laptop and scrolled down the page. An image of overflowing sloppy joes filled the screen.

"Where's everyone else?" Richard leaned on the wall, ankles crossed. "I thought you had a whole group helping with this."

"There was a miscommunication." Ainsley clicked on the link for recipe. A quick scan verified, with some multiplication, it would work.

"What do you mean?" Richard moved closer to Ainsley.

She bristled and widened the distance between them once again. "Apparently the youth director forgot to mention the women's shelter event in the newsletter."

Amanda relayed the rest of the story, adding a great amount of detail as to why, what the other students were doing this evening, and why she and her sister decided to serve at the shelter instead. "But Ainsley may wish we hadn't by the time we're done." She grinned. "Like I told her, I'm not the most talented cook around. Last time I made cookies for youth group, I was told they looked like scabs. But that they tasted good."

Ainsley laughed. "That's all that matters. Besides, remember our prayer earlier?"

The girl nodded. "We just have to do our best and leave the rest to God." She raised her paring knife to the ceiling then returned to chopping tomatoes faster than her sister could wash them. Their mother peeled cucumbers at the sink while Chris stood in the center of the kitchen looking about as awkward as a football player at a Tupperware party. She needed to assign him a task.

She grabbed an onion and handed it over. "Would you like to wash and chop this?"

He smiled. "I'd be happy to."

Richard rose and stepped forward, attempting to wedge himself between them. "I'll get that."

Ainsley frowned. "Fine." She handed him a knife and the remaining bag. "While you're at it, we need three more peeled, washed, and chopped." He wouldn't be so anxious once the fumes hit his eyes and tears started gushing. Come to think of it, a bit of tear-induced humility would do the man good. Suppressing a laugh at the image, she turned to Chris once again. "Would you mind browning the meat?"

"Not at all."

Chris looked at Richard. "So, what do you do?"

"I'm a psychiatrist, specializing in neuropathology, borderline personality disorders, and dissociative disorders, most often resulting from multiple personalities."

"That's a mouthful." Chris grabbed a tube of ground beef and sliced it open.

Ainsley met him at the stove with a saucepan then returned to the cupboard for three more until one occupied every burner. Next, she handed Richard a cutting board and knife.

He took both to a nearby counter and began hacking away the outer onion peels. "What about you, Mr. Langley? I seem to remember seeing you at the corner café serving coffee." His tone dripped with condescension.

Ainsley stiffened, waiting for Chris to react. To her surprise, he didn't. Instead, he grinned and replied, "Yep, that was me."

A man who didn't feel the need to dominate or compete? Now that was a first.

Either that, or he was oblivious to Richard's attempts, something that only irritated the man all the more, based on the way his left eye had begun to twitch.

Not that this deterred him any, for he continued to drill Chris while everyone else scampered about preparing the meal. Initially, Ainsley felt bad for Chris, thinking that perhaps she should defend him. But after a while, Richard's childish tactics became comical.

What had she ever seen in the man?

Three hours later, ground beef slathered in ketchup, mustard, and brown sugar filled the slow cookers. Tupperware filled with salads — fruit and vegetable — lined the counter.

Ainsley tested her sauce. "Not bad." She glanced at the clock. "I'm surprised Gina's not here yet." Moving to the window above the sink, she rose on her toes and leaned forward.

"She's not over at my house, is she?" Chris stepped behind her. "I'll be back." He turned and exited the kitchen.

"Wait, I'll come with you." She followed him out, leaving Richard to fume.

Chris inhaled the crisp evening air, relieved to be free of Ainsley's boyfriend — or perhaps former boyfriend — and his constant psychobabble investigation. The tension between those two sizzled throughout the house. Something told him this was more than a romantic spat. At least he hoped so, because Ainsley was much too good to date such a loser. Surely she knew guys like that only got worse after marriage. Some even turned abusive.

He tried to remind himself yet again it was none of his business, but the protector in him refused to settle.

He sighed and raked his hand through his hair. "What are You doing here, Lord?"

"You OK?"

He turned to see Ainsley studying him with a furrowed brow. He forced a smile. "Yeah. Just catching my breath."

She laughed. "That was a workout, wasn't it? I appreciate your help. I can't imagine trying to pull it off myself."

"No problem." He stopped at the edge of the driveway and waited for Rusty to lumber to his feet. Poor dog, his joints must have stiffened in the cold. Even so, the fresh air had been good for him.

He knelt and massaged the dog's hindquarters to help loosen them up. "Come on, old boy. Let's get you inside." They cut through Ainsley's yard to his, finding Gina on his porch.

She stood with hands cupped around her face, nose pressed to a fogging window. She wore a silver jacket with a furry hood, polka-dotted gloves, and lime-green rubber boots.

Resembling a fictional character named Pippi Longstocking, she stirred a brotherly affection within him. "Hello." He lowered his voice, a grin emerging with full force.

Gina jumped and whirled around, her cheeks pink. "Oh, hi." She brushed a patch of dirt from her jacket and straightened. Her nails were painted a mint green. "I thought I was to meet you here."

Ainsley stepped forward and looped her arm in Gina's. "The *guys* came over a bit early, to help." She raised an eyebrow.

Gina's eyes widened. "Oh, did they now?"

Chris sensed a hidden meaning laced their conversation, but then Gina faced Chris, her tense posture visibly relaxing.

Gina faced him. "You're a cook, I take it?"

"I don't know about that, but I can stir a mean lump of meat." He fell into step beside her and the three of them traipsed back to Ainsley's.

"Add a few gallons of ketchup and a healthy dose of mustard, and you've got a meal fit for a king," Ainsley said.

Chris stared into her green eyes. "Or a family shelter."

She smiled but it vanished when they reached her front steps to find Richard standing like Robot Man.

Richard eyed Chris then turned to Ainsley. "How are we going to get all this food to the shelter?"

"I thought we could use your Lexus with its luxuriously roomy trunk." Eyes dancing with laughter, Ainsley shot Gina a wink. But then her face warmed as she recalled his earlier comment about acting like adults. Just because she wasn't dating the man, just because she was finding him more infuriating by the day, didn't mean she could act like a jerk.

This group could only handle one of those. "No." Shaking his head, Richard backed toward his car. "Absolutely not."

Ainsley rolled her eyes. "Relax. I was kidding. Although, truth be told, I hadn't thought of that one. I'm not sure I can fit everything in my car."

"I've got a van." Norma hooked a thumb toward her vehicle parked along the curb.

Ainsley smiled. "Perfect."

"I call shotgun!" Amanda shot her hand in the air, and everyone laughed. Everyone except Ainsley, who shot a glance toward Richard only to find him watching her.

Childish or not, she did *not* want to sit next to him. Because if she had to listen to his sarcastic, condescending comments for one more minute, she was liable to scream.

And she really didn't want to do that in front of the girls.

Chapter 26

earing the North Kansas City Ray of Hope Women and Children's shelter, the houses and buildings grew increasingly run-down. A vacant lot bordered a dilapidated liquor shop and a shotgun house with boarded windows. Across the street, a kid in a gray sweatshirt glided by on skateboard.

"You know these kids don't stand a chance." Richard leaned back and looked out the window.

Ainsley glared at him. "How can you, a mental health professional, say such a thing?" And in front of impressionable teenagers, no less. "Of course they have a chance. Jesus can transform even the worst of lives, even the most hopeless of situations. You know that."

"In theory, perhaps, but research suggests a child's self-esteem is developed by the time they are five. Their overall belief system is established by age twelve." He motioned toward a two-story brick apartment complex with barred windows. "Most of these parents — and I use the term quite loosely — are too busy smoking crack, among other things I am sure, to care where their children are."

The girls exchanged glances, their eyes growing wide.

Their mother visibly tensed, her brow plummeting. "You don't know that. There are countless reasons why families end up in poverty from job loss to illness and disability to single parenting." A plastic bag whipped through the air, bouncing off her windshield. "Which is why we're doing this. Right, girls?" She shot her daughters a grin through the rearview mirror. "Making no assumptions and coming with the grace of our Savior, we're going to show these women and children that there is indeed hope in Christ."

Richard muttered something under his breath but Ainsley ignored him. She wasn't interested in continuing this conversation with such a hard-hearted man. In fact, he shouldn't even be here. Acts of goodwill her foot!

Lord, please never let my heart grow hard. Fill me each day anew with Your love for Your prodigal sons and daughters, and let us be instruments of Your grace tonight.

They turned left, the brick building of the shelter coming into view. Ivy climbed up its walls, making the old, gothic building look foreboding. Women with children of all ages crowded the sidewalk, waiting for the doors to open. The shelter had limited beds, offered on a first-come, first-served basis. How many families would be turned away tonight?

Norma pulled into a fenced lot sandwiched between the shelter and a dark stone building. Two flickering street lights manned each corner and a single bulb hung above a metal door cut into the wall. Windblown plastic bags and bits of newspaper dangled from the thick strands of barbed wire lining the chain-link fence.

Richard craned his neck, looking around. "Do you really think it's wise to leave your vehicle here?"

As Norma cut the engine, Ainsley scooted to the edge of her seat, ready to be out of the car and away from Richard and his negativity. "It'll be fine."

Everyone piled out, gathering around the trunk.

Richard stepped too close for Ainsley's comfort. "You're beautiful when you worry. Do you know that?" He raised his hand to her cheek.

She grabbed his wrist. "Don't. If you want to help serve, fine." Heat flooded her face when she realized everyone else, now silent, was watching her. Even so, it needed to be said, so, lowering her voice, she continued. "But if you came to try to weasel your way back into my life, you may as well leave."

Awkward silence continued, making Ainsley regret her words. Or more accurately, allowing Richard to come in the first place. Norma's cheerful voice broke the tension. "Fellas, do you want to grab the slow cookers? They're pretty heavy." She unlocked the trunk with a beep.

"But be careful. They're hot." Ainsley moved aside to let the guys through. "At least, I hope they're still hot."

Chris peered over a steaming slow cooker, the skin around his eyes crinkling. "Hot enough to take the bite off the cold."

Richard grabbed a second slow cooker; the women carried the rest. From the looks of it, they had enough to feed an army, and yet, Ainsley still worried. This was the last place she wanted to come up short. For some of these families, this could be their first and last meal of the day. But they'd done their best with what they had, and like Amanda had said earlier, the rest was up to God.

After offering up a quick prayer, Ainsley stacked two large containers of salad on top of one another then carried them across the lot where the others stood gathered around a metal door. She pressed a broken doorbell and waited, shivering in the cold, salad containers shoved under her chin.

"Does the doorbell work?" Gina scrunched her neck in her jacket, teeth chattering.

"I don't know." Ainsley tried again.

"Excuse me." Richard nudged her aside and kicked the door three times, waited, then kicked again.

A moment later a woman with braided hair streaked with gray appeared. "Who are you with?"

"Northside Youth Group, without the youth." Ainsley offered a nervous laugh. How in the world would they pull this one off, considering none of them — not one — had ever done anything remotely like this before? Although they'd already done the hard part — cooking. But the real test would come when everyone tasted the concoction.

The woman's face softened and she opened the door wider. "I'm Rose." She held out a wind-chaffed hand and closed icy fingers around Ainsley's. Her smile revealed a mouth full of crooked teeth. "Do y'all need help?"

Within seconds, women emerged from numerous directions, hoisting containers from their arms and disappearing with them down the hall. Ainsley and her crew followed to a large room filled with rectangular tables.

"Kitchen's this way." Rose led them to an industrial-sized kitchen. A partial loaf of bread sat next to a tub of butter. On another counter freezer bags full of leftovers lay next to a tub of powdered drink mix. She gathered them up. "Guess we don't need these. We'll save them for Sunday."

What did they do for food when the leftovers ran out and volunteers failed to come?

She turned to Chris and Richard who stood just inside the door, still holding their slow cookers. "Why don't you plug those in, on low. That way food won't get cold." She glanced at the clock. "What time do we start serving?"

"We open the doors at 6:30 for worship and the message." Rose looked from one face to the next. "So who's preaching?"

Richard frowned. "What message?"

Ainsley offered a sheepish smile. "I suppose I forgot to mention that. I thought one of the youth boys would take care of it."

"Doesn't have to be fancy or nothing." Rose grinned. "Just read one of the Psalms. Like Psalm 121 or something. "I will lift up mine eyes unto the hills, from whence cometh my help" (v. 2 KJV; paraphrase).

"I know that's right!" A woman with stringy black hair hanging over bony shoulders entered the kitchen carrying a ten-quart juice container. "My help cometh from the Lord, the maker of the heavens and the earth" (v. 2 KJV; paraphrase).

The two women burst out in song, "We'll be standing on the mountaintop, looking out upon the valley. You carried me. Father, You carried me."

Ainsley giggled and turned to Gina. "Would you mind stirring the meat a bit while it reheats? I'm going to get my guitar."

Chris rushed to her side. "And I'll get mine."

She raised an eyebrow. "You play?" She'd seen a second guitar in the van but assumed it belonged to one of Norma's girls.

"I dabble."

"When did you . . ."

"Gina said you'd be playing. I told her I did too. She said you might feel more comfortable if one of us went up with you, so I grabbed my guitar back at your house when all you females were taking turns with your bathroom."

Her cheeks warmed. "Right." They walked side-by-side to the van.

"So, how long have you been playing?"

She retrieved her instrument from the trunk of Norma's van. "Since I was twelve. At one time I thought I wanted to be the next Amy Grant."

"There's always time." He grabbed his case and slung it over his shoulder. "Guess tonight will be our first duet, huh?"

Ainsley smiled, her heart giving a little jump. When they reached the shelter entrance, he opened the door and held it for her. "If you're ever interested, I'd love to have you come play at the café sometime."

"I didn't know you had live music."

"We don't, yet, but it's on my list." He chuckled. "Among other things."

They returned to the kitchen to find Richard leaning against a counter, scowling. Gina hovered over three slow cookers, vigorously stirring the bubbling meat. The compact kitchen smelled of garlic, tangy beef, and fresh brewed coffee. It set Ainsley's mouth watering, reminding her it'd been a while since her last meal.

She propped her guitar against the wall and crossed the kitchen, breathing deeply of the spicy, sweet aroma.

Voices floated in from the other room. Ainsley peered into the cafeteria. Women and children milled around tables, gathering in packs of fours and fives. Her breath caught, and, palms pressed together, she brought the tips of her fingers to her mouth. Was that . . . ?

Yes! Sitting near a far table with her shoulder's hunched, head drooped forward, sat Wanda, the battered woman from the apartment. Her son sat beside her with the same down-trodden posture. He wore a pale green sweatshirt, the hood pulled over his head. Every once in a while, he'd glance up, scan his surroundings, then stare at his hands again. Poor kid. But at least he and his mom had found a safe place. For tonight.

"Showtime, folks." Grinning, Rose poked her head through the doorway. "Y'all ready?"

Ainsley nodded, swallowing hard. She glanced at Gina who shot her a wink.

Richard placed a hand on her shoulder. "Surely you're not nervous, my princess."

Ainsley turned to Chris. "Shall we?"

He nodded and followed her down the center aisle toward a small, black podium in front of the cafeteria. Three wooden stools of alternate height lined the far wall. She pulled one forward. It wobbled on uneven legs. She returned it and tried the second one. Chris followed suit and settled on a stool beside her.

He held her gaze, the warmth in his eyes sending a flutter through her heart and heat to her cheeks. She quickly glanced away, scanning the crowd for Wanda and her son. Upon making eye contact, she smiled. Would she get a chance to talk with them later? What would she say? That she thought about them constantly, prayed for them daily?

Richard sat at the far end of the room at an empty table, back rod straight, arms crossed. Gina sat beside him. She smiled and gave Ainsley a thumbs-up sign.

Ainsley cleared her throat. *Lord, this one's for You. Please, overcome my insecurities, for their sake. Love these women through me today.*

She turned to Chris. "'You'll Never Leave Me'? In G?"

He nodded then awaited her lead.

Ainsley strummed her guitar and let the softly played chords envelope her. Wanda watched her intently, her fingers twined and pressed to her mouth. Tears shone in her eyes. She reached for her son's fisted hand, placed hers upon it. He visibly relaxed and leaned into her. Lifting his head, he centered his gaze on Ainsley.

Her voice cracked as intense emotion swept through her, nearly stealing her breath. It was as if God was loving them through her. And in that moment, she felt more alive than she had in some time, if ever.

Chapter 27

*A*insley swept cookie crumbs into her hand while a group of giggling children scampered between the tables. Unfortunately, William and his mother weren't among them. Had they come for the meal only? Or had they sought shelter, only to find the beds already assigned? *Oh, Lord Jesus, please watch over Wanda and her son. Hold them tonight. Keep them warm. And fed.*

A woman with frizzy red hair pulled back in a loose ponytail approached, looking from the floor to Ainsley's face. "That was a great meal, thank you." An infant dressed in soiled pajamas squirmed in her arms.

"My pleasure." Ainsley stroked the baby's cheek, a lump lodging in her throat. "You have a beautiful little girl."

The woman's eyes moistened. "Thanks."

"Assignments!"

Startled, Ainsley turned to see Rose standing at the front of the room holding a clipboard.

"Sammy, you've got the downstairs bathroom. Tiffany, the hallway . . ."

As she continued assigning tasks, women scurried in different directions. Some wiped tables, others gathered leftover food items, while others carried brooms and mops down the hall. Meanwhile, the children ran about the cafeteria, playing with one another and laughing.

Ainsley hoisted a slow cooker with leftover sloppy joe mixture and heaved it into the kitchen. Richard's narrowed gaze followed her, though he made no move to help. He appeared much too busy throwing visual daggers at Chris, who, as usual, didn't notice or didn't care.

Gina came in carrying an empty salad bowl. "I'd say we were a hit." Her eyes danced. "Great music, inspiring message, and halfway decent food."

Ainsley placed the slow cooker on the counter. "I'm just glad there was enough."

A woman, with spiked gray hair and feather earrings, wearing a gray sweatshirt entered carrying a tray topped with half a dozen cookies. "What do you want us to do with the leftovers?"

Two women at the industrial sink, elbow deep in soap suds, spun around, and the kitchen went quiet as a dozen eyes looked her way.

Ainsley swallowed. Such hope for a few morsels of food many Americans threw away. "We'll leave them."

The silence broke into cheerful chatter. The women scampered around the kitchen, filling plastic storage bags with food.

"Save that juice!" An older brunette pointed a long, curved nail toward one of the near empty slow cookers. "That's some good juice right there."

Agreement sounded and women dashed into the storage area, reappearing with more ziplock bags.

A large woman with long, silver-streaked hair and jaundiced-looking skin wrapped the remaining cookies in a napkin. "Some of the ladies are at work. They'll like this. Yes, indeed, that was a fine meal."

Chris approached carrying a stained rag. Richard was close behind, his entire body visibly tense. Planting himself in the doorway, his narrowed gaze followed Chris's every move. Ainsley rolled her eyes. To think she once found him charming. Once again, she thanked God for His guidance and protection.

After wiping down the stovetop and a counter, Chris dropped his rag in a sudsy tub and faced Ainsley. "Gotta job for me?"

The woman at the sink spun around, lather splattering across the floor and counters. "I want a job."

Ainsley's heart ached. She and Chris exchanged glances.

He turned to the woman, eyes soft. "No, *I'm* looking for a job, to help clean up."

The woman's shoulders slumped. "Oh." She returned to washing dishes.

Rose entered a moment later, still clutching her clipboard. "Thank you for coming. The ladies really appreciated it."

Ainsley studied the women in the kitchen, a lump lodging in her throat. A desire to do more than fill their bellies welled within. Sometimes life cut deep. She couldn't fix these ladies' problems but she could point them to the God who would carry them through. "I'd like to come back."

Chris nodded. "Me too."

Rose smiled. Her charcoal eyes sparkled as if they'd just offered her a new Mercedes. "Come with me." She led Ainsley and Chris through the cafeteria; the narrow hallway, and into a small, cluttered office. Bible verses printed on thin sheets of paper dangled from tacks on the wall and odd little knick knacks covered the desk. An orange troll with green hair stood on the top right corner of an archaic computer screen.

Chris leaned against the doorway, hands shoved in his pockets.

Ainsley sat on the edge of a metal folding chair.

Rose grabbed a paper calendar off the wall and placed it in front of Ainsley, then handed her a pencil. "When do you wanna come?"

She skimmed the sheet in front of her, numerous days unfilled. "When do you need us?"

Rose laughed. "Girl, we always need warm bodies to come in here."

Chris stepped forward, carrying with him the faintest scent of spiced cedar. "Monday's work best for me."

A nervous flutter filled Ainsley's stomach, and she lowered her gaze.

Rose looked at each of them in turn, a hint of a smile tugging on her lips. "Perfect. We're always shorthanded at the beginning of the week. What was your name again?"

"Chris. Chris Langley."

Rose jotted down his name then looked at Ainsley. "What about you, Miss . . . ?"

"Ainsley. Meadows."

"Ah, I like that. Makes me think of a field of flowers in spring." She grinned. "Monday work for you?"

"I . . . Uh . . ." Ainsley straightened. She glanced at Chris, blushed beneath his lingering gaze, then looked away. "Sure. Monday's fine." The words tumbled out, leaving her wringing her hands as the flutter in her stomach increased.

"Well then." Rose extended her hand, shaking first with Chris then Ainsley. "I'll see you both Monday. And bring your guitars, if you don't mind. Y'all play so beautifully together."

Ainsley nodded and started to rise, then settled back in her seat. "A woman and her son came tonight — named Wanda and William. Do you know them?"

Rose tapped her pen against the palm of her hand. "Hmm . . . Can't say I do." She picked up and studied her clipboard. Flipped the page, then another, before returning it to her desk. "Don't have them listed. But we get a lotta folks comin' here. Some come to eat, others hoping for a bed. Once we fill up." She shrugged. "I wish I could shelter them all. The fact is, I can't."

Ainsley nodded then stood, lingering a moment longer before slipping silently out. In the hall, a toddler sat strapped in a stroller tucked against the wall. She reached out a chubby hand as Ainsley passed, her high-pitched squeal echoing through the hall.

Ainsley chuckled and stroked the baby's cheek. "Aren't you a bottle of sunshine?" The skin beneath the baby's nose was red and cracked. Dried snot covered the edge of her nostrils and streaked across her rosy cheeks. She wore tattered and food-stained pajamas, her bare feet sticking from cut openings on the bottom of each leg. Where was the child's mother?

Chris stopped beside her. "Children are such precious gifts."

"Who are you?"

Ainsley turned as a woman with long, tangled hair emerged from a nearby bathroom. She carried a mop in one hand and pushed a wheeled bucket with the other. She twitched when she walked like a detoxing addict.

"I'm Ainsley, and this is Chris." She smiled. "What's your name?"

The woman pushed her bucket against the wall and plopped the mop in it. "Who's asking?" The skin above her thin eyebrows creased. "You from the CIA?"

Ainsley and Chris exchanged glances. Either drugs saturated the woman's brain or she suffered from schizophrenia.

"No, we're not from the CIA." Ainsley spoke as if coaxing a timid child. "We're from . . . Well, I'm from Northside Community of Christ."

The woman's shoulders relaxed. "You're an angel, then. Just like Miss Rose."

Ainsley's heart gave a tug. "Not angels. Just believers in Christ who long to share God's love with others."

"For God so loved the world that he gave his one and only Son that whosoever believes in him shall not perish but have everlasting life. For God demonstrated his love for us in this, that while we were yet sinners, Christ died for us." The woman spoke fast, hardly pausing for air. "For I have loved you with an everlasting love, I have drawn you with loving kindness. Sing to the Lord a new song, praise his name in the congregation of his saints." Verse after verse spilled from her mouth without pause. When finished, she leaned forward, face red, as if she'd used every last ounce of air, then sucked in a loud breath.

Chris chuckled. "Wow, that's a lot of great Scripture."

"For the word of God is living and active, sharper than a double edged sword, dividing soul and spirit." She popped off four more verses, her face growing even redder than before. Halfway through her fifth verse, someone cleared their throat and Ainsley turned to see Richard standing beside her, frowning

He glanced from Chris to Ainsley. "Are we ready to leave?" A tendon in his jaw twitched.

"I . . ." She looked at the baby again, wondering if she should wheel her into Rose's office. Before she could, a tall, blonde woman dressed in flannel pants and a baggy T-shirt tromped down the stairs and to the stroller.

"Hey." She looked from Ainsley to Chris then continued on down the hall, pushing the baby with her.

As Ainsley watched them leave, her heart completely overwhelmed by all she'd seen and experienced that night. Loss, pain, hope, love, God's provision and grace poured out on these women. On these precious children. She couldn't imagine a baby living on the streets. That didn't happen, did it? And yet, she knew it did. According to an article she'd read, the average age for a homeless person was nine. Fourth grade. She couldn't image. The problem seemed insurmountable.

Lord, show me what I can do!

With a heavy sigh, she turned toward the cafeteria. A woman with long, gray hair swept while two younger women wiped down tables. Behind them, two more folded the tables and shoved them against the far wall.

She nodded. "Seems they've got everything under control."

Gina stood in the center of the room surrounded by a handful of children. She glanced up, caught Ainsley's gaze, and winked.

"Would you fellas mind gathering up our dishes while I round up Gina?"

"I'm all over it." Chris disappeared into the kitchen.

Once Chris left, Richard turned to Ainsley with a scowl. "There's something unsettling about that guy."

"Not now."

"I don't like the way he looks at you. It's not right. Be careful."

"You've read one too many neuropathology books."

"Just be careful," he repeated. "And remember how many people Ted Bundy fooled with his charming smile."

"Seriously, Richard, you need to join the real world once in a while. Not everyone's a sociopath."

"Not everyone's altruistic either." His phone chimed and he pulled it from his front pocket. "Excuse me."

"Gladly."

Singing drifted from the cafeteria, Chris's low voice audible over the others.

Her heart warmed as she thought of him standing over the toddler tucked in the stroller. The look in his eyes had been so tender.

Could a man fake compassion? She remembered all the afternoons she waited in vain for her father to call—the man who once called her his little angel. Yes, a man could, and love for that matter.

It'd be easier, and safer, to avoid romance all together. She'd be like those old women in the movies with lots of cats, books piled on every surface, and cobwebs clinging to every corner.

Chris carried the last slow cooker to Norma's van. He glanced at Richard who rested against the side of the vehicle, phone in hand, apparently glued to the door. Quite the servant. He'd gone from sitting in a far corner, scowling, to standing in the parking lot while everyone else worked double-time.

His heart warmed as an image of Ainsley standing over the snot-faced toddler, eyes radiating with love, came to mind. She and this guy were Sun and Moon from each other. Or perhaps, Sun and Pluto was a more accurate analogy. Ainsley's light shone so bright, it brought smiles to everyone she encountered. Except for Richard. He hadn't smiled once, other than the lip-stretching attempt he gave Rose on occasion. Maybe Ainsley's servant heart would soften the guy. Either that or he'd snuff the life from her.

Footsteps crunched on the gravel as Ainsley and Gina exited the shelter, chattering. Rose stood in the opened doorway.

Her shoulder rested against the silver metal, her body acting as a doorstop. "Thanks again for coming." She flicked a wave. "And Chris and Ainsley, I'll see you Monday."

Chris gave a thumbs-up sign. "Looking forward to it."

Richard slipped his cell phone in his pocket, shoulders pulled back as if trying to appear larger than his willow branch five feet nine. He glowered at Chris before turning to Ainsley with narrowed eyes. "What's that about?"

Ainsley frowned. "Serving." Her tone was clipped. Crossing her arms, she turned her back to him and stared at the shelter entrance. Richard's scowl deepened, and he shifted his gaze to Chris, looking like a testosterone-loaded teenager itching for a fight. Chris suppressed a smile. *Nice try, man, but I have no interest in masculinity wars.*

Ignoring the fuming man catty-corner from him, Chris sat on the van bumper, waiting for Norma and her girls to meander out. Apparently, they'd enjoyed a bit too much punch and needed to use the facilities. Meanwhile, he listened to Gina share a story of a black-haired toddler with the "cutest lisp." She began to mimic the child, alleviating the awkward tension with much-needed humor. She had just launched into a second tale when Norma approached with her girls, unlocking the van as she did so.

Ainsley opened the back side door. "That was something else. I don't know how to process it all." She smoothed a loose curl from her forehead. "I loved being here, but it's hard too. Know what I mean?"

Chris nodded, climbing into the van behind her. "I do." He'd never even considered all the children living on the streets. Or the joy he'd experience spending an evening with them, serving them. "This is what it's about, huh? God's pretty amazing, and to think, He allows us to be part of what He's doing, right here in Kansas City."

Chapter 28

The light turned green and Chris accelerated. He eased into the intersection, tiny specks of snow dotting the windshield.

To his right, a woman in a thin, white nightgown shuffled down the sidewalk, head swiveling, shoulders hunched. The wind whipped through her hair. Chris slowed and leaned forward.

His heart cramped. *Mom!* What was she doing out here?

He veered to the curb and slammed on his breaks. Horns blared as cars swerved around him and into the center lane. His mom looked up with wide eyes. He threw the truck in Park, jumped out, and ran to her side.

"Mom, what are you doing out here?"

He reached for her, but she jerked away, her teeth chattering behind blue-tinted lips.

"Who are you? What do you want with me?" She shifted right then left, white fingers touching her face. "Where am I?"

Chris's blood coursed hot, his muscles constricting. He cupped his mother's elbow. "Why don't we go inside to figure this out?"

Lord, please don't let her fight me on this. Give her a moment of clarity, or acceptance—anything to help me get her out of this cold and back to the nursing home. Before she catches pneumonia.

With an extended pause, she looked at him, her chin quivering. Then she nodded and let him guide her to his truck. After securing her seat belt, he closed the door, rounded the truck, and hopped in.

"Where are you taking me?" She shivered against the passenger door, hugging her torso.

"Do you see that building over there?" He pointed toward the nursing home.

She nodded.

"The lights are on. I bet someone in there can help us." Hopefully the nursing home lobby and staff would trigger her memory. Otherwise things could get ugly. His teeth ground together as a memory of the staff dragging his mother hitting and screaming to her room flashed through his mind. They said they wouldn't restrain her, but God only knew what happened behind closed doors.

He pulled into the lot, parked, and turned to his mom, still trembling beside him. How he longed to reach out to her, to hold her hand, to soothe her fear. But that might only frighten her more. So instead, he breathed deep and put on his best smile.

"Here we are."

Lord, please, help me bring her inside.

She studied the nursing home entrance, creases deepening the wrinkles on her forehead. "I recognize this place. Have I been here before? Where are we?" When she turned back to him, her eyes softened. She touched his chin with an icy hand. "My Chris, how good to see you. And look at you, all grown up. You've got your father's eyes, you know."

He placed his hand over hers and gave it a gentle squeeze. "It's good to see you, too, Mom. Shall we?"

He hurried to her door before she had a chance to open it. The last thing he needed was for her to slip on a patch of black ice and break her hip. Cupping his hand under her elbow, he led her onto the sidewalk and up the front steps.

Heather, one of the night staff, met them at the door with a frown. Her dull, brown hair draped from a loose ponytail, stray locks sticking out in frazzled clumps.

"Mrs. Langley, where have you been?"

Chris inhaled, his hands balling into tight fists. He didn't speak until he knew he could keep his voice steady. "How did she get out?"

Two other staff members joined them, talking fast, chastising his mom, making excuses for what had happened, talking about "wandering residents" who slipped past the staff. Meanwhile, his mom grew increasingly agitated, her gaze darting between them.

"Stop." Chris spoke firmly. "Let's take care of Mother first. We'll talk about the situation once she's settled."

The staff fell silent. Two left, muttering under their breath, leaving Heather and Chris to guide his mom back to her room.

"Where are you taking me?" She pulled back, straining against their grip.

"Sh. It's OK." Chris rubbed his mother's back. "You're cold. Let me get you a blanket and a warm cup of peppermint tea."

She nodded. As they continued down the hall, her quivering lessened. Air fresheners lined the ceiling, an overpowering aroma of gardenias and talcum powder mixing with the stench of dried urine.

At the end of the hall, a man in mismatched clothes sat in a wheelchair, dried food caked in his beard and mustache, hair matted to one side. His head fell forward, his mouth slack.

Chris stopped and turned to Heather. "Is anyone going to put that man to bed?"

"Yes, when they get a chance. We're understaffed today."

Which was probably why his mother managed to wander out into the cold. What if she did it again and he wasn't there to find her? That was a chance he wasn't willing to take. He needed to make different arrangements, but he'd have to move fast, before Matilda filed for guardianship and the courts got involved.

Chapter 29

onday evening Ainsley arrived at North Kansas City Ray of Hope ready to serve. She felt more alive during the few hours here than any other time during the week. And yet, she always left with a heavy heart, worrying about where the women and children would spend the night. Wondering if William and his mother would be among them. She checked the temperature on her dash. Thirty-eight degrees and dropping.

"Holy Father, please watch over these ladies, and those who won't make it into the shelter tonight. Please help them to find You."

A moment later, Chris pulled into the parking space beside her. She scrambled out, clutching the collar of her jacket as an icy breeze swept over her.

He glanced around. "Where are all those pretty lights and wreathes strung through the Plaza? Guess the city forgot to decorate this part of town, huh?"

"Funny how that happens." She popped her trunk, stacked three large containers of pasta salad on top of one another then hoisted them between her forearm and her chin.

Chris ran to her side. "You need help?"

"I got it, but thank you. Did you bring your guitar?"
Chris gave a thumbs-up sign. "I'm all over it."

Across the lot, a brunette emerged and held the door open. "Hey, y'all. Best hurry before that wind up and carries you away. Woo-wee, is it a cold one tonight."

Guitar case balanced on his shoulder, Chris turned to Ainsley and extended a hand. "After you."

Inside, they encountered a cluster of chattering voices

surrounded by the rich aroma of warm bread, garlic, and basil. Ainsley paused in the hallway to inhale, her stomach, neglected since morning, growling.

"My two favorite volunteers!" Rose emerged from her office loaded down with toilet paper rolls. "And tell that wonderful pastor of yours, many thanks for the tissue!"

Ainsley nodded then moved aside to allow Rose to hurry past them toward a small bathroom to their left. Once out of earshot, Ainsley stepped closer to Chris. "One day our pastor came to drop off flyers for a life-skills class; he found Rose sitting in her office cutting toilet paper down the middle."

His eyes widened. "Why?"

"Because their supplies had dwindled, and she wanted to make what they had last."

"Toilet paper, huh?" He shook his head. "Sure puts life in perspective."

She nodded and led the way to the kitchen where a group of teens flowed in and out carrying cookie packages, brownies, plastic utensils, and napkins. Industrial-sized pots simmered on four burners, each manned by a different student. Two teens emerged from a back storage area hefting a bright-orange drink tub between them.

Chris set his guitar down and dashed to their side. "I got it."

Ainsley placed her salad on a cluttered counter. She checked the clock — 6:20. Soon, Rose would open the doors, allowing all the women gathered out front for food and warmth.

Until then, she and Chris helped where needed. By the time the front doors banged open, food and drinks lined the tables.

The teens hung back as women and children crowded into the eating area, hollowed eyes sweeping back and forth, toddlers running between them. They gathered in threes and fours throughout the room, some slumped forward, eyes downcast, others rigid, scowling.

Ainsley wove her way through them, pausing to rub the back of a wide-eyed toddler before sitting next to an ashen-skinned woman engulfed in a ripped ski jacket. Chris followed a few feet behind and set his guitar near the front beside two folding chairs before joining her.

"I'm Ainsley." She smiled.

The woman nodded, her gaze darting about. She rocked in her seat, arms wrapped around her torso.

Ainsley's heart ached for a connection, to find words able to break through the barrier this woman hid behind. After a few attempts, the woman grumbled and scooted further down the table, indicating she wanted to be left alone.

Offering a silent prayer, Ainsley studied the wind-chapped faces all around her. A few she recognized. A woman with two elementary school-age children slouched on either side of her. A woman with waist-length hair and bright-red lipstick. Two chubby-cheeked, shoeless toddlers squirmed in the arms of a blonde with dark circles shadowing her eyes.

Rose moved to the front and took the microphone. "Good evening." Everyone grew quiet. "Many of you remember our dear friends, Ainsley Meadows and Chris Langley." She motioned toward them, eliciting a chorus in the affirmative.

"Mmm, hmm."

"You know that's right."

"Sure do!"

Ainsley studied her hands, cheeks warming. Her stomach knotted and she asked herself the same question she did every Monday night: *Why do you do this to yourself?*

Because she loved the women and loved to sing — so much so, it overshadowed her shyness.

"You ready?" Chris nudged her arm.

She nodded and followed him to the front of the room. Settling onto a stool, she inhaled and repeated her favorite mantra. *Just You and me, God. Just You and me.*

When Chris's fingers strummed the guitar, filling her ears with the soft melody of "Amazing Grace," peace settled over her nervous heart. She closed her eyes, lifted her voice in harmony, and lost herself in praise.

"Amazing grace, how sweet the sound, that saved a wretch like me. I once was lost, but now I'm found. Was blind, but now I see."

With each verse, memories surfaced—of the day she first heard the gospel message and the immense love that swept over her when she stumbled, quivering, down the aisle. Of the countless nights God met her as she lay in bed, broken and afraid, while her parents fought in the next room. How God had stayed with her, helped her find peace, when after her parents' divorce, they attempted to pit her against one another. Her Savior had carried her through it all.

Launching into the second verse, she reached her hands toward heaven, tears slipping through her closed lashes. With each line, God's love penetrated deeper, until it filled her completely.

When Chris played the last chord and the melody drifted into silence, Ainsley opened her eyes to see tear-streaked faces staring back at her, children wrapped in their mother's arms.

She turned to Chris, captured by his gaze.

"That was beautiful." He spoke barely above a whisper.

Chris sat next to Ainsley, guitar tucked under his feet. A man with a gray T-shirt, the word *Transformed* printed on the front in fluorescent green letters, took the mike

"Wow, amazing." He smiled at Chris and Ainsley. "If you're ever free on a Sunday, look me up. Our congregation would be blessed to have you."

Chris stole a glance at Ainsley who studied the ground, cheeks pink.

The man continued. "I'm Pastor Jeffreys and that lovely lady in the back," he motioned to a woman with short, black hair seated amidst a cluster of teens, "is my beautiful wife, Elaina."

Heads turned, followed by murmuring, which lulled to silence once he started to speak again. "You've probably heard the story of the boy with the richly decorated robe? Broadway created a show sometime back based on the biblical account. Joseph was the second youngest of twelve brothers, born to his father's favorite wife."

He continued to lay out Joseph's history, explaining the mounting tension filling Joseph's home and the hatred his brothers felt toward him. "Then one day, they saw their chance for revenge. While tending their father's animals, Joseph approached them, wearing his richly ornamented robe. Fueled by rage, they plotted to kill him." He turned to his Bible and read Genesis 37:18–36, then continued his paraphrase. "These traders brought Joseph to Egypt where he was sold to a man named Potiphar, an Egyptian officer. So, here was Joseph, betrayed by his brothers, stripped of everything he cared about, living as a foreigner. Just as things began to turn around, Mrs. Potiphar accused him of attempted rape, and he was falsely imprisoned. So what'd he do? Turn bitter? Hateful?" He shook his head. "Young Joseph became a beacon of light in an incredibly dark place."

Chris focused on a kid who looked to be twelve or thirteen, slumped over the table, and a lump formed in his throat. Memories of his junior high years surged to the front of his mind. Surviving eighth grade was hard enough. What increased difficulties did this young man face, shuffling from one shelter to the next? And where was his father? In prison? Or kept at bay by a restraining order?

When the message concluded, everyone migrated toward the food lined along the back wall.

Standing, Chris gave Ainsley a smile. "Shall we?"

She nodded and they wove through women and children until they reached their stations behind the salad bowls.

Mrs. Jeffreys waddled over and slid behind a pan of garlic bread. "You two were something! Rose said you have your own café, said you were trying to set it up as a believers' retreat. Ever think of singing live, for your customers?"

"Actually, yeah. Just haven't launched the idea yet." He looked at Ainsley. "What do you say? Think you could pop in for a few hours next Saturday for a duet?"

She blinked. "I . . . Next Saturday?"

"I've got an idea!" Mrs. Jeffreys snapped her fingers then turned to a teen standing beside her. "You got this? I'll be right back." The girl nodded, taking Mrs. Jeffreys's place as the woman hurried to where her husband manned the dessert table.

Chris chuckled. "If that idea of hers generated that much excitement, I gotta admit, I'm rather intrigued to hear it."

Ainsley scooped a mound of salad onto a plate extended in front of her. "I'm not so sure. Something tells me it won't be in my comfort zone."

"Which means it's probably from God." Chris winked.

"What do you mean?"

"Last thing God wants His children to do is settle into the comfortable. Nope. He's in the stretching, growing, teaching business."

Ainsley frowned, her delicate forehead creasing above deep green eyes. His pulse quickened as he watched the color spread through her cheeks, fighting against a sudden urge to draw her close.

Whoa, time to step it back.

Looking away, he focused on the task at hand — feeding the long line of hungry, broken women and children God placed before him.

A moment later Mrs. Jeffreys returned, out of breath. "What do you think about hosting a benefit concert at your café?"

"What do you mean?" He plopped a scoop of potatoes onto a little boy's plate.

"Nothing fancy." She flitted her hand. "Just you and Ainsley, unless you know of other musicians. We could take a love offering at the end to support the mission. I know they're running low on funding."

Chris grinned. "Love it! And 15 percent of all sales could go to the shelter as well." He turned to Ainsley, nearly chuckling at her furrowed brow and flushed face.

Finally, her contorted features smoothed into a smile. "Guess it's time for a bit of spiritual aerobics, huh?"

Chapter 30

Chris pulled into the North Oak Landing apartment complex. Matilda's periwinkle four-door sat across the lot beneath a long, multislot steel carport.

Lord, give me the words today. Please help my sister understand the urgency of Mom's situation.

And yet, even as he prayed, one question nibbled at his gut — what if his sister was right? Would Lily of the Valley really take better care of their mother, or were they merely putting on a show for potential clientele?

Thick clouds blanketed the sky, mirroring patches of snow melting on the winter grass. Gray and tan rocks lined the empty stream bed, bare trees swaying in the crisp midmorning breeze. A man in a blue ski jacket and heavy knit hat strolled down the sidewalk, leash in hand, while a snowy white poodle scurried behind him.

Chris grabbed the brochure for Lily of the Valley and got out, the wind biting at his ears and cheeks. Turning up his jacket collar, he strode toward his sister's apartment.

He pressed the doorbell, initiating a faint chime, followed by the rattling of a chain. A moment later, Matilda stood before him dressed in a pink housecoat, her gray-streaked hair set in rollers.

"Chris, what a surprise. Is everything all right?" She moved aside, touching her curlers.

He peeled off his jacket and gloves and deposited them on a nearby couch.

Matilda shuffled into the kitchen, separated from the tiny living room by a long laminate counter. "Would you like a cup of coffee?" She pulled two mugs from the cupboard.

"Yes, thank you." He sat in a floral recliner.

She placed a steaming cup in front of him then moved to the couch, watching him, her face void of emotion. "You've come to discuss Mom's care, correct?"

"Yeah." He lifted his mug, breathed deep of its rich steam, then set it down. "I went to see her last night. Found her wandering the streets in her nightgown, confused and near frozen."

Matilda gasped. She pressed her hands on her thighs and stared at them. "Did you talk to the director?"

He shook his head, his jaw tightening as the callous looks on the staff's faces came rushing back. "She'd already left for the night. I spoke with the night nurses, but they acted like Mom's little evening jaunt was an unavoidable annoyance."

Matilda's lips pressed together, the lines around her mouth deepening. Her eyes grew moist. "I'm sure to some extent that is true. You and I both know how hard it is to manage patients with Alzheimer's, which is why we decided to place her in a care facility in the first place, remember?"

"So it's OK for Mom to wander the streets, then?"

Her eyes narrowed. "Tell me, Chris, what would you have them do, restrain her?"

He rubbed his face. "Of course not, but there has to be some way to keep her safe, without locking her up."

"That's what the security alarms are for. You remember what they told us during the tour? She must have followed a visitor out or something. Did you ask the staff what happened?"

"They didn't realize she'd left, remember?"

Matilda shook her head slowly. "I'm not sure we'll find better."

He pulled the brochure for Lily of the Valley from his back pocket and slapped it on the table. "I already have. I know it's pricey, but they have a much lower patient-to-staff ratio. Plus, the personnel seems much kinder than those shift-cyclers where she's at. You should have seen the look on Heather's face when I brought Mom in. Not a hint of concern, no, 'Are you OK, Mrs. Langley?' She acted annoyed! Like Mom had inconvenienced her."

"No one is going to care for Mom quite the way we'd like. Alzheimer's is a very trying disease. You know that. You can't expect the staff at Shady Lane to demonstrate patience all the time. They're human, and they're going to get frustrated."

"Listen to yourself." Chris spoke louder than he'd intended, and Matilda flinched. He lowered his voice. "What if I hadn't showed up? It was thirty-eight degrees out, with a wind chill factor of twenty-five."

"And you think taking her to this . . . this . . . home — " she lifted the brochure then let it drop, "is going to fix all that?"

"Any place has to be better than where she's at."

"We went over all this last fall, after Dad died. Shady Lane was the best we could find."

"But that's only because we didn't know about Lily of the Valley. Just look at the brochure. It's like a home. The owners live on the property, and I met with the staff. To them, this is more than a job. It's a calling."

"So they say."

"I believe them. Come with me and see for yourself. The home is peaceful, and the residents are neatly dressed, clean-shaven, with their hair brushed; no dried food clumps on their faces."

Her shoulders sagged and her eyes moistened. "We can't afford it. You know that."

"I'll cover the charges."

She snorted. "With what, the money you bring in from your café? Because correct me if I'm wrong, but I saw quite a few empty tables."

"It's in transition, that's all."

"And if your business goes under, what then? We can't move Mom from place to place. That would only frighten her more." She stood. "Is there anything else? Because if not, I have to be at work in forty-five minutes."

Chris rose and grabbed his jacket and gloves. "No, there's nothing else." He stomped to the door. "Have a good day."

Chapter 31

*R*ichard leaned against the kitchen doorframe, phone to his ear. He gazed through the sliding glass door overlooking his patio to the Plaza skyline beyond. "No, Eric, that is not the wisest decision. I have no doubt Ainsley and I will have worked everything out long before then." He couldn't believe they hadn't already. In fact, he was beginning to worry about it. She appeared to be following in the footsteps of her irresponsible, relationship-burning mother.

"And if not?"

"I'll simply tell them she caught a cold, or perhaps encountered a family emergency." He looked at the clock. She would be out of church soon and likely in an amiable state of mind. Unless that close-minded pastor of hers further swayed her thinking. Originally, he found her religious fervor endearing. But now, clearly it had become a problem. Of course, helping her to see that was another matter. But once they married . . .

If they married. Every muscle in his body tensed as he reviewed their previous conversation and the obvious contempt — anger even — in her eyes.

"Richard, are you listening?"

"What?"

"I said, that will go over real well. Remember, you invited the press. 'Richard Hollis throws an engagement dinner, without the bride.' Is that really the headline you want?"

He stalked out of the kitchen, down the hall, and into his bedroom. "I don't know what you expect me to do." He sifted through his neatly arranged closet and pulled out a light-blue shirt with a buttoned-down collar. Too formal. He returned it to the rack. "Certainly the alternative isn't any better, especially since she's bound to change her mind before the wedding date. You of all people know how indecisive women can be." Not that Eric's long list of failed marriages helped Richard's case any, but at least it illustrated the need for patience and confidentiality.

Eric chuckled. "Women. Does she play these games often? Because if so, I suggest you find another bride."

"Are you intentionally irritating me? You should know, you're already treading a very thin rope." After selecting a cream sweater and tan corduroy pants muted enough to soften what others coined his "pit bull" eyes, he closed the closet door and exited the room.

He paused in the kitchen to pour a glass of orange juice, grabbed the newspaper lying on the table, and meandered into the living room. "Your track record isn't adding to my confidence here, Eric." With a flick of the switch, he turned on his gas fireplace and settled into a leather recliner.

"Listen, the KCGW thing wasn't my fault."

"Really? Then whose, pray tell, was it? Perhaps if you'd taken the time to listen to a few broadcasts before booking my appearance, you would have realized the circus that station encourages."

"Again, I'm sorry, but could we please return to the issue at hand. I strongly suggest you cancel the engagement dinner."

"Many of Kansas City's most respected mental health professionals have already RSVP'd. Do you realize how irresponsible I would appear?"

"I'm sure you'll think of something. Anything would be better than showing up alone."

"Clearly you are not listening, Eric. I told you, everything will be back to normal by then. Now, why don't we spend the rest of our conversation discussing positive action, instead of worrying over potential crises? You spoke with my editor about the second book I proposed?"

"Unfortunately, their contingency remains. They want to see how well this book does before contracting another."

"The problem with signing with a small press, I am sure."

"The larger presses felt—"

"I'm not interested in rehashing that conversation again. Is there anything else?"

They discussed other interview options, none of them promising, and concluded the conversation with an agreement to speak again, once Richard secured a few more academic endorsements.

With a growl, he tossed his phone onto the coffee table. Everything hinged on his finding a way into his colleagues' inner circle. They claimed they provided endorsements based on merit, but an evening of drinks and well-worded conversations could be quite influential. Success rested on the strength of your connections. Forming the right ones required a delicate balance of knowledge and likeability. He needed Ainsley, with her soft curls and large, green eyes, to balance him out. As much as her timid, wildflower heart needed his determined strength. They complemented one another perfectly.

Somehow he needed to help her see that.

Ainsley collapsed on the couch, her lungs screaming for air while Gina fell into an adjacent recliner. Her cheeks blazed red and her chest heaved.

"What a waste of sweat." Gina took a large gulp from her water bottle.

"You have a reservoir to maintain, do you?"

"Very funny." She grimaced and stretched her legs. "Next time, maybe we should—"

"Oh no." Ainsley shook her head. "My quads can't handle a next time." Extending a leg, she reached for her toes. "You're my best friend and all, but even our friendship doesn't run that deep, pun intended." She laughed. "You remember what I told you in high school when you asked me to join the track team?"

"Not buying the running allergy, Ainsley."

She stood and moved to the mirror hanging on the wall. "Yeah, then what are all these red blotches on my face? Looks like hives to me." She turned around and planted her hands on her hips. "I'm thinking I deserve a piece of cake or something, after that self-induced torture you finagled me into. You did bring treats, right?"

"But of course. I'll be back in a few." Gina dashed out to her car, returning with a package of chocolate chip cookies — the chewy kind.

Ainsley followed her into the kitchen and pulled two saucers from the cupboard. "So, what's up with you and Chris? Any phone calls? Email messages? Romantic candlelit dates?"

"Nah."

Ainsley's pulse quickened, a smile tugging at her mouth. "So you've given up completely, huh?"

"Pretty much. He's nice and all. But I get the feeling he's not really interested in romance."

"Now that would be a first. A man not obsessed with women."

"I know. Weird, huh? Because there's certainly nothing wrong with me." She grinned, framing her face with her hands. "Not that I'm all cut up about it."

Ainsley raised an eyebrow. "You've got a date?"

Gina nodded.

"With who?"

"A very handsome and intelligent librarian with lumberjack shoulders." She shoved the remainder of a cookie in her mouth and grabbed her hand towel and water bottle. "Anyway, thanks for the run, but I gotta hose off this dried sweat before my nostrils rebel. I'll call you later?"

"OK." Ainsley walked her to the door then returned to the couch, her muscles uncoiling into strands of limp rubber.

Crazy Ginger. That girl had more vigor than the Energizer Bunny on espresso.

But at least one of them had a social life.

The coffee-stained magazine she'd purchased at the convenience store a while back sat on a nearby end table, opened to the article highlighting the log cabin. She picked it up and studied the tall maples and flowering dogwoods encasing the quaint little cottage. A stone pathway surrounded by blossoming rose bushes led to a white gazebo nestled beneath a flowering vine. Her heart pricked, not in mourning for Richard, but for the fairy-tale happily-ever-after ripped from her dreams.

The doorbell rang. Her legs burned, wobbling like overstretched taffy, as she rose and trudged across the room. Parting the blinds, she peeked out the window. Her mother stood on her doormat in an orange jacket and matching shoes, a heavily sequined purse draped over her shoulder. A glittery scarf surrounded her neck, accentuating her salon-tanned skin.

Ainsley opened the door and forced a smile. "Mother, how good to see you."

Her mom rushed into the room like a midwestern blizzard. She carried a paper grocery sack. After peeling off her jacket and gloves, she waltzed down the hall and into the kitchen.

Ainsley followed. "What's all this?"

"Did you forget about our ornament making?"

"That was supposed to be last week, Mom."

"Oh, honey, I'm so sorry!" She rubbed her forehead. "Do you want me to leave?"

"No, it's fine."

"Great!" Grinning, she fished through the bag and began unloading items onto the counter. Flour, a tub of salt, a box of plastic cookie cutters, thread, and straws. Diving into her bag once again, she pulled out a container of cocoa mix and a board game. "Thought we could make a night of it, just us girls. Do you have a boom box?"

"What?"

"A boom box, to play Christmas music." She held an old—like ancient—cassette in the air.

Ainsley shook her head sarcastically. "I've got Pandora."

Her mother scrunched her nose then flicked a hand. "Never mind. We'll sing."

Ten minutes later, flour covered their clothing, clung to their hair, and dusted their faces, the initial tension abated by the occasional giggle.

Her mother grabbed a mound of dough and plopped it onto the island. Flour poofed in her face. "So, how are you feeling, with the breakup and all?"

Ainsley chewed her bottom lip. How often had she longed to have a deeper relationship with her mother—the type that allowed them to share their hearts? But was her mother really asking or merely "conversing"? Her mother was great at talking without really *talking*.

She came over and wrapped her arm around Ainsley's waist. "If you don't want to talk about it, that's OK."

She studied her mother. She seemed genuinely concerned. And she was here, salt dough ingredients and all. "It's been weird not to have him around, but I know I did the right thing. He wasn't the guy for me."

"Not your soul mate. Right. I get it."

"Really? I didn't think you believed in that stuff."

"Oh, honey, the universe knows!"

"How can the universe . . .? You know what, never mind. So, how are things with you and Stephen?"

"Oh, great! We're starting a catering business together. Hope to launch it by the end of the year, as soon as we get financing."

Ainsley's jaw dropped. "A what? Do you cook? And no, boxed macaroni doesn't count."

"I'm learning. Everything's on the Internet, you know."

Love, joy, peace. Now wasn't the time to draw battle lines. "Gina and I went running today."

"Oh, good for you. I need to join the gym. Maybe yoga."

After a few more random tidbits of information, the tension dissipated again and their giggling resumed. Perhaps Ainsley and her mother could maintain a relationship after all, so long as they remained within non-teeth-grating parameters.

She gave her mother a sideways hug. "This was a great idea, Mom."

Using her forearm, her mother pushed her hair out of her face, leaving a streak of flower across her forehead. "I agree. Just like old times, huh?"

"Almost." Ainsley smiled. Maybe she'd been too hard on her mom. "You know, next Friday there's a — "

Her mother's cell phone chimed and she raised her hand.

"Hello? Oh, Stephen. . . . Right now?" She looked at Ainsley with a frown.

Ainsley sighed and focused her attention on a mound of salt dough, pounding it with more force than necessary. Their little get-together had lasted all of, what? Twenty minutes? *Thanks, Mom.*

"What a lovely idea. Give me a bit to clean up. OK. See you then." She snapped her phone shut then surveyed the mess of dough and partially made ornaments. "Looks like we made a pretty good dent here. Let's get your kitchen back in order and set another date to finish, maybe next week?"

"Sure." Like she'd save salt dough. "Have fun."

Her mother smiled and kissed Ainsley's cheek. "Oh, I will, dear. I'll call you."

Yeah, like five hundred times, yet you can't stay for half an hour.

Chris opened his ice-covered mailbox and pulled out a stack of envelopes. He sifted through the abundance of junk mail, tucked the bills and green, red, and gold envelopes under his arm, and headed up his walk. A small UPS package lay on his stoop, addressed to Ainsley Meadows. After tucking his mail between his door and the glass pane, he grabbed the box and headed to his neighbor's.

His sneakers crunched on ice crystals. A thick blanket of clouds covered the sky, threatening snow or sleet. He surveyed the rest of the driveways surrounding the small, tree-lined cul-de-sac. How many of his neighbors would need a steady dose of help come blizzard season? Many who used to help his parents out.

Reaching Ainsley's porch, he climbed her stairs and rang her bell, then stood, shivering in the brisk morning wind.

When the door opened, a woman with burgundy hair and bright-red lipstick stood before him. A thick layer of makeup settled in the deep creases around her eyes, nose, and mouth.

"Hello. Can I help you?" She looked Chris up and down, her smile widening.

He nodded and raised the package. "Hi. I live next door. UPS left this package on my doorstep."

Ainsley appeared, her green eyes sparkling beneath delicately arched eyebrows. The pink sweater she wore accentuated the olive glow of her skin.

The older woman held the door wider and moved aside. "Come in, come in. I've been wanting to meet Ainsley's new neighbor. Where I'm from, we take great pride in our open door hospitality. I'm Mrs. Meadows." She held out her hand, stressing the word *Mrs.* Glancing at his box, she dropped her arm.

Chris crossed the threshold, held the package out to Ainsley, then turned back to her mother. "So where are you from?"

Ainsley set the box on the coffee table. "We're both longtime Kansas Citians."

"Although I spent my childhood in Texas." Mrs. Meadows cupped her hand under Chris's elbow and led him to the sofa. "Please, have a seat and tell me where you're from and what brought you to the Midwest."

He sat on the edge of the cushions, looking from Ainsley to her mother, not sure whether to politely excuse himself or accept Mrs. Meadows's hospitality. "I moved here from Rancho Cucamonga, California, to be closer to my mom. She's got early-onset Alzheimer's."

"I take it she's divorced?"

"Mother!" Ainsley's cheeks colored. "Please excuse her. She meant no offense."

He shook his head. "That's OK. None taken. My father died a year ago."

Mrs. Meadows sat across from him. "Oh, my. I'm so sorry! But you look so young. How old was your father when he passed?"

Chris swallowed as years' worth of rushed phone calls and quickly scribbled Christmas cards flashed through his mind. If only he'd taken time to be there for his dad when he'd had a chance.

He cleared his throat. "He died young, and I was a twilight baby. My mom was forty-one when she had me."

Mrs. Meadows laughed. "Ainsley, I guess your biological clock isn't ticking as fast as you think, huh?"

"Mother!"

"Just saying, if Richard's not the one, you need to throw that reel back in the water. Don't you agree, Chris."

His face warmed, and swallowing, he stared at his folded hands. Apparently he'd stumbled into an ant hill. Best thing he could do was politely excuse himself before things turned ugly.

He stood. "Good to meet you, Mrs. Meadows." He turned to Ainsley. "Have a nice weekend. I'll see you Monday."

Mrs. Meadow's eyebrows shot up. "Oh?"

Ainsley rolled her eyes. "He serves at the women and children's shelter with me."

"Oh." Mrs. Meadows tilted her head, studying Chris.

He shifted. "Yeah, I've enjoyed it. Really puts your life in perspective."

She rubbed her pinkie nail with her thumb. "I imagine it does."

"Did Ainsley tell you about the benefit concert she and I are hosting in a few weeks?"

"No, I haven't heard anything about it. What's it for?"

Frown lines creased around Ainsley's mouth. "I assumed you wouldn't be interested."

Chris felt like a gnat caught between a flame and an ember. "An informal concert of sorts. Your daughter will sing while I play the guitar. Fifteen percent of sales will benefit the shelter, and we'll accept a love offering at the end. Your daughter has the voice of an angel. You should come."

"Yes, well, I have heard Ainsley sing on many occasions." She flicked a hand. "As a teen, she felt certain God wanted her to devote her life to music." She patted her daughter's shoulder. "I'm not sure what I have going on that day. Send me an evite? And please, do take pictures." With that, she rose and glided across the room. "Anyway, I must be going." With a wave, she disappeared out the door.

Ainsley visibly tensed. She turned back to Chris. "Thanks again for bringing the package by."

"My pleasure." He showed himself out.

That was awkward, to say the least. Why did he have the feeling those ladies had an arsenal of firecrackers hidden beneath their forced pleasantries? He shook his head, remembering all the times he and his father argued when they could have connected instead. Only now it was too late.

Chapter 32

*R*ichard yanked on his winter jacket, dashed outside, and slammed the door behind him. He clicked the deadbolt in place. Next door, Laurie Manning supervised as a crew of men hung lights on her house. In an effort to avoid needless conversation, he stared straight ahead and strode down the cement walkway.

"Richard, good morning." Footsteps rustled on the grass as his neighbor approached.

"Good morning, Mrs. Manning. They're doing a lovely job on your lights."

"Would you like their phone number?" She pulled a business card from her back pocket.

"Thank you." He scanned the rest of the neighborhood, lights draped across every house save one or two.

Manger scenes, wooden reindeer, and snowmen dotted the adjacent lawns. In less than a week, slow-moving cars and horse-drawn carriages would clog their streets while carolers filled the sidewalks. Oh, the joys of living near the Plaza. Although he held his neighbors, not the city, primarily responsible for the surge of gawkers. Must they really turn their homes into heavily lit spectacles?

"Are you bringing your fiancée to Jeff and Janet's Christmas party?"

He frowned, an image of Ainsley's angry face coming to mind. How long would she continue to spurn his attention?

"Honestly, I haven't given it much thought."

"I haven't seen her in a while. Is she doing OK?" She edged

closer and Richard bristled, taking a sideways step to preserve the distance between them.

"She's fine. In fact, I'm heading to her house now."

"Oh, I see."

Lengthening his stride, he hurried to his car and slid behind the steering wheel. As he pulled away, he glanced in the rear-view mirror to find Mrs. Manning watching him, which struck him as odd.

He pulled out his cell phone, snapped his earpiece in place, and called Ainsley.

"Hello."

"I . . . Ainsley . . ." Expecting her voice mail, he faltered over his words. "What's your schedule like today?"

"You must quit calling."

Specks of ice dotted Richard's windshield and thick fog spread across the inside of the glass. Tapping his breaks, he turned on his defroster and cranked up the heat. "I really feel we need to discuss this — us — further. Can we meet for coffee?"

"There's nothing to talk about."

"You need more time. I understand."

"Actually, I don't. For the hundredth time, it's over."

His grip tightened around the steering wheel. "How can you say that after all the time we've been together?" He exhaled, regaining his calm. "You're nervous. Unsettled. Considering your upbringing, I understand that completely. But I'm concerned — "

"I don't love you, Richard."

He refused to accept that. She was confused, overwhelmed. "Certainly you aren't expecting prom-night butterflies to last forever." He tensed as an image of Chris Langley flashed through his mind. "It's your neighbor, isn't it?"

"What? You can't be serious."

"If you think your doubts will lessen with another man, you're bound to be disappointed."

"Our breakup has absolutely nothing to do with Chris Langley. You and I are too different. It wouldn't work."

"You're being absurd and assigning a false cause to your anxiety."

"I'm sorry it had to end this way, but please quit calling. Otherwise I'll have to change my number."

The call went dead in Richard's ear. Traffic merged around him as he continued on in a daze, staring at the gray road in front of him. Ainsley's words replayed in his mind. *"Quit calling . . . I'll have to change my number."*

This was all Chris Langley's fault. Everything had been fine until he had moved in. The conniving, low-class loser. Perhaps he had sparked Ainsley's curiosity, but Richard refused to let the man steal her heart.

Chris paused outside Matilda's door to take in a deep breath then pressed the doorbell. Footsteps approached and the blinds covering the adjacent window parted, revealing Matilda's gray and blue-swirled eye. A moment later, the lock clicked and the door swung open.

She blocked the entrance with her square frame. "Chris."

He shifted, memories of Thanksgiving and Christmases past forming a lump in his throat. They were once so close. How could decades worth of friendship shatter in less than a year? "Can I come in?"

She hesitated for a full two seconds before moving aside. "Want tea?"

"That'd be great, thanks."

He followed her into the kitchen and sat at the table while she set the filled kettle to boil. She occupied the chair across from him. The skin beneath her eyes sagged, although whether from sorrow or fatigue, he couldn't tell.

He rested folded hands on the table. "The court date's scheduled for next week."

She nodded.

"I don't want to fight with you, Tildie."

Her gaze flicked upward, holding his, and tears welled behind her lashes. But then she inhaled and straightened, her features hardening. "Neither do I, but I cannot allow you to uproot Mother, no matter how wonderful you believe Lily of the Valley to be."

"I know you love Mom and only want the best for her. For her to feel safe. At home."

Silence stretched between them.

"There's gotta be a way we can work this out. Outside of court."

Her lips pressed flat, accentuating the tiny lines feathering from her mouth.

"Can we at least delay the proceedings?"

"Let me guess, your café isn't doing as well as you'd hoped, and you're afraid the judge will rule against you."

Well, yes and no, but that wasn't why he came. "Do you remember the slumber parties Mom used to throw us when Dad went out of town? How we'd fill the living room with sleeping bags, books, and massive amounts of junk food?"

She nodded. "I do. Her fresh-baked monster cookies were to die for! In fact, that's the only reason I participated." She laughed. "Mom said I couldn't eat the cookies otherwise." She shrugged. "I might have acted like a stink, but in truth, I loved it. Of course, you always demanded the best spot — the one closest to the fireplace."

Chris chuckled. "Yeah, but Mom never let me. You remember why?"

"She said her kids would never get their way by fighting."

"Because we were a family and families drew together, in love."

Matilda studied her hands.

"Can we at least pray about it before forming legal battle lines?"

Her eyes moistened.

"For Mom?"

"OK."

Chapter 33

he blare of the alarm pulled Ainsley out of bed. Early morning sun filtered through her blinds, striping the carpet in bands of light. She slipped her feet into her fuzzy slippers, crossed the room, and peeked out. Tiny ice crystals glistened on blades of grass, and icicles hung like ornaments from tree limbs.

She glanced toward Chris's, the far corner of his house barely visible from her angle. How would the California boy fare come blizzard season? She might need to give him a few pointers, like why one needed to keep snow shovels and ice scrapers in their trunk. Never knew when your car would get buried or stuck.

Thirty minutes later, she sat at her kitchen table nursing a vanilla-cream cup of coffee and searching career databases. She'd sent her resume to half a dozen businesses and had yet to get invited to a single interview. Luckily, she had a chunk of savings — funds she'd hoped to put toward tuition. Although this wasn't her plan, at least it'd help her stay out of debt, so long as her joblessness didn't drag on too long. She figured she had maybe five months. Six, if she lived off PB and J.

The doorbell rang, and she glanced at her watch. Who would stop by so early on a Sunday morning.

She shuffled to the front door to find Chris on the stoop dressed in jeans and a sweater. Oddly enough, Rusty wasn't with him.

"Hey." He gave a sheepish, almost boyish smile.

"Good morning." Her heart fluttered when her gaze met his.

He shifted, ran his fingers through his hair, then shoved them in his front pockets. "I . . . Do you go to church?"

"Yes." What an odd question.

"Mind if I join you? Well, not join you exactly, but like . . . go to the same place?" He shifted again, looking like an elementary student about to give his first book report. "I've been looking online, in the phone book, trying to find a good to church to join, but there's gotta be more than a hundred. And the last one I visited kind of freaked me out."

"There are quite a number of churches in the Kansas City Metro. Mine's rather small, and not fancy by any means. Although it's kind of far. Up north, near Smithville."

"Sounds perfect. What time is service?"

"Nine forty-five. Hold on." She dashed inside and returned with a pen and pad. "I normally take 435 to SkyView then follow the roads to . . . She wrinkled her brow. "On second thought, it might be easier if you follow me . . . or we might ride together. It's somewhat complicated, but in case you wanted to Mapquest it." She wrote down the address and handed him the slip of paper. "It takes about twenty-five . . . She glanced past him to the street to gauge the roads. A thin sheet of ice speckled with salt crystals glimmered in the morning sun. "Maybe thirty minutes to get there."

Chris checked his watch. "So I'll be back just after nine?"

Warmth crept up Ainsley's neck and filled her chest. "Great. See you then." She closed the door before the shy smile tugging at her mouth took hold.

Her mind instantly turned to Richard and her stomach soured. She could already hear the rumor mill:

"Look who Ainsley brought to church. I bet that's why she broke it off with Richard. Five years, and she threw it all away for a California hottie. She's just like her mother."

She stared at her reflection in the hallway mirror. *Am I?*

The words from a long-forgotten verse filled her mind, "Every good and perfect gift is from the Lord, and He adds no trouble to it."

What in the world did that mean? Pondering the words, she plodded to her bedroom, unable to shake the feeling that God was trying to tell her something. Maybe an hour-long worship service would cut through all the clutter in her head and heart.

But first she needed to call Gina. For backup, or more accurately, a safety net.

Unfortunately, she got her voice mail.

Ainsley ended the call then redialed. So long as Gina's phone wasn't on silent, the shrill ring would wake her eventually.

"Hello?" Gina spoke through a yawn.

"How quickly can you get ready?"

"Why? I don't have to be at church for another hour and a half."

"No, you need to be come to church with me this morning, and since you live so far south, I'd suggest you leave as soon as possible. Like now."

Gina sighed. "What are you up to? Did I miss the 'take your best friend to church day' memo?"

"No. Chris's coming."

"Oh. OK."

"So, you gonna join me, or what?"

"Why? To make sure he tithes?"

"Drop the sarcasm, please. I don't want to start any rumors, especially after my recent breakup."

"But those poor prayer-chain ladies. Whatever will they talk about now?"

"Ha, ha. Very funny, and Christlike, might I add." Phone wedged between her shoulder, Ainsley grabbed her Bible and tucked it into a canvas tote. Her spiral notebooks, extra pens, and a pocket calendar were already packed.

"Sorry. I forgot, your church isn't like mine. On second thought, yeah, I'd love to come." She laughed. "I'll be there in a few."

She hung up then turned to the mirror, chiding herself for her rather drab appearance, then chiding herself further for caring.

Chris tidied his kitchen, a grin forming. The way Ainsley's eyes had widened, those thin little lips opening in a near perfect O, you would have thought he'd asked her to go to the Bahamas. What he wouldn't give to catch a glimpse of the many thoughts swirling through that dainty little head of hers.

How had he never noticed how beautiful her eyes were before? Chestnut and green swirled together, surrounded by thick, dark lashes that extended to her arched brows.

He blinked and shook his head, as if doing so would clear her image from his mind and the longing building in his heart. Not like a Hollywood movie trash scene, but more like a . . . like a . . .

An image of his father standing in the kitchen, his arms wrapped around his frail, recently diagnosed mother, came to mind. His determined, unwavering look of love that had radiated from his eyes mirrored the desire taking hold of Chris.

He wanted to be Ainsley's protector, her steady rock that would quiet her fears and sooth those deep wounds away. But she was taken by a man with as much heart and gentleness as a starved pit bull.

Lord, are You calling me to pray for her? Is that why I feel such love for a near stranger? Please draw Ainsley to You. Heal the pain in her heart — the pain reflected in her eyes no matter how hard she tries to hide it. He paused, swallowed.

And please, don't let me fall in love with her.

Inside, Rusty waited near the kitchen. The bald patches scattered throughout his gray-splotched fur showed more dominant than before. Squatting down, Chris scratched the dog's muzzle.

"You hungry?"

Rusty gave a low whine.

Chris laughed and scruffed the dogs ears before wrapping an arm around his neck in a tight hug. His gaze lingered on a patch of silver fur, and Chris's heart cinched. It'd hurt something awful when this dog died on him.

His eyes burned, and he blinked furiously to keep tears from forming. "No dry dog food today, buddy." He moved to the fridge and pulled out crisp pieces of bacon left over from his morning breakfast.

Rusty was at his feet in an instant, ears perked, drool forming.

Chuckling, Chris dropped the treat on the ground, giving the dog's musky mane another scratch.

Thirty minutes later, the doorbell rang. He grabbed his wallet, tucked it into his back pocket, and hurried to the door. His pulse quickened as an image of Ainsley's soft face and marbled eyes came to mind.

He opened the door to find Gina standing in front of him. She flashed a toothy smile. "Hi!"

"What's up?"

"You're coming to church, right?" Her eyes sparkled. "No sense in us all taking separate cars. Besides, Ainsley's church is out in the boondocks of the boondocks, at the end of winding country roads. I'd hate for you to get lost. Why not ride with us?" She spoke quicker than a toddler on Kool-Aid.

"Did she send you over?" He sounded like a prepubescent middle schooler. *Does she like me? Check yes or no.*

"Something like that." Her grin widened. "Can you meet us in five?"

He shoved his hands in his pockets, his thumbs hooked through his belt loops. This situation was more than awkward. But then again, it was just a car ride. And he did need to find a good, Bible-preaching church. "Sounds good."

Gina beamed, waved her hand like a parade float queen, and spun around. She bounced down the steps and across the lawn. Shaking his head, he closed the door softly.

Why do I feel like I'm about to step into something?

He looked at his watch. His mom was probably in full fight mode, giving the nursing staff enough flack to keep them from taking her to chapel. Which was why he needed to call and defuse their flimsy excuses at the start.

He grabbed the phone and dialed his mother's private extension.

"Hi, Mom. It's Chris."

"Good morning, dear. It's so good to hear your voice. Are you coming by today?"

Mornings were her best times, and apparently, this one was especially good, although there was no telling how long reality would remain.

"After church. Which is why I'm calling. Are you going to chapel?"

"You know I don't like to go down there. All they ever talk about is having peace like a river—every Sunday. Same old message. Most of those folk don't pay attention, not that I blame them. Then there's the piano music, if you can call it that."

He waited patiently while his mother vented. This had been a hard transition for her. Losing her husband, her independence, her church home. He'd bring her with him, but new situations scared her. Besides, he didn't have a church home himself. Although, Ainsley's sounded nice. Small and quiet.

"You need to go, Mom. You can't stay locked in your room all the time."

"Those people are crazy, you know. They've all lost their mind."

Chris pleaded with her for a while longer then hung up and headed to Ainsley's. The garage door was open and the car running. He started to go to the front door when the girls walked out carrying nearly identical purses.

Ainsley glanced up, her green eyes filling with the same childlike timidity that had colored her features when she answered the door earlier. Her pink lips hovered near a smile.

"Good morning, Chris. I'm glad you can join us." She walked to her car then paused with her hand on the door. She glanced first at Gina then Chris.

"I'll sit in the back." He slid in before either of them could protest.

Ainsley's face smoothed into a smile. She moved into the driver's seat and tucked her purse beside her.

A handful of gray clouds dotted an otherwise clear, blue sky, but a band of black lined the east horizon, poised to swallow the midmorning sun. Bare trees covered in melting ice bent beneath the steady wind.

Gina angled her body to look Chris in the eye. "So, how are you adjusting to the midwestern winter?"

He caught Ainsley's gaze through the rearview mirror. Her green eyes rounded and a splash of pink colored her cheeks. "I'm adjusting."

"It's been a warm winter so far. Well, minus the occasional storm." Gina talked fast, as if she had a head full of words and a limited amount of time to release them. "Although it's still early. Wait until February when blizzard season hits."

She launched into one story after another while Chris pretended to be engaged, nodding at the occasional pause and offering a smile here and there, but mostly he watched Ainsley. The more Gina talked, the more Ainsley appeared to relax, and although she rarely joined in the conversation, she smiled and laughed. She had the sweetest laugh.

They continued north. Storefronts gave way to long stretches of brown grass covered in patches of snow. The road narrowed and wove around quaint farmhouses surrounded by barren trees.

Fifteen minutes later, Ainsley turned onto a narrow gravel road cutting between two fields. After another five minutes, she turned onto another dirt road and continued toward a single-story church with a tarnished wooden cross. A handful of cars filled the makeshift lot.

She parked beside a brick-colored Camry and cut the engine. "As I said, it's small, and not fancy by any means, but . . ." She smiled. "It's home."

Chris and Gina followed her across the lot and into an entryway about the size of a bathroom stall. Wood paneling covered the walls and soft organ music poured from a wooden archway leading from the foyer to a nineteenth-century sanctuary.

"Ainsley, good morning." A woman with silver hair, a wooden cane in her hand, enveloped Ainsley in a hug. She pulled away and her smile widened. "And Gina, I'm so glad you are here! How have you been, dear?" Before Gina could answer, the woman turned to Chris. "Who's your friend?"

"This is Chris, my new neighbor. Gina brought him." She spoke quickly and glanced around as if avoiding the woman's gaze.

The woman offered Gina a knowing smile. "I see. Well, welcome, my dear. I'm Deborah Eldridge. Ainsley's old third-grade teacher."

Chris raised an eyebrow. "Is that right?"

Ainsley smiled. "Deborah was the first person to tell me about Jesus and the first one to invite me to church. Drove me every Sunday for almost nine years."

"Until you grew up on me and started driving yourself." Deborah squeezed Ainsley's hand. "How are things with your mother?"

She shifted, her smile vanishing. "Good, thanks."

Deborah gave her a sideways hug. "We'll talk later." She stepped aside, scanning the area. "If you see Michelle, can you tell her I'm looking for her?"

Ainsley nodded then led the way into the sanctuary. She slid into the pew farthest back and moved to the center.

Gina giggled. "Ainsley likes to barricade herself in. Make it near impossible for anyone to say hi."

Frowning, Ainsley blushed.

Gina gave her a squeeze. "You know I love you, my sweet little hermit friend." Then she launched into three stories in quick succession, not stopping until everyone else stood and broke into song.

*a*insley slid onto the driver's seat and waited for Chris and Gina. When they hopped in the back, she angled the rear-view mirror to catch Gina's gaze. "Nothing I like better than playing chauffer."

Gina's cheeks colored. "I'm sorry. I thought Chris would . . . Want me to come up there?"

"No, it's fine." She turned the engine and eased out of the parking lot, waving to Deborah as she left.

"Oh, my! Is it that late already?"

Ainsley glanced back to see Chris staring at his watch.

"Is everything OK?"

"Yeah, I guess I didn't realize your service went so late. I normally eat lunch with my mom on Sundays. How long does it take to drive back? Twenty minutes?"

Ainsley shrugged, a lump forming in the back of her throat as she thought about her own mother. They hadn't spoken since the salt-dough experience.

Love initiates, expecting nothing in return. How many times had she heard that message? How many prayers of surrender had she offered? But somehow her determination dwindled once she left the sanctuary.

She studied Chris's reflection in the mirror. "We're about twenty to thirty minutes out, depending on how many tractors or escaping cows we encounter along the way."

"It'll be close. I hate to ask, but . . . A crooked smile began to emerge. "You guys wouldn't happen to like overcooked country fried steak and mashed potatoes, would you? My mom does much better with routine, although there's a good chance she'll forget our luncheon. But if she does remember and I don't show up, or I show up late . . . His forehead creased.

A turkey wobbled across the road and Ainsley slowed. "No biggie. I'll drop you off. Where is it?"

Gina leaned forward. "But how would he get home?"

"Right." There could be worse ways to spend her Sunday. "Country fried steak sounds lovely."

They spent the rest of the drive engaged in small talk, Gina asking enough questions to fuel a national trivia contest while Ainsley stifled a giggle at Chris's two-to-three-word answers. They pulled into the Shady Lane Parking Lot exactly twenty-two minutes later.

Once parked, Chris jumped out and led the way up the sidewalk, into the nursing home, and through a sparsely furnished lobby. Ainsley and Gina scurried after him.

The rich aroma of roasted meat and melted butter drifted down the hall, followed by a steady clanking of silverware and the agitated chatter of voices. One woman's voice dominated them all.

"Hermon, I just took you to the bathroom. Eat already before I take your food away."

Chris stormed down the hall and around the corner, hands fisted. He didn't slow until he stood in front of a woman dressed in a faded smock. Gina and Ainsley gathered behind him, exchanging glances.

Upon seeing Chris, the woman's scowl smoothed into a stiff smile. "Mr. Langley, I thought perhaps you weren't coming today."

Chris's eyes blazed. He turned to an arthritic man sitting beside him and placed a hand on his shoulder. "Hermon, my buddy! How you like them mashed taters?"

Hermon's gray eyes lifted and a smile emerged on his food-speckled face. He mumbled something, every third word punctuated by a chuckle.

"You better eat your supper, buddy, before these hungry ladies steal those tender peas of yours." He shot Gina and Ainsley a wink. "Mind if I take a taste?"

After a little more banter, Hermon picked up his spoon.

The nursing assistant muttered something under her breath then wandered to another table, her plummeted eyebrows casting a long shadow over her face.

Ainsley stared after her. "That lady's a little low in the compassion department, huh?"

Chris's steely eyes softened when he turned to Ainsley. "You know what they say about those who are overworked and underpaid, although most of the staff's pretty good." He scanned the dining room then strolled toward a woman sitting three tables down at the end. The woman glanced up when they approached.

"How are you?" Chris leaned over to kiss her, but stopped short when she flinched and pulled away.

"Do I know you? You look so familiar." She wrung a napkin in her hands.

He motioned to an empty seat. "Mind if we join you?"

She studied each face in turn, smiling when her gaze met Ainsley's. "Now aren't you a pretty little thing, just like an angel dropped straight from heaven. Have you eaten yet?"

"We were about to fill our plates." Chris smiled. "Will you hold this seat for us?"

Ainsley followed Gina and Chris to the buffet counter, smiling at the residents she passed. Most of them lit up when their eyes met.

A woman in a paisley sweatshirt grabbed Ainsley by the arm. "Such beautiful curls. They're natural, aren't they?" She lifted a wrinkled hand to touch Ainsley's hair. "I used to have curly hair." She ran her hands across her silver locks. "Used to be a blonde too."

"Least you still have hair." A baldheaded man with age spots speckled across his arms rubbed his head. "What do you say? Think you can spare a few strands for me? Get me some Super Glue, and I can make myself a wig."

When she finally made it to the tray table, Chris grinned and handed her a plate. "You ladies appear to be quite the hit. I'd say you're gonna have to come back next Sunday."

Ainsley turned around and found the woman who'd touched her hair still watching her, still smiling. Like those down at the shelter, it took so little to make these women happy. "You may be right. They certainly pull on one's heartstrings." She looked at the partially empty tables all around her. "Do many of them get visitors?"

Chris's face fell. "No, not normally." He motioned for the girls to go ahead of him. "If you scoop from the middle, you'll avoid most of the clumps."

Once food filled their plates, they meandered back through the residents to Mrs. Langley who appeared to have lost all interest in eating.

Her face caved in a deep set frown and she clutched the collar of her shirt. "It's freezing in here." She struggled to stand, entangling herself with her chair. "Where's my husband? James, where in the heavens have you gone?"

Chris set his plate down and grabbed his mom's elbow. She flinched like his hand felt hot and turned on him. "Who are you and what do you want?"

He stepped back and spoke in a low, soothing voice. "I'm here to help you. Would you like a blanket?"

Ainsley clasped her hands in front of her, at a loss as to how to help. Her heart ached for Chris and his mom.

Mrs. Langley glanced around, chin quivering, shoulders hunched. "I left my sweater in my apartment." Her gaze swept right then left. "My apartment is . . . My apartment . . ."

"Your apartment is at the end of the hall, remember?" Chris guided her through the cafeteria and around the corner.

Ainsley and Gina followed a few steps behind while Chris continued to speak softly to his mother. Rounding another corner, they nearly ran into a nurse with spiked hair and big hooped earrings.

The nurse smiled and came to Chris's aid. "Mrs. Langley, would you like to rest?" She nodded to Chris and he moved aside.

Mrs. Langley trembled. "Where's my husband? Have you seen my husband?"

Chris stopped in the middle of the hall and shoved his hands in his pockets. When the nurse and his mother disappeared through a wooden doorway, he turned back around. "So, you wanna finish, or should I say, start, your lunch, or would you rather hit a burger joint?"

Gina glanced back toward the dining hall. "Uh . . . burgers sound great."

Silence fell over them as they passed the cafeteria and continued to the parking lot.

Once in the car, Ainsley paused with her hand on the ignition key. "You're so patient with her. How do you do it? I mean, that's gotta hurt, to have her forget who you are."

Chris shrugged. "I mourned her a while ago, although I suppose I still mourn her. But I've come to realize this is who she is, and I love her for who she is and not who I'd like her to be." He stared out the window, as if remembering times past. "It's hard, but it's beautiful, too, because it helps me see God's love for me."

"I don't get it."

"When Heather, the nurse from the dining room, looks at my mother, all she sees is her behavior — her mood swings and agitation. But that's not how I see her. When I look at my mother, I see her sickness, Alzheimer's. Often we have the same shortsightedness. When we look at each other, all we see is the behavior — bouts of anger, selfishness, snide comments. But when God looks at us, He sees our sickness, sin."

Ainsley swallowed, her thoughts jumping to her mother. Like Chris's mom, her mother was sick. Only her sickness, sin, wasn't as easily diagnosed. And yet, did loving her mother for who she was, and not who Ainsley wanted her to be, mean giving up hope for change? She could understand it in Chris's case, but her mother chose her disease. Jesus offered a cure for sin.

Then again, a cure only proved useful to those who sought treatment.

Chapter 35

*A*insley's cell phone trilled on the coffee table. She checked the number then answered. "Good morning, Mom." Sleet pattered on her roof, adding rhythm to the moaning wind. Nestling into the corner of the couch, she pulled the blanket tighter around herself. "Are you on your way to work?"

"No. I quit my job."

"You what?"

"It stressed me out, and the way my boss treated me. It wasn't right."

"But how will you pay your bills?" Like mother, like daughter? How did the saying go? You can trim the foliage but can't sever the roots.

"Oh, I've got a few months' worth of unemployment coming."

"You don't get unemployment when you quit. Only when you're fired."

"Oh . . . then Social Security? With all the money the government's stolen over the years, I've gotta have something coming."

Ainsley closed her eyes and rubbed them. "Was there something you needed?"

"Are you going to Aunt Shelby's for Christmas this year?"

"Same as I do every year. Although I'm planning on spending time at the women's shelter. Why? Has something changed? Did Aunt Shelby decide not to host this year?" A smile emerged as the idea of Christmas, minus the drama, blossomed.

"No, of course not. So you're going then?"

"Why wouldn't I?"

"Then you won't mind if I don't? Stephen's taking me to the Bahamas." Her tone lightened. "Isn't that exciting?"

"Minus the whole, 'my mom's shacking up with a guy she met a few months ago'? Sure, yeah. Exciting."

Her mother huffed. "You and your religious babble. In case you've forgotten, I'm an adult, not a teenager in bobby socks. In fact, girls don't wear bobby socks anymore. They even wear," she gasped, "pants."

"Listen, Mom, I'm not interested in a debate, and I know you aren't calling to invite me to join you. Since you don't have any pets needing to be cared for, I'm stumped."

"Aren't you edgy today? Your boss pile on the workload again?"

No, I'm fired, and not up for a "stick it to the big guy" mantra either. "What can I do for you?"

"I wanted to make sure you're OK with me going, and to see if perhaps we could meet for dinner, for an early Christmas celebration, just the three of us — unless you have a date you could bring, of course."

"Thank you for considering my feelings." *Or more accurately, allowing your thoughts to drift in my direction after the fact.* Not that Ainsley expected anything different.

"Of course, sweetie. I always worry about my sugarplum. But I should probably let you go. I'm sure you've got a busy day ahead. How about if I call you later tonight to talk about specifics?"

Yeah, terribly busy — drinking coffee, dusting shelves, and maybe, if she got real crazy, cleaning toilets. "Good idea."

They said their good-byes and hung up. Tossing her phone aside, Ainsley grabbed her Bible. Tears welled in her eyes, the initial liberation she felt when Mr. Holloway let her go now replaced by fear and doubt.

Lord, I know You've got a plan here. You've always got a plan. Please help me to see it. Help me to walk through whatever doors You open with surrendered obedience.

Her stomach soured as an image of the women huddled

around tables down at the shelter flashed through her mind, the sermon Pastor Jeffreys spoke resurfacing.

"To what lengths would you go to reach the lost? Joseph brought glory to God in the depths of an Egyptian prison. What about you? What if God has you here, in this shelter, in order to love your bunkmate through you?"

Clutching the Bible to her chest, she closed her eyes. *Lord, You know how accustomed I've become to comfort, and the thought of losing my home and living at the shelter, among those ladies, terrifies me.* A shiver ran up her spine and she gripped her Bible tighter. *But if that's what it takes to reach their broken hearts . . .* She swallowed. *Then not my will but Thine be done.*

Opening her Bible, she leafed through the pages until she landed on Isaiah 43:19–20. "For I am about to do something new. See, I have already begun! Do you not see it? I will make a pathway through the wilderness. I will create rivers in the dry wasteland, . . . Yes, I will make rivers in the dry wasteland so my chosen people can be refreshed."

Closing her eyes once again, she sat in the Lord's presence until her anxious heart settled and a warm peace washed over her. Then she slid her feet to the floor and shuffled to her bedroom to get ready for the day — whatever it entailed.

Thirty minutes later, she stood on her front step bundled in a heavy jacket, knit scarf, and ski gloves. A brisk wind swept across her yard. Sunbeams pierced through the blanket of clouds, creating a faint rainbow partially hidden by the adjacent rooftops.

Shoving her hands deep in her pockets, face angled downward to ward off the icy wind, she strolled to the corner café. She intended to spend the next hour or two nursing a hot vanilla latte. After that, she'd scour the want ads for another job.

The door swooshed open, ushering in a gust of cold air. Chris glanced up to see Mrs. Jeffreys and a pack of chattering ladies bustle in, purses clutched to their chests. He set his rag on the counter and migrated over to meet them.

"Mrs. Jeffreys, how good to see you."

She shucked off her gloves and tucked them in her pocket, bobbing her head and smiling. "Good morning, Mr. Langley. These ladies are from my women's Bible study." She swept her arm from one woman to the other, making introductions. "We normally meet at the Starbucks on 64th, but," the skin around her eyes crinkled, "we decided to give your café a try."

Chris led them to the counter. "So, what can I get you ladies? A peppermint mocha? Or, my personal favorite, eggnog?"

"Now don't those sound lovely?" She plopped her purse on the counter and studied the menu. "How about a white chocolate raspberry latte?"

He took the rest of their orders while Candy, his lone remaining employee, filled them. Cupping their hands around the steaming coffees, the ladies traipsed to a table next to the window.

Candy glided to his side and leaned forward, her back slightly arched, a few too many buttons on her shirt unfastened. "Your friend's quite the recruiter. Maybe you should give her flyers."

Diverting his gaze, Chris chuckled. "I have a feeling she's already printed them up for our upcoming concert. Which reminds me, we really do need to get the word out." He glanced at the clock. "How about you drop some flyers around town, at the library, grocery stores? Maybe take some to a few to area churches? Ask if they'll distribute them to their Bible study leaders."

She poked her bottom lip out. "But it's so cold outside, and my car's heater is broke. How about we go together after closing?" She moved toward him.

He stepped aside. "That's OK. I'll take care of it."

"You go to church, right?"

"Yeah."

"I've never been. Well, once, in elementary school with a friend." She twirled a lock of hair around her finger. "Maybe you could take me sometime."

Chris cleared his throat, glancing at his "What Would Jesus Do?" bracelet. Sure, Jesus ate with sinners and prostitutes, but He also told them to leave their life of sin. And the pouty smile Candy gave him whenever she looked his way suggested sanctification never crossed her mind. "I . . . Yeah, maybe." He pulled a package of napkins from a bottom shelf then strolled across the room.

The door chimed open and Ainsley rushed in bundled in winter clothes, her nose and cheeks rosy. Her green eyes sparkled beneath her knit cap, her curls cascading beneath it.

"Good morning." Chris smiled.

"Hi." She pulled off her hat and scrunched up her hair, each curl bouncing back into place. "Love the smell of fresh brewed coffee and baked goods." Peeling off her gloves and jacket, she walked with Chris to the counter. "And a hot vanilla latte sounds amazing."

While he rang up her order, three more women entered, waved to the group of ladies gathered near the window, then ambled to the counter.

"Looks like things are starting to pick up a bit." Ainsley fished through her purse and pulled out her wallet.

"Thanks to Mrs. Jeffreys and her Bible study group." Chris tipped his head their direction and Ainsley turned and waved.

"You're here later than usual. No early morning meetings today, I take it." He punched her order into the cash register. "Or do you have the day off?"

Ainsley looked down. "You could say that. I've been fired."

"No way. Seriously?"

She nodded.

"Perfect!"

Her head shot up, her eyes widening.

"I mean, that's unfortunate. I'm sorry to hear that . . . but if you're looking for something to do, I could sure use some help."

Ainsley's eyebrows shot up, and she studied him, before her features settled into a frown. She shook her head. "I appreciate the offer, really. But I'll find something. I've got plenty of prospects." She pulled a crumpled newspaper add from her purse. Red ink circled numerous ads.

"Well, what if you helped me in the meantime?" The door opened again as two more ladies scurried in, falling in line. "Because I have a feeling we're going to be busy today."

She looked around. "I suppose it won't hurt. But only when you're busy. I don't want charity."

"Charity suffers long."

"What?"

Chris chuckled. "*Charity*, the word used for love in 1 Corinthians 13:4 in the King James Version."

Lowering her gaze, Ainsley wrapped her hands around her coffee then moved out of the way. She lingered near the counter while Chris took drink orders. Ten minutes later, things quieted enough for him to talk with her.

"Would you like to start today?"

Her mouth parted. She glanced down at her jeans and sweater, then from Chris to Candy. "I . . .

"Don't worry. You look fine. Although . . . He looked at Candy who leaned over the counter, twirling her hair. If he allowed Ainsley to come in street clothes, Candy would demand the same right, low-riding pants, midriff shirts, and all. Not that the polo he bought her appeared to help any, the way she stressed the buttons. Note to self—next employee meeting, explain new policy number 375—No more than two buttons unfastened at any time.

He motioned for Candy to take his place behind the register then turned to Ainsley. "Follow me for a brief lesson on latte construction."

"Are you sure you wanna reveal your coffee-magic secrets?"

He stared into her beautiful eyes, his chest warming. "Nothing would please me more."

Chapter 36

*R*ichard examined Jolino's parking lot, relieved to see only a handful of cars, and only two he recognized. Eric's black two-door occupied the last stall on the right. His parents' Lincoln Continental sat beneath the dim streetlight next to the handicapped slot. Of all people to show up early. His pulse quickened in anticipation of his mother's relentless questioning, knowing his clichéd excuse wouldn't suffice.

Men in designer suits and women in long wool jackets crowded the lobby. A tall man with gray-flecked hair dressed in a suit and tie stood behind a marble-topped podium.

He offered a stiff-lipped smile when Richard approached. "How many, sir?"

"Hollis party." He scanned the dining area.

"Follow me, please." The maître d' led him around a grand piano, through a high archway, and up a wooden staircase. Cream trim accented the rich, golden hues of the venetian plaster on the walls, and soft music poured from hidden speakers.

Richard stiffened with every step, the anxiety nibbling on his gut when he first entered mounting to near nausea. Chiding himself for his childish emotions, he lifted his chin and centered his gaze straight ahead. At thirty years old one would think he could address his father without fear. And yet, it seemed each encounter only increased his angst.

"Here you are, sir." The maître d' left Richard standing in a private dining room surrounded by floor to ceiling windows.

A long table centered the room, decorated with golden

napkins folded to resemble blossoming flowers. Candlelight complemented the dimmed lighting.

Richard looked for Eric. He stood next to a long buffet table conversing with the wait staff. Richard's parents occupied the far corner, sipping what appeared to be cocktails.

Squaring his shoulders and donning a firm smile, he strolled across the room.

"Mother." He kissed her cheek then straightened. "Father, glad you could make it."

His mom's forehead wrinkled. "Where's Ainsley?"

He stepped back, buying some time. "She is . . . Having an early midlife crisis, not that he could verbalize such. Luckily Eric approached, providing the perfect distraction. "Ah, look who's here."

"Richard, good to see you." Eric held out his hand and the two shook. "I had the pleasure of meeting your parents in the lobby. Although as I told your mother, she's beautiful enough to pass for your sister."

Richard's mom appeared undaunted by the compliment. "Son, where is Ainsley?"

"Feeling ill."

"Oh, my! Nothing serious I hope? I wanted her to join me at my women's tea this Thursday. The ladies are dying to meet her. Quite honestly, they're beginning to think she's a figment of my imagination." She gave a slight smile.

"No, nothing serious, but I suspect she might be unavailable for some time, gauging by her condition when I spoke with her this morning. I fear she has the flu."

"How unfortunate. Perhaps next week." She sipped her drink. "On second thought, how about giving me her number and I'll speak with her directly. After all, she will be my daughter soon enough. No sense asking you to be liaison."

The knot in Richard's stomach tightened as everyone focused on him, including Eric. Richard clenched his jaw and shot Eric a warning glare before turning back to his mother.

"That's a wonderful idea. Remind me to get that to you before the night's end."

"I have a pen —"

He rotated to face Eric. "I believe you and I have a few things to discuss before our guests arrive. Mother, Father, enjoy your drinks." Stepping forward, he talked as he walked, forcing Eric to follow. "Have you spoken with the *Kansas City Star*?"

"Yes. I left messages with the senior editor and sent numerous emails to their editorial staff."

"But you haven't received a confirmation?"

Eric cleared his throat. "You know how editors are about returning calls."

Shoes clicked on the marble floor. Everyone turned as the maître d' escorted two primly dressed couples into the room. Another followed a few steps behind.

Richard forced a smile and hurried to greet them.

"Dr. Shavonaugh, Dr. Foster, so glad you could make it." He waited for the men to introduce their wives then turned to the third couple now standing by their side. "Dr. Cook, thank you for coming."

A waiter approached holding a tray of deep fried calamari. "Can I get you something to drink?"

"A glass of Sauvignon Blanc."

The waiter nodded then continued to the other guests, taking each one's order.

Richard's father approached, dragging his wife with him. "Dr. Shavonaugh, my son never told me you were coming."

The room filled up quickly, couples gathering in groups of fours and sixes. A few more doctors came alone, clustering in the center of the room, arms crossed tightly or hanging stiff at their sides. Richard made his rounds, looking each guest in the eye and offering a firm shake, followed by a saccharine-laden compliment or two. Numerous questions regarding Ainsley's absence surfaced, but most appeared to accept Richard's response. His father, on the other hand, watched Richard closely. At least his mother appeared to be enjoying herself, laughing among the other wives.

After drinks had been distributed and hors d'oeuvres passed a few times, Richard grabbed a silver fork and clanked it against his wine glass. Heads lifted and the room quieted.

"Thank you all for coming. As many of you already know, Ainsley, my fiancée, couldn't make it due to a rather unpleasant case of the stomach flu. She sends her regards and sincere apologies. Now, if you would be so kind as to find your seat, the wait staff will take your order shortly."

The rest of the night dragged. Richard attempted to engage numerous colleagues in small talk, but the minute he spoke of his book, their eyes glazed over and they quickly changed the subject. By the end of the night, he left with nothing more than handshakes and a few "Best wishes to you."

Afterward, Eric joined him on the curb. "Did you have any luck?"

He scowled. "They were not impressed with my publisher."

"I told you, the bigger publishing houses felt your book lacked—"

"Originality. Marketability. I know. But that's what I hired you for, isn't it? To create a market for me."

Footsteps sounded behind him, the scent of expensive perfume signaling his parents' approach. He turned and smiled, his overtaxed cheek muscles stiff from a long night of playing host.

"Father, Mother, thank you for coming." He stepped back and stared at the street to avoid eye contact. Hopefully, he could slip away before his mom mentioned—

"I do hope Ainsley feels better soon." She dug into her purse and pulled out a small, spiral notebook. "Give me her number. I'll bring her soup."

Richard tensed. "She's got the stomach flu. Soup likely won't sit well. And she's really not up for phone calls right now. I'll tell her to contact you as soon as she feels better."

"Fine. So I'll bring soda and saltines. Does she still live off Vivian?"

Richard swallowed. If he said no, she'd likely call information and wonder why he'd lied. If he said yes, she'd show up on her doorstep with a care package.

He checked his watch then kissed her cheek. "I hate to dash, but I have a lot of work to catch up on. I'll call you."

With a plausible reason why she couldn't possibly show up at Ainsley's, which barring an unforeseen disaster, wouldn't be easy.

Ainsley surveyed the restaurant, the knot in her stomach tightening when her gaze landed on her mother and Stephen seated at a corner window booth. Even from this distance, her gold blazer and heavily sprayed hair commanded attention. Attention Ainsley preferred to avoid.

Inhaling, she tucked her hair behind her ears and straightened her posture. Moving toward them, she wove between tables and extended feet, offering polite nods as she passed.

Standing behind her mother, she smiled at Stephen.

"Ainsley, good to see you again." He rose and extended a hand.

Her mother swiveled in her chair with a lipstick-cracking smile. "Sweet pea, so glad you could make it." She rose to give Ainsley a brisk hug. "Have a seat. You remember Stephen, the charming man who steals my every thought." She shot him a wink.

Ainsley draped her purse over the back of her chair and sat, hands folded in her lap. "Yes, of course."

"How pleasant to enjoy lunch amidst such attractive company." Stephen leaned forward. "Beauty must run in the family."

She fought an eyeroll. Real creative, this guy, and about as smooth as a snail, slime included.

She studied her menu while searching for an appropriate conversation starter. She had no desire to hear about their upcoming trip, how they spent their time, or how many illegitimate children the man left in his wake. Which, considering his snaky smile and John Travolta dress shirt, covered all potential topics.

Setting her menu down, she forced a smile. "So, Stephen, you work for Burlington Northern, correct?"

He nodded. "I work on trains." Grabbing his glass, he gulped his water, opening his mouth wide enough to allow the ice to funnel in.

"Interesting."

"Oh, it is!" Ainsley's mom batted her eyes in a way reminiscent of Tammy Faye. "I've never seen such an engine before! Those, oh, what are they called, those long, cylinder-like things you showed me?"

He chuckled. "I showed you a bunch of stuff—valve bridges, camshafts, rocker arm assemblies."

She waved her hand. "Whatever. All I know is they were big, and the engine was loud."

The two continued batting eyes at one another for the rest of meal. Ainsley attempted conversation every once in a while, to no avail. Clearly she occupied the third wheel as yet another man dominated her mom's attention. Come January, her mother's infatuation would fade. Then her focus would return to Ainsley until another slug took her place. And was it really worth it? At what point could she wash her hands of it all, mourn her mom and move on?

Chris's words spoken at the nursing home resurfaced, tugging on her heart and stinging her eyes with the threat of tears.

"I've come to realize this is who she is, and I love her for who she is and not who I'd like her to be. When I look at my mother, I see her sickness."

Yeah, well, some people's illnesses run deeper than others.

Chapter 37

*B*lack storm clouds advanced across the sky, swallowing the moon and stars as sleet pelted Ainsley's window. A semi barreled past her, splattering her windshield with salted slush. Hunched forward to see through the thick haze, she flicked on her wipers and sprayed the glass with washer fluid.

Slowing to a stop on the corner of North Oak and Vivian, she thought once again of William and his mother and all the other women who frequented the shelter. How many of them huddled on the street somewhere, drenched by the icy rain? The temperature gauge on her dash read thirty-five degrees. The weather man predicted a twenty-degree drop by morning.

She repeated what had become her most frequent prayer: *Lord Jesus, please watch over those precious women and children tonight. Help them find shelter. Help them find You.*

As she eased into her cul-de-sac, her cell phone rang. Richard. She hit Ignore.

A text message followed: *"Can't we talk?"*

Two minutes later, he sent another: *"My mother might stop by this week."*

She grabbed her phone and jabbed her finger on his number. "Hello—"

"What? So you're sending in reinforcements now? Figured harassing me yourself wasn't enough?"

"I under—"

"No, you don't. Let me clarify. I am not now nor will I ever marry you. So do yourself—and your mother—a favor, and stop the theatrics. Now." She ended the call and tossed the phone into the console, then gathered her things.

A cold gust of wind swept over her as she stepped onto the slush-covered drive. Using her hip to close the door, she stalked up the steps, face angled to the ground to ward off the driving sleet.

She fumbled through her purse for her keys, rain and hail pelting her face and soaking through her thin blazer.

"Where in the world." Grumbling, she searched deeper into her purse, coming up blank. A few minutes later, teeth chattering and completely drenched, she dashed back to the car. She cupped her hands around her face and pressed her nose to the icy window. Lovely. Her keys lay on the passenger side floorboard and her cell phone remained in the console.

"You've got to be kidding me." She grabbed the door handle and yanked — locked — then stood, shivering.

Now what? Hugging her arms to her body, she canvassed the homes on either side of her. Mr. Johnson's house sat dark and quiet, curtains drawn. Light streamed through a few windows down the block, but she didn't know the owners and certainly didn't feel comfortable ringing random doorbells. Especially not at 10:00 p.m. Chris's porch light glowed and the gleam of a television flickered behind partially closed curtains. Finding no other option, she scurried to his house then stood, shivering, on his front porch wishing she could rewind her day. OK, maybe her month.

Or perhaps the past five years to when she first met Richard. Where would she be right now if she'd walked away that day? Likely still shivering on her neighbor's, now boss's, porch.

After doing her best to smooth back her drenched hair, wiping smudged mascara from under her eyes, she rang the doorbell. The curtain beside her rustled and she stared at the ground, cheeks flushing hot. A moment later, the door swung open and Chris ushered her inside.

"Are you OK? Hold on." He ran out of the room and returned carrying a thick, velvety blanket which he wrapped around her shoulders.

"I'm fine." Her tense muscles relaxed as warmth spread through her. "I locked myself out of my car. And house. My cell phone's in my car." Water dripped from her jeans, pitter-pattering on the floor. She glanced down at the growing puddle, wishing she could bury herself in the blanket. "Sorry."

"No problem." He disappeared down the hallway and returned with a mound of towels and folded clothing. After dropping most of the towels on the floor, he handed one to her along with dry clothes. "Why don't you go get dry and slip these on? I'll call the locksmith."

Ainsley's stomach flopped. She clutched the warm clothing, which felt like they came straight from the dryer, and chewed her bottom lip. Old Sunday School lessons flashed through her head, Deborah's kind yet stern face hovering in her mind.

"Can't go dancing with the devil and expect not to get burned. Most girls never plan to get themselves into trouble, but if you put yourself in a provocative situation, trouble's bound to find you."

What could be more provocative than standing in a man's house, drenched to the bone? Standing in a man's house waiting on a locksmith, wearing his clothing. And if the neighbors saw her?

The puddle beneath her grew drip by drip. Water streamed down her face, soaking into the blanket while her feet continued to saturate the towels beneath her.

Chris cocked his head, laugh lines crinkling around his eyes. "You're not planning on standing there all night, are you? Cuz it could be an hour or more before the smith shows up. Those clothes are clean. Promise."

She met his gaze and nodded. "Yeah, I guess that'd be better than making a mess of your floor."

"Down the hall, last door on the left."

Chris pulled out a telephone book still wrapped in cellophane — a present from the Kansas City Welcome Wagon. Poor girl would've caught frostbite if he hadn't been home. He paused and closed his eyes as a memory of himself and his mother nestled on the couch while she read *Princess and the Pea* in glossy print. She loved the fairy tales, and read them all. At first, he balked at the idea, claiming it was a girl's story. But the way she told it, changing her voice deep for the prince and stern for the mother, it made him feel like a prince. Like a knight who one day would rescue his princess.

"Despite her rather rough exterior, drenched in rain with mud splattered along the hem of her dress, the prince knew this girl was the one. His heart told him so. Only his mother was not convinced, and it wasn't long before the mean old queen hatched a plan to expose this girl dressed in rain-soaked attire."

"What'd she do?"

Momma pulled him close and wiggled her fingers into his ribs until he succumbed to a fit of giggles. "She made her eat her peas!"

Chris blinked the memory away and grabbed his phone. A few moments later, soft footsteps padded across the carpet. He exited the kitchen to find Ainsley dressed in his hooded sweat-shirt and running pants. They hung from her slender frame, giving her an image of almost childlike vulnerability. Spiraled curls surrounded her face and her cheeks glowed pink. A hint of a smile graced her lips.

His breath caught when she lifted her long, dark lashes to meet his gaze. He cleared his throat, willing his pulse to slow. "Have a seat." He motioned to the couch then settled in an adjacent loveseat. "Called all the numbers listed with no luck." He glanced at the clock on his DVR. "Left a few messages. Hopefully we'll get a bite soon." And if not? He wasn't ready to think about that yet, nor was he ready to deal with the surge of emotions welling within.

Lord Jesus, I could really use some of that strength made perfect in weakness here.

"You ready for the concert?" *Keep talking. It'll distract you.* Although reality told him no conversation, regardless how stimulating, could make him forget the beautiful angel sitting in his living room.

Ainsley smiled, the pink in her cheeks deepening. "Sort of. I've never liked the idea of performing in front of people. In junior high, I joined the school choir. Loved it too. Rehearsals anyway. Thought for sure God wanted me to be a singer, like He created me for that very purpose, until my first solo." She shook her head. "But in this case, the cause is too important to let stage fright get in my way." Her forehead wrinkled. "Those poor women. Makes me feel ashamed really. I'm worried about looking bad in front of a group of people while they're worried about finding their next meal."

"Yeah, I know what you mean."

They sat in silence for a while. Ainsley perched on the edge of the seat cushions while Chris's gaze shifted between her and his phone, which lay silent on the coffee table. His thoughts instantly shifted to Gina and his stomach soured. She seemed nice enough, but never made his heart race the way Ainsley did, standing on his porch like a drenched stray searching for a home. Only problem — the two were best friends, tighter than tight. He certainly didn't want to do anything to chisel a crack in their friendship.

"Is this your mom?" Ainsley pulled a picture frame from a box at her feet and held it up.

In the photo, Chris's mom nestled beneath his dad's muscular arm, her cheek resting against his chest. They looked so happy, in love.

"Yeah. My sister took that picture five years ago during a family reunion in Hilton Head, South Carolina. Sweetest couple I ever saw. My sisters and I used to cut jokes about them dancing through the nursing home halls in their old age, still acting like a pair of newlyweds." A lump formed in his throat as a memory of his parents waltzing in the kitchen emerged. "My dad died just over a year ago of a heart attack."

"I'm sorry. Were you close?"

"Not as close as we should've been. I was too wrapped up in my career as an up-and-coming lawyer. Always said I'd call later, visit next year. Never even said good-bye." His chest ached as old emotions rushed to the surface. "I was in a meeting when I got the call. Only I never took the time to answer. Saw my sister's number and hit Ignore. I'd like to say I thought she wanted to talk about something trivial, but truth is, I didn't give it much thought. Couldn't take my mind off that next big win long enough."

He inhaled, releasing his breath slowly. "Sold my practice a couple months later, determined not to make the same mistake with my mom." He shook his head. "Dad's death has been especially hard on her. He used to take care of her, once her mind started to go. She'd probably still be living here, under his watchful eye, if he hadn't died. I'd take care of her, but honestly, I don't know how."

Ainsley's eyes moistened. "Can I pray with you?"

"I'd like that."

She rose, her bare feet shuffling across the carpet, and knelt before him, holding out her hands. "Do you mind?"

He shook his head and encased her soft, warm hands in his. Closing his eyes, he said a silent prayer of his own as her words poured over him.

Lord Jesus, barricade my heart here before I fall in love with this woman.

The dull ache in his chest told him it was too late for prayers.

Richard pulled behind Ainsley's car and studied her dark house. Her porch light, normally lit, lay dormant, and thick shadows enshrouded her front door. He checked the clock on his dash—10:30. Odd. Maybe she'd blown a fuse? He smiled. How convenient. A perfect knight-in-shining-armor opportunity. With her fear of the dark, she'd welcome him in with gratitude. Then, he'd disappear into the basement to "save the day," flip a switch, and return her long-forgotten her.

Taking her steps two at a time, he reached her door and rang the bell. Silence, save the low rustle of wind following the tails of the early winter storm. He rang again, twice this time.

Nothing. Perhaps she fell asleep? But even so, surely the doorbell would awaken her. Pivoting on his heels, he glanced at her car to the door then tensed. Only two scenarios made sense: Either she and Gina went bar hopping, which was highly unlikely, or . . .

He stared at the house next door, teeth grinding. Chris's pickup occupied his driveway, light streaming from the house's windows.

Fisting his hands, he stalked across the lawn and bounded up Mr. Langley's front steps. He punched the doorbell three times, waited, then punched it again. The door creaked open a moment later and Mr. Langley stood in the entry way, eyes wide. Ainsley stood a few feet away, face flushed, mouth ajar.

"Richard, what a —"

He pushed past him, muscles twitching, fingers digging into his palms. The image of Ainsley, hair damp and disheveled, dressed in men's clothing, seared his brain. "Oh, I get it now." Spittle flew from his mouth. "Why get married when you can play the field?"

Ainsley stepped forward. "It's not what you think."

"Really? Then tell me, what is it?"

The weasel started to speak but Richard raised his hand. "Did I ask you?" He stared at Ainsley. "Haven't you learned enough from watching your mother? I thought you were smarter than this. Guys like this care about one thing." Expletives flew from his mouth.

"Out. Now." Chris pointed to the door, eyes blazing.

Richard's chest heaved. Chris stepped forward, thick veins pulsating in his neck. They locked eyes.

"You're not worth it." He turned to Ainsley. "And you . . . His voice quavered. "Mark my words, you'll come running back to me once this guy uses you like a sheet of toilet paper, then tosses you aside to sully someone else."

He stomped outside and slammed the door behind him, then stood on her neighbor's porch gasping for air.

So that's why Ainsley broke their engagement? For a coffee boy? He snorted.

That poor, naive girl, conned by a smooth-talking playboy.

Oh, you're good, Mr. Langley. But not nearly good enough.

Marching back to his car, he chuckled as a plan took form.

May the best man win.

Chapter 38

*a*insley shifted her guitar case to free her hand and swung open the café door. She paused to inhale the rich chocolate and cinnamon aroma. "Silent Night" poured from the overhead speakers like a soothing balm. A sharp contrast to the nerve-firing, gut-churning stress she experienced at Voltex. Almost made the minimum-wage pay worth it.

If only she could find housing to fit her salary. But that was God's department. Her job was to surrender and obey. He would take care of everything else.

Chris caught her gaze and meandered over. He swung a coffee-stained dish towel between his hands.

"Sorry if I got you in trouble last night."

"It wasn't your fault. Richard's just having a tough time accepting our breakup." Not that they'd left him with a very palatable image. The door behind her clinked open. She turned and smiled at a group of women ushering inside, buried in jackets, hats, and scarves.

"Business seems to be picking up." She surveyed the handful of customers seated throughout the room. In the corner, toddlers stacked blocks while their mothers chatted in nearby chairs. A group of elderly women occupied the tables near the far wall.

Chris nodded, his blue eyes sparkling. "All thanks to Mrs. Jeffreys. Guess she's been talking us up to all her church friends quite a bit."

"That's awesome."

"Can't wait to see the turnout for our benefit concert next Saturday."

Her stomach churned. She'd back out if her conscience would allow. But she gave her word and intended to keep it.

Except when it comes to engagements, apparently.

The thought swirled through her mind, causing her already soured stomach to cramp tighter.

"You OK?" Chris touched her arm, sending a shiver through her. "You got all serious on me. You're not thinking of backing out, are you?"

She studied him, his soft eyes soothing her hyperalert nerves. "I . . . no, not — "

"Oh, Chris?" Candy's syrupy voice drifted toward them.

Ainsley turned. Across the room, Candy leaned over the counter, twirling a lock of hair. Her gaze darkened when it met Ainsley's and her coquettish smile hardened into obvious disdain.

"Glad to hear it. We'll talk details later." Chris gave her a parting grin before crossing to the counter where Candy waited with pouty lips and fluttering eyelashes.

Ainsley shook her head and slipped into the back hall to deposit her winter gear. Almost reminded her of high school, and the way the "popular" girls flaunted themselves at every passing jock. Most of the guys took them up on the offer, too, so long as there were fringe benefits.

But Chris was different.

Right? And yet, even the good guys had weaknesses. How long would it take Miss Barbie Doll to chisel through Chris's good-boy boundaries? The idea caused the muscles in her neck and shoulders to twitch.

Seriously, Ainsley, as if you care.

She blinked as reality set in. She did care, much more than she wanted to admit.

Pinching the bridge of her nose, she closed her eyes and leaned against the wall.

I am becoming just like my mother! Oh Lord, help me. Steel my heart.

Chris rounded the counter and tossed his dishrag into a nearby bus tub. "Listen, I told you last week, your shirt needs to stay buttoned no less than two from the top. And perhaps you need to go a size bigger."

She arched her back and made an O with her lips. "I'm sorry. Didn't even notice." Cocking her head, she lowered her lashes and tugged on the bottom hem of her blouse. "My shirts must've shrunk."

Chris sighed and punched open the cash register, then sifted through the bills. Business had picked up, but his bank account still hovered in the red. "I'll order you another." He grabbed a notepad from under the counter. "What size do you wear again?"

Candy ran her hands down her torso and along her hips. "Inches?"

He certainly didn't need to hear her measurements. "Never mind. I'll get you the catalog then let you pick." Assuming she'd actually select an appropriate size. What was with this girl anyway?

Footsteps clicked on the stained concrete and Ainsley emerged from the back hall wearing a pressed uniform and a radiant smile. "You know, this place really brightens my day." She planted her hands on her hips and surveyed the tables in front of her. "So, where do you want me?"

He checked his watch. With Ainsley here, perhaps he could leave for a few hours. "My mom's getting blood work done today, and I'd really like to be there. I'm hoping to keep her calm enough to prevent them from strapping her down."

"Oh, Chris, I'm so sorry." Her eyes softened. "I'd offer to come with you, but I know that'd only make things worse."

And he'd love to have her there, if only for mental support, but he couldn't leave Candy in charge. Besides, strangers would only add to his mother's agitation.

"I appreciate the offer. If you'll excuse me." He dashed into his back office and grabbed his winter gear, pulling it on as he walked. With a smile and a wave, he rushed out into the bitter cold.

Pressed against the cold brick wall, his homeless friend, Albert, huddled beside a large, cloth bag. Chris turned up his collar against the wind and squatted until their eyes met. "Missed you this morning. Worried something might have happened."

Albert shook his head, his charcoal eyes darting right to left. "Nope."

"You want to come inside, get a cup of coffee? Have a bite to eat?"

Albert leaned sideways and peered into the glass window, then settled back against the brick, rocking. "No. No. No. People rancid running falling, pouring coffee on my head. On my head. On my head. Hot, boiling, steaming. Be careful, Albert. Burn my tongue. Be careful, Albert."

"Would you like me to bring a cup to you?" He spoke slowly to give Albert time to make sense of his words.

Albert nodded and talked through chattering teeth, one sentence merging with the next. "Hot coffee, warm coffee, steaming from the cup. Be careful not to burn your tongue. It's hot, Albert, hot coffee. Steaming from the cup of plastic foam. They make cups from plastic foam. Who's they? You know who's they, but they won't find you here. How do you know? I know. You don't know. I know. They won't find you here."

Chris hurried inside and returned a moment later with a bag of pastries and a steaming latte made from vitamin D milk.

Albert's eyes brightened and his rocking slowed. "Be careful. It's hot. Don't burn your tongue. Don't burn your tongue." He brought the cup to his lips, his chattering ceasing as the steam fogged his face.

"It's OK. You can take a drink. I added a few ice cubes."

Chris waited a moment longer, asking God to watch over and protect Albert, before hurrying down the street toward his neighborhood and his ice-covered pickup.

Thirty minutes later, he pulled into the parking lot of Shady Lane Assisted Living and surveyed the row of vehicles on either side of him. Matilda's car was parked three stalls down. She was probably pretty stressed. She couldn't handle these appointments, which usually resulted in their mother being pinned down by at least three nurses, eyes flooded with fear, as the doctor searched for a vein in her heavily wrinkled arm.

Lord, keep things amiable today, for Mother's sake.

Inside, warmth swept over him from large vents in the ceiling. Men and women dressed in their finest, hair neatly combed and faces scrubbed free of food residue, dotted the lobby. Nursing staff hurried between them.

An attendant in crisp scrubs rolled a woman with thinning hair in front of the television. As soon as the doctors left everything would return to normal and these seemingly well-cared-for folks would be shoved in their rooms, forgotten between the assembly-line rounds.

Take out dentures. Check. Pull off day clothes and slap on nightwear. Check. Toss in bed then move to the next resident. Check. At least some of the staff took their time, offering a kind word or hand squeeze between rotations. Truth be told, Heather was the only one he had a problem with, but her biting words sliced deep enough to undo every dash of compassion the rest of the staff sprinkled. Unfortunately, although her words left countless wounded in her wake, nothing she did proved illegal or worthy of dismissal. But one of these days her short temper would get the best of her and seal her fate.

Sadly, probably at the expense of yet another resident, maybe even his mother.

Rounding the corner, his stomach did a 360 at the sight of Matilda standing outside their mother's doorway, rubbing the back of her neck. As he approached, his mother's agitated voice, seeping through the thin walls, ignited a fight-or-flight response.

"They kick you out?"

She shook her head. "They're trying to get her ready."

"Why? The doctor can't give shots if she stays in her night-gown?" He threw open the door, a knife stabbing into his chest as he beheld his mother trembling in the center of the room, nurses on either side holding her arms.

"Chris! Who are these people? Tell them to leave. Make them leave me alone! Why won't they just leave me alone?"

He looked from one face to the next before locking eyes with Heather. "I'll take care of this."

"But Mr. Langley, we can't let you —"

"Out."

She stared at him with wide eyes. His mother clutched her hair, torso caved inward, and inched backward until she ran into the wall.

Chris's muscles quivered. He pointed to the door. "Now!"

The nurses scurried out and Matilda hurried in, her face blanched. "Chris, you can't order the nursing staff around like that. They're only trying to do their job."

"Are they?" A series of fresh bruises splotched his mother's arms. "What do you call this?" Breathing deep in an effort to calm himself, he turned to his mother and softened his voice to a near whisper. "Everything's fine, Mom. You're OK. Everything's OK. Let me help you." He checked the clock and searched his mind for soothing words, but nothing came. The doctor would be here in less than fifteen minutes with a needle.

Lord, I could use some help here.

Stepping closer, he started to sing softly, as his mother used to sing to him. "Jesus loves you, this I know, for the Bible tells me so. May His love ease your fears, may He keep you through the years." As he sang, her quivering eased until it stopped completely. Placing an arm across her shoulder, he pulled her close and continued singing. She nestled against him and buried her face into his chest.

"Where's your father, Chris? I need your father. Please, tell him to come get me. Why won't he take me home?"

"Sh. Everything's fine." He rubbed her back, tears stinging his eyes.

Three hours later, shot administered and his mother sufficiently calmed, he and Matilda stood outside the main entrance, flecks of snow swirling around them.

Chris faced Matilda head on. "Now do you see why I want her moved? Why she can't stay here?"

"And you think another home will do a better job? She's agitated, paranoid, and combative. The staff is doing the best that they can."

"It's not good enough. Did you see those bruises on her arm? They're too rough with her."

"She could have gotten those any number of ways. She bruises easily, you know that."

"So they should be extra gentle with her."

Matilda shook her head. "We've had this conversation before, and frankly, I don't have the energy to rehash it now. Honestly, I believe they're doing the best they can, all things considered."

"Fat lot of good it does them. From where I sit, their 'best' only made her more agitated. I calmed her down in less than five minutes."

"That's because she recognized you. This time."

"Dad would never have stood for this, you know that."

"Really? How do you know what Dad would or wouldn't have done? From what I remember, you weren't around much."

Chapter 39

*A*insley hugged her knees and rested her chin upon them. Her last paycheck from Voltex lay on the coffee table, promising one more month of rent. When Chris hired her, they never discussed salary, but she doubted making lattes, tips included, would cut it. But at least she hadn't had to dip into her savings yet.

She smiled as an image of Mrs. Jeffreys's rosy face came to mind and the five- to ten-dollar bills she dropped in the tip jar. Not that Ainsley expected charity, but the generosity behind the gesture touched her deeply.

But even that well would run dry eventually, which meant she needed to find another job soon.

And spend less time with Chris.

Oy! What silly schoolgirl reasoning, and yet, she suspected her feelings for her him were more than a passing crush. When he looked into her eyes, it felt like he could see in the depths of the soul — even more than that, like somehow their hearts longed to be united. It was an emotion she'd never felt before, and she didn't quite know how to deal with it. Her first instinct was to quit her job and run, but her budget prevented it.

Her doorbell rang. Glancing at the clock, she smoothed her hair and crossed the living room, mentally sifting between three possible visitors: her mom, Chris, or Richard.

More than likely, Richard, coming with more psycho-babble on why their breakup was caused by her unresolved issues. Uh-huh. *She* was the one with issues. Right.

"Oh!" Wide-eyed, she stared at Richard's mother.

Her gaze swept Ainsley's frame and her face puckered. "You look well."

"Why thank you." *I think.* "Uh . . . would you like to come in?" She stepped aside to allow Mrs. Hollis in.

"I stopped by the other day with soup and crackers, but you were out."

Uh, OK . . .Thank you." Did Richard put her up to this? She almost laughed. *"Here's some soup. Do you like it? Enough to go through with the wedding?"* "What can I do for you, Mrs. Hollis?"

"Richard said you were ill, so I—"

"He what?"

"He said you were ill. You were ill, weren't you?"

"Not in the last year, no." And to think, Richard accused her of being irrational. Seriously, what was this about?

"Then tell me, Ainsley," she crossed her arms, "why you neglected to come to your formal engagement dinner?"

Ainsley blinked. "Why? Surely he told you . . . She let out a whoosh of air. "I'm sorry you had to hear this from me, but your son and I are no longer engaged."

"I don't understand."

Ainsley guided her to the couch, explaining, as gently as she could, what had happened.

"But why would Richard . . . ?" Her face hardened. She rose, clutching her purse to her chest. "Apparently my son and I need to talk. Have a good day."

Ainsley followed her to the door, unable to find an appropriate parting phrase. Somehow, "Great to see you," didn't seem right.

Chris cruised through the aisles of Big Savings in search of quality toys at bulk prices. "Jingle Bells" played from overhead speakers, adding a bounce to his step. He paused in front of a Matchbox Car display, multiplying the price times four then adding the total to the toys already in his cart. Logically, the kids at the shelter needed more practical gifts like gloves, socks, and underwear, but he couldn't bring himself to buy those things. Besides, logic and Christmas didn't belong in the same sentence, and every child deserved something fun in their stockings.

Did those kids even have stockings? Sighing, he pulled out his wallet and sifted through the cash tucked inside. A long list of upcoming expenses ran through his mind. At least business at the café appeared to be picking up.

Give and you will be given, with good measure, right? *Lord, I'm taking You on Your word here, because I would love to see each one of those little faces light up when I hand them a stocking full of goodies. And candy.*

Richard massaged his temples, his mother's sharp voice grating in his ears. "I didn't feel it worth mentioning." He moved to the couch and dropped into it.

His mother hovered in the middle of the room, back rod straight, clutching her purse. "Not worth mentioning? Ainsley tells you it's over, and you don't think it's worth mentioning? You'd rather I learn of this after a formal announcement is made to all of your father's colleagues?"

"You know her history, Mother. Surely you expected a moment's hesitation to arise."

"A moment's hesitation doesn't last for weeks, son."

"It's difficult to put a timetable on these sorts of things, but I know her. She'll come around."

"I don't think so. She's made up her mind. I could tell. We need to tell your father."

Richard stiffened. "There's no need for that. Not yet. Give her time. She just lost her job — "

"Whatever for?" Her lips pressed together. "I'm concerned, Richard. If Ainsley is as irresponsible as she appears, then I'd rather you find someone else to carry on the Hollis family name."

"She's not unstable, just confused. Surely you felt as much when Father asked you to marry him?"

She perched on the edge of a recliner, hands cupped over her knees, and angled her head. A slight smile emerged. "Yes, I do. I wanted the exciting romance I saw all my friends experience, but then I grew up and realized marriage is much more than physical attraction or fluttering hearts. It's a formal agreement to work together, as a team. The question I have for you is, do you really believe Ainsley to be your life partner?"

"I do. And I am certain everything will right itself by the end of the month."

"Perhaps. But in case you're wrong and her concerns run deeper, I think it's best if we hold off on making any more arrangements. Although I do hope it'll be resolved before August."

In order to meet the conditions of the trust, which affected more than his inheritance. "It will be; I assure you."

He showed his mother out then paced the living room. If only his grandfather were alive today, he'd tell him how ludicrous those conditions were. To think that Richard's marriage, or lack thereof, could affect his family's standing, potentially even cost his father his practice. Likely his grandfather received great satisfaction knowing his son, whom he deemed a colossal failure, would in turn raise another failure, thus sealing his fate.

As if the old coot had room to talk, dying alone on a hospital bed with only a handful of people by his side, most of whom were paid to be there. Even then, with tubes stuck up his nose and lungs rasping for breath, he'd used every last opportunity to level both Richard and his father — to show them once again how worthless he thought they were.

"I imagine the bulk of my estate will be going to the Audubon Society, but I welcome your attempts to prove me wrong."

And now Ainsley threatened to make good on Grandfather Hollis's predictions. Richard's jaw clenched, every muscle in his body tightening, as an image of Mr. Langley, her snake-charming neighbor, came to mind.

Richard refused to admit defeat yet. He just needed to determine a logical course of action. Thinking, he tapped on his chin. He smiled as a plan took form — one guaranteed to send his little princess running back to his arms.

He crossed the room, pulled open a filing cabinet, and sifted through old cases, mentally reviewing each one. Most were useless — a college professor who suffered a nervous breakdown, a middle-aged housewife looking for a doting ear. Two of them, however, offered potential. Holding his thumb as a place marker, he sat behind his office chair and turned on his desktop. Fifteen minutes later, refreshed by a large file of therapy notes, he grabbed the phone and dialed Lyle Wheeler's number.

A woman answered. "Wheelers' residence. May I help you?"

He leaned back in his chair. "Good morning, Mrs. Wheeler. May I speak with your husband, please?"

"Who's calling?"

He cleared his throat to suppress a chuckle. "Dr. Hollis from Hollis Psychiatrics."

Silence hung between them, and Richard's smile widened as an image of Lyle's wife, forehead creased in confusion, came to mind.

"In regard to?"

He twirled a pen in his fingers. "He will know, I am sure."

"Hold on." The phone clanked against something hard, followed by the sound of muffled voices, what appeared to be footsteps, then a door closing.

A moment later, Mr. Lyle came on. "Mr. Hollis, I'm surprised you're calling me at home. You may remember, my wife had no knowledge of our visits, or . . . the situation."

"I remember. And how have things been, with your wife I mean?"

"Fine." His voice sharpened. "As I mentioned in my last appointment, now that the past is behind me, I'm determined to do everything I can to make our marriage work. Thanks to you, of course, and your impulse-control-behavior-modification approach."

"Then I'm sure you're unwilling to allow anything from the past resurface that might create unnecessary marital tension?"

"Are you asking if I continue to engage in risky behavior? Absolutely not. And if there's nothing else, I really need to — "

"I've been going through my notes from our therapy sessions, and it occurred to me how damaging it would be if anyone ever got ahold of them."

He waited for his words to take hold.

"What are you saying?" Mr. Lyle's voice dipped to a coarse whisper.

"It appears, Mr. Wheeler, you and I can be of help to one another. Are you still working for Mega-tech Security?"

"Yes."

"Excellent. Then you will have no problem locating the information I need." He draped his ankle over his knee, explaining, in detail, what Mr. Wheeler needed to do in order to secure silence.

"You can't do that. As my psychiatrist, you're legally bound to maintain confidentiality."

"As your former psychiatrist, you mean? And of course you are right, but could I help it if information leaked out? You know as well as I the security risks with using online databases. Unfortunately, I'm afraid I saved files to an insecure server."

Mr. Wheeler cursed. "If I do this, you'll permanently delete my files?"

Richard rubbed his lips with his index finger. Now why would he do that, when Mr. Wheeler proved so helpful? "Of course."

Chapter 40

T hanks for coming." Aunt Shelby walked Ainsley to the door. "So sorry your mother couldn't make it. Do tell her we missed her."

When I talk to her next, you mean? Which, considering how much money Stephen shoveled her way, wouldn't be for quite a while. Nope, now that Ainsley's mom found a solution to her cash-flow problem, she'd have no reason to call her only daughter.

Ainsley said good-bye to a few more relatives then scuffed down the walk to her car. She slipped behind the driver's wheel, tears stinging her eyes. Why had she expected this Christmas to be any different? As if her mom would suddenly wake up and realize how incredibly selfish she was . . . as if she'd suddenly care. Why did Ainsley continue sticking her heart out only to be trampled?

A passage from her morning Bible reading resurfaced. *"If you love those who love you, what reward will you get?"*

The more accurate question was: If you love those who couldn't care less about you, what reward did you get? A smashed heart filled with bitter memories. The same emotions she saw shadowed in so many eyes down at the shelter. How many of those women experienced similar rejection and worse? Probably a lot, otherwise they wouldn't be there. Family didn't let family sleep on the streets.

Easing out of the neighborhood, down Barry Road, and onto I-29 South, she flicked through radio stations until praise music emanated from her speakers. Smiling, she thought of Kiara and Janalyn, two young girls from the shelter, snuggled on either side of her, waiting to hear a story. And tonight, their eyes would twinkle especially bright when they saw what she brought. OK, so maybe her homemade Barbie doll food items weren't toys and games quality, but they worked.

By the time she pulled into the North Kansas City Ray of Hope parking lot, excitement swallowed the bitterness poisoning her heart. Among all the materialistic tinsel, nothing more clearly illustrated the Christmas message like spending the evening among the homeless. Quite a fitting scenario, actually, considering the location of Christ's birth.

Her stomach fluttered when she noticed Chris's pickup parked beside the chain-link fence. She paused to check her appearance in the mirror, smoothing a few stray curls and adding a bit of gloss to her lips.

The gravel crunched beneath her thick-soled boots as she approached the building. A cold wind moaned through the adjacent buildings. When she swung open the heavy metal shelter door, singing poured from the hall, punctuated by rhythmic clapping. The scent of chocolate and roasted ham filled the air.

Good. Someone brought dinner then. She picked up her pace, hurrying down the hall and into the cafeteria. She stood in the archway, the air caught in her throat, and stared at Chris. He knelt in the center of the room, clutching a large, white trash bag. Dirty-faced children surrounded him, bouncing on socked feet, arms waving at their sides like hummingbirds. He glanced up as she approached and held her gaze, causing her heart to flip.

She set her package of homemade toys beside her and watched, laughing, as Chris distributed stuffed animals, crayons, and coloring books to the children huddled around him. When finished, he folded the plastic sack into a square and turned to Ainsley.

"How come you're not with your family?"

"I went earlier. But I had to come here, to distribute a few things." She held up her small package, heat pricking her cheeks.

Chris smiled. "Yeah? What'd you bring?"

"Nothing as elaborate as all this." She hugged a few of the giggling children bouncing all around her. Their mothers sat a few feet away, smiling. Some laughing. Two fighting tears — happy ones.

"I'm sure it's splendid. What do you say, kiddos? Wanna see what Auntie Ainsley brought for you?"

Cheers erupted, eliciting more laughter. Kiara, a toddler with braided hair, crawled into Ainsley's lap and looked up with big, brown eyes. "Did you bring sumsing for me, Nantie Nainsy?"

Ainsley giggled and gave her a squeeze. "Did I ever!" She pulled the clay food wrapped in tissue paper from her sack, and handed them out. Footsteps approached. She glanced up and froze. *William!* He walked toward her in a sweatshirt, most likely provided by Rose, that looked at least three sizes too big. A hole marked the toe of his right shoe, but his face was clean and his hair was brushed. Behind him, his mother lingered in the doorway, hugging her torso. Rose stood beside her and draped an arm over the woman's shoulders.

Tears lodged in Ainsley's throat as she looked from the mother to her timid son. Then, smiling at the boy, she picked up a nerf football Chris had brought and tossed it in the air. "Hmm . . . Something tells me this football has your name on it. What do you say, Chris?"

"Absolutely." He grinned. "Course, I hope you'll let me toss it around a bit." He winked at Rose. "What do ya say? How about us fellas play some football?"

William's head jerked up. Looking from Chris to his mom, it was clear he was doing his best to hide a ginormous smile.

Rose stepped forward, her face stern. "Uh-uh. Not in here you don't." She jerked her thumb toward the back hallway. "Take it outside, boys. And no tackle. You hear me, right?"

A handful of boys sprang to their feet. "Right!"

Laughing, Chris spun the football on his finger and approached William. "You're my defender. Can you handle that?"

Ainsley's heart felt like it would explode as she watched the group leave. *Holy Father, You are so faithful. So incredibly faithful.*

Sweat sticking his shirt to him despite the icy chill, Chris wiped his brow with his sleeve. Heaving for air, he planted his hands on his knees. "I've been had! A bunch of ball-throwing beasts, that's what you are." He smiled and nudged William with his elbow. "What do ya say we go back inside, see if Rose won't make us some hot chocolate?"

Beaming faces nodded and the children skipped to the door and clanked it open. Their laughing voices echoed through the hall.

Ten minutes later, steaming mug in hand, Chris leaned against the doorframe separating the hall from the cafeteria. He watched Ainsley read stories to a group of girls. She sat cross-legged on the linoleum, back rested against the wall, nearly buried by affection-starved children. She glanced up and met Chris's gaze, pink splashing her high cheekbones, before turning her attention back to the book in front of her.

"Real angel on earth, isn't she?"

He turned to see Rose standing behind him, eyes glistening with unshed tears.

"Most folks come here out of obligation." She frowned. "During the weeks before Thanksgiving and Christmas, do-gooders swamp the place, bringing food and lofty sermons. From a distance, mind you. Come mealtime, they all huddle around that back table over there." She pointed toward an empty table near the far wall. "Guess they're afraid poverty's contagious. Or maybe they think these ladies here got some sort of disease."

She shook her head. "Then there's Ainsley. She gets in the thick of it, sitting plop-dab on the floor, surrounded by dirty children. Only you know what? I bet she don't see the dirt. No sir, because she's too busy looking into their hearts."

A voice called for Rose from down the hall and she excused herself with a nod. Although Chris could have watched Ainsley and the children all night, the almost frantic milling in and out of the kitchen beckoned his assistance. But not until he said a silent prayer asking God to bless her for her continual acts of kindness. Hopefully with a new, higher-paying job.

His stomach dropped before the prayer concluded. He'd grown accustomed to seeing her at the café each morning. She brought a vitality to the place, like a ray of sunshine on a dreary day. But she deserved more than he could afford to pay her.

Although, if God blessed the shop, he could increase her wages.

Cheered by the thought, he rounded the corner and surveyed the kitchen. Dirty pans lined the counters as women poured leftovers into large ziplock bags. Two other women manned the large industrial-sized sink while a third leaned against the stove, cell phone pressed to her ear.

When two women entered heaving a seven-quart slow cooker between them, Chris ran to their side and took it off their hands. At first, it seemed as if the women wouldn't release it.

"That's good juice in there." A brunette he didn't recognize locked eyes with him. "Don't throw it away. We can use that for our meal tomorrow."

His chest tightened as the women around him continued to scrape each drop and crumb into bags. So many needs. So much heartache. What could he, but one man, do, other than offer a meal or buy an occasional Christmas gift?

As if in answer, the chorus of his favorite song filled his head. It reminded him God didn't expect him to save the world, but instead, to obey with full surrender. Full surrender in pursuit of a glorious God.

Thirty minutes later he and Ainsley stood in an empty and clean cafeteria, the residents ushered upstairs to spend a long-sought night in a heated room with a roof over their heads.

Ainsley tucked a curl behind her ear. "I'm not sure which breaks my heart more, to see familiar faces or new ones."

"What do you mean?"

"I guess I hope these ladies hit a temporary patch of bad luck, but some of them have been here since you and I started serving, and likely long before then. And yet, when I see new faces, I'm reminded of how many more are out on the streets right now, either unable to make it here or unable to get in once the beds are full. No one should sleep on the streets on Christmas."

They stood in silence for a moment, staring down the dim hall leading to the stairwell.

"And on a lighter note . . . He offered what he hoped to be a soothing smile. "You wanna get some coffee, or are you coffee'd out after slaving over an espresso machine all week?"

"Can a woman ever have too much coffee?" But then her brow furrowed as if sifting through a mental debate.

"You know Gina and I aren't dating. Not because I ditched her or anything. I mean . . . OK, that sounded stupid. "We both decided things wouldn't work out."

Ainsley smiled. "I know. She told me. And coffee sounds great."

As agreed, Ainsley parked in a garage off Broadway and waited for Chris to pull his truck beside her. He met her at her door as she stepped out.

"You going to be warm enough?"

She nodded. "Especially when I get a nice, hot peppermint latte in my stomach."

"Let's get you to Starbucks then." He looped his arm through hers, causing her heart to jump and face to flush. Conflicting emotions battled within as she thought of Richard and their canceled engagement. *Was it wrong to be out with another man so soon after their breakup? Was this a rebound thing? No.* The quickening of her pulse every time Chris glanced her way told her otherwise.

"Joy to the World" poured from hidden speakers tucked within the storefront awnings as they strolled down the sidewalk toward the bookstore. Thousands of twinkling lights glimmered on every store front, building, and tree. It gave the shopping center a fanciful feel — like they'd stepped into a midcentury fairy tale.

A gust of hot air met them when they entered the bookstore. Ainsley paused beneath the heating vents to savor the rich aroma of fresh-brewed coffee mixed with the scent of new books. Her skin, numbed from their walk, tingled as warmth spread through her toes and fingers. She peeled off her gloves and coat then allowed Chris to lead her through the aisles and toward an escalator leading to the second floor.

Halfway up, she turned to face him. "So, was it your love for coffee that motivated you to buy the café?"

"Honestly?" His smile evaporated and his eyes searched hers.

"Honestly."

When they reached the second floor, he guided her past decorative display tables and leather recliners filled with bookstore patrons. His hand rested on the small of her back, sending a jolt of electricity up her spine.

They filed in line behind the counter then slowly inched forward.

His smile returned. "In answer to your question, it's more like a calling, like an urban mission of sorts. A mission and a ministry. After my dad died . . ." He paused, his expression sobering. "I never had the chance to say good-bye."

"I remember you telling me that. Did he die suddenly?"

"Yes and no. He'd been complaining of chest pains for some time, but honestly, I attributed it to heartburn. When he went to the ER, I figured they'd hand him some aspirin and send him home. Got a call the next morning from my sister. She said he had 85 percent blockage and needed a bypass." He shook his head. "At that point, most sons would've hopped a plane, but I was in the middle of a big case and told myself those kinds of surgeries were routine. Figured my dad was too young for anything serious. He died the next afternoon."

Silence hung between them, but Ainsley made no effort to fill it.

"So anyway, on the tails of that, and dealing with how to care for my mom, I realized I needed to make a change — to find a way to free up my time. One night, after spending hours tossing and turning, I drifted into a restless sleep filled with the weirdest dreams." He shook his head. "In my dream, I worked at a coffee shop similar to Java Bean, only a bit different." He chuckled. "It was more like a soup kitchen slash café, filled with contrasts — women in Sunday dresses served by women with missing teeth, giggling children running around between them. I'm not sure what God's plan is for me or the café, but I'm moving forward, trusting," he sighed, "hoping He'll work out the details."

Ainsley studied him, unsure of what to say.

A few moments later, steaming cups in hand, they meandered toward a long window lining the far wall. Shoppers filled the sidewalk below, brightly colored bags in hand. A horse drawn carriage covered in twinkling lights, a couple cuddling in its seat, pulled to a stop behind a red Camry.

Chris stopped. "Wanna go for a ride?"

She looked at him, her breath catching when his eyes locked on hers. "That'd be lovely."

Chapter 41

*R*ichard sat in a leather loveseat, staring at the revolving doors in front of him. The parting comments Mr. Wheeler made during their phone call concerned him, indicating perhaps he might not show—that perhaps Richard's threats of disclosure weren't enough to override the man's ridiculous value system.

A cab pulled to the curb, and Richard leaned forward, hands tightly twined. He relaxed, settling back into his seat, when Mr. Wheeler stepped out clutching a briefcase. The man examined the sidewalk on either side of him, dashed inside, then stood in the center of the hotel lobby. Upon seeing Richard, he crossed the marbled floor and sat in a vacant chair, holding his briefcase like a shield.

Richard chuckled. "Relax. You act like I'm asking you to commit high treason."

Fire filled Mr. Wheeler's eyes. "No, just a bit of Internet hacking, dredging up someone else's baggage."

"Does that mean your search proved successful?"

Mr. Wheeler set his briefcase on a glass-topped coffee table in front of him. "Not highly. I did a search on the address you gave me. The house belongs to a Mrs. Langley, the man's mother."

"I'm not interested in a genealogical account, Mr. Wheeler, nor do I care what steps you took to uncover your information."

The man's eyes darkened but he nodded. "After deducing the man's last name, I searched for records pertaining to him. The results were extensive. He previously practiced business law in Southern California."

"Any shady clients or associations?"

"To the contrary. It appears he took numerous pro bono cases for small, struggling businesses, and I found a fair amount of ministry connections."

Richard frowned. "This is not helpful, Mr. Wheeler." He knew that weasel Langley had secrets. The man acted much too ... cheerful, even when there was no reason for such. Clearly he was hiding something. Either a personality disorder or perhaps something shameful from his past. But having been a lawyer, the man was probably quite adept at keeping his record clean. On the surface. "Apparently you are not as committed to your marriage as I thought." He started to rise.

"Wait. I did find something."

Richard sat again as Mr. Wheeler snapped open his briefcase and sifted through various papers. His hand trembled when he pulled out a stapled stack, a Los Angeles County Circuit Court seal stamped across the top. He handed it to Richard then leaned forward, hands clasped.

Richard studied the documents page by page, his smile growing with each one. "A sexual harassment suit? Just as I suspected." He dropped the file on the coffee table. "You did read the court transcripts?"

Mr. Wheeler nodded.

"And?"

"The charges appear to be trumped. From what I could tell, a disgruntled employee sued her boss to get rich, although the jury ruled in her favor."

"Really?"

Mr. Wheeler nodded. "According to a juror interviewed by the local papers, they didn't believe Mr. Langley harassed the plaintiff. However, although they agreed she deserved to lose her job, they didn't like the way he fired her. Or more accurately, they disapproved of many of the company's policies. I imagine their ruling had more to do with the economic downturn occurring during that time than the merits of the woman's case."

"And yet, the jurors ruled in her favor. Excellent. Anything else?"

"Maybe." Mr. Wheeler sifted through his briefcase again, producing low-quality images. "I found these on a college alumni website." He handed them over. "They appear old and based on the captions — I couldn't find anything more than that — they are from a past spring break trip. Inconsequential, I'm sure."

Richard studied the images of three guys dressed in Bermudas and ball caps, each holding a beer. All except for Mr. Langley, who raised what resembled a bottle of Vodka to his mouth. The men looked to be in their early twenties. They were at the beach, posing with very curvy girls dressed in string bikinis. Though the girls were well-endowed, they looked young, maybe underage. Richard couldn't be sure.

He looked at Mr. Wheeler. "Who are these girls?"

The man, still scowling, shrugged, and Richard didn't push it. It didn't matter. The images, along with the man's legal issues, were condemning enough. He glanced at the photo again, smiling. Yes, these were very condemning indeed, especially considering Ainsley's issues with her father.

Mr. Langley, the neighbor with the choirboy image stood sandwiched between two blondes, posing quite provocatively. A brunette stood behind him, her arms draped around his chest. Making a kissing face at the camera, she held a beer in one hand and a bikini top in another.

He set the photo on the table in front of him. "This confirms my suspicions, Mr. Wheeler." Clearly, Mr. Langley was after one thing, and he'd set his lustful sights on poor, naive Ainsley. He needed to make sure the man's efforts proved unsuccessful, and now he had the means to do just that.

Standing, he grabbed the photo and court papers. "Combined with the court documents you found, this image is quite telling. Quite telling indeed."

Chris straightened the already tidy café. Funny how anxious a simple concert made him, although something told him it was more than that. If all went according to plan, tonight had the capacity to launch his dreams. And if it flopped? Well, then he'd have to try again at a later date.

But would Ainsley be so willing to join him the next time?

"How many people are you expecting tonight?" Candy leaned over the counter, hair twirling as usual.

"Don't know. Twenty? Ten? Sixty-five?"

Her eyes widened. "How can I handle all those people by myself? Cuz Ainsley's singing with you, right? Meaning, I'll have to take all the orders single-handedly?"

Chris raked his fingers through his hair. Something he hadn't thought about — how to deal with the influx of people. He scanned the handful of customers seated throughout the café. "Can you handle it here for a minute?"

Candy shrugged. "Yeah, whatever."

"Great. I'll be back in a few. An hour tops." Running outside, he cinched up his jacket and raced home. Twenty minutes later, he pulled into the gravel parking lot of North Kansas City Ray of Hope, smiling. The midafternoon sun glistened on freshly fallen snow and tiny icicles sparkled in the chain-link fence. He practically bounced across the parking lot, stomped his snow-packed shoes on the concrete stoop, then threw open the door.

Rose met him in the hallway. "Everything all right? Aren't you supposed to be leading a concert?"

He glanced past her into the dark cafeteria then toward the long stairwell to their left before returning her gaze. "Yep, but I'm a bit shorthanded."

She shook her head. "It's just me and about half a dozen residents today."

"Perfect. Any of them need a job?"

"I know what you're up to, boy." She clapped her hands and laughed. "Yes sir. And do I have the perfect workers for you. You wait a moment while — " She frowned and snapped her fingers. "Blast it all. She's got two young 'uns, and I don't think she'd feel safe leaving them here with me. Not yet. Poor girl's as timid as a beat-down horse."

"Then tell her to bring them."

"For real? Well, all right then!" She turned on her heels and hiked up the stairs, pulling on the railing for support, laughing and shaking her head the whole way.

She returned less than five minutes later with two women and three kids — William and Wanda among them. The other two children were strapped in strollers.

Chris offered his biggest smile. "Looks like I've got a winning crew." He grabbed William in a headlock and playfully rubbed his fist in the kid's hair.

Ainsley added a dash of mousse to her damp locks, scrunched the curls, then surveyed her reflection in the mirror. Her stomach fluttered, making her laugh. Twenty-nine years old, acting like that awkward waif of a seventh-grader about to bomb the junior high talent show. It was a café performance for goodness' sake, not Madison Square Garden.

Her doorbell chimed. After a quick glance at her nightstand, she spun around and darted down the hall. She opened the door to find Gina standing on the other side with a cheek-bunching grin and a camera dangling from her neck.

Ainsley stepped back, shaking her head. "Oh no, you don't. Absolutely no pictures. You may as well leave that thing behind."

Gina breezed past her. "But then how would I Facebook tag you? You know I created a page for this event, don't you?"

Ainsley's already somersaulting stomach flip-flopped as heat flooded her face. "You didn't."

"Of course I did. It's not every day my best friend gives a concert performance, you know. Besides, it's for an excellent cause. Imagine how many meals you guys can provide with this thing."

Gina had a good point. Images of dirty, smiling faces from the shelter surfaced, adding perspective to her trivial concerns. While Ainsley worried about flubbing it in front of a crowd, the women feared spending yet another night on the street.

She threw her hands up. "OK. Fine. You're right. Wanna help me choose an outfit? If I'm going to fall on my face, I'd like to at least look good doing it."

"Absolutely!"

When Ainsley entered the jam-packed café twenty minutes later, her courage waned. Lingering in the doorway, she sucked in three successive breaths and willed her stomach to uncoil with each exhale. It didn't work.

Gina looked at her. "You all right? Not gonna hyperventilate, are you? Because that could get messy. I never learned CPR."

"So funny, and so not helpful. Besides, it's too late to ditch now." Although the idea had crossed her mind.

Chris approached. "Good morning. Hey, we've got the paparazzi! Awesome. I'll tell Stan from the *Star* you'll be handling the pictures."

Ainsley swallowed, her hands growing clammy. "Reporters from the *Kansas City Star* are here?"

Chris's eyes gleamed. "Crazy, huh? I guess they caught wind of this event somehow. They said it was a perfect community piece — local businesses helping out the underprivileged. And what a great way to generate community awareness for the shelter." He draped his arm across William's shoulder who now stood by his side. "And here's our drummer."

William's gaze fell to the floor.

"Really?" Ainsley smiled, resisting the urge to wrap the boy in a hug. "We're really going to rock the house then."

William's head snapped up, a toothy grin exploding across his face. "Yes, ma'am!"

"Well, ladies." Chris gave a parting nod. "Guess we better find some percussion instruments for our friend here." The two wandered off through the crowd toward the back hallway, likely in search of an empty coffee can and a pair of wooden spoons. Unless Chris had drums stashed somewhere.

Gina looped her arm through Ainsley's and gave a squeeze. "See, this is way bigger than you. Think you can die to yourself for a few hours to give that kid the time of his life — a chance to hold his head high?"

Ainsley nodded. "Absolutely."

Ten minutes later, Chris quieted the room by clinking a spoon against a ceramic mug. "Sorry, folks, but our sound system's on the blink today." The audience laughed. Chris looked around then locked eyes with Ainsley. He motioned her forward.

A wave of nausea swept through her, threatening hiccups. Walking on wobbly, adrenaline-pricked legs, she joined William and Chris in front of the crowd. Three stools stood behind them.

Chris pulled a tall accent table from the wall and positioned it in front of one the stools. He plopped an overturned coffee can on top of it. "Thanks for coming out. What better way to spend a Saturday then praising God and helping His children?"

Amens echoed throughout the room and a whistle split the air. Ainsley glanced at Chris, who spoke words of encouragement through his steady gaze.

Once the crowd quieted, he introduced the rest of his band then gave William a nod.

William's cheeks colored as he perched behind the coffee can. Using two wooden spoons, he tapped on the metal surface, softly at first, but gaining strength as he continued.

Chris shot Ainsley a wink and a nod, picked up his guitar, and started to strum.

Ainsley closed her eyes as the melody swept over her.

Just You and me, God. Just You and me.

Chris's voice plunged her heart into the song until the words poured from her. By the second verse, a peace so deep it permeated every part of her took hold.

When all else fails, I run to You, for You alone shield me from the storm.

When the icy current crashes through, Your love alone keeps me warm.

I surrender now to the lover of my soul.

Take my heart and make me whole

I run to You, to Your arms of grace

I run to You, the lifter of my face
Be near me now
Hear me now
Cleanse me now
Remove my sin-ravaged heart and make me whole.

William slowed the beat, and they ended with a melodious hum.

They played three more songs, two crowd-stirring fast, and one tear-jerking reflective. Halfway through the third chorus, Ainsley opened her eyes to see families gathered close, mothers holding their children, chins rested on tiny heads, swaying to the music.

Chapter 42

Chris stuffed a wad of cash into the bank bag, zipped it closed, then shut the register. Ainsley peered at him from the other side of the counter. She glanced around for Gina, anxious to share this moment with her, but her friend appeared to be engaged in conversation.

Ainsley faced Chris with anticipation. "Well?"

"Well . . . Laughter filled his eyes. "Take a guess."

"Eight hundred?"

He shook his head.

"Nine?"

"Nope."

"A thousand?"

William's chestnut eyes grew rounder with each raise.

Chris reached into his back pocket, pulled out a 3-by-5 index card, and recited the verse printed on it. "Now to him who is able to do exceedingly more than all we ask or imagine, according to his power that is at work in us, to him be the glory in the church and in Christ Jesus throughout all generations, forever and ever. Amen!" (Ephesians 3:20–21; paraphrase). Dropping the card, he drummed his fingers on the counter. "And the grand total is . . . $1,575.63."

The girls squealed, and Ainsley gave William a high five. "Amen is right!"

Wanda threw her head back and laughed. "Amen, amen, amen!" She enveloped her son in a sideways hug.

"Much more than William and I could imagine, that's for sure. Got food in our bellies and cash in our pockets." She teared up. "Thank you for letting us work. Most folks don't give me the time of day."

Chris smiled. "I could use you Monday too. If you're available."

"Available? Honey, I got all the time in the world." White teeth flashed before fading beneath a frown. "So long as the bus comes out this way." She looked at her son then lifted her chin. "But don't you worry none. I'll make it work."

Chris's smile grew. He pulled a business card from his back pocket and handed it to her. "And if you can't, give me a jingle. I'd be more than happy to pick you up."

William nestled in the crook of his mother's arm, peaceful smiles on both of their faces.

Ainsley could've soaked in the moment forever. God had showered them all with so many blessings, well beyond what she could've hoped for. And her first official concert. The thought still made her giddy.

As if sensing her joy, Chris smiled and reached for her hand, twining his pinky with hers. "I better get you all back to the shelter." He glanced around at the remaining customers, who seemed in no hurry to leave. "Would you mind locking up for me?"

"Not at all."

He tossed her the keys, rounded the counter, and pulled a paper sack from the shelf, handing it to William. "Would you like to pick out a few pastries before we go?"

The boy's eyes widened and his tongue flicked across his bottom lip. He looked at his grinning mother. She nodded.

While he scoured the pastry shelf, Chris turned to Ainsley, the intensity in his eyes causing her pulse to quicken. "I'll be back in a few, if you'd like to hit a movie or something."

She smiled. "I'd love to."

Ainsley watched Chris leave, her heart swelling from the day and all God had done. It felt so good to sing again. She couldn't quite explain the feeling, except that it was as if God Himself had reached down to her, was smiling over her.

A verse swept through her mind, threatening sweet, joyful tears. "For the Lord your God is with you. . . . He will rejoice over you with joyful songs" (Zephaniah 3:17; paraphrase).

Oh, how she longed for that to be true! To hear God say, "Well done, good and faithful servant!" (Matthew 25:23 NIV)." She wasn't sure what the future held, or even what God was calling her to. But one thing she knew for certain: she planned to spend the rest of her life discovering what that was.

Breathing deep, she turned to see Gina approaching with an older gentleman, her lips twitching toward a smile.

The man appeared to be in his midthirties. His hair in a loose ponytail, and his face clean-shaven except for a strip of hair running from his bottom lip to just below his chin. He wore a T-shirt and ripped jeans and held a coffee mug in his hand.

Gina wasted no time with small talk. "Remember that friend of a friend I told you about?"

Ainsley tilted her head, sifting through past conversations.

"My friend, meet Matt Wharton from New Life Records."

Her stomach bottomed out as her memory kicked in, and for a moment, she felt as if her legs would buckle beneath her. Face hot, she stared from the man to her friend then back to the man, all intelligible words suddenly erased from her brain.

The man smiled, obviously accustomed to seeing grown women scared mute. He extended a hand. "Good to meet you, Miss Meadows. As your friend said, I'm from New Life Records, a Christian record label, and I'm always looking for fresh talent. Is there a place we can talk?" He glanced around.

"Yes." She cleared the squeak from her throat and motioned to a nearby table. "Would you like something to drink? A coff—"

The man raised his mug. "I'm fine, thank you." He sat, and Ainsley did the same in the chair across from him. "So, your friend tells me you like to sing?"

Laughter bubbled in Ainsley's throat as dreams she'd only recently allowed to resurface rushed to the forefront of her heart. Breathing deep to maintain composure, she nodded. "I do. More than anything."

"Great. Because I'd like to sign you."

Her mouth dropped open, and she stared at him long enough for it to become awkward. "Excuse me?"

"I'd like to sign you. You have the look—modern, yet chic without being . . . inappropriately so. I'm sure you've been told how beautiful you are."

She dropped her gaze, her face heating.

"And yet, you have an endearing shyness about you I know fans will love. Combined with your sweet voice." He grinned. "I am confident you will be a perfect fit for New Life Records. What do you say?"

Her heart leaped, with no trace of her usual fear and hesitation. And yet, even so, she needed to be absolutely certain this was God's will. "It sounds amazing, Mr. Wharton. Truly. But if you don't mind, I'd like to take some time to pray over this."

His grin widened. "Of course." He pulled a second business card from his pocket along with a pen. "Can I send you information via email?"

A shiver of excitement ran through her, but she did her best to maintain appropriate composure. "Yes, please do."

Richard pulled his cell phone from his pocket and skimmed through his missed alerts with a scowl. If Ainsley continued to avoid his calls, he'd have no choice but to allow the post office to deliver his scandalous news. But she couldn't fall into his arms for comfort if he wasn't there. No, he'd wait. She'd answer her phone eventually. If not, he'd show up on her doorstep ready to offer condolences.

"Richard, are you listening?"

He glanced up and gave Eric a dismissive wave. "Yes. You were explaining how you intended to generate more publicity for my upcoming book launch. I hope you don't plan to include more no-name radio station interviews."

Eric fiddled with the papers in front of him. "I've scheduled one hundred blog tours, and I need you to provide answers to these interview questions by next Friday." He pushed a stack of papers across the table.

Richard read the typed questions. Why did he choose to write about schizophrenia? What made his book different than the others already available on the topic? How many years of clinical research backed the theories he presented? At least these questions were pertinent to the subject matter. On the first page anyway. After skimming a few more pages, he folded his hands on top of the table and stared at Eric.

"Is this a joke?"

Eric shook his head and started to speak but Richard raised a hand.

"*Suzie's Homeopathic, Aromatic, and Soul-centered Meditations?* What possible benefit could I find in appearing on her site?"

"Blog."

"Even better."

"I told you, Lancaster Publishing doesn't have much of a marketing budget, which means you need to generate your own sales."

"Isn't that what I pay you for?"

"You mean what you *paid* me for?" Eric cleared his throat. "Because those funds are gone. They've been swallowed by marketing expenses."

"Which is why we negotiated 10 percent on the back end."

Eric's face tightened, and his gray eyes locked on Richard's. "Exactly. The very reason we need to drive sales any way we can."

"Perhaps you forgot that was why I hosted the engagement dinner like you suggested."

"Well, that didn't go as well as expected, did it?"

"You're the expert — the one who knows which market best fits my book."

"There is no market, Richard. Unfortunately, I can't work magic with the promises you made to your publisher. Contrary to your claims, academia is not anxiously awaiting your material and the general public really doesn't care. So unless you find a way to make them care—"

"This conversation is pointless." Richard checked his watch. "As enjoyable as your lectures are." He strode toward the door.

"Wait."

Richard turned, his right eye twitching.

Eric sifted through his briefcase and produced a stack of glossy postcards. He handed them over. "Take these with you."

Richard scanned the bold type across the front: *Discussing the Deep Shadows Haunting the Schizophrenic Mind. Join Dr. Hollis on Saturday, February 10, for an engaging discussion of neuropathology and its effects on society. Autographed copies of his latest release,* The Schizophrenic Next Door, *will be available for 20 percent off.* A time and address followed.

Richard snorted. "And what exactly would you like me to do with these?"

Eric shoved the remaining papers into his briefcase and snapped it shut. "I'm sure you realize face-to-face invitations are much more productive than random mailings. I imagine you'll encounter colleagues at the country club, gym, or wherever you frequent between now and your signing."

"I'm meeting my father and a few other family members and close friends. I doubt they'd be interested." His stomach soured in anticipation of the humiliation fest his father was sure to initiate. One of these days Richard would do something so extraordinary the old man would be rendered speechless. Delivering spam wasn't one of them.

He returned the postcards. "I am content with the mailings, Eric."

Ainsley trudged down her driveway toward her snow-covered mailbox. Thick mounds of gray sludge barricaded her drive, thanks to the city road crew who plowed the neighborhood.

A steady scraping sounded to her right. She turned to see Chris shoveling his driveway in a gray ski cap, thick knit scarf, and a jacket so puffy it gave him the appearance of an overinflated Stay-Puft Marshmallow Man.

Glancing her way, he propped his shovel in the snow and rested on the handle. "Quite a storm last night, huh?"

She nodded, grabbing her mail and tucking it under her arm. "Don't you love the city's plowing job?"

He strolled over, flecks of snow dotting his head and shoulders. "I'll dig you out when I'm done here."

"Oh no. I've got it. My boss gave me a couple days off, so I'm good."

"Sounds like a great boss." He winked. "But if you don't mind sparing a chunk of ice or two, I need the exercise. I'd much rather shovel a few driveways than pump iron."

Ainsley started to argue, but he'd already resumed his shoveling, apparently oblivious to her protests. A giggle tickled her throat as an image of him heading from one walk to the next surfaced. Last weekend, she caught him salting Mr. Dander's walkway. The week before he'd done something under the hood of Mrs. Prinkton's car.

"So . . . Chris rested his arms on the end of his shovel. "Any decisions made regarding the record deal?"

Ainsley smiled, warmth creeping into her face. "I signed the contract. We should start recording in a month or two."

His grin widened. "Seriously?"

She nodded.

"Way to go." He raised his hand for a high five. Laughing, she complied, then he ushered her off, telling her it was much too cold for her to be hanging around outside. Considering her feet were already beginning to grow numb, she didn't argue too heartily.

God had truly blessed her, in so many ways.

Once inside, she peeled off her winter garb then focused on the mail. Sifting through the stack, she shuffled into the kitchen to trash the junk mail, pay the bills, and file the fourth collection notice sent on behalf of her mother's Visa company.

A pale-blue envelope shaped like a greeting card, Richard's blocklike lettering scrawled across the front, elicited a sigh. She almost tossed it into the trash, along with all the other cards he'd sent her since their breakup, but as usual, curiosity bid her.

Same sentiments, different card: I'm thinking of you, miss you, long to see you again, repeating his regular closing, "Call me. We need to talk."

No, we don't. She threw it away.

Twenty minutes later, her cell phone rang and Richard's number flashed across the screen. She hit Ignore. Shortly after, her voice mail icon lit up. She reluctantly played the message.

"We need to talk. There's something you need to know. About your neighbor. Please return my call."

She massaged her forehead. The man acted like a jealous teenager fighting for his prom date, and Ainsley had no interest in regressing.

A text message chimed in. "I've learned something you need to be aware of. Your altruistic neighbor is not the man you think he is."

Nice try, buddy. Depositing her phone on the counter, she plopped into a kitchen chair.

Was she a drama magnet or something? Between her mom's creditors and Richard's childish antics, she felt like she'd ventured into an episode of *Real Housewives of New Jersey*.

Chapter 43

Chris set his bank statement down and turned it toward Matilda.

She leaned across the table, frowning, as she studied the long list of debits and deposits.

When finished, she sat back and folded her hands. "Your business is doing quite well. You should be proud of yourself and all you've accomplished." Her face softened. "Dad always said you'd be a force to reckon with."

He fiddled with the straw in his iced tea.

"I understand your concerns, and I would give more than anything to see Mom spend the rest of her days surrounded in love, pampered. If I could, I'd take care of her myself." She sucked in a breath of air and shook her head. "But I don't think it'd be wise to move her, nor am I convinced this facility you talk about will be any better than the one she's at now."

"Will you at least check it out?"

"And what if the move is too hard on Mom? She's in a familiar setting. She knows what to expect."

Chris tensed. "Yeah, she expects to be berated for soiling her bed and not eating fast enough."

Her lips pressed into a firm line, the skin around them growing white.

His shoulders went slack. "I'm sorry. I'm not trying to be argumentative. But can't we at least try? Bring Mom for an orientation. See how she responds?"

Matilda studied him for a long moment. "I'll think about it." She stood. "I'll call you."

He saw her out, thanking God for the miniscule crack etching through her resolve and asking for a sledgehammer to finish the job.

Although the real battle would start once she conceded to his plan. Then everything would rest on his mother's response. A rather disconcerting thought.

He checked his watch — 6:45. Ainsley would be getting off work soon, freeing her for yet another stroll through the Plaza, as had become their Saturday evening custom. He smiled at the memory of their first carriage ride and how the glistening Christmas lights adorning the buildings reflected in Ainsley's eyes. As they drove past a jewelry store, his mind jumped to thoughts of a wedding. Which he shoved aside, of course, having dated the woman for such a short period of time. Yet he knew. He had no doubt she was the one.

So how long should he wait? He chuckled, considering they'd only been officially dating for a few weeks.

Slow it down, my man. Otherwise you'll scare the girl away. Like her last fiancé did.

His mirth dissipated as thoughts of Richard and the recently broken engagement arose.

Am I a rebound?

He squelched the thought.

Richard parked in front of Ainsley's yard and inspected the adjacent lot. Based on the empty drive and darkened windows, her neighbor wasn't home. Good. He cut the engine, tucked the photos and documents beneath his leather jacket to shield them from the snow, and stepped out. A smile twitched as he made his way to Ainsley's door. After pausing to smooth his windblown hair, he chimed the doorbell. The blinds cracked, and the door clicked.

Ainsley scowled. "What are you doing here?"

"Give me five minutes. That's all I ask."

She kept her hand on the door, her body blocking the entrance.

"Five minutes. Please."

She sighed and stepped aside. "Fine. Five."

He followed her into the living room where she stood with arms crossed.

He moved to the sofa, pulled his documents from his jacket, and placed them on the coffee table. Then, settling into the couch, he propped an ankle on his knee and waited while Ainsley inspected first the images, then the documents.

"What's this about?"

"Isn't it obvious? Your neighbor appears to be quite the ladies' man. As I suspected."

"And you thought this would suddenly change everything and I'd come running back, is that it? Unbelievable." She stomped to the door and flung it open. Snow drifted in and fluttered across the floor. "Leave. And take these with you." She flung the papers at him. They splayed across the floor.

Richard gathered them up then closed the distance between them. "I'm concerned, that's all. As I told you when we were dating, you'd be wise to steer clear of that man. Because as far as I can tell, your lives have become quite entwined."

Her eyebrows shot up. "Have you been spying on me?"

"Just an observation — you both work at the shelter, and now he's your boss, right? A rather precarious situation, considering the lawsuit."

"Good-bye, Richard." She pressed her back against the open door. "Don't force me to file a restraining order."

He dropped the papers and photo on an accent table in the foyer. "I'm sorry to be the one to break this to you. I really am."

Ainsley slammed and locked the door. The nerve of that man! Most likely, those documents were a farce. She shook her head and marched into the living the room. Seriously, what had she seen in Richard? Oh, he'd charmed her well enough, but even then, hints of his manipulative side had poked through. Only she was too stupid to pay any attention.

As she paced the kitchen, the image of the official Los Angeles County Circuit Court seal stamped on the documents he'd left drew her. With papers in hand, she resumed her pacing, scanning the pages as she went.

Sexual harassment? What did that mean, exactly?

She studied the photo, fighting back images from her high school days and the "stacked-pack" as the chauvinistic jerks used to call themselves.

No. Chris was nothing like them. Although in this picture, he sure looked like a playboy.

Not to mention the fact that she was a terrible character reader. Richard had fooled her for five years.

But that was different. She knew with Richard. Although she tried to deny it, looking back she'd had her doubts, her concerns, for quite some time. Not with Chris.

Yet.

Flipping to the second page, she read the claims raised by the plaintiff, the knot in her stomach tightening.

Unwelcomed sexual advances . . . threats of termination . . . hostile work environment . . . retaliation.

Punitive damages: $75,000.

She tossed the papers on the coffee table and resumed her pacing, but no matter how hard she fought it, unsettling questions dominated her thoughts: *How well did she know Chris? What if she'd misread him?*

She closed her eyes as her mind drifted to her father and the plastic floozy draped over his arm. A phrase her mother often repeated flooded her brain, "Men are pigs. All of them. Some just come in fancier packages that take longer to unwrap."

Not Chris.

Surely he had a reasonable explanation for this.

Chapter 44

"Another great day." Grinning, Chris zipped his money bag and closed the register.

"That good, huh?" Wanda drew near, swinging a dish towel, her chestnut eyes sparkling.

He nodded and clasped William's shoulder who stood beside him, plunking leftover pastries into a paper bag. "Better than I estimated. And I couldn't do this without you all."

Wanda's eyes glistened as she looked at her son. "We move into our apartment next week, thanks to you. A month and a half ago, William and I spent our first night on the streets, slept beneath an overpass." Her voice quavered. "I thought for sure God had turned His back on us. But I never stopped praying, for William's sake. Figured I'd die in a heap of garbage, but not my son."

She shook her head, her eyes like chiseled flint. "Nope, not my son. I determined then and there to do whatever it took to see he got a better life. Begged God for mercy on William's behalf." She grinned. "He's about to finish third grade and never missed a day this year, did ya boy?"

William puffed out his chest, shaking his head. "No, ma'am."

"Even kept a B average."

Though Chris rejoiced with them, his heart felt heavy thinking of all the other homeless kids he'd seen come in and out of the shelter. How many of them made it to school? How many mothers knelt on the ice-covered ground each night begging God for better, asking for aid? What might the world look like if every Christian lived out their faith in surrendered obedience?

He looked at Wanda. "Can we pray?"

She and her son nodded and they all joined hands. Chris glanced across the café toward Candy who leafed through a leather-bound Bible. "Wanna join us?"

She shook her head and looked away.

Chris bowed his head. "Lord, may this café be a sanctuary, a place of hope and healing. Rain down Your blessings, Lord, so we can be instruments of Your love and grace."

"Amen!" Wanda squeezed his hand before letting go. "And I'd say God already answered that prayer."

Chris followed her gaze through the front window where Albert shivered, breath fogging the glass. A woman with long, gray hair protruding from a brown ski cap stood beside him, gnawing on a fingernail.

Chris turned to William. "Think you can hand me a couple of those pastries? And one of the gospel tracts."

William nodded and selected three blueberry scones. He pulled a glossy flyer from beside the cash register and loaded everything into a paper sack.

"Thanks." Chris grabbed the food items, crossed the café, and held the door open. "You wanna come in for a bit?"

Albert stepped forward, his gaze darting from one face to the next, bushy eyebrows scrunched together. Chris held his breath, praying for God's love to sweep over this man and give him the courage to step inside.

Footsteps clicked behind him, and Albert's eyes widened. He darted around the corner.

Chris sighed and stepped outside, letting the door close behind him. Albert huddled against the brick wall, teeth chattering. The woman stood beside him, staring at the street in front of her.

"Here. Blueberry scones with lemon icing." He held out the package and Albert snatched it up. He and the woman studied Chris then looked away.

Chris lingered, hands shoved in his pockets, watching the two devour the pastries. When they finished, he squeezed Albert's shoulder. "See you tomorrow?"

Albert nodded, a smile emerging beneath his crumb-speckled mustache.

Chris returned to the café to find everything cleaned, swept, and in order. He turned to Wanda "You guys ready to go?"

"Don't need a ride today. Rose is picking us up. Gonna take us to Operation Breakthrough so's we can talk to other moms standing where we once were." She gave William a sideways hug. "Like that verse you always tell us about. 'To him who much has been given, much is required.' Finally got a chance to give back some."

A horn beeped and Chris turned to see Rose parked along the curb. She smiled and waved while Wanda and William scurried out.

"Wait, don't forget the pastries!" Chris chased after them with the paper bag. He returned to find Candy lingering near the counter, a coffee-table devotion in her hand.

"What's this mean, walk by the Spirit?"

"That's kind of confusing." He lifted a Bible from a nearby shelf and placed it on the counter between them. Flipping through the pages, he located John chapter 3. "Back in Bible times, there was this guy named Nicodemus. To the observer, he appeared to do everything right. Read the Scriptures, went to the synagogue, followed all the rules."

"Taking the direct route to heaven, huh?"

Chris smiled. "Well, he thought so — until he met Jesus." He read the passage, starting with verse 3. "Jesus replied, 'Very truly I tell you, no one can see the kingdom of God unless they are born again'" (NIV).

"Ha, ha. Yeah, I've heard about that — the rebirth experience. From where I sit, if that's what it takes to get to heaven, I'm outie!"

Chris chuckled. "Nicodemus had a similar reaction." He continued reading. "Jesus answered, 'Very truly I tell you, no one can enter the kingdom of God unless they are born of water and the Spirit. Flesh gives birth to flesh, but the Spirit gives birth to spirit.' You should not be surprised at my saying, 'You must be born again.' The wind blows wherever it pleases. You hear its sound, but you cannot tell where it comes from or where it is going. So it is with everyone born of the Spirit" (John 3:5–8 NIV). He marked his spot with a napkin then closed the book. "It's a spiritual birth that happens when a person turns from a life of sin and surrenders to Jesus as their Lord and Savior."

"Still don't get it." She leaned closer, her shoulder brushing against Chris's, a small pout on her lips.

"I think I've got something in the back that will explain it better. Hold on."

He dashed into his office and scoured his shelves in search of anything that might explain spiritual life to someone who might have no concept of sin. Settling on a spiral-bound notebook filled with commentaries, he pulled it down and leafed through the pages. Footsteps scuffed behind him. Candy appeared at his side, the fruity scent of her perfume filling his office.

"My old neighbor used to tell me stories . . . about a Samaritan woman who slept with a bunch of guys." Her eyes intensified as she traced her finger along the book spines lining the shelf. "And of another woman caught in adultery."

Chris swallowed and stepped back, clutching the notebook to his chest.

Candy slid closer, gaze locked on his. "She said Jesus loved those women despite what they'd done." She moved closer, her breath warm on Chris's face. He tried to increase the distance between them, but his heel hit the wall. "What about me? You think there's hope for a girl like me?" Angling her head, she touched his arm and leaned forward. Chris raised a hand to push her away moments before her lips met his, his hand squished between them.

"Excuse me."

Chris gave a shove, sending Candy tumbling backward.

Ainsley stood in the doorway. Color seeped up her neck, matching the fire in her teary eyes. "To think I thought you were different." She flung a stack of papers toward him, spun on her heels, and ran out.

"Wait! It's not what it looks like!" Chris chased after her, slipping on the pages strewn across the floor. By the time he reached the front of the cafe, she'd already made it to the door. "Please, let me explain."

Without turning around, she raised a hand and left, the door swinging closed behind her.

Chris grabbed his cell phone and punched in her number. Her voice mail picked up halfway through the first ring. She'd hit Ignore. With a sigh, he turned around and lumbered back to his office, pushing past Candy.

She rolled her eyes. "Touchy."

Chris marched down the hall to his office and the mess of papers spread across the floor. The Los Angeles County Circuit Court official document glared back at him, causing his stomach to catapult. Beside them lay a picture of him and some college buddies, looking like a pack of playboys. It was downright shameful, and thanks to Christ, he'd left that kind of lifestyle behind. Surely Ainsley could see that. And yet, stacked with the court case and flirty Candy pressed against him, Ainsley had drawn her conclusion.

He closed his eyes and rubbed his face. The image of her wide, tear-filled eyes tumbled through his skull. He opened his desk drawer and pulled out an ad he clipped from the local paper and stared at the photo of the diamond ring.

Lord, please don't let me lose her.

Ainsley jumped into her car and cranked the engine. Praise music poured from her radio. She snapped it off and eased behind a pale blue pickup.

Men were pigs. All of them. Why should Chris be any different? But at least it hadn't taken her five years to figure it out.

Tears stung her eyes as she gripped the steering wheel, memories of riding through the Plaza tucked beneath a warm blanket while Chris shared his dreams for the café resurfacing.

And she bought it all, going so far as to plop herself in them.

Now what? Her entire life revolved around the man, and she certainly couldn't quit her job. Not yet anyway. She'd have to give her two weeks notice.

Rounding the corner into her cul-de-sac, her gaze fell on Chris's house and her heart plummeted.

How stupid could she be? *Way to box yourself in, Ainsley.* How many times had she rolled her eyes at women who got involved with their bosses? And here she was, dating not only her boss and ministry partner, but her neighbor! With Richard, breaking up had been as easy as hitting the Ignore button whenever he called. With Chris, it'd require a complete life change. Maybe even a move.

She gathered her things, got out, and hurried inside, slamming the door behind her. Silence settled over her house. Pulling her cell phone from her pocket, she thought about calling Gina then tossed the phone aside.

It's just You and me, God. Like always.

Collapsing into the corner of the couch, she grabbed a throw pillow and hugged it, tears pricking her eyes as questions that once haunted her nightly as a child rose to the surface.

What's wrong with me? Why doesn't anyone love me?

An old photo album lay on the bottom shelf of her coffee table. She'd salvaged it from her mother's trash years ago. The memories tucked inside were bittersweet. It was like a timeline of her life, from carefree toddler to broken home to isolation.

She flipped the album to the first page and studied an image of her father holding her. Nestled in his arms, only the top of her peach-fuzzed head remained visible. A smile crinkled the skin around his eyes as he looked down at her.

Turning the page, she skimmed through five more years to when she turned six. The year her dad took her to Kmart to buy her first bike. Pink with glittery tassels. Her helmet swallowed her head, and thick pads encircled her knees and elbows. In the photo her father stood beside her, clutching the back of her seat as she death-gripped the handle bars. His smile was huge.

By the time she turned twelve, the pictures grew scarcer, most of them class photos. She paused to study a snapshot of her thirteenth birthday — an afterthought when her mother came home to find her in tears. The year her mother forgot and her father never sent a card.

That was the year she barred her father from her heart. The year she told herself she didn't — wouldn't — care.

She glanced up, reading the verse on an embroidered wall hanging.

"I have loved you with an everlasting love. I have drawn you with unfailing kindness."

Yeah, well, You're the only one. And Gina. And Deborah. Thank You for bringing such caring women into my life, Lord.

As she crumpled against the couch cushions, one image rose to the surface — her father. She tossed her pillow aside.

This is not about my father. It is about a sleazeball who charmed me into believing he was different, who broke down my walls only to slash through my heart once he laid it bare.

And yes, Chris was like her father. Carbon copy, minus the gray hair and paunch belly. Lesson learned.

Her Bible beckoned like an ever-faithful friend. She grabbed it and flipped through the thin pages, landing on Matthew 7 (NIV).

"First take out the plank in your own eye, and then you will see clearly" (v. 5).

She snapped it shut and dropped it back onto the coffee table.

The issue wasn't clarity. She'd seen enough already, but somehow the prick in her heart wouldn't go away, as if God wanted her to dig deeper — to draw nearer, to somehow catch hold of something just beyond her reach.

Then you will see clearly. She reread the passage again, beginning with verse 3 (NIV).

"Why do you look at the speck of sawdust in your brother's eye and pay no attention to the plank in your own eye? How can you say to your brother, 'Let me take the speck out of your eye,' when all the time there is a plank in your own eye? You hypocrite, first take the plank out of your own eye, and then you will see clearly to remove the speck from your brother's eye.'"

OK, God, You want me to resolve things. Then can I quit?

The phrase, "then you will see clearly," echoed in her mind, causing her to read the passage a third time, more analytically.

What are You trying to tell me, God? What's my vision-distorting plank?

Once again an image of her father surfaced and this time she didn't shove it away.

Closing her eyes, she pinched the bridge of her nose as tears welled behind her lids.

She knew what God wanted. He wanted her to release her bitterness, to forgive her father for all the times he hurt her, but doing so would only invite fresh pain.

I can't. I'm sorry, but I can't.

But that wasn't true. Not really, because with God, all things were possible. This wasn't a question of her ability but instead of her surrender. To give herself fully to God, wounds and all.

Closing her eyes once again, she slipped to the floor. On her knees, she pressed her folded hands to her forehead. "Help me, Lord. Help me to forgive him. To move on. Help me learn to trust."

Chapter 45

With one eye trained on the door, Chris wiped down tables and straightened books in the shelves and windowsills. Would Ainsley come in today? He'd called her numerous times, stopped by her house, left messages, with no response. The television light flickering through her blinds told him she'd been home.

Shoes clicked behind him and he turned to see Candy approach with a pouty smile, hips swaying like a pendulum. She twirled a lock of hair around her finger and lowered her lashes. "You're not still angry with me, are you?"

He stepped back to lengthen the distance between them. Now what? If he fired her, she'd probable file a sexual harassment suit. "Is the counter stocked?"

"Yep." She moved closer and traced a finger along the table in front of her. "I didn't mean to make you uncomfortable the other day."

"There's no sense discussing it again. I'm confident you understand the parameters of our relationship now." He crossed his arms. "You might want to see if Wanda needs help in the kitchen."

She lifted a Bible from the nearby shelf and leafed through it. "If you're not too angry, I have a couple questions."

He sighed and rubbed the back of his neck. So how does one reach out to sinners without getting dragged through the gutter?

"OK." He moved toward her.

The door to the café chimed open and he turned to see Ainsley enter, her eyes going from wide to narrow as a deep scowl spread across her features. Dropping his towel on the table, he raced to her side.

"Ainsley, can we talk?"

"There's nothing to talk about." She tucked her purse beneath the cash register. "It's not like we had a formal commitment or anything." Her eyes darkened as her gaze shifted to Candy who glided over with lowered lashes and a slight smile.

"Good morning, Ainsley." Back arched and mouth pouty, she fiddled with a container of pens.

Customers milled in, lining behind the counter. Moving aside, Chris turned to Ainsley. "Please, can we talk? Give me five minutes."

After an extended silence, she nodded.

He followed her to his office, his heart wrenching at the sight of her clenched hands. *Oh, sweet Ainsley.*

She stopped in the center of the room and picked at her thumbnail. "I'm sure I'm overreacting here, but the truth is, I'm not interested in the dating scene. And . . . She swallowed and looked at her hands. "I think it would be more comfortable for both of us if we limited our time together."

"You're quitting?"

"As soon as I find another job. It'd be better if we didn't serve together at the shelter anymore either. I think one of us should switch days."

"Ainsley, please. I didn't do anything. Candy came on to me, but I pushed her away. And that picture —"

"You don't need to explain. As I said, we weren't committed. I hold no claims to you. I'm just . . . Honestly, I'm . . . I wish you well."

"But I want to be with you. Can't you see that?"

She blinked and her chin dimpled. For a moment, the angry lines in her face softened, but then Chris's phone rang, and she spun around and left.

He glanced at the number displayed on the screen and sighed.

Lord, can we start this day over?

"Matilda, good morning."

"I stopped by the nursing home this morning to have breakfast with Mom."

"Is everything OK?"

"I found her lying in dried feces, and there were fresh bruises on her arms."

His stomach dropped.

"You're right. Mom deserves better. I've scheduled a meeting and tour with the director of Lily of the Valley, if you'd like to join me."

"What time?"

"Ten thirty."

He checked the clock. "I'll be there."

Tucking the phone in his back pocket, he hurried down the hall, and out onto the café floor. Ainsley and Candy manned the counter, side-by-side. Based on the Candy's crooked grin and Ainsley's scowl, he'd be lucky to find Ainsley here when he returned. Although he longed to hover, countering the crazy ideas swimming through her head, he couldn't leave his sister waiting. Not when so much hinged on this meeting.

He approached Ainsley and tried to make eye contact, but she concentrated on scrubbing an old coffee stain from the counter.

"Do you think you guys can handle the place for a while?"

Ainsley nodded and Candy's smile widened. "We'll keep the coffee hot and the cash register clanking."

An hour later, he stood on the curb outside Lily of the Valley.

"What do you think?" He held his breath as Matilda's inspected the single-story brick building lined with windows and the occasional wind chime.

"It appears lovely. And I like that it is faith-based."

Chris nodded.

"Although I'm still concerned about how Mom will handle the change." She fiddled with the strap of her purse.

"I know."

"I've given this much thought. This must be her last move, which means, if your business fails . . ."

"I understand. I'll do whatever it takes to see the bill gets paid. When would you like to move her?"

"You don't mind losing out on two months worth of rent?"

He shook his head.

She glanced at her watch. "They're probably getting Mom ready for lunch now."

"Let's go."

Chapter 46

hris and Matilda gathered on the curb outside of Shady
Lane Assisted Living.

"Shall we pray?" She held out her hands and Chris took
them in his.

Chris nodded and bowed his head. "Holy Father, we need
Your help today. Mother's been through so much." His voice
cracked at a memory of his mother crumpled beside their
father's coffin, her trembling hands reaching for him. "Please
calm her anxiety and let this be a peaceful transition. Please go
before her and keep her safe."

When they finished, Matilda wiped a tear from her cheek
and lifted her chin. "Shall we?"

They filed into the facility, backs rod-straight.

Heather met them at the reception desk, face blanched. The
facility director stood beside her holding a manila file. Chris
glared at Heather, his muscles quivering. She avoided his gaze,
but the director stepped forward.

"I highly recommend against this course of action." Her
eyes darkened behind wire-rimmed glasses. "Why don't we go
into my office to talk about this?"

Chris spun around. "Perhaps we can talk about the best way
to file abuse charges?"

The director's eyes widened and her lips quivered.
"Incontinence is quite normal at your mother's stage —"

"Incontinence I understand. Inflamed skin beneath
dried feces, I do not." Matilda's eyes narrowed on the
director.

"That was an unfortunate —"

"Accident?" Chris scoffed. "You were understaffed? And the bruises on her arms, which resemble human hands, arose out of nowhere?" He increased his pace, Matilda matching him step for step. The director scurried behind them.

A few heads popped out of doorways, eyes wide. A woman with short, silver hair smiled at Chris, nodding. She appeared on the verge of tears. Chris swallowed, eyes burning, as her unspoken plea settled deep in his heart. As soon as they got Mom settled at Lily of the Valley, he'd head to the courthouse. This place needed to be shut down.

They reached their mother's room to find her sitting in front of the television while a CNA straightened her bed.

She glanced up and smiled. "What a pleasant surprise. I wasn't expecting company." Her face blanched, her hands clutching at her neck, when she noticed the director. "No, no, no, no, no, no!" She shook her head and waved her arms in front of her.

Chris reeled around. "Out! Get out, now!"

"As the director of this facility I am responsible —"

"I said out!"

The director gasped and stumbled backward, the CNA scurrying close behind. Matilda closed the door in her face then turned back to their mother who white-knuckled the armrests of her chair.

"Sh. Everything's fine." Matilda knelt in front of her and started to hum. Chris moved to her side and joined the melody.

He flipped off the television, shooting up silent prayers while Matilda soothed their mother's back, her soft humming now expanded into song.

You are my ever-present shield, the strong tower at my side.
Your strength is like no other, in Your love I hide.
Though my enemies assail me,
Though my strength is wearing thin,
You alone will carry me,
You strengthen me from within.

By the second verse, their mother relaxed her grip on the armrests and settled back into the chair.

She glanced around. "Where's my angel?"

Matilda stopped singing. "God's angels are always with you, Mom."

She shook her head. "No, my curly-haired angel with the voice from heaven."

Chris swallowed. Matilda looked at him, but he averted his gaze.

He stepped closer to his mother and placed his hand on hers. "Have you seen the birds yet. I know how you like to watch them fly." He rotated her chair, careful not to jolt her, while Matilda opened the blinds. Outside, the vibrant pinks and purples that once filled the sky had faded to a pale blue. Cotton-ball clouds hovered above the city skyline.

While they admired the horizon, Matilda resumed her singing and began to pack their mother's things. Ten minutes later, she held a filled tote.

Chris clutched his mother's hands again and looked into her eyes. "Would you like to go on a trip? It's such a beautiful day." He held his breath.

The room went silent as his mother looked from face to face. Chris fought to keep his muscles relaxed and his gaze warm and steady, although his pulse quickened.

Please, Lord, let her come willingly.

"Is your father coming?"

"No. It'll just be us today."

She smiled and nodded. "Yes, that sounds lovely. A mommy-and-kids day. We haven't had one of those in quite some time."

Chris continued to pray as they led her down the hall and into the crisp morning air. His stomach flopped when his mother stopped in the center of the sidewalk, the muscles in her arm tightening beneath his hand. But then she giggled, pointing out a bushy-tailed cat hiding beneath a pickup.

"Here, kitty, kitty." She leaned forward and extended her hand, wobbling on her feet.

Chris secured his grip and placed his free hand on the small of her bony back.

A chilled breeze swept over them and his mother shivered.

He pulled her closer to shield her from the wind. "Let's get you out of the cold."

Matilda waited at her car, holding the back door open. "Mind driving? I'd like to sit with Mom."

Chris took her keys. "Not at all."

Exhaust streamed from the muffler and heat poured from the interior, drawing their mother like a stray to a heated barn. Soft, classical music drifted from the speakers.

Sliding across the leather seat, she inhaled. "What a lovely smell. Like flowers. Just like spring flowers." She leaned against the headrest.

Matilda eased the door closed then rounded the car and poked her head into the opposite door. "Mind if I sit here?"

"By all means. You must be new to our group. I'm Mrs. Langley. And you are?"

Tears glistened in Matilda's eyes. "Matilda."

Once they were settled, Chris got in the driver's seat and cranked the engine. Fifteen minutes later, they pulled up to a single-story structure Chris hoped would soon be his mother's new home.

Chris parked the car and got out. Waiting on the sidewalk, he shoved his hands in his pockets, eyes trained on his mother. His tense shoulders relaxed when she exited the car with a smile.

"Where are we?"

"Mother, I want you to meet someone. A sweet Christian couple." Matilda looped her arm through their mother's and guided her up the walk. Sarah and Donald Lovington, the facility owners, met them at the door dressed in jeans and T-shirts. Their eyes sparkled when they looked at Chris's mom.

"Welcome." Sarah stepped aside. A candle burned on a white pine accent table, filling the air with the scent of spice cake.

Inside, an elderly man and woman relaxed in recliners, newspapers spread on their laps. Ferns draped across end tables and books lined numerous shelves. A worn leather Bible with slips of paper poking from the pages lay on the coffee table.

Matilda led their mom inside.

She stood with her hands laced in front of her and examined the quaint surroundings. Her gaze landed on the Bible. "What passage are we studying today?"

Sarah came to her side and extended her hand. "I'm Sarah Lovington. You must be Mrs. Langley."

Chris's mom smiled. "You must be the study leader. And this must be your husband." She frowned. "My husband appears to be running late." She checked her watchless wrist.

"Would you like a tour?" Sarah touched their mom's elbow and looked at her husband. "Could you ask Laurie to bring some coffee to Mrs. Langley's room?"

Chris's mom straightened, looking from one face to the next. "My room? What room? What is she talking about?"

Matilda rubbed her back. "Isn't this a lovely place, Mom? Listen." She paused and their mom angled her head. Soft music poured from hidden speakers. "Do you remember when Aunt Jane used to sing that hymn to us?" She started to hum.

"Ah, yes. I do." Their mother joined in.

They led her down a picture-lined hallway half a step behind Sarah.

They stopped in front of a rose-colored room with thick, beige carpet and lace curtains. A floral quilt adorned a queen-sized bed and stuffed animals filled a corner shelf. An opened Bible lay beneath a pink reading lamp. The faint scent of vanilla and lavender drifted from decorative air fresheners tucked in the ceiling corners.

A soft knock rapped on the opened door, and a young woman with a bright smile that extended to her eyes entered carrying a tray of coffee, porcelain mugs, and a saucer of sugar.

An hour later, after kissing their mother good-bye, Chris and his sister gathered on the sidewalk outside.

Matilda pulled her gloves from her purse. "You were right, Chris. This is going to be a wonderful place for Mom. Very calm and loving."

Chris smiled. *Thank You, Father.*

Chapter 47

*R*ichard checked his phone for the tenth time that day. Ainsley still hadn't returned his calls. It didn't make any sense. He knew she was no longer seeing that Langley character. He'd watched them at the café: her scowling face, his slumped shoulders. He'd even followed her some, wondering if she'd started seeing someone else. But no. She went to work, the shelter, ran her normal errands. Although there was that guy from New Life Records.

He rubbed his face, his hands scraping against newly grown stubble. That poor, confused woman. Though she needed him desperately, and yet, she continued to spurn him, the very one who could help her most.

His phone chimed, and he started, hope stirring in his heart. A glance at the screen soured his mood. Eric.

He answered. "I'm here."

"You're late."

Richard hit Call End and slipped the phone in his front pocket. Stepping out of the car, he scanned the near vacant lot and frowned. He checked his watch—4:05. Either his readers were even later than he, or this endeavor would be a waste of time. Where was this place anyway? The meeting area Eric had scheduled was nothing more than a vacant storefront in a failing strip mall. The only businesses that appeared even remotely successful were a seedy liquor store and a tiny Chinese restaurant.

He grabbed his books from the trunk and crossed the lot. A rusted bell above the door dinged as he pushed his way into a square room bordered by wood paneling.

Eric hurried to meet him, then stopped and stared at Richard. "What happened to you?"

Richard ran his hands through his hair. It felt greasy. "And good afternoon to you too." After grabbing his notes from the top, he shoved his books at Eric. His jaw tensed as his gaze swept the room. The ceiling was made of drop-down plastic foam, a handful of which was missing, revealing insulation.

Maybe a dozen men, most wearing button-up shirts and slacks, three in thick, square glasses, occupied the tables placed throughout the room. They looked to be in their late teens or early twenties. College freshmen, most likely. Eric said he'd invited the university's psychology club. As if college students had money for extracurricular book purchases.

None of them held cameras. Scowling, Richard turned to Eric. "Where's the press? You did invite them, didn't you?"

"They're not coming." His entire countenance went slack, as if devoid of energy. Clearly, the man lacked the enthusiasm necessary to fulfill his job requirements. "I'm afraid they don't consider your book newsworthy. You reviews are . . . lacking. Your sales to this point are dismal, and arriving late to scheduled events isn't helping." He shook his head, his expression showing more pity than frustration.

A pity that soured Richard's stomach and was completely unfounded. "Yes, well, perhaps if you scheduled events worthy of my time, I would offer more of it." Lifting his chin, he swept an arm to indicate his surroundings. "Where did you find this place? Craigslist?" He gave a snide laugh.

Eric rolled his eyes and opened his mouth to speak, but Richard raised a hand.

"Surely you would agree, now is not the time to discuss your job performance."

Turning his back to his publicist, he looked for a podium. Of course there wasn't one.

Frowning, he turned to face his . . . guests. "Thank you for coming. As you are probably aware, I am Dr. Richard Hollis, author of *The Schizophrenic Next Door*, a book that discusses neuropathology and its effects on society." He went on to explain the diagnostic criteria of the illness, briefly describing the four main types. From there, he talked about reasons individuals don't seek a diagnosis, have delayed diagnoses, or are misdiagnosed, and how this affected their treatment plan. "As I'm sure you're aware, there is a stigma attached to mental illness. This inevitably leads to shame, which in turn can make one reluctant to seek help. Obviously, denial is another factor."

His mind drifted to Ainsley, and he soon began analyzing her behaviors. Though she held no neuropathology, much of her behaviors were caused by emotional wounds and barriers, and of course, a great deal of denial. And now she intended to make her career in music? Surely she had more sense than that. Did she plan to spend the rest of her life singing in coffee shops and at church socials? It was quite disconcerting. He had been the only stabilizing factor in her life, and now that their relationship was severed.

"Mr. Hollis?"

Richard's focus jerked back to the men in front of him, all of whom were staring at him. "Excuse me." He cleared his throat and fumbled with his notes. "Where was I?"

"You were discussing the comorbidities and differential diagnoses of schizophrenia."

"Yes, of course."

Ten minutes later, he concluded with a short reading. Though he had plenty more material, and quite fascinating at that, to share, he felt it a waste of time, considering his audience, to do so.

He folded his speech outline and tucked it in his pocket. "Any questions?"

Hands shot up, and he exchanged glances with Eric who shrugged, motioning for him to continue. He sighed and pointed to a kid with jet-black hair that was so straight, it jetted from his scalp like porcupine quills. One question led to ten which led to a debate on the value and dangers of electroconvulsive therapy in modern psychology.

Richard forced a cough. He shot Eric a scowl and made a deliberate act of checking his watch. This engagement proved pointless. The group in front of him continued to engage in their fruitless debate, so Richard coughed again, more forceful this time.

"I appreciate you coming." The talking ceased and all eyes turned to him. "Should you wish to purchase an autographed copy of my book, I will be signing at that table." He pointed to the far wall where a stack of books and promotional material had been arranged.

When the men made no effort to rise, but rather, returned to their childish arguments, he exhaled and kneaded his forehead. Crossing the room, he breathed deep, slow and steady, in an effort to calm himself.

He held Eric's gaze. "If I were less charitable, I would fire you."

Eric didn't flinch. "That would imply a paid arrangement."

Richard stared at him, his hands fisting with such intensity, a cramp shot from his thumb to his elbow. "Mrs. Ellis mailed you a check last week."

"Which was returned for insufficient funds."

Richard blinked, halted as he processed his publicist's words. "Ridiculous." Then, with a huff, he grabbed a stack of books and began signing. He would leave these with Eric, should any of the guests ever conclude their discussion and choose to purchase one. "Clearly there's been an error. You should get that straightened out."

"I'm concerned, Richard." Eric moved in front of him, as if commanding his attention. He could command all he wanted. Richard was done with this absurd conversation.

"What's become of you?" Eric's breath expelled, flooding Richard's nostrils with the stench of stale coffee and onions. "You're losing it." He softened his voice. "This is because of Ainsley, isn't it?"

Richard's head snapped up, his eyes narrowing. Muscles tense and free hand fisted, he returned to signing, stacking each book in turn. As he rose to leave, his phone rang. He yanked it from his front pocket and stared at the number on the screen. Mrs. Ellis. Why was she calling on a Saturday?

He stabbed his finger on the Answer icon. "Yes?"

She responded by calling him a very unpleasant name, one quite uncharacteristic for his normally mild-mannered secretary. "I knew this would happen, the moment you asked me to begin canceling appointments and referring your clients elsewhere."

Sensing Eric's unwavering stare, Richard turned his shoulder to the man and switched the phone to his other ear. "Calm down and tell me what this is about."

"My paycheck bounced, which caused me to bounce numerous checks I'd written."

"Bounced?" Richard's mouth went dry. How had this happened? "Your bank must have made a mistake." Surely his accountant would've mentioned this. Although he had called on more than one occasion, urging Richard to call him back, which he fully intended to do. But somehow, it had slipped his mind.

Because he'd run into one of Ainsley's church friends shortly thereafter and had learned of her record signing. This led to an afternoon of Internet searching in the hopes of finding out if she'd been scheduled to sing anywhere. So he could find a way to talk with her in person, to reason with her, to help her see —

"Did you hear me?" Mrs. Ellis's voice rose, snapping him back. "I expect you to pay the bounced check fees. I will also be writing a letter to each business affected, explaining, in detail, what has happened."

His stomach recoiled, sending a rush of bile up his throat. "That is completely unnec —"

The line went dead, the deafening silence broken only by the throbbing in his skull.

"Let Ainsley go, man." Eric moved into Richard's line of vision. "Your obsession for her is destroying you. In your effort to control her, you've allowed her to control you."

He lurched to his feet. "This conversation is done." He slid the few books he'd autographed across the table and shoved the rest, along with his crumpled notes, in the box. "Good day. Call me when you have a profitable event scheduled."

"This is it, Richard. This is the best I can do for you. At some point you're going to have to accept the fact that this book is a complete dud. Perhaps it's time you cut your losses and move on. That's what I plan to do." He pulled a slip of paper from his inside blazer pocket and set it on the table. "I am resigning as your publicist. Effective immediately."

His words hit like an elbow to the gut, leaving Richard speechless. Rotating on wooden legs, he left, stalking across the parking lot in rhythmic yet rapid steps. His pulse pounded in his ears, the rush of adrenaline heady. By the time he reached his car, beads of sweat had accumulated along his forehead and upper lip.

"You're losing it. . . . She's destroying you. . . . Controlling you."

He yanked open his car door, thrust his books onto the passenger seat, and sank behind the wheel. Eric's words replayed like a relentless tornado siren, merging with Mrs. Ellis's threats. His reputation would be destroyed.

Tears, hot and furious, rushed to the surface as he stared back at the dive Eric had chosen for his book launch. Everything — everything! — had rested on this book. His practice, his finances, his self-respect. And he'd failed. More than failed, he'd destroyed his relationship with Ainsley and lost control.

He stared at his reflection in the rearview mirror. His stubbled chin and sunken eyes shadowed by the deep purple of sleep deprivation.

"You're losing it. Let her go."

In truth, he'd never really loved her. Rather, he'd loved the idea of her. Of having a doting and supportive wife, one who would admire him, listen to him. Honor and respect him. But in his effort to gain that, he'd shattered every ounce of respect he'd worked ceaselessly to acquire.

Falling forward, he pressed his forehead against the steering wheel and sobbed.

Chapter 48

*A*insley cradled the phone between her ear and shoulder and pulled a bag of rice from the cupboard. "I'm fine, really. It's not a big deal." Her sheet music lay on the counter, sent by Mr. Wharton. She hoped to have it mastered by the end of the week.

"Yeah, no biggie," Gina said. "You're only talking about quitting your job, buying out of your lease, and finding a new place to live. All signs that your heart's been shattered."

"We didn't date long enough for that." But the ache in her chest belied her words.

She measured a cup of rice into a pan of boiling water and pulled a wooden spoon from a drawer and stirred.

"Too bad emotions rarely run according to our timetables, huh?"

"Ha, ha. Real funny, Gina."

"Do you think you misjudged him? I mean, you said he was in college, right? Surely he's changed since then, as have we all, thank goodness."

Ainsley glanced through her window toward Chris's house, fighting memories of his boyish smile and deep laugh. "It doesn't matter. I'm too messed up to be in a relationship." Her voice cracked. "How can my heart ache for someone I barely know?"

"You two spent a lot of time together."

Ainsley's phone beeped. She glanced at the unfamiliar number flashing on the screen. Hopefully one of the business owners she'd left her application with called for an interview. "Listen, Gina, can I get back to you later? I've got another call coming in."

"Sure."

She switched to the next caller. "Hello, Ainsley Meadows speaking."

"Miss Meadows, this is Mrs. Webster from North Kansas City Hospital. Your mother listed you as an emergency contact."

Her pulse raced. "Is everything all right? Has there been an accident?"

"She swallowed a large amount of lorazepam. We pumped her stomach, but she remains confused and complains of dizziness."

"I'll be right there."

Grabbing her keys, she ran out the door. She peeled out of her driveway and onto Vivian. Her speedometer hovered between seventy-five and eighty by the time she hit the freeway. Ten minutes later, she screeched into the hospital parking lot, bolted through the emergency entrance, and to the reception desk.

A woman with black hair and porcelain skin looked up from a computer screen. "May I help you?"

"I'm here to see Angela Meadows." Ainsley spoke in bursts, her lungs heaving for air.

The woman swiveled to the monitor and typed, each tap accelerating Ainsley's pulse until she felt ready to explode. A moment later, a woman dressed in scrubs emerged from a side door.

"Miss Meadows?"

Ainsley nodded.

"Follow me."

The woman led her through a fluorescent-lit hallway, past large red bins labeled *Biohazardous Waste*, and around a nurses' station to an examination room. Her mother lay in bed, clutching a thin, white sheet to her chin.

The doctor glanced up when Ainsley entered. He held a clipboard in his hand.

"What happened?" She looked from the doctor to her mother, but her mother refused to make eye contact.

The doctor motioned for his nurses to leave then turned to Ainsley. "I'll leave you two to talk and will return to check vitals later."

She waited until the door clicked closed before hurrying to her mother's bedside. She sat in an adjacent chair. "Mom, what happened? Did you have a reaction to your medication?" Was she even on medication? Maybe if Ainsley returned her calls once in a while, she'd know.

A tear slid down her mom's cheek. "I'm sorry, Ainsley. I was just so . . . lonely."

Her chest constricted. "You mean you did this on purpose?"

"Stephen left me."

"What?"

"Stephen left me."

"What are you talking about? You've only known the man for a few months. You'd take your life for him?" Her mother flinched. Ainsley sucked in air and counted to three before speaking again. "Mom, he's a man." And all that entailed — pond scum included. "You've got so much more to live for." Tears lodged in her throat as she thought of all the times she'd ignored her mother's phone calls. Could she have prevented this?

Her mother shook her head. "What, Ainsley? What do I have to live for? I'm fifty-six years old, can't keep a job, can't keep a man, and I'm about to get kicked out of my apartment." Tears streamed down her face. "Where's the hope in that?"

Ainsley grabbed her mother's hand, words from a sermon spoken the previous Sunday flooding her mind and burning on her tongue. Looking into her mother's glistening eyes, her heart sank at the deep emptiness that stared back at her.

"There is hope, Mom. There's hope and love and goodness, only you're looking for it in all the wrong places. Don't you see? You're running from one man to the next hoping they'll fill that hole inside, only they don't, because they can't. There's only one person who can give you the love you need, and that person's Jesus."

Her mother shook her head. "He'd never take me, not after all I've done."

Ainsley smiled and squeezed her ice-cold hand. "That's why it's called grace, Mom. Undeserved favor based on unconditional love. If you confess your sins, He is faithful and will forgive your sins and make you new."

"There's something I've got to tell you. About your father."

"I don't want to talk about that, Mom. You've got to let that go. You've got to forgive him and move on."

"No, it's he who needs to forgive me, for what I did, and for all those terrible things I've told you all these years. Oh God, forgive me." Her voice trembled as fresh tears surfaced. "Ainsley, dear, I'm so sorry. I'm so very, very sorry."

"What are you talking about?"

Her mother grabbed a tissue from a nearby box and blew her nose. "Your dad didn't leave me. I'm the one who left."

"But you said . . .

"I know what I said, and I'm sorry. We got married so young, and after a while I started to get restless, like I was missing out on something, only I didn't know what that was." She sniffled. "So I joined clubs and went to the movies with friends."

"I remember."

"I thought it would help, but it only made me more agitated. The more fun I had, the more I wanted." She looked away. "Then one day, I met a man."

A wave of nausea swept over Ainsley. "I don't want to hear this, Mom."

Her mother grasped her hand. "I need to tell you. All these years I've wanted to tell you, but whenever I started to, another lie popped out. After a while there were too many lies to unravel." She sniffed and wiped her nose with the back of her hand. "I cheated on your father, and he found out. I thought for sure he'd divorce me, but he said he wanted to work things out. Begged me to go to counseling."

Ainsley pulled away and pressed her spine against the seat backing.

"I told him I needed space and moved out. He waited for a year, and fought against the divorce once I filed."

"Then what about that floozy he's with?"

Her mother shook her head. "Don't know. Maybe he wanted to make me jealous. Either that or he finally gave up." She wiped her tears. "I lost the best thing that ever happened to me then turned his daughter against him. So tell me, do you still think this Jesus of yours has love for me?"

Ainsley stood, her mother's words swirling through her mind. Shaking her head, she backed out.

"Please, Ainsley, don't go. Forgive me. Please forgive me. I'm so sorry!"

Chapter 49

Chris cradled the phone between his ear and shoulder to free his hands for packing. Most of his belonging sat in boxes lining the walls, leaving the living room free of clutter. Three or four more boxes to go and he'd be ready for the realtor to take pictures.

Silence stretched across the phone line before Matilda's soft voice broke it. "Are you sure this is what you want to do? I know I pushed you pretty hard to sell, but I've changed my mind. If you want to stay in Mom and Dad's house—"

"No. This is for the best."

"Would you like me to come over? Do I need to sign the papers or anything?"

"I'll have the realtor fax them to you when we're done here."

He hung up, tucked the phone in his back pocket, turned his attention to an old photo album lying on top of the coffee table.

After a quick flip through the pages, he dropped it into the box. Holding on to this house and his parents' things wouldn't bring his father back, nor would it prevent his mother from slipping further into dementia. Besides, a two-bedroom, low-maintenance condo would free up his time for the café.

The doorbell chimed, and Rusty yipped. Dropping the roll of packing tape onto the sofa, he answered the door, Rusty trailing behind him.

Darcy Trieman stood on his stoop holding a briefcase, camera, and a tripod. "Ready to sign the paperwork?"

He glanced toward Ainsley's house with a heavy heart. Such a sweet, godly woman. Too bad it hadn't lasted. Turning back to Darcy, he nodded and moved aside to allow her in. "As ready as I'll ever be, I imagine."

She surveyed the living room, her gaze lingering on the six-foot-tall box wall stacked between matching bookshelves. "I suggest you get a storage locker. You'll want to clear as much of this away as possible."

"I'll probably donate most of it." He swallowed. "Although I hate to part with it, too many people struggle to make ends meet to justify holding on to things they don't need."

"Are you OK?" Her eyes softened. "I know this must be hard for you. If you're not ready —"

Chris shook his head. "I'm good." As if sensing his sorrow, Rusty watched with droopy eyes before sliding his belly to the floor.

"Wanna give me a walk-through?"

He made a sweeping motion with his arm. "This is the living room." He chuckled, although it fell flat.

Continuing across the room and down the hall, he showed her the guest bathroom, the master bedroom, and a small sitting area. Next, they moved upstairs to the three bedrooms that at one time created his safe haven. Rusty remained near the door, laying on his belly, muzzle resting on his forepaws, eyes sad as if he could sense Chris's mood.

They entered his childhood room first, with its pale-blue walls and a sports-themed border. His bed, a twin with a metal frame, sat in the corner, a bedspread covered in footballs and field goals spread across it. His throat ached as a memory of his mother kneeling beside him as they said bedtime prayers surfaced.

Darcy paused in the middle of the room, watching him with a wrinkled brow. "You need a break?"

"Nope." He inhaled and lifted his chin. "There are two more rooms down the hall, both about the same size."

After showing her the other rooms, the second bathroom and a small office where his father used to pay bills and crunch numbers using an old, handheld calculator, he led her back downstairs.

"Is there someplace we can sit to go over these documents?" She lifted her briefcase.

"Follow me."

They moved to the kitchen. He cleared the table, pulled out a chair for her, then sat beside her.

She plopped her briefcase in front of her, snapped it open, and pulled out a thick stack of papers. She went through each sheet word for word. When finished, she turned the documents toward Chris and handed him a pen. "Time to sign your life away." She grinned.

How true those words were. Fifty years worth of history and thirty years worth of personal memories would soon be sold to the highest bidder. But no matter what they did to the house, no matter who purchased the donated furniture, nothing could erase the images forever engraved in his heart.

When they finished, he walked her to the door.

"Based on the comparables, I think your house will sell quickly." Darcy smoothed back her hair. "Let me know when you'd like to go condo shopping."

"Will do."

With a parting nod, she turned around and traveled down the walk, returning to his lawn a moment later carrying a For Sale sign. Her face contorted as she struggled to stab it into the semi-frozen earth.

Chris ran to her side. "Let me get that for you."

Holding the sign, he glanced up as Ainsley pulled into her driveway. They locked eyes for a moment. His breath caught in his throat as he stood, frozen.

Undo this, Ainsley. Tell me not to leave. Tell me you believe me. Tell me you love me.

Ainsley stared at the For Sale sign clutched in Chris's hand, tears burning her eyes. Inhaling, she gripped the steering wheel tighter and looked away. Her wounds would heal. Slowly perhaps, but they would heal.

Then why did the ache in her heart grow worse every time she saw him?

Her heart cramped as she glanced at the apartment rental guide lying on the passenger seat. It sat on top of classified ads from three newspapers — one from Kansas City, one from Overland Park, and the other from Belton.

Lord, help me out here. How am I supposed to forget Chris when my entire life is entangled in his?

But at least he changed days at the shelter. That remained her one safe haven, even if his absence actually produced the opposite effect.

Once inside, she dropped her things onto the kitchen table. Gripping the counter, shoulders slumped, she stared across the lawn toward Chris's house. The realtor's sign stood like a sharpened dagger, glimmering in the low-lying sun.

No matter how hard she tried to bar him from her heart, memories arose. A thousand times a day she fought against them. Now that her gut-reaction dimmed beneath rational thinking, she knew he told the truth in regard to Candy. But it didn't matter. Her heart was too bruised to go another round. Regressing fifteen years, she felt like that frightened child who waited for her father to come home, waited for her mother to notice her.

Love hurt and men stank. The years of pain enshrouding her mother attested to that.

Only her mother's pain had been her own doing. Ainsley blinked as her mother's words replayed once again in her mind.

Oh, Daddy! If Mom lied about the divorce, did she lie about your desire to see me as well?

She pulled her cell phone from her pocket and sifted through her contacts for her father's number. Her stomach churned as she pressed Call Send. It rang four times before going to voice mail. And extended beep followed. She took a deep breath, opened her mouth. Then closed it, ending the call.

Chapter 50

*A*insley snapped the book shut and enveloped Kaily and Miranda in her arms. Leiland, a toddler with pitch-black hair and dimples, wiggled beside her. Raising her arm, she included him in a group hug and squeezed.

"Again, again, again!" Kaily tugged on the book, forcing the pages open once again.

"Again, again, again!" The other children chorused.

Ainsley giggled. "Then *The Muffin Who Lost His Berries* it is, for the tenth time." She shot Rose a wink who sat at an adjacent table reading through documents.

"Chris!" Kaily bolted to her feet and ran across the cafeteria, the other children following close behind.

Ainsley stiffened, her gaze locked on Chris's as a handful of kids barreled into him, nearly knocking him down. William stood beside him clutching a paper bag, his mother and Nancy, another resident recently added to Chris's crew, close by.

Rose set her papers aside and stood. Sauntering over to Chris and the others, she broke into conversation. "Thanks for coming down here. That rickety old bus drives me crazy." She rolled her eyes. "Always breaks down at the last minute. But Pastor Jenkins from Faith Community says his congregation plans to buy us a new one. Should be bringing it by in a few days, so this'll be the last time you gotta play taxicab.

Course, you know Wanda's done got herself an apartment smack-dab on the bus line. Moves in next week, so you won't be driving her around no more."

Chris smiled and squeezed William's shoulder. "Heard all about it. God is good!"

"All the time!" William beamed and gave Chris a high five.

Kneeling, Ainsley gathered the pile of books with a heavy heart. Rose and Chris's conversation drifted toward her. She watched them from the corner of her eye.

"So, that café of yours has become quite the happening place, huh?"

Chris chuckled. "Thanks to my fantabulous crew."

Rose flicked the paper bag in William's hands then crossed her arms. "So, you workin' them or feedin' them?"

"A bit of both."

"Like I always said, will work for food." Wanda laughed.

Chris nodded. "Love seeing the body of Christ in action. They've been amazing. We must have at least ten different Bible studies meeting at the café, and many come with cans of food. We're talking about turning it into a soup kitchen, minus the soup, on Thursdays. Giving the less fortunate a warm place to hang out, a toasted bagel, and a hot latte. Along with a little dash of Jesus, of course."

Rose turned to Ainsley and planted her hands on her hips. "You're not still looking for another place to work, are you? Cuz it sure seems Brother Chris could use your help."

Ainsley stood and brushed her hair from her face. "It sounds like a wonderful endeavor."

Chris shifted and looked at his watch.

"Don't let me keep you." Rose gave him a sideways hug. "Always good to see you. One of these days I need to come get me a mocha."

"Yes, you do." He looked at Ainsley and held her gaze.

A loud crash sounded through the ceiling.

Rose frowned, staring up. "Guess I better see what's going on up there." She whirled around and clomped up the steps, her long, floral skirt swishing around her feet.

Ainsley searched for something to say. "I see you're moving."

"Yeah. Figure it's time to downsize. You, too, right?"

"Thinking about it. It's either that or sign on for another six-month term."

Silence stretched between them.

"I didn't sexually harass that lady."

"I know."

"There's nothing between Candy and me."

She nodded.

"About those pictures — they were before I came to know Christ. I was in college, drank way too much, and some buddies and I — "

"You don't have to explain anything to me."

"Then why are you so angry?"

Tears lodged in Ainsley's throat. "I'm not angry. I just . . . *Don't want you to break my heart*, only it was too late for that.

His shoulders slumped and he shoved his hands in his pockets. "Well, I guess I better go."

Her pulse quickened as he turned to leave, words of protest flooding her mind, warring with her heart. But the sooner he left, the sooner she found a new job, the sooner she moved, the sooner she could return to her old life. Pre-Richard, pre-Chris, just her and Gina. And a whole slew of cats.

The door shut, leaving Ainsley to stare down the dim, empty hallway. Images of Chris sitting on the floor, large garbage bag stuffed with toys plopped before him, flashed through her mind.

Why did love hurt so bad? When would her heart mend?

"Hurts most when you fight it."

She whirled around to see Dixie standing beside her, propped against the kitchen doorway. "I used to have me a man like that but I let him get away. Done settled for a life of regrets instead."

Ainsley blinked and stared at the closed door.

Chris straightened some papers on his desk and closed his laptop. Crunching numbers for an hour didn't erase the memory of Ainsley's soft eyes, moistened with unshed tears. With a sigh, he pushed himself to his feet. There was nothing more he could do. At least when he thought she believed the lawsuit, he had something to fight against. But now he knew. The woman didn't love him. How could he fight against that?

He flicked off the light and shuffled down the dim hall, his footsteps echoing through the empty café. Standing at the counter, he dipped his head in prayer.

You've done some amazing things here, God. And I'm grateful. I really am. Pain stabbed at the back of his throat. *But somehow I thought Ainsley would be part of this.*

He grabbed his keys and turned off the lights, the glimmer of streetlights and passing cars casting long shadows on the stained concrete floor.

A silhouette filled the doorway, flanked by two others bundled in tattered garb. Chris hurried to the door and threw it open. He ushered his guests inside.

"I didn't think you'd come." He guided Albert and his friends to a table and grabbed a Bible from a nearby shelf. "Vanilla latte, whole milk, right?"

Albert nodded. "Don't burn your tongue. It's hot. Steaming hot in a plastic foam cup."

"And for your friends?" Chris studied the wind-chapped faces in front of him, trying to catch their darting gazes. "Three lattes it is."

He returned a few moments later with a tray loaded with toasted bagels slathered in strawberry cream, and steaming espresso. After distributing the drinks and food, he set the tray on an adjacent table. He flipped a chair around and straddled it, draping his hands across the backing. "So, I told Albert I'd introduce him to my best friend, Jesus." He flipped to John chapter John 14:1-2. "Don't let your hearts be troubled. Trust in God, and trust also in me. There is more than enough room in my Father's home." He continued through verse 6. "Jesus told him, 'I am the way, the truth, and the life. No one can come to the Father except through me.'"

For the next twenty minutes, he answered questions and read numerous other passages while Albert and his friends drank their coffees. As he spoke, his heart swelled within. The pain of losing Ainsley remained, but the joy of seeing wounded hearts turn to Christ numbed his sorrow.

"Let's pray." He held out his hands and Albert and his friends stared at them. "It's OK." After exchanging glances, they slid their hands in his. Everyone bowed their heads as Chris prayed. "Holy Father, thank You for sending Your Son. Thank You for Your free gift of eternal life. And thank You for the promise of heaven."

The door chimed open and he looked up. Ainsley stood in the doorway.

His heart burned as he rose to his feet. "Excuse me." Balling his hands, he fought the urge to run toward her.

"Ainsley, I . . . He reached for her, stopping with his fingers an inch from her face, then let his hand drop. Why was she here? To quit? Tell him she'd found a job sooner than expected?

"I'm sorry. I . . . Can we . . . ?" She pulled her lips in over her teeth as a tear slid down her cheek. "I'm so sorry."

His heart leapt. "Oh, Ainsley." He wiped her tear away with his thumb then traced it along the edge of her jaw. Her skin was so soft. "There's nothing to apologize for. I can't imagine how it must have felt to see that picture." He shook his head. "I was disgusting. Completely selfish and irresponsible."

"You don't have to explain your past."

"I want to." He searched her eyes, his reflection mirrored in them. "I need to." He motioned toward a table a few feet away, and they walked there together. They sat across from each other. "Before I became a Christian, I was a complete jerk. Nothing but a cocky jock who felt entitled." He took in a deep breath. "I'm ashamed at who I was." He shook his head. "But then I met Christ, and everything changed. I changed."

She studied him. "And that lawsuit?"

He shrugged. "The lady who made those claims once worked as my assistant. She was OK for a while, but then she started slipping. I think she was an alcoholic who fell off the wagon, but I could never be sure. Long story short, she wasn't cutting it, so I fired her, and she became bitter, vindictive." He paused. "The case was long and drawn out. Cost me a boatload of money in lawyer's fees and lost time. Obviously, I wasn't stupid enough to represent myself. Through discovery, we learned she'd filed bankruptcy half a dozen times, but the judge wouldn't allow that in." He shook his head. "Even so, she had a weak case. We thought for sure it'd be dismissed, but it wasn't. We were shocked when the jury ruled in her favor."

"Any idea why they did?"

He nodded. "A reporter talked to one of them later. She said they never believed I harassed her, but they were upset with me for firing her." He shrugged. "She was a single mom with a kid at home, and this was at the height of the recession when conspiracy theories and employer hatred ran high. Of course, that wasn't what the headlines read."

"I'm sorry you had to go through all that, and that I wasn't more . . . understanding. Trusting."

"You're here now. Oh, sweet Ainsley." He stood and moved to her, his gaze locked on hers, his heart hammering so fast it hurt. "If you only knew how much I love you." Folding her hands in his and pulling her close, burying his face in her hair as her tears dampened his shoulder. Pulling away, he looked her in the eye and dropped to one knee.

"Oh, Chris!" Hand to her neck, laughter lit her eyes, her entire face.

"I didn't realize how much I loved you until I thought I lost you." His voice went husky. "I don't want to lose you again. I don't have a ring, but . . . He searched his pockets for something that might work then sighed. "But I'll get one."

She giggled, her eyes dancing.

"Will you marry me, Ainsley Meadows?"

She bent down and cupped his face in her hands. "Yes, Chris Langley. Yes!"

Clapping sounded behind them. They rose to find Albert and his friends gathered around, grinning.

Chapter 51

*A*insley stood behind a wooden partition and peered out into the crowd. Women from the shelter, customers from the café, and a few of their street friends, cleaned up and dressed in thrift store suits, filled the folding chairs lined in front of the simple gazebo. To her right, a hummingbird flittered around the flowers lining the quaint cabin while a red-breasted robin serenaded them from the trees.

Ainsley once again read the card in her hands, tears stinging her eyes. It was from Richard, apologizing for his actions and wishing her and Chris the best. Her heart warmed as she thought of how hard she'd prayed for him. That somehow God would break through to his hardened, deceived heart. Though she had no idea where the man stood spiritually, clearly God had been at work. Such an ever-faithful, ever-patient Savior, proving yet again, no one was beyond His reach.

Gina approached, her eyes dancing. "You ready?" She bounced on the balls of her feet.

Ainsley nodded and handed the card over. "Hold this for me?"

Gina looked at it, her eyes widened, then smiled. "Of course."

"Let's do this." Ainsley grinned and pulled her veil over her face.

Music drifted from a gilded harp nestled in the shade of an oak tree, and the wedding party — Gina, Rose, William, and Wanda — assumed their places.

Ainsley's father came to her side and looped his arm through hers. "You look so beautiful. My little angel." He cupped her chin and brushed a kiss against her cheek.

Unspoken words drifted between them, and Ainsley blinked

away a rush of tears as she thought how closely she'd come to missing this — to robbing her father of the privilege of walking her down the aisle.

"Shall we?" Her dad smiled, and she let him guide her around the corner and down a petal-strewn pathway. All eyes turned to her as she made her way to the altar. She paused at the final row to look at her mom, who sat with tissue wadded in her hands, tears streaming down her face. For once a man didn't sit by her side.

Ainsley reached out and squeezed her mother's hand.

Her father took his seat, and she joined Chris at the altar.

His eyes glimmered in the early morning sun.

The reverend stepped forward and read from a well-worn Bible. "The Lord God said, 'It is not good for the man to be alone. I will make a helper suitable for him'" [Genesis 2:18 NIV]. A helpmate — a partner, united as one, not for personal pleasure or self-fulfillment, but to demonstrate the love of Christ. Ainsley Meadows and Chris Langley, may your marriage be a living testimony of grace and may the two of you, united, serve God with reckless abandon." He closed his Bible and looked at Chris. "Do you, Chris Langley, take this woman, Ainsley Meadows, to be your lawfully wedded wife, to have and to hold, in sickness and in health, for richer or poorer, till death do you part?"

Chris grinned. "I do."

The reverend turned to Ainsley. "And do you, Ainsley, take Chris Langley to be your lawfully wedded husband, to have and to hold, encouraging, uplifting, and offering respect, till death do you part?"

Joyous tears filled her eyes. She blinked them away. "I do."

"Then by the power invested in me, I now pronounce you husband and wife."

The music stopped and everyone moved to the edge of the dance floor. Ainsley giggled, clutching the bouquet to her chest. She shot Gina a wink, but Gina stepped back, shaking her head and waving her hands in front of her.

Turning with her back to her guests, Ainsley offered a prayer for blessings over whoever caught her bouquet then hurled it over her head. She turned around to see it sail through the air before landing in her mother's arms. Her mom stared at her with wide eyes and for a moment the room went silent. Then a whoop sounded near the back and everyone clapped.

Ainsley smiled. Her mother was a miracle waiting to happen, but God was in the miracle-making business.

Bible Study On the Go!

Interact. Engage. Grow.

New Hope Interactive is a new digital Bible study platform that allows you to unlock content to download your favorite New Hope Bible study workbooks on your tablet or mobile device. Your answers and notes are kept private through a profile that's easy to create and FREE!

Perfect for individual or small group use!

To learn more visit NewHopeInteractive.com/getstarted

NEW HOPE
PUBLISHERS
Gospel-Centered. Missions-Driven.